ECLIPSE

**Center Point
Large Print**

**This Large Print Book carries the
Seal of Approval of N.A.V.H.**

ECLIPSE

RICHARD NORTH PATTERSON

CENTER POINT PUBLISHING
THORNDIKE, MAINE

This Center Point Large Print edition
is published in the year 2009 by arrangement with
Henry Holt and Company, LLC.

The text of this Large Print edition is unabridged.
In other aspects, this book may vary
from the original edition.
Printed in the United States of America.
Set in 16-point Times New Roman type.

ISBN: 978-1-60285-353-9

Library of Congress Cataloging-in-Publication Data

Patterson, Richard North.
  Eclipse / Richard North Patterson.
      p. cm.
  ISBN 978-1-60285-353-9 (alk. paper)
  1. Petroleum industry and trade--Africa--Fiction. 2. Large type books. I. Title.

PS3566.A8242E25 2009b
813'.54--dc22

2008036390

For Nancy

PROLOGUE

The Devil's Light

IN A WEST AFRICAN VILLAGE, MARISSA BRAND Okari watched her husband prepare to risk his life for the act of speaking out.

It was night. Hundreds of villagers, old and young, gathered in the center of town, their faces illuminated less by moonlight than by the huge orange flame that spewed out of the vertical stem thrusting from an oil pipeline. Torchlike, the stem backlit the line of palms behind the village, its thick residue of smoke blackening the air, its roar a constant ominous presence. Every day in the life of any villager under thirty, this terrible eruption— the flaring of gas from the oil extracted by PetroGlobal Luandia from beneath the deep-red clay—had never ceased, its searing, poisonous heat denuding trees, killing birds and animals, and turning the rainfall to acid, which corroded the roofs that sheltered the people's thatched homes.

The "devil's light," Bobby Okari called it. Now his people, the Asari, bore him on their shoulders to a rough-hewn platform at the center of the village, past the open-air school, its four poles holding up a canopy of wood and palm leaves; the white wooden Pentecostal church, where boisterous celebrants sang and prayed each Sunday morning; the marketplace, now dark for the night, where women peddled an ever-dwindling harvest of fish and fruit, the legacy of oil spills that fouled the oceans, creeks, and farmland.

To Marissa's anxious eyes, her husband looked elated, as though the festive scene that typified Asari Day, the annual expression of Asari heritage and harmony, carried no undercurrent of fear. The young men around him, Bobby's core cadre of followers, held him higher, his burgundy African shirt resplendent, his reading glasses hanging from a gold chain around his neck. On this Asari Day, as ever, the villagers had gathered here at dawn for the singing, drumming, and dancing by groups of girls and women in bright dresses, their celebration pulsing from morning to night. But this Asari Day was different: at Bobby Okari's urging, in every village in Asariland, people had come together— three hundred thousand Asari in all—to protest the devastation caused by the partnership between PetroGlobal Luandia and the regime of General Savior Karama, which, in Bobby's pungent phrase, "drills and kills without remorse."

This village, Goro, was Bobby's ancestral home. His father, Femi Okari, was its chief; though Bobby's fame as a novelist, and then as a spokesman for his people, had taken him to many lands, he still kept a home here to maintain his tribal roots. On this day, Bobby and Marissa had driven here from their compound in Port George, and his followers sang or chanted or beat their sheepskin drums to announce his advent. Now, as the young men thrust him atop the platform, the throng pressed forward to hear him—some men in shirts and pants, others, mostly elders, in the traditional round cap and long robes; the women adorned in head scarves, earrings, and beads set off against bright blouses, the young women's dresses single-wrapped in contrast to the double wrapping of the matrons. As suitable for a married woman, Marissa, a matron at thirty-six despite her slim body and lineless skin, wore a double wrapping, in contrast to Omo, the fifteen-year-old girl whose hand she held and whose beautiful eyes shone with adoration for Bobby Okari.

"Ma'am," Omo said simply, "your husband is a great man."

Looking into the girl's face, still so innocent, Marissa tried to quell the sense of danger she had felt ever since Bobby had conceived this, the first mass protest in the history of Asariland. In its place came a fleeting amazement at the choices that had brought her, an American of mixed race, to this life and this man; to this astonishing and deeply accursed country; and to the Asari, a mere half million people among Luandia's two hundred and fifty ethnic groups and two hundred and fifty million citizens, whose perverse blessing was that beneath their land lay the richest oil reserves in one of the world's most oil-rich regions, the Luandian Delta. Until Bobby Okari, the Asari had endured

11

the consequences in silence, robbed of heart and hope. But now Bobby, through his eloquence and relentless work, had summoned a grassroots movement, offering the restless young a vision beyond that of the armed militia groups that hid in the swamps and creeks that made the delta a trackless maze. It was Bobby's strength—or blindness—that his belief in the movement he had summoned from nothing overcame his fear of an autocracy whose leader, General Karama, caused those who displeased him to die or disappear.

"The Asari," Marissa answered Omo softly, "are a brave people."

Bobby held up a hand for silence. As Marissa scanned the crowd, she spotted Bobby's father, Chief Femi Okari, his face grim beneath his broad fedora, his eyes slits of disapproval and resentment. But he seemed an island to himself, alone amid the collective admiration of his son, the pride of the Asari. As the cries for Bobby receded into a deep silence, her husband stood taller, his slight form radiating an energy that suffused his proud bearing and made him seem larger than he was, less vulnerable than the flawed and troubled man Marissa knew him to be. As he began speaking, even his voice—deep yet lilting—belied any hint of frailty.

"Haah Ama," he began in Asari, then translated the phrase into English, Luandia's colonial tongue: "Community, I greet you."

Men's and women's voices answered with cries of varied timbres. Then Bobby turned, pointing to the giant flame that lit the dark behind him. *"This,"* he called out, "is the bastard child of a rapacious oil company and a corrupt and brutal autocracy. Together, PetroGlobal Luandia and the Karama regime have polluted our streams, killed our fish, denuded our land. Now they are taking all that is left—the oil beneath our feet."

"Yes," a chorus of voices called out.

Bobby's voice rose above the din. "For years we have suffered. But now, at last, we demand an end to their tyranny. We insist on our rightful share of oil monies for schools, roads, clinics, clean water to drink. The United Nations itself has recognized our oppression. And yet the government and PGL pretend to be deaf and dumb.

"When I sent them the Asari Manifesto five months ago, demanding our rights, they did not answer." Bobby's deep voice became slow and somber. "And six weeks ago, when the people of Lana gathered to protest an oil spill, our government sent Colonel Okimbo and his soldiers to kill eighty-two Asari of both sexes and all ages; rape women and girls; amputate the limbs of men and boys; and burn their village to the ground."

Marissa knew the stories, all too well. So did the villagers: their lowered voices receded into silence, the only sound the deep roar of flaring oil. In the light from the giant orange flame, a shadow crossed Omo's face, and she gripped Marissa's hand more tightly. "Tonight," Bobby said in the same low voice, "we are out in force, three hundred thousand strong, calling for an end to this exploitation in every village in Asariland. Even for General Karama, that is too many villages to raze, too many people to kill."

Calls of approval rose from the Asari. But Marissa's voice caught in her throat: in Luandia her husband's words were sedition, and surely somewhere among his listeners was an agent of the state security services, armed with a tape recorder.

Bobby's face glistened with sweat. "And yet the government and PGL are already committing genocide against the Asari people. When we cannot farm or fish or drink our water—*that* is genocide. When more Asari are dying than are born, and those who survive their infancy can find no work—*that* is genocide. When we are riddled with diseases but have no electricity for hospitals—*that* is genocide.

"That is what oil has done to the Asari—the same oil that runs the factories, heats the homes, and fills the gas tanks of the Americans, the Europeans, and our new exploiters, the Chinese." Bobby stared out at the crowd, moving his gaze from side to side, as though to seal their bond. "In Luandia, oil blackens everything it touches. It fouls the hands of the ruling class that misappro-

14

priates its profits. It stains the ambitions of the young, who in their desperation will pick up a gun, sabotage a pipeline, kidnap a foreigner to grab their pitiful share of the riches. It elevates the powerful, and drowns the weak. And it degrades the character of our people, unleashing greed, envy, dishonesty, and corruption. Oil is dirty—as dirty as the slave trade and the craven Luandians who helped the British sell our ancestors."

"Shame," a man called out.

"Yes," Bobby answered. "But now it is not some colonial governor who rules us. It is a Luandian who has suspended our constitution, banned our political parties, jailed our leaders, and shut down our newspapers. Karama's police extort money from the innocent; his prisoners rot for years without a trial; his judges take bribes before pronouncing sentence. And he uses ill-gotten petrodollars to pay off the generals, bureaucrats, governors, and chiefs who help maintain his power, the better to siphon the billions he steals from us into American jets, Italian sports cars, and bank accounts in Switzerland."

No, Marissa thought—not at the sound of truth, but from fear of its consequences. For a moment, she shut her eyes, instinctively listening for alien sounds, perhaps a powerboat landing on the beach nearby, the first warning of an invader. Through the roar of flaring she heard a faint but familiar whir. "This must not be," Bobby was saying.

"People are not made for states—states are made for people."

Marissa opened her eyes. From the sky behind her husband came a streak of light, blurred by the orange glow of the flare. Then the sound she heard merged with the silhouette of a helicopter, hovering above the palm trees with an arrhythmic thud, its beam aimed at the villagers, whose heads turned from Bobby to stare upward at the dark metallic bird. Marissa glimpsed a white circle painted on its side, framing the large black letters PGL.

On the platform, Bobby looked from the helicopter to his people, their connection to him severed by the fear stamped on their faces. Part of Marissa wished for Bobby to send them home.

Instead, his voice carried above the sounds of blades chopping air. He pointed to the intruder. "PGL, too," he cried out, "is our oppressor. It banished peace from our land from the day it laid its first pipeline, letting nothing stand in its way—not trees or farms or rivers, nor even beast or man."

As did the others, Marissa saw, Femi Okari looked from the helicopter to Bobby. *"Why?"* Bobby shouted. "Because we are *Africans*. PetroGlobal does not rape the land in the United States or Europe—only in Luandia. And now we've become its pawns in a ruthless competition among superpowers frightened that terrorists will cut off the flow of the oil from the Middle East, their lifeblood . . ."

As though in answer, the helicopter swooped down over the platform, the swirling blades drowning out Bobby's voice, its shaft of light impaling him like a lone figure in a passion play. Following the beam upward, Marissa could make out the fleshy face of a blond man gazing down from the chopper at Bobby Okari. And then, with a leisure that made its departure as ominous as its presence, the helicopter floated away until at last it became a shadow, vanishing in the half-light of an illuminated sky.

Only then did Bobby speak again, his voice softer but still resonant. "Tonight, we demand that those whose lives depend on oil respect *our* lives and *our* lands. That the United States, PetroGlobal Oil's home, require its subsidiary PGL to follow the high standard of human rights it professes to value and open its courts to our claims against it. That PGL renounce its pact with General Karama and his machinery of death and open its books so that we can see how much our government has stolen from us. That the Karama regime grant us the right to run our own affairs, and free elections where our ballots are counted, not burned."

With each demand, the crowd seemed more inspired, its outcry louder and more sustained. "The people of Lana," Bobby continued, "asked these things and were slaughtered for it. So now I tell Karama this.

"Tonight, throughout Asariland, Asari women are blocking the roads to PGL's oil facilities. And, a few moments ago, Asari men in boats seized the offshore oil platform that mars the serenity of our fishing waters." With the voice and manner of a prophet, Bobby pointed over the heads of his listeners. "Look, and you will see."

Turning with the others, Marissa looked toward the mouth of the creek that ran beside the village to the ocean and saw the flicker of torchlights from the oil platform, as though suspended above the dark waters. Only then did she fully comprehend how much her husband had dared; when Bobby spoke again, the Asari turned to him in wonder. "The time has come," he told them, "for General Karama to help us build the Asariland of our hopes.

"We know that he can do this. In four years he raised a new capital city from nothing, then named this glistening creation after himself." Bobby's lips formed a broad but ironic smile. "So we will promise him that every road, school, and hospital we build will bear his name. We will do this for him, yes?"

Amid the cheers and laughter someone called out, "Yes."

"It must be so," Bobby answered, his voice strong again. "For this has become a dangerous country. Too many of our young men, deprived of any future, drink gin and smoke weed from morning to night. Too many others have taken up arms and vanished to hideouts in the creeks, killing one another for the right to live as criminals. If Karama does not yield, we will descend into an unending darkness of corruption, criminality, murder, and reprisal, condemning those who survive to a permanent hell. And among the things that will *not* survive is PGL—"

"Kill them all," a young man called out.

Glancing through the crowd, Marissa spotted him, a youth taller than most others—restrained from joining the militia, rumor had it, only by his attraction to Omo. Glancing at the girl, Marissa saw her downcast eyes fill with doubt and worry. "No," Bobby answered. "To act with violence will only bring to our door reprisals far more terrible than what we saw in Lana. I want no more blood spilled in Asariland."

Uncertainty filled the young man's face; though some around him nodded their approval, others wore expressions grimmer and more opaque. As though to reassure them, Bobby continued: "But the government's time is short. Every day our patience frays, and our youth slip beyond our power to restrain them. Karama and PGL must give us justice now, or there will be no peace for the powerful and PGL will be driven from Asariland."

"*Fuck* PGL," a voice called, and then a ragged

chant came from a cluster of young men near Marissa. "PGL, go to hell. PGL, go to hell . . ."

Bobby held up a hand, his face impassive until, at last, there was silence. "Let us march to join our brothers and sisters," he told them, "and pray for the souls of our dead."

As CONCEIVED BY Bobby, the climactic event would be a meeting with demonstrators from a neighboring village at the site of a recent oil spill, which, bursting into flames, had incinerated men and women from both villages who had come to scavenge for oil. Tonight those assembled would gather in memorial. But at least one of the villagers would be missing: Chief Femi Okari, Marissa noted, had gazed across the water at the torches flickering on the oil platform and then, shaking his head, turned away to walk home.

With Bobby and Marissa at their head, the people of Goro gathered where the road began, many with cigarette lighters held aloft. As the march commenced, the villagers began singing their anthem: "Be proud, Asari people, be proud."

A few feet ahead, Marissa spoke to Bobby beneath the chorus. "Women blocking roads, men seizing the platform. Did your council approve?"

"Is it dangerous, you mean?"

His voice held a hint of challenge. "I already know that," Marissa answered calmly. "So do the others."

"Do you doubt me?"

"Only when I should. What did Atiku say?"

Bobby did not look at her. "Atiku is rallying support in England," he answered in a weary voice. "Our young need more than words from us, or more will drift away."

Through her misgivings, Marissa sensed that he had made this decision in the face of resistance from his lieutenants and found it painful to consider how this might end. Taking his hand, she asked, "Is today all you had hoped for?"

Bobby summoned a small smile. "Do you see their eagerness, the joy on their faces? For a day they are free of docility and fear." He paused, then finished softly, "Were I to die right now, Marissa, I would die a happy man."

His faintly autumnal tone reminded Marissa of the gray flecks she had begun to notice in his hair, the deepening grooves in his face that betrayed that he was not only older than she, but suffering from an exhaustion he tried to conceal from the others. She grasped his hand more tightly.

For a mile they walked at the head of the Asari along a dirt road forged by PGL repair crews between mangroves and palm trees, the orange glow of flaring gas lighting their path. Then Bobby stopped abruptly.

Marissa followed his gaze. At a fork in the road ahead, three silhouettes hung from the thick branches of a tree, specters in the devil's light.

Turning, Bobby held up his hand. The marchers fell quiet, save for cries of shock from those who saw what Bobby saw. "Wait here," Bobby told Marissa.

But she did not. Together, they moved toward the tree, stopping only when the three shadows became corpses. As Bobby held up his cigarette lighter Marissa saw that strangulation had contorted their faces and suffused their eyes with blood. All were Luandian; all wore denim shirts bearing the letters PGL.

Her stomach constricting, Marissa turned to Bobby. Tears shone in his eyes. "Now what will happen to us?" he murmured.

A stirring in the grove of palms behind the corpses made Marissa flinch. The figure of a large man emerged, followed by three others. As the men stepped into the light, Marissa recognized the familiar uniform of Luandian soldiers and saw their leader's face.

Instantly she felt herself recoil: though she knew him only by the patch over his right eye, by reputation Colonel Paul Okimbo was a mass murderer, a rapist, and, the survivors of Lana whispered, insane. Okimbo wore the eye patch, it was said, to conceal a walleye and, bizarrely, to evoke the Israeli general Moshe Dayan. Stopping beside the hanging bodies, he trained his remaining eye on Bobby, then Marissa, letting his gaze linger.

Facing Bobby, he said, "This is your work, Bobby Okari."

"No," Bobby answered. "Not mine, and not ours."

Okimbo emitted a bark of laughter. "So you say. But soon you will face the justice of Savior Karama."

Marissa watched Bobby exert the full force of his will to meet Okimbo's stare. A spurt of anger broke the colonel's impassivity. "Unless the Asari withdraw at once," he snapped, "there will be consequences. Some will die."

Feeling the dampness on her forehead, Marissa saw the sheen of sweat on Bobby's face. With palpable reluctance, he answered, "As you say. But this will not end here."

"Of that you can rest assured," Okimbo responded with the flicker of a smile. "I know two hundred ways of killing a man, and more men than that who deserve to die."

To Marissa, the silence that followed felt suffocating. Involuntarily, it seemed, Bobby looked from Okimbo to the corpses, hanging with eerie stillness in the dense night air.

Seeing this, Okimbo placed his hand on the back of the body nearest him, idly shoving it toward Bobby as though propelling a child on a swing. As the dead man slowly swung between them, Okimbo said softly, "For you, hanging will do nicely."

The Dark
of the Sun

1

THE DAY BEFORE HIS DIVORCE BECAME FINAL, Damon Pierce sent an e-mail to a friend, a woman he cared for deeply, the one who had chosen another man and another life. Pierce was alone at Sea Ranch on the last weekend before the house became Amy's, contemplating the rugged California coastline and what his own life had brought him. Now it was early evening, and the sun slowly setting over the cobalt-blue Pacific was so bright that Pierce squinted at the screen. Despite this, he composed his words with care: he had met her in a creative writing class and, even now, their exchanges strove to capture events in a way the other would appreciate and make a good-natured effort to surpass. It was a pleasure that Amy, far more literal and less romantic, had never understood; still less did she appreciate that this complex blend of admiration and remembered attraction, surviving time and distance, had come to hold a mirror to their marriage.

His e-mail reflected his mood, the ironic yet sober assessment of a man on the cusp of midlife—a partner in a fifteen-hundred-lawyer megafirm caught between an increasingly thwarted professional desire to do good and a former blue-collar boy's appreciation of fine dining, good wine, and travel undreamed of in his youth. Among Pierce's specialties was complex international litigation, in which he enjoyed a considerable reputation; as he had told his correspondent several years ago, "not everyone has put away for life the murderous president of a former Balkan rump state."

Perhaps this experience as a war crimes prosecutor, the clearest expression of his still flickering idealism, reflected his admiration for her commitment to others, the harder choices she had made. But his work in Kosovo was now years in the past. For Pierce, the chief residue of this time was the several hundred dead men, women, and children— the defendant's victims—on whom the world's attention had focused far too late, and whose images still came to him in dreams.

"Since returning to the firm," he wrote now, "my practice has become more or less what you predicted. My principal clients are investment bankers and tarnished corporate titans staring at a stretch in prison for ambitions that exceeded the law. Some strike me as almost tragic; others as loathsome. A few are even innocent. Many of them I like—it's me I wonder about. Often I remember what Charlie Hale, my best friend at the firm, said after our first week as associates: 'Damon, my boy, us two will do well here. In ten years, we'll be partners; in twenty we'll have more money than time; in forty we'll be looking back at our careers. And after *that* . . . ,' he finished with a sardonic grin, 'there's only one big move left.'

"Charlie, however, has a nice wife and three bright-eyed daughters he adores.

"As for me, I have a condominium with a view of the Golden Gate Bridge and sufficient cash to indulge in pleasures you might think superfluous. But remember that when we met I was mired in student loans; compared to me you were born to have a restless conscience, and to act on it. Still, I question myself every time I imagine you asking, 'Is this a life of meaning?' Then I imagine the conveyor belt of life leading straight to my premature demise, keeling over at my desk on another weekend of too much work for no great cause. Perhaps that's why I spend so much time at the gym."

Pierce paused there. Any fair external inventory would count him lucky: he was even fitter than when they had last seen each other, and the twelve years since had lent a keenness to his face without thinning or graying his dark shock of hair, leaving the Damon Pierce of the courtroom a still youthful but commanding presence, tall and slim and quick of tongue and mind. "Nevertheless," his e-mail conceded, "my career thrives more each year. And I arm myself for Judgment Day by giving pro bono advice in international human rights cases, a faint echo of my time at The Hague.

"As for my former literary ambitions, the only real writing I do is to you.

"Which brings me, I suppose, to Amy.

"We're divorcing. It's really not her fault. The most critical thing I can say is that Amy never questions her life. If her client is a crook, he just is. My tendency to ponder the meaning of it all strikes her as a waste of time.

"Why did we marry? To begin, Amy's a gorgeous strawberry-blonde, so tall and elegant that she looks more like a ballerina than a lawyer. And wicked smart—smart and beautiful, you'll recall, tends to get my attention. Amy is also the most self-possessed person I know, so that even her bursts of anger seem less spontaneous than chosen. The same spartan discipline governs her exercise and diet: at thirty-five, she remains so youthful that I once teased her that when she dies at ninety, they'll have to cut off her leg and count the rings to figure out how old she was. She had the grace to find that funny—of course, she herself is often funny in a matter-of-fact observer's sort of way. A lawyer's way.

"But then we lived like lawyers. Every Saturday we sat at breakfast and updated our professional and social calendars for the next four weeks. Our conversations were like telegrams—no words wasted. For two trial lawyers, time is always a problem, and there was never enough.

"The question became, For what?

"Expensive dinners alone. Vacations in Fiji. More expensive dinners with other childless couples who trumped Fiji with Montenegro. Fundraisers for abortion rights or battered women or the Democratic candidate for whatever. Comparisons of trial tactics: Amy was so delighted with the exercise of her considerable skills that I once told her she would have cheerfully represented Martin Bormann. 'Only for the cause,' she retorted, a slight dig at my pro bono work. Her most grotesque clients became her babies.

"There it is. I wanted them; Amy didn't.

"Not her problem, but mine. Amy has no illusions, least about herself: that she never wanted kids was just a fact, and Amy never fudged facts. But as you so often suggested, I'm a bit of a romantic, and sometimes still believe that I can make life, even people, turn out as I hoped. And what I hoped for was two small Pierces.

"A couple of years ago, I realized that I was the only one who heard Amy's reproductive clock ticking. When I said as much, she countered me with jaundiced humor: 'Have you checked out your partners' lives postchild?' she asked. 'Moving to the dullest suburb for the "best schools"; planning car pools and sleepovers and after-school enrichment programs; going to parent-teacher conferences and obsessing about how to propel their obviously sociopathic seven-year-old toward Stanford Medical School, until their only friends are the other lobotomized couples whose only subject is "the kids"—'

" 'Beats hearing about Montenegro,' I interrupted. 'Somewhere during that last dinner, I realized Chris and Martha are the biggest waste of time since reality TV.' Suddenly I became serious. 'Amy,' I said slowly but clearly, 'just loving *you* is not enough.'

"For a long time she just looked at me. 'It might be,' she answered, 'if you still did.'

"All at once I realized how good she was at stating facts.

"*That* fact, once she brought it to my attention, was fatal. I may not be as surgical as Amy, but I'm no more inclined than she to lie about what I know. I had stopped loving the Amy Riordan I had married, and the life she had never questioned. Only the distraction of our work had allowed us to drift apart with our eyes shut, not seeing what Amy now saw so clearly with those beautiful blue eyes— which, for once, were filled with tears."

Pierce paused. There was more he might have said—not just that Amy and he were different but that the difference between his wife and the woman to whom he was writing had grown in Pierce's mind. He knew this was unfair: he had taken Amy on her terms, and it was not right to compare her to a woman whose path in life was driven not just by her virtues but by her scars. Nor could he fully explain, to this woman or himself, how much he valued their ongoing connection amid the deterioration of his married life. It

32

was best, he concluded, to stick to that life itself.

"Our decision to divorce was sad," Pierce continued. "But it was this hollow quality that makes me the saddest now. We're lucky, friends tell us, that we have no children to pay for our own failure. Still, without kids or money to fight over, there is too little to keep us from drifting ever further apart, until we become again the strangers we once were. The saddest fact is this: when the first of us dies, the survivor will likely learn of it, if at all, by reading the obituary page.

"Sorry. It's the black Irish in me, and this St. Patrick's Day I turned forty. As you're not divorcing, certainly not Irish, and only thirty-six at that, I hope you'll forgive this side trip into morbidity." After rereading this passage, Pierce added, "In truth, the confluence of divorce and a major birthday may be God's wake-up call. My work at The Hague, however hard, was about something of fundamental importance—vindicating human rights through law. Though leading the prosecution team wasn't easy, I think I was at my best, and I never doubted the worth of what I did. So it seems I've got some things to think about, and the freedom to do so. Perhaps, in its way, that's not so bad a birthday gift."

This was a good place to end, he thought. "Tell me how you are," he concluded. "From what I read and hear, I worry that I haven't heard from you lately. And you still write a pretty good sentence.

"Affectionately, Damon."

Pierce sent the e-mail. When he looked out the window again, still pensive, the sun was an orange sliver descending beneath the blue-gray line of the ocean. He went to the kitchen, poured himself a chill glass of Chassagne-Montrachet, and made himself dinner.

Two hours later, as he returned to his computer, an e-mail appeared. Opening it, he found himself staring at its first sentence.

"Seven nights ago," Marissa began, "I saw the corpses of three oil workers hanging from a tree."

2

FINISHING MARISSA'S E-MAIL, PIERCE STARED AT the screen.

From hard experience, he knew that media attention to human rights abuses was fitful—let alone in a remote region of West Africa shut down to outsiders. His only hope for news was the BBC, the source he had followed since danger had begun enveloping the Okaris after Bobby had issued his manifesto.

Shortly before nine P.M., he found a brief news item on the BBC Web site. By cell phone, a journalist had managed to reach Bobby Okari. On this day, a little after ten o'clock in the morning, a solar eclipse would darken Goro; at the moment of eclipse, Bobby had insisted, he would stage another demonstration, a successor to Asari Day, his symbolic defiance of Savior Karama's ban on nighttime demonstrations. Pierce checked his watch, calculating the time in Luandia—if the planets stayed on course, the eclipse would begin in a little more than four hours.

Damn you, his inner voice said. Yet what he felt was not anger but fear. As he knew too well, her life had trained her not to listen.

FROM THE FIRST words of her short story, Damon Pierce had watched Marissa Brand and known that it was hers.

Each Thursday night, fourteen men and women clustered around a table, listening to Larry Banks—a gifted novelist whose tenure at Berkeley allowed him to write without starving—read one of their stories aloud. His purpose was to conceal the author's identity, enabling the group to critique without compunction. In Pierce's estimate, this conceit of anonymity promoted a certain savagery, licensing the arrogant to eviscerate their peers. But Pierce, a sensitive observer, could often guess the identity of the author and, depending on what he saw, frame his comments to offer a dollop of mercy.

On this night what tipped him off was the woman's studied veneer of blankness, belied by an intensity of focus so complete that she was utterly still. Though they had never spoken, Pierce's interest transcended art: clearly biracial, the woman had light brown skin and small, perfect features accented by a cleft chin and dark eyes that conveyed an almost startling intensity unleavened by more than a passing hint of humor. Seemingly indifferent to her beauty, she did not wear makeup or attempt to tame her tight black curls. Yet what Pierce perceived in class was the opposite of indifference: that she was trying so hard to show no feeling suggested, in his mind, a woman who felt so deeply that it scared her.

But he was here for the writing. His interest piqued, he listened to her story as closely as she.

Its surface was nearly flawless. She wrote with a jeweler's eye—each word precisely chosen, each sentence polished, their rhythms varied to add energy and avoid the soporific effect of sentence upon sentence with too many clauses and commas. Her facility made Pierce smile to himself.

But the story was more problematic—deeply personal and yet oddly abstract. Its core was the blighted relationship between a father and daughter, so mutually uncomprehending that they were doomed to flay each other's wounds until the man's last breath. The writer dissected him in telling detail: his narcissism, his emotional aridity, his resentment when his attempts at reconciliation, having failed, revealed how little he saw any woman except as the mirror of his own self-regard. The daughter was different. Though Pierce tried to give her his sympathy, she was less victim than observer, inspecting her father with the merciless scrutiny of a recording angel. The effect was to create more compassion for this man than, Pierce suspected, his real-life model deserved.

The other students were not fools. When Banks finished reading, they nailed its flaws with equivalent charity. "Airless," a male poet sniffed. The graying lesbian called it "slight as a pianist's finger exercise." The pallid woman next to Pierce labeled the story "a lacquer box with nothing inside." Looking at the author's face, Pierce wished her critics literary lives of rejection letters and desperate pleas to academic presses. Her eyes betrayed the hurt her words had not.

When Pierce's turn came, he stressed the story's virtues. "I wouldn't add or subtract a word," he concluded. "And I feel that I know a man I'll never meet—the essence of characterization. Flaws in a story can be fixed. Mediocrity in a writer can't."

By the time class ended, twilight had fallen on the campus. Pierce paused on the steps of the building, gazing at the looming bell tower whose spire split the darkening sky. He felt a presence close behind him.

"Thank you," she said simply.

He turned to her. "For what?"

"For liking my story."

Her steady gaze discouraged evasion. "How did you know I knew?"

"Because you looked at me so closely as it began, but not at all when you spoke. Or after."

Damon waited for the last stragglers to pass them by. With a smile, he told her, "You're every bit the observer your story suggests. Liking it was easy enough, except for wishing I wrote that well."

It was the wrong thing to say: her eyes signaled an instant distrust. "Please don't," she said in a flat tone. "They were right, and you agree."

"About the problems? Okay, the female character is too withheld. But as I said, that's fixable."

For a moment, she studied his face. "Maybe in stories. 'Write what you know,' they say."

The conversational hairpin turn caught Pierce off guard. But as he well knew, writing, once shared, creates a curious intimacy; despite her obvious attractions, it struck him that this woman might be lonely. "Are *you* withheld?" he asked.

She gazed down at the cement between them, her shoulders finally twitching in a shrug. "I don't know. I don't like to think of myself that way."

Pierce decided to take a chance. "Because you don't see yourself that way? Or because you don't like to think about yourself at all?"

She seemed to consider this, and then looked up at him again. "Both. People often aren't who they think they are, let alone who they say they are. Only actions don't lie."

Pierce shook his head in demurral. "That would

make us nothing but nerves and reflexes. If we don't think about what we do, and why, how will we ever change?"

To his complete surprise, she laughed, a sound expressing wonder but not rancor. "And you think that's so easy?"

"Not easy. Possible."

In her renewed silence, Pierce realized that darkness had closed around them. "I'd better go," she said at length.

Pierce suppressed his disappointment. "If you drove here, I'll walk you to your car."

The smile she gave him was slightly skewed, as though fending off an antique gallantry. "Facts are facts," Pierce told her. "Nighttime isn't safe here. And I'd be happy for the company."

After a moment, she shrugged. "If you have time."

With that, she skittered down the remaining stairs and headed across the grass, Pierce straining to keep up. Her small frame moved with a whippetlike efficiency that, for Pierce, held a tomboyish appeal. As though remembering her manners, she asked, "What do you do besides write?"

"Practice law. After college I weighed my student loans against my literary gifts and chose law school over a master's in creative writing. Now I'm paying off my debt on the installment plan, one year at a time, hoping to stay out of debtor's prison. And you?"

She glanced over at him. "I'm like you, I guess—a would-be writer who decided that the smart move was a master's in education. I look at the bestseller list, and it seems like no one who's any good writes for money."

"Tell that to Philip Roth," Pierce answered with a smile. "Or, for that matter, Stephen King."

She shot him a swift grin, as though caught in an alibi. "So maybe I was a coward. But now I've made other plans."

To Pierce's practiced ear, the last phrase sounded significant. "I'd like to hear about them. Any chance I could buy you dinner?"

She stopped abruptly and stood in the moonlit shadow of the spire, appraising Pierce with an enigmatic smile. "Thanks," she said. "But I've got somewhere to go. My boyfriend's giving a speech."

Once more, Pierce felt a stab of disappointment. "Concerning what?" he asked.

"West Africa—and oil." She hesitated, then added, on seeming impulse, "If you're curious, come with me. The more people who hear him, the better. The first time *I* did may actually have changed my life."

To refuse, Pierce sensed, would sever whatever tenuous link they had—especially since, having invited her out, he lacked an excuse. "If he's that good," he answered, "I'll buy you both dinner."

Pierce had thought of it as reconnaissance, at

most the waste of an evening. Now, twelve years later, he gazed intently at the BBC Web site, recalling fragments of half-forgotten prayers from his Catholic boyhood as he worried for them both.

3

As THE FIRST LIGHT DAWNED, MARISSA STOOD AT the center of Goro—seven days ago the scene of her husband's greatest triumph—awaiting the passage of the sun with far more apprehension than she had expressed to Damon Pierce.

Around her the village stirred to life. Children arose for school; Omo arrived at the marketplace to prepare her mother's stall; the few remaining fishermen paddled ancient canoes out to sea and cast their fishing nets, a snapshot of a timeless way of life. Soon more villagers would leave their thatched huts, and struggling enterprises like the Happy Fingers Saloon—a hairdresser, to Marissa's persistent amusement—would open at idiosyncratic hours. In the freshness of dawn, the grass beside the polluted creek was verdant, and the sandy beach where it met the ocean unstreaked with oil. But Marissa feared that this day, already marked by nature, would be unlike any other.

Inside their house, Bobby was at his desk, awaiting word from his lieutenants across Asariland. His father, Femi, peered out his door. Today he wore the robes of a chief, the formal vestige of a power that had dwindled as his son rose and youth fell away. Now he gazed up at the sun with a misgiving as palpable as that which Marissa chose to conceal.

At precisely 10:17, the astronomers said, a total eclipse of the sun would cast the village into darkness, relieved only by the unrelenting glare of oil flaring. It was Bobby's luck, or fate, that nature would cause this to occur six days after General Karama had forbidden all nighttime gatherings, citing the lynchings that had ended Asari Day.

For two days Bobby had stirred a debate among his cadre by cell phone and e-mail. "We cannot crawl back into our holes," he concluded. "And not even Savior Karama can stop the movement of the planets."

His plan was provocative: a mass demonstration that would conform to Karama's edict due only to the intervention of the moon, the Asari people's defiance signaled by lighters thrust toward the dark of the sun. Karama's response was to close the major airports; cordon off Asariland; and expel all foreign journalists from the Luandian Delta. His directive did not mention Bobby's plan: the fact that PGL had simultaneously shut down operations provided Karama, in Marissa's mind, with sufficient pretext for whatever he chose to do.

Since this edict Bobby had barely slept.

Restless, Marissa crossed the muddy clay and reentered their house. On another day, she would have found its character fondly familiar: a balky fax machine, an erratic cell phone, the generator whirring, cartons jammed with speeches and manifestos, documents strewn across Bobby's desk in a chaotic jumble he allowed no one to touch, the sturdy but sclerotic ceiling fan whose revolutions barely disturbed the listless air. Bobby sat with his back to her. Beside him, signed the day before, was a final iteration of his will.

Now he was writing his speech in longhand, so focused on this task that he did not hear his wife. Only the sound of helicopter blades caused his hand to pause.

Marissa preceded him to the door. Hovering above the line of palms was a helicopter with the black logo: PGL. From behind her, Bobby murmured, "I thought they were gone."

Marissa faced him. Reading her face, he spoke with quiet urgency. "If I back down, the movement ends. I'm the one they trust, and the world community sees them through what I say or do."

"What about your writing?"

Bobby shook his head. "It is not the same as action—not to the world, and surely not to our people." This last phrase, pointedly inclusive of Marissa, was followed by a fleeting smile. "However brilliant, my prose cannot rally a semi-literate populace. That's why I schooled myself, frail vessel though I am, to not just speak but to act as a symbol for them and others."

Outside, the deep beating of chopper blades slowly receded. Marissa touched his arm. "The others are gone," she answered. "Karama has expelled them. No one hears us now."

The doubt in Bobby's eyes revealed how well he knew this. "The Asari do, Marissa." He paused, his next words betraying that he, like she, could not forget the killings at Lana or the dangling corpses or Okimbo's threat. "I cannot let them down, or they would be right to lynch me."

When Bobby resumed writing, Marissa gazed out the door again, hoping the women in the marketplace would distract her from her anxiety.

She fixed on Omo and her mother, covering their sparse offering of pineapples in anticipation of what was to come. Their expressions were less animated and, to Marissa's mind, their movements bore the weight of uncertainty. Every so often Omo cast her eyes at the sun: the pendency of an eclipse created a sense of awe among a people for whom the natural world held more mystery and meaning than it had in Marissa's childhood. Watching the girl, her favorite, she barely heard the fax machine ringing.

A moment later Bobby appeared at her side, gazing down at a fax with a look of such devastation that Marissa felt her throat clutch. "What is it?"

When he shook his head, as though unable to tell her, she took the document from his hand.

It was signed by four of his lieutenants, including Eric Aboh, his second-in-command. Marissa scanned the agreement, more heartsick with each phrase. "On behalf of the Asari people," the four leaders had met with "representatives of the government and PGL" and had "amicably resolved the current tensions in exchange for further talks." Therefore they urged the Asari to "disclaim violence and provocation" and "allow all lawful economic activity to resume unimpeded." For his part, Colonel Paul Okimbo had promised to "stabilize Asariland to prevent the unwarranted loss of life." Slowing, Marissa read the final paragraph: "We urge Bobby Okari to place the good of the Asari above his own ambitions, and to call on his remaining followers to resume their normal lives."

Watching her face, Bobby said softly, "How many pieces of silver it required, they do not mention." He took the paper from her hand. "This is a hunting license, Marissa. Karama and the oilmen have isolated me. Now I will bear sole blame for whatever they choose to do."

Before she could respond, an elderly subchief appeared at their door. Formally addressing Bobby, he said, "Your father, Chief Okari, must speak with you."

Bobby glanced from Marissa to the man. "With both of us," he answered.

4

RESTLESS, PIERCE SCANNED THE INTERNET FOR descriptions of an eclipse.

In the middle of the day, he read, a shadow moves across the sun. For a few moments, the sky becomes like that of a moonlit night; animals and birds go silent, and nature seems in suspension. Though the sun has vanished, its outer edge is visible as a ghostly hole around the black disk of the moon. But for that, and the gas flaring Marissa had so vividly described, Goro would be plunged into darkness.

Anxious for news, Pierce returned to the BBC Web site. A new bulletin was reporting an agreement. For a moment he was hopeful. Then he read Colonel Paul Okimbo's promise to restore Asariland to a state of order and knew, from weeks of following the Asari movement after the massacre at Lana, that his friends' peril had only deepened. In that moment, he thought of Bobby and Marissa twelve years ago, heading blindly toward this day, and imagined what might have happened had he met Marissa sooner.

THE AUDITORIUM WHERE Bobby Okari would speak was small. A scattering of white and black students mixed with some older people from Berkeley—the men often distinguished by ponytails or beards, the women by an absence of makeup—whose world-view, Pierce surmised, had been shaped by the sixties. At Marissa's behest, she and Pierce sat close to the stage, where Bobby Okari waited behind a cadaverous professor of international relations who had begun to introduce him. After describing Bobby as a visiting professor of literature and one of Africa's most gifted young novelists, the man's voice became a pipe organ of piety: Bobby Okari's true mission, it transpired, was to speak for the embattled people of West Africa who, for too long, had suffered from the oppression of neocolonialists, arms merchants, purveyors of diamonds, and, most deadly, petroleum companies who fed the Western world's rapacious thirst for oil.

Immediately, Pierce was bored. The professor struck him as a man whose impact on these problems consisted of ringing declarations to groups who could have recited them in their sleep. The more fruitful study was Bobby Okari. From his biography and appearance, Pierce put him at a good ten years older than Marissa; small and bright-eyed, he awaited his turn with an obvious restiveness. When at last the professor finished his peroration, Marissa leaned forward in anticipation, and Pierce wondered what about this diminutive figure Marissa found so captivating.

The first seconds were not promising—Bobby Okari looked barely taller than the podium. With an engaging smile, he stood briefly on his toes, accenting the moment of unintended comedy. "I don't worry if you can't see me," he assured his audience in a resonant voice. "If you can hear me, you can also hear my people."

For the next half hour, Bobby Okari enthralled his audience as completely as, judging from her rapt expression, he enthralled Marissa Brand. In mesmeric cadences, he limned the paradox through which oil riches in the hands of klepto-crats and oil companies deepened the Asari people's misery. Nor did he exempt his listeners. "When you use our oil," he told them, "you facili-tate our exploitation.

"Without knowing it you help them steal our land, enslave our children, turn our girls into pros-titutes who service the men who fill your gas tanks. Nor can you alleviate our suffering merely by developing more gas-efficient cars."

This drew a ripple of nervous laughter. "When the white man came to Luandia," Bobby con-tinued, "our people had the land and the white man had the Bible. Now the Asari have the Bible and the white man has our land. As in so many things, this reflects the toxins of Western society—racism and greed."

Seeing Marissa's mouth curl in a bitter smile, Pierce divined that much of her response to Bobby was visceral, and perhaps involved race. "When Luandians hate Americans," he said, "it is because Americans allow the oil companies to embody the evils you claim to deplore." Pausing, Bobby surveyed his audience as though looking into each face and heart, and then his voice softened. "But I do not come here to abuse you.

"So many of you were once soldiers of conscience in the struggle to make your country what it claims to be. *All* of you can be that now. Today, your moral imperative must be to improve the lot of humanity—not just among your own people but in the world. Even, I dare to hope, in Luandia."

The audience applauded warmly. But for Bobby Okari, Pierce knew, this night was merely practice for an enterprise more challenging than pricking the nerve ends of Berkeley progressives. Touching Marissa's arm, he murmured, "I'd very much like to meet him."

"I HAVE A modest goal," Bobby told Pierce wryly. "To start a movement among the Asari, like that of Martin Luther King, which will spread throughout the delta until we are too mighty to resist."

They sat in a Thai restaurant on Shattuck Avenue, a favorite of Bobby and Marissa's. To Pierce, Bobby's entire being belied his self-deprecating tone: his eyes were filled with hope, even confidence, and his slender frame radiated a kinetic energy. With a smile that mingled challenge with humor, Bobby said, "You are skeptical, I see."

Marissa looked from Bobby to Pierce. "It's a

reflex," Pierce answered with a laugh. "I'm Irish—caught between an immigrant's optimism and a certainty that the world is about to break your heart."

Bobby's smile lingered. "You're also a lawyer, Damon. Lawyers shun delusion and cherish facts. And so, the facts. The Asari are poor, uneducated, unarmed, and scorned by the many ethnic groups who far outnumber them. When nonviolence is one's only choice, it is best to embrace the moral high ground.

"To paraphrase Robert Kennedy, even the humblest among us can create ripples of hope and daring which, when they cross, create a wave so powerful that it overcomes the mightiest wall of oppression. Kennedy said this in South Africa. In the quarter century that followed, Mandela and a handful of prisoners overcame apartheid by seizing the imagination of the world."

Bobby's aspirations for his people seemed no more modest than for himself. But though he appeared confident in his persona as leader, he glanced often at Marissa, as though gauging her reaction. "Our leaders exist in a world of their own," he continued. "But PGL exists in the wider world that turned on corporate malefactors in South Africa. Engaged Americans can compel PGL and your government to demand more from our leaders than oil. That was my business tonight. Perhaps someday you can help us."

Already, Pierce realized, Bobby saw him as a potential instrument of his will. It struck him that in Marissa's eyes this small but vibrant man might make other men seem smaller. Looking from Marissa to Pierce, Bobby asked politely, "How did you two meet?"

Pierce glanced at Marissa. "We're in the same creative writing class."

"Yes," Marissa added with a pointed smile. "Damon even liked my story."

In a rueful tone, Bobby inquired, "The story I haven't read?"

Marissa shrugged. "One of them," she replied.

Something in this exchange caused Bobby to look at Pierce more closely. "Tell me about yourself, Damon."

Briefly, Pierce outlined his life from parochial school in Boston, to Harvard, and at last to San Francisco. "A classic Irish-American story," he told Bobby. "I'm more curious about yours. How did you become a writer? How did you become an activist? How in the world did you wind up *here*?"

Bobby's chuckle was as deep as his voice. "From childhood, my father said I had the devil's own way with words—many of which displeased him. I also have a mother who found her husband's interest in other women less than charming. My father is chief of our village; perhaps as a favor to himself, or perhaps to her, he used some of the

51

money PGL paid for his passivity to dispatch me to an English boarding school.

"There I learned to love the written word. English is the white man's only gift to Luandia: the Brits taught me to value Dickens and the principles of liberty they cherished for themselves, if not us. The intoxicating experience of discovering both language and hypocrisy simultaneously made me a debater and, eventually, a novelist and journalist in my native land, bent on exposing the outrages I now saw with clarity. But soon I perceived that my scribbling alone would not transform Luandia." Bobby's smile embraced both Pierce and Marissa. "A long journey from bad to worse, my father would say—which is what brought me here two years ago. Friends within the government made it clear that my alternative to a sabbatical abroad was jail. Out of what I suspect remain mixed motives, my father once again encouraged me to decamp. He seems to think I will bring trouble to his door." With a grin, Bobby finished: "Of course, there's no wind so ill it fails to blow a little bit of good. It was here I met Marissa after giving a speech much like this one. The same speech, in fact."

Pierce found his seeming openness engaging, all the more for the lightness with which he treated the difficulties that had compelled him to leave. "Are you going back?" Damon asked.

"*We* are," Marissa said.

Her answer seemed more for Bobby than Pierce.

Watching Pierce, Bobby appeared to read his thoughts. "For a time," he said, "I worried that to go to this strange place would impose on Marissa hardships no man could ask. Especially one who hopes—no, expects—to be consumed with the cause of his people." Bobby gave Marissa a glancing smile. "Not to mention that my father is both a Christian and a polygamist. Though I pledge her my utter fidelity, I fear that Marissa finds my background novel."

"Not that novel," Marissa interposed in a tone both mild and sardonic, and Pierce remembered the father of her short story.

Bobby smiled at her. "In this matter, as in others, I'm my own man."

Dinner arrived—the dishes heavy on curry and spices. "If one can't replicate Luandian food," Bobby explained, "at least one can evoke its zest."

He began to consume his portion, wielding chopsticks with rapacious deftness, driven by an appetite surprising given his slightness. "Bobby's eating for his people," Marissa explained with the air of a color commentator. "He burns off calories just sitting around."

Hungry, Pierce occupied himself with dinner. Only when Bobby's plate was clear did Pierce ask him, "About returning, do you worry for your safety?"

"Is it dangerous, you mean? Possibly. But it is my lifeblood—where I come from, what I care for, what I write about. What would I become in America but a random black man with an advanced degree, an ornament for some faculty, trained to teach young would-be writers who, when they fail, will themselves become teachers." Bobby scowled at the table. "What would I feel *then,* when I read some truncated report in the *New York Times* about the misery of my people? What would I be to my friends but a stranger who sends them gifts and money? What kind of shadow life would I substitute for a life of meaning, even if that life is all too brief?"

The last phrase, though casually stated, struck Pierce so forcibly that he wondered at its impact on Marissa. "And you?" Pierce asked her.

"I'm an American by birth," she answered calmly. "But when I watch our politicians on TV, or listen to talk radio, Americans seem so insulated from reality that they're narcotized.

"And yet I know that my mother's cases as a social worker are worse than ever, the neighborhood she works in more hopeless than before. There's another generation of black men in jail, and Americans have no interest in or will to change what they conveniently believe is all the black man's fault. In Luandia, perhaps I can make a difference."

Bobby did not comment. But Pierce read a message into his silence: that life in Luandia would be harder than she knew. Perhaps, he intuited, Bobby wanted her too much to say this. Reflecting on the short story that Bobby had not read, he wondered whether—however fond of each other they were—their relationship relied on such strategic silences, and whether she was drawn to Bobby less from passion than the need to heal the wounds of identity and family. But all he chose to say was "I admire you both."

It was true. Still, at that moment he guessed he and Bobby would never become close. In the days before the next writing class, when he found himself thinking of Marissa, he identified the reason why, and sensed that Bobby Okari already knew it.

5

PIERCE STARED AT THE MOON ABOVE THE OCEAN, casting pallid light on the windblown line of cypress trees that marked land's end. He checked his watch again. It was eleven-fifteen, and in two hours the eclipse would darken the village of Goro. The BBC had no more news of Bobby Okari. Pierce's only antidote to worry was memory.

"I've always been lucky," he had told her. Now he wished that, like his father, he believed that luck could be passed from one person to another.

THEY HAD BEEN lingering over dinner at Rivoli, an elegant Italian place near campus. By tacit consent, their postclass dinners had become a ritual, facilitated by Bobby's immersion in teaching, writing, speaking, and planting the seeds of a movement in Luandia through incessant late-night phone calls. Their conversations, largely concerned with the craft of fiction—theirs, and others'—rarely became personal, and only once or twice did Pierce wonder if Bobby knew of them. But tonight Marissa seemed curious about his life.

"It's true," Pierce told her. "My dad insists that I was *born* lucky."

The smile this elicited was quizzical. "Born white, you mean?"

"Even better," Pierce responded amiably. "Born on St. Patrick's Day, and blessed by a future president. Or so my father thought."

HIS FATHER WAS a storyteller. Sean Pierce had told *this* story so often that Damon could recite it.

"On March 17, 1968," Sean would declaim in his immigrant's brogue, "at St. Margaret's Hospital in our neighborhood of Dorchester, I learned that my seventh and last child was, after six blessed daughters, a son. Tears in my eyes, I answered, 'You've made my heart sing, Dr. Lowell.' "

In those days, Sean would continue, there was little for a new father to do but celebrate with other men. So after kissing the exhausted Patrice on her forehead and noting with pride the miraculous infant's shock of black hair, Sean departed on a tide of elation. Reaching the street as the metallic clock of a bank chimed twelve times, signaling noon, Sean briskly walked one and a half miles to the precise midpoint of the St. Patrick's Day parade. Amid the revelers at the corner of D Street, some flushed with the excitements of whiskey, Sean awaited the Hibernian marchers—the intricate floats evoking Ireland on flatbed trucks; the familiar faces of the local politicos who always led the way.

But he could tell this day was different. The cheers were louder and, up the street, the crowds pressed closer than normal. And then Sean saw the two Irish princes at the head of the parade who, though he had never met them, were woven into the fabric of his psyche. With each confident stride Edward and Robert Kennedy, senators both, came nearer, drawing cries of surprise and delight from the onlookers—in many of their homes a picture of their martyred brother Jack hung beside that of the pope. And just yesterday, in the caucus room of the Senate, Robert Kennedy had declared that he, too, would reach out for the presidency.

One on each half of the two-lane street, the brothers paused to shake hands as they passed, Robert on the side nearest Sean. Propelled by this confluence of wonders—the birth of his son and now Robert Kennedy walking toward him—Sean felt himself drawn into the street. "Go get him, Bobby," he heard someone call. "Lyndon can't hold a candle to you."

Laughing, Robert Kennedy looked about for his well-wisher and spotted Damon's father coming toward him. For an instant Kennedy froze, before seeing the rapt expression in Sean Pierce's eyes. Then they were face to face. In the one moment they would share on earth, Sean blurted, "My first son was born four hours ago. Both of us wish you well."

Looking up at the taller man, Bobby Kennedy grinned. "What's your boy's name?"

"Damon. Damon Pierce."

"A fine Irish name. He'll thank you for it." Bobby glanced toward the crowd for another hand to shake. Then, on impulse, he turned back to Sean. "What's your parish?"

"St. Gregory's, in Dorchester."

"My grandfather's parish." Kennedy's voice softened. "Let's each say a prayer that the luck of the Irish blesses your new son. And I'd be grateful if your prayer included a bit of luck for me."

"I will," Sean promised. Then the future president was gone and, instead of seeking out a bar, Sean went to St. Gregory's to keep his promise to Robert Kennedy.

"AND THEN HE was dead," Marissa said to Damon. "My mother cried, she tells me."

Damon nodded. "As did my father."

"But he still thought you were lucky?"

Pierce smiled a little. "It became part of the

58

myth. For a time he pondered whether his prayer dwelt too much on me, and had failed Robert Kennedy. But he was quite sure that Kennedy had kept his end of the bargain.

"In the end, he concluded that I had gotten all the luck two men's prayers could give me—and the luck meant for Bobby Kennedy, as well. Everything that's happened since persuades him that he's right. For him, my success in life is less an achievement than a gift."

Marissa tilted her head. "Not an expectation?"

Pierce sipped from his glass of rich Brunello di Montalcino, the last of the bottle they shared. "You have to understand my world, Marissa. Did your parents go to college?"

"That and more. My father has a PhD in English, my mom a master's in social work. I've got no room to be a wonder."

Pierce briefly scanned the dwindling crowd, so clearly of the rarefied environment spawned by the Berkeley campus, so far from the pubs of Dorchester. "Neither of my parents got past grade school. Their world was a bounded one, their greatest fear that us kids would be tainted by malign influences." A memory made Damon smile wryly. "So they were mortified when my sister Meg applied for a scholarship to Barnard."

Marissa looked amused. "An all-girls school? What could possibly go wrong?"

"It was in *New York,* may the saints preserve us.

So my parents enlisted the help of the mother superior. As Meg tells it, Sister Agnes warned her in sepulchral tones that a priest in New York reported that any girl who went to Barnard lost her faith *and* her virginity within six months." Pierce grinned. "For a rapturous moment my sister was galvanized by visions of sexual deliverance. But, for our parents, that was that. They dispatched her to Boston College, where she met the man she married before they settled down close to home. Life was like that."

Marissa finished her wine. "But not yours?"

"I was the youngest, and a boy. Still, until I was eighteen all my friends had names like Milligan and McNamara, and the biggest event in our lives before then was when Pope John Paul said Mass for a hundred thousand of us on Boston Common. Now all but a handful are firemen or cops or in their father's construction business and, with variations in piety, still Catholic."

"Aren't you?"

"Only when I visit my parents. Like Meg, all that sexual repression got to me, but with a healthier result—a quiet but *very* persistent rebellion."

Marissa touched a curled finger to her lips, her narrowing eyes signaling a speculative amusement. "So now you're cured?"

"Mostly. Though whenever there's a news flash about some sexual deviant being caught, my first reflex is that he's Catholic."

She laughed, displaying even white teeth whose only imperfection, the slightest gap in front, Pierce found charming. "I know about guilt," she said, "if not repression. My father's side is Jewish."

"Lucky for you. In my observation, Jewish kids grow up believing that aspiration is not only good but imperative—you *must* be educated, you *can* succeed, you *will* outstrip your parents—"

"*Who,*" Marissa interrupted, "will never believe you've achieved enough."

For the moment, Pierce suppressed his curiosity. "Maybe. But the voice my friends and I too often heard said, 'Don't aim too high or stray too far when the greatest aspiration is the afterlife.' And so I, like my sister, went to Boston College. Then I graduated summa cum laude and really *did* rebel."

"You decided to become Jack Kerouac?"

Pierce shook his head. "In the end, I was too steeped in practicality. But, to my parents' horror, I decided on Harvard Law School, that coven of atheists. Instead of going to B.C. law school on the scholarship they offered."

"How did you manage?"

"Luck, of course. The financial aid office at Harvard didn't have enough to pay my way. So they directed me to a book with the daunting title *Restricted Scholarships*. Nothing doing: the restrictions were things like 'Latvian-Americans,' or 'graduates of Yale.'" Pierce smiled. "Then, on the second-to-last page, I found the 'William Stoughton Bequest.'

"The bequest dated back to 1750. Stoughton was, as I recall, a colonial governor of Massachusetts. His only stipulation was that the recipient of his largesse had to come from Dorchester . . ."

"Like it was written for you."

Pierce laughed. "Stoughton was a total WASP—judging from the oil painting I saw later, the last thing he'd imagined was empowering the Irish hordes. But in 1750 there *were* no Irish living in Dorchester. So William Stoughton became my benefactor. Even my father saw the humor in it. And, of course, the luck."

Marissa gave him a keen look. "Do you still feel lucky?"

"Yes," he answered seriously. "I take nothing for granted—least of all, despite its faults, this country. If my father hadn't come to America, God knows who I'd be."

Marissa frowned, then shrugged dismissively. "It probably makes a difference if your ancestors came as volunteers. My father's did. My mother's didn't."

Something in her tone suggested that the subject was closed—perhaps because its complexities, as suggested by her short story, involved far more than race. Pierce decided to leave it there. Only later did he perceive that this caution was a form of caring, and that he did not wish to lose a woman he did not even have.

6

CHIEF FEMI OKARI AWAITED BOBBY AND MARISSA in the main room of his home. By village standards, it was sumptuous, with rugs covering the floor and another hanging on the wall behind him, depicting the chief in ceremonial robes. He sat in his ornate carved chair, holding his cane of office, and his robes and gold-beaded headdress reflected those in the portrait. His face was somber, his voice low. "A word," he told Bobby. "Before darkness comes."

Bobby hesitated before nodding. The curt gesture spoke to Marissa of the deep conflict between them, their years of estrangement, and the ingrained deference of the young for the old, a son for his father. "I have heard from Eric Aboh," the chief said. "Leave your plans for another day."

"So *you* are part of this," Bobby burst out with an anger so raw that Marissa flinched. "You conspire with Eric and the others to betray me."

"Betray *you?*" his father asked in a tone of incredulity. "We are *frightened,* as would be any man of reason. Tell me, do you think Okimbo's offer of 'protection' made Aboh feel *safe*? Eric understands well enough what that could mean, and so do you." His voice lowered again. "I am still chief of this village. If I ask my people to disperse, they will."

Bobby managed a dismissive smile. "Will they,

63

now? It is thirty years since you became chief, scarcely longer than the time you have taken PGL money and allowed 'your' people to scavenge for themselves in the cesspool you have left them. Especially our youth." When his father stiffened with outrage, Bobby continued, "Take Marissa's favorite. By next year Omo may be a prostitute in Waro; in five years she may be dead of AIDS. But you will still be 'chief of this village.'

"Do 'your' people know of your fine house in Port George, the young women you keep there with the money PGL gives you to 'compensate' them for this ruin of *their* land? If they do, it is not because I've told them. I am, despite all, a dutiful son."

His father scrutinized him with weary eyes. "So this is still about your mother."

Watching, Marissa wished she could turn away. Bobby's gaze expressed only pity and contempt. "How much weight you give, Father, to the most paltry of your sins."

Femi Okari gazed at his only son as his face sagged with regret. Then he stood, abandoning all ceremony to place a hand on Bobby's shoulder as he looked into his face. "I have made mistakes. They are painful. I do not wish for you to make a mistake more painful than losing a son, at a cost to many more people than one old man. Please, heed me."

Bobby met his eyes. Then, his face closing, he slowly shook his head. "Too late, Father. For us both."

Without waiting for his father's answer, Bobby left. Glancing over her shoulder, Marissa saw Femi Okari shake his head.

At the center of Goro, the villagers had gathered, their mood shadowed by fear of Karama and by the passage of the moon, its edge now appearing to touch the sun. As Bobby moved toward them, his cell phone rang.

He answered swiftly, eyes fixed on Marissa as he listened. Briefly, they shut. Before hanging up, Bobby said quietly, "Be safe."

Once more his gaze met Marissa's. "That was Atiku," he said. "In Ebu, the demonstration has collapsed. In most villages people are afraid to leave their houses. There are whispers that our youth lynched those workers on my orders."

"Is that possible?" Marissa asked. "Not on your orders, but despite them?"

Bobby stared at the ground with hooded eyes. "So many of our youth are filled with hatred. It's as though violence is in the water we cannot drink and the air that singes our lungs." He came to her, placing his hands on her shoulders. "We are truly alone, Marissa. Those rumors about me are part of it."

Looking into his face, Marissa searched for a way to ask him to disperse the crowd. "Think of what you've already done. You've given the Asari identity and purpose."

Bobby smiled faintly. "And now I should stop?"

"Not stop. Pause."

He angled his head to indicate the gathering. "In ten minutes the eclipse will be upon us; in another ten I will send them home. But now is not the moment for me to show fear. Please, Marissa, do not make me afraid."

He held her gaze for one more moment. Then he took a cigarette lighter from his pocket and snapped it once, then twice more. When it did not light, he took out another. As this one produced a flame, Bobby laughed softly.

"Always prepare," he said. He straightened, standing taller, and walked toward the crowd and into the lengthening shadow of the eclipse.

7

AT SEA RANCH, PIERCE GLANCED AT HIS WATCH again.

It was just after midnight. In the deep black surrounding him, unfiltered by city lights, he imagined the darkness moving toward Goro. Then, as vividly, he recalled the night his relationship to Marissa proved as complex as he had begun to sense it was.

THAT EVENING HAD begun no differently than others. The two of them emerged from class, debating a classmate's story that she liked and he disdained. "I call it 'ennui fiction,'" he said as they reached the sidewalk, "where the main character wakes up, discovers his hair dryer doesn't work, perceives that as a metaphor, and decides not to leave his apartment—"

"I thought it was sensitive."

"What about 'enervated'? If the guy in that story came to life, you wouldn't give him a nanosecond." Pierce turned to her. "So where are we going to dinner? Stories that go nowhere make me hungry."

Marissa considered this. "I don't feel like being waited on," she said. "Tonight I feel more like pizza from a box."

"Fine with me," Pierce responded on impulse. "Let's go to your place and order one."

Marissa scrutinized him in the dark, then gave what passed for a careless shrug. "Only if you like anchovies," she answered.

They stopped at a corner store for a bottle of cabernet, then drove to her walk-up in a venerable three-story building. When she opened her door, hesitating for just a moment, Pierce followed her into a cramped efficiency apartment. Its con-tents—a fold-out couch, chair, desk, bookshelf, and kitchen table—included only modest clues to her life: a photograph of Bobby, another of a pleasant-faced black woman Pierce took to be her mother, and, to his surprise, a black-and-white poster of a perspiring Michael Jordan. "Do you like basketball?" he asked.

"Nope," she answered crisply. "That's only there 'cause Michael's hot. What else do you like on your pizza?"

AFTER DINNER THEY sat facing each other on the couch, Pierce at one end, Marissa at the other, still sipping the spicy red wine. "So I'm waiting for your story," he said.

She sipped from her glass, eyeing Pierce over the rim. "You've read them all, thank you. There aren't any more."

He smiled at this deliberate misunderstanding. "Of your life."

Her wary expression deepened. "Why does it matter?"

Though his smile lingered, Damon chose to meet her gaze with new directness. "Friends talk about lot of things, I always thought."

"We do talk."

"Rarely about you. For example, all you've said about your parents is that he's Jewish and an academic, and she's an African-American social worker. My guess is they're divorced, though I don't even know that much."

She seemed to study him more closely. "Oh," she said softly, "I think you know a lot. Sometimes when you look at me I can see your mind at work. And I wonder why."

Feeling caught out, Pierce covered this with a shrug. "When I like someone I want to know them. Tell me, how did your parents meet?"

After a moment she gave an almost imperceptible nod, suggesting both acquiescence and reluctance. "They were civil rights workers in Mississippi," she began, "during the Freedom Summer of 1964. My mom describes it as a time of idealism and change—both of them were from the North, and they'd stepped into this place so alien and filled with hate she began to worry they might not get out alive. Every moment took on an immediacy, she tells me—when they made love, it was not only the *best* time, but maybe the *last* time." Marissa's smile was knowing, as though she had perceived the ending of the story before her parents. "So at the end of the summer they celebrated their survival by getting married, two people who saw themselves as symbols of the new order. My existence is an accident of history—the country's, and theirs."

Though she spoke easily enough, a slightly caustic undertone suggested that affecting detachment was the carapace for far more complex feelings. "Were you born down South?" Pierce asked.

"In New Orleans—my father was getting his doctorate at Tulane." Marissa paused. "The hospital had been integrated, and I was one of the first overtly biracial babies the place had ever seen. Years later my mama told me that on my birth certificate—next to the box for my mother's race, 'Negro,' and my father's, 'Caucasian'—was the handwritten notation 'Is this correct?' She insisted they couldn't raise me in such a place."

The last sentence contained a quiet irony, an awareness that questions of identity and race were not so easily escaped. "So that's when they moved to Cleveland?" Pierce asked.

"Uh-huh. My father landed a job as an assistant professor, my mother as a caseworker for the county. They chose to live in a suburb noted for its public schools—which translated into 'lots of Jews, not many blacks.' That's where I discovered, without quite knowing it, that the bewilderment on my birth certificate extended to my Jewish grandmother."

"How so?"

Marissa stretched her legs in front of her, her feet nearly touching Pierce's, a hint that she was feeling more comfortable and, perhaps, even enjoying this relief from the solitude she seemed to carry with her. "Grandma Ruth would hug my father, but never Mom. And when she was just with my mother, she'd never look at her, even when they were talking.

"Now I realize we *scared* her. Her parents had fled Russia after most of the Jews in their village were slaughtered by Russian soldiers. Her first memories were of that story." Marissa's voice softened. "What that taught her was a fear of standing out—that being different could be fatal. Not only were Mama and I different, but we marked *her* as different, the Jew whose granddaughter was black. But all I knew then was that she never kissed me."

She said this in a tone of remembered puzzlement, but no self-pity. "If she's anything like my grandparents," Pierce ventured, "she could never acknowledge any of that."

"Of course not. The nearest we ever came was when I was twelve. For Christmas, of all things—which my mother insisted on celebrating—Grandma Ruth gave me Anne Frank's diary with a card saying, 'You must read this.'

"So I did. For some time afterward I woke up terrified that they were coming for me. Only I didn't know who *they* were, or whether they would kill me for being Jewish or black. What I really didn't know, I guess, was who *I* was supposed to be."

Pierce absorbed this. "One thing about my childhood," he remarked. "I always knew who I was supposed to be. Sometimes to a fault."

Marissa cupped the glass in her hand. "My mama tried to tell me I was 'special'—to be proud of my heritage, Jewish *and* black. But the message I'd begun to absorb was that I didn't get to choose. When we did *The Wizard of Oz* in sixth grade, I was the Wicked Witch of the West, a black girl in a very black dress. It made me feel uncomfortable—by then my dance teacher had told me that black women's bodies weren't well suited for ballet."

Marissa paused, looking down, and her dispassionate tone became tinged with self-

71

contempt. "But not as uncomfortable as realizing that I wanted Grandma Ruth to come see the play instead of Mama. I had a crush on the Jewish boy who played the scarecrow, and didn't want him to think of me as black. When my mother came up to hug me, I folded my arms and looked away."

Pierce squirmed inside. "You were a kid, Marissa."

She looked up at him. "What I'd begun to feel, and believe today, is that there's a need hardwired in the human species to define itself in relation to some lesser, dismissible race. That's why Bobby's people are so disposable—Luandians dismiss the Asari as an inferior ethnic group; Westerners dismiss them because they're black. But back then I blamed only *myself* for that."

Pierce searched for common ground—perhaps one of Sean Pierce's many stories of being disdained as an Irish Catholic. But the comparison struck him as superficial: he had never been confused about who he was; nor did merely entering a room set him apart.

Marissa's voice broke through his thoughts. "Do you know what I remember most from that time?" she told him. "When my mother showed me a sepia-tinted photograph of an ancient black woman and told me it was my great-grandmother, a slave. She meant it as a history lesson. But all I felt was this terrible shame."

She stopped there, pensive. "Where was your father in all this?" Pierce asked.

Her downward gaze persisted. At last she answered, "He's the part I struggle with. All the reasons I didn't tell my parents how confused I was came from suspicions about their marriage that turned out to be true.

"Their relationship had stopped being an act of glorious defiance. More and more my father spent time with whites, my mother with blacks. When I was small, I used to crawl into bed between them, holding their hands like I was some sort of human bridge." She paused again, then looked up at Pierce. "Sometimes I look back at myself as a girl of nine or ten, and it's like I'm someone else. That's the person I feel sad for."

Pierce felt them coming closer to truths that had eluded him. "Is your dad the man in your short story?"

The smile at one corner of her mouth did not change her eyes. "More or less. But there's one scene I'll never write."

Unwilling to push her, Pierce settled into silence. For a long time, Marissa contemplated her wineglass. "I was twelve," she said abruptly. "My mom was visiting her sister and her new baby. It was late at night, and I guess he figured I'd sleep right through. Instead my Anne Frank paranoia turned into a nightmare of men in uniforms breaking into my room—some black, some white. I was so afraid I wanted to find my father.

"My bedroom was at the top of the stairs. When

I cracked open the door, I heard voices." Marissa sipped her wine, as though reflecting back. "The light in the alcove was dim, but I could see them clearly enough. My father, kissing a woman who had slipped in through the door, running his hands all over her body.

"She was young and slender—not at all like my full-figured mother—and very white. They turned and started up the stairs, smiling at each other. I closed the door as softly as I could, so they wouldn't see or hear me. Then I pressed my back against the door, listening until I heard the door to my parents' bedroom close as softly as I'd closed mine."

Pierce remained silent until she looked up at him again. "That's all," she said. "Were you expecting more?"

"I was just wondering if you ever confronted him. Or told your mother."

"Neither. As time went on I discovered that my father had constant affairs, typically with graduate students, young women who reinforced his need to feel his own magnetism. All of them were white." Her tone became cool. "To him my mother wasn't a person—just part of an image he once had of himself. Having me was the sacrifice he made to keep her before realizing he didn't want either one of us. Eventually he got so blatant that even Mama couldn't take it.

"After the divorce he moved to a condominium,

where everyone was white and everything was symmetrical. When I visited on weekends it felt like I was trapped in a Fisher-Price village on Astroturf. I hated it. I hated the women he saw. Most of all, I hated *him*." Pierce saw her jawline tighten, and slivers of anger entered her voice. "When I told him I didn't want to come there anymore, he accused me of being an anti-Semite. He was so completely solipsistic that he looked at his own daughter and saw nothing but an angry black woman filled with all the rage my mother had never shown, all because she was too patient, too caretaking, too concerned with how I'd feel. And he never, ever *saw* her. So I rejected him, *all* of him, with all the fury I could muster."

Abruptly she fell silent, caught in the emotions of her narrative, yet perhaps regretting that she had taken it so far. To lighten the moment, Damon said laconically, "You should have put *that* part in the story."

To his surprise, Marissa gave a rueful laugh. "That part's mine. At least it was until now."

Though nothing in her tone underscored the last remark, it suggested that she had not fully revealed herself to Bobby Okari. But all Pierce said was "I guess things got better."

"Not for a while. I'd just started high school, where there were blacks mixed in with whites. And I was remote and angry all at once—the white kids found me intimidating; blacks thought I was 'snobby.' For a while I slipped back and forth between them, trying on attitudes and not fitting in anywhere. Then my father's example gave me direction."

"Which was?"

Marissa looked at him with renewed directness. "Sleeping with black guys. I didn't stop until I realized people were laughing at me, white *and* black, and that my reasons were no better than my father's. So I pulled myself out of it and hid behind a veneer of toughness. My own solitude became the safest place I knew."

"And that's when you started writing."

Her teeth flashed briefly. "How did you ever guess?"

"Sheer brilliance. Plus the fact that feeling different from everyone around me was what got *me* started."

She gave him an ironic look. "You felt special. *I* felt different. It's taken some time to separate myself from the identity laid out for me by other people and sort out who I was meant to be."

Pierce reached for the wine bottle, helping himself to another half glass. "Is that what Luandia's about?"

"I think so." She gave him a keen look. "Just to clear something up for you, I was drawn to Luandia *before* I met Bobby. Over a year ago I went with a human rights group to Waro, the major city. The services were collapsing; the roads were

76

congested; there were piles of garbage in the street; the power failed for hours on end. But there was a vitality I'd never seen before." She began to speak swiftly, passionately. "I was scared and enthralled and thought the people were amazing—filled with energy, directness, and the will to survive. Suddenly I felt that anything was possible for me there, that I could have an impact way bigger than anything I could accomplish here. Now I can't wait to go back."

Pierce did not analyze his impulse to object. "*Then* you were a foreigner who knew she was coming back here. From the sound of Bobby's plans, the next time coming back won't be so simple."

Marissa shrugged. "Then I'll have to become Luandian, won't I."

Pierce sipped his wine. "I wonder if fitting in will really be that easy."

Marissa bit her lip, lending her expression a stubborn cast. "In America I'm already twice a minority. Granted, less than half of me is black—Mama tells me there's at least one slave owner in the family tree. But for everyone except blacks I'm black. So I've chosen to embrace that. I can't be white, and don't want to be."

"And I can only be me, Marissa—an Irish Catholic with as open a heart as I can manage. That has to be enough."

Perhaps it was the wine, Pierce realized, that had made him say more than he should, or the sense that his time with Marissa was running out. She looked down again, seeming to draw a breath, then met his eyes with an expression of deep gravity. "For who?"

"Maybe for you."

She held his gaze, head slightly tilted, as though she were replaying his tone of voice. Then she said, "It can't be, Damon. It just can't."

The quiet insistence in her voice hinted at an inner struggle. With equal quiet, he answered, "I'm not your father. Or Bobby Okari. What matters to me is that I see you as you are."

Her eyes and body froze. "That's pretty condescending."

"Is it? I thought part of respecting someone was speaking honestly. That's what we've been doing." He softened his tone again. "Do you talk this way to Bobby?"

"I don't need to," she snapped. "I already feel stupid for saying this stuff to you. How much dumber would it be for me to whine to Bobby about adolescent angst or my parents' crummy marriage? For him I'm what he sees right now— and yes, that *is* enough."

"For who?" Pierce shot back. "Didn't you say your mother was too concerned with others' needs to speak out for herself? Or do you need Bobby to see you as someone too consumed by higher causes to bother him with herself?"

"That's completely unfair." Marissa stood, trembling with anger. "Damn you, Damon, for drawing me out and then turning that back against me. I gave you credit for being sensitive, when all you are is manipulative."

Standing to face her, Pierce felt himself flush. "All I've done was listen to you and, because you matter, challenge you. I think you know the difference. That's one of the reasons tonight happened the way it has. You can say anything to me you need to say, and that you *don't* say in the stories Bobby never reads." He lowered his voice again. "I care about you, Marissa. But then you've known that for a while."

Slowly the stiffness left her posture, and then she looked into his face. "What I know is that we're different. You're a poor boy from Boston who's grabbing what America has to offer you—a partnership in a corporate firm and the money to buy a Victorian in Pacific Heights, fill the cellar with fine wine, and have enough left over for liberal causes. It's only human for that to appeal to you. But I'm going where I can help people in a way that I think matters. The life you're headed for would be slow death to me."

"And yet you've imagined it," Pierce said softly. "Can you tell me you love Bobby as much as the cause he stands for?"

To his surprise, Marissa said nothing. Nor, despite her stricken expression, could she seem to look away.

Pierce touched her face. "It seems you're out of words."

Still she didn't speak. Gently, Pierce brought his face to hers.

As they kissed, he felt her hesitate, and then their kiss went deep. When it was done, she rested her forehead against his chest. In a strained voice, she said, "You have to go now."

Cradling her chin, he raised her head. Twisting away, she said, "*Please.* If you don't go I can never see you again."

She made it sound like a matter of her own survival. He touched her face with curled fingers and then, against his will, walked slowly to the door. When he turned again, she looked as vulnerable as the child she had described.

Out of compassion and the fear of losing her, Pierce left.

8

IN THE DARK OF NIGHT, PIERCE READ THE BBC'S latest bulletin.

General Savior Karama, the report said, had announced the imminent arrest of Bobby Okari. Karama's statement ended simply: "The necessary measures will be taken to maintain civil order as the arrest is carried out." But Pierce, familiar with war crimes, knew too well that bland phrases and the passive voice often signified unspoken horrors.

There was nothing more. In silence, more profound for what he could imagine all too well, Pierce recalled the last time he had seen Marissa Brand.

THE FOLLOWING WEEK, Marissa had not come to class. Afraid that he had offended her, Pierce forced himself to wait. But then she missed a second class, and a third.

He did not have her phone number; directory assistance could tell him nothing. Only his fear of making matters worse kept him from going to her apartment.

The next week she reappeared.

She would not meet his eyes. When class was over, she left before he could catch her.

He hurried outside, then stopped abruptly. She was waiting at the bottom of the steps, as though nothing had changed. But when he came closer, the anxiety he felt was reflected in her eyes.

Touching his sleeve, she asked, "Can we walk a little?"

Together they moved across the moonlit grass. She did not speak or look at him until they stood beneath the shadow of the campanile. Quietly, she said, "I'm leaving, Damon."

"Class? Or school?"

"America. Bobby's returning to Luandia—it's time, he's decided. I'm going, too."

A dull shock silenced him for an instant. "To do what?"

"Marry him. *Help* him." Her eyes held uncertainty and a hint of pain. "I don't expect you to understand. But I won't be sad to leave a place where so many take so much for granted, and go where the simplest thing—the survival of your child—is precious."

He drew closer, looking down into her face. "Is this about Bobby, or the cause?"

"I don't separate them. The work is part of who he is." Her tone, though sharper, contained a plea for understanding. "It's also about me."

"But do you love him? Does he love you? If he doesn't *see* you, Marissa, all the good works in the world won't make you feel less alone."

For a moment she looked away. With fresh urgency, he asked, "Why didn't you come to class?"

"You know the reason."

"Do I? Then look at me and say it."

When she gazed up at him it seemed an act of will, though she answered in a soft, deliberate voice. "I love him. I want the life we'll have together. But you have the power to confuse me."

He tried to restrain himself from showing hope. "Then maybe you shouldn't go yet."

"I'm going. But right now it's like jumping into the unknown, the biggest thing I've ever done or will do. Just by *being,* you make me doubt myself."

"Are you sure that's about me, Marissa? Or is it

also about Bobby and the choice to be with him?"

She shook her head, an ambiguous gesture he could not decipher. "Please, Damon, help me. This is something I need to do."

He looked into her face, caught between the sense that he might still dissuade her and the instinct that a man less selfish would respond as a friend. As though someone else were speaking, he heard himself say, "Then I hope your life in Luandia is all you want it to be. Keep safe for me, all right?"

For a moment she tried to smile at him. Then she reached up, fingers grasping the hair at the nape of his neck, and kissed him swiftly on the lips.

"I have to go," she said, and hurried away into the darkness.

THOUGH MARISSA HAD disappeared, she had not vanished.

Her first letter had surprised him. He answered promptly; her next letter, more discursive, had a warmth and comfort that surprised him more. She had come to understand that she did not want to lose him, she said—from eight thousand miles, friendship was possible, even essential. And so they began writing, trading stories about their different worlds and observations about the world at large.

He had been wrong about her. Though she struggled in Luandia, she persevered. As the years passed, Pierce could feel her growth: he still remembered entire passages from the early letters that she had written, and he had saved, before e-mail became their way of speaking to each other.

"When I first arrived," she wrote after two years in Luandia, "I was as clueless as you thought I'd be. My American family was fractured and dys-functional; in Luandia, families share everyone's business in a way that takes some getting used to. I was outspoken about everything; here even strong women resort to subterfuge.

"In Goro, polygamy still exists. Women aren't allowed to cook during their period, or to appear at social events if they've just had a baby. Marriage is usually arranged—with the appropriate bride price, of course. And despite everything, I've come to love it here.

"That's taken some work. I was married in Goro as a true Luandian bride. I walked to my wedding with a large tin bucket balanced on my head, filled with gifts from Bobby suitable to my new life as a married woman—native wraps, shoes, a watch, a handbag, an umbrella, and some cooking utensils. In my entire life, I'd barely cooked. But then I'd never walked a hundred feet beneath a bucket I was forbidden to touch, to the beat of a line of native drummers. By my bridal day, I could actu-ally dance to the beat a little. Even Chief Okari seemed impressed.

"But becoming a wife was easier than being

accepted as Bobby's partner. I know Luandian women who've forged a place of influence based on sheer character and will. But at first all I could do was avoid getting hit on: in Luandia, sexual taboos are minimal. Never was I more alluring. But never once was I unfaithful to Bobby.

"Like everything else, married life was an adjustment. In many ways Bobby reverted to the traditional male role—spending time with other men, expecting me to do household chores without a lot of thanks. What I wanted was to be part of Bobby's movement. It helped that he respected my judgment; maybe it helped more for me to learn patience.

"After a time, I began going to meetings with Bobby and his advisers. I was careful to parcel out my advice sparingly, or to save it for when he and I were alone. Now, I think, no one doubts my commitment to his cause. Just the other day, I realized that Luandia truly is my home. People have started addressing me with honorifics like 'auntie' or 'madam.' The little village girl I most love, Omo, always calls me 'ma'am.'"

In the letters and e-mails she sent him over the years, her precarious existence seemed almost exotic. But her inner life remained, at most, a subtext. Even when he had known her she had been more guarded: now, given the gulf between how they chose to live, to explain herself might seem beyond the power of the printed word. Or perhaps it was the way they had parted. Whatever the case, he divined that she, too, was childless solely because the only children she mentioned were, like Omo, those whose futures she had come to fear for, just as Pierce now feared for her.

Once more, he checked his watch. It was one-fifteen; in Luandia, ten-fifteen in the morning. The eclipse was moments away.

9

MARISSA WATCHED BOBBY AS HE CLIMBED THE platform around which silent villagers clustered.

Most were gazing upward, hands shading their eyes. The sun was partially covered now, reduced by the black disk of the moon to a diminishing crescent of light. The air was still; the birds soundless. In the gathering darkness, narrow bands of light and shadow raced across the red earth.

Omo came to Marissa's side. The crescent diminished to a sliver, then broke into pinpoints of light that vanished one by one. "Look, ma'am," Omo exclaimed.

Marissa smiled at her wonder. "Those dots are the last sunlight," she explained, "shining through the valleys on the face of the moon."

The sole remaining light became as brilliant as a diamond. Then its glimmer vanished, and the black moon was framed by the faintest of orange halos.

The village, for once unlit by flaring oil, was swathed in eerie darkness.

From atop the platform, Bobby called out, "Let the world see *our* light."

Along with Omo and Marissa, people began snapping cigarette lighters, their glow illuminating somber faces that now turned from the sky to Bobby. He stood straighter, preparing to speak, and then became still, as though seeing something the others did not.

The first sound Marissa heard came from the ocean.

Turning, she saw the stream of lights on the obsidian waters, heard the growl of outboard motors heading toward the beach. From above, a sudden beam of yellow cut the darkness, causing Omo to shrink back against Marissa. The black form of a helicopter appeared over the palm trees, blades chopping as it rotated to turn its searchlight on Bobby. A second helicopter appeared, then a third, their thudding so loud that Marissa could hear no other sounds. As their searchlights crossed, she saw the black logo of PGL.

She swirled to look at Bobby, suddenly small and stricken. She drew Omo closer. Pressed against her, the girl trembled.

From the ocean the throb of outboard motors grew nearer. Turning, Marissa saw men emerging from the first boat as it struck the sand, weapons projecting from their shadow. "Oh my God," she cried out. Then a spark came from a figure running toward them, and Marissa heard the soft moan of the man beside her falling to his knees.

Yanking Omo by the arm, Marissa pulled her to the ground.

Bullets flew from all directions. The man beside her, gut-shot, shuddered and was still. In the darkness Marissa saw the flash of guns firing, heard their cracks amid pounding footsteps and yelps of pain and panic. An acrid smell sifted through the air, and Marissa's eyes began to water. Omo pressed so tightly against her that they seemed to breathe as one. "Please, God," the girl whispered.

Marissa shut her eyes. From the darkness came the haunting sound of soldiers singing and chanting, the cries of women and children, the muffled sound of bodies falling, the crackling of fire. The smell of tear gas mingled with that of burning wood.

Marissa swallowed convulsively. Through slitted eyes she saw the village burning. Backlit by the rising flames, a soldier shot a kneeling man in the back of the head. The soldiers kept up their eerie, warlike chant, their deep voices a terrible counterpoint to the piteous pleas of men and women and children, the shouts of their comrades, the dull thud as a soldier kicked a girl writhing on the ground. A dry retching sound issued from Omo's throat.

"I'm still with you," Marissa whispered. From

behind them Marissa heard boots stomping, the sounds of slaughter coming closer. The heat of conflagration brought dampness to her forehead. Closing her eyes, she prepared to die in Luandia.

She lay there, Omo whimpering in her arms. Minutes passed. The cries subsided, the gunfire grew scattered. The chanting stopped. In the eerie silence, glowing cinders brushed her face.

She opened her eyes again. The eclipse was passing, and the smoke of fire and tear gas drifted through the false dawn. A few feet from her lay Omo's would-be suitor, an arm stretching toward them, eyes sightlessly peering from his nearly decapitated head. Omo trembled soundlessly.

Fearful of notice, Marissa did not move.

Nor did she wish to. Arrayed in front of her were the bodies of once vibrant villagers in the grotesque postures of violent death. Two soldiers wrenched a man outside her line of vision; gunshots followed. A small boy darted into the bush, seeking cover. Another soldier, his pants around his ankles, sodomized the wife of a village elder as she lay on her stomach groaning; the plump head teacher stared dully at the soldier and his victim, blood dribbling from her severed ear. Three soldiers poured gasoline on a wounded youth, then wrenched the cigarette lighter from his grasp and set his clothes afire, adding more gasoline as he began to twitch and scream. Beside him, Omo's mother clasped a head scarf to her face, as though to ward off the stench of burning flesh. A soldier ended the boy's misery with a gunshot and then, turning, put a bullet through Omo's mother's head.

"Good," a deep baritone intoned from behind Marissa. She knew it was Okimbo before he stood in front of her.

She gazed up at him, Omo's face still pressed against her. "You came to hear a speech," he said. "Listen, and I will give you one."

Marissa sat up, mute. Okimbo walked to the platform and climbed it to stand where Bobby had, the colonel's audience corpses strewn amid slaughtered goats and chickens and the few villagers not yet dead—a woman covering her face; a six-year-old boy wailing without tears; a grizzled man, eyes dull with shock, contemplating his missing arm. Their sole kinship now was fear. Of the buildings, only the church and Bobby and Marissa's home survived.

Pausing to adjust his eye patch, Okimbo drew himself up as though imitating Bobby, addressing the dead and traumatized with mock solemnity. "Asari people," he proclaimed, "this is your day of liberation."

He pointed to the charred remnants of the village, the gesture stately and grandiose, as though this were a miracle of renewal. "What you see," he called out, "is the eclipse of the Asari movement— the consequence to those who follow Bobby Okari into the charnel house of murder and sedition. This will happen in every village where people gather in his name. I will come in the night. After my soldiers kill your men and enjoy your women, they will burn your empty houses to the ground." He stared across the bodies at Marissa. "This is how we will sanitize Asariland, Marissa Okari. So watch, and learn."

Lying in Marissa's lap, Omo remained as still as the dead. "Bring Okari's father," Okimbo ordered.

Two soldiers dragged Chief Okari to the foot of the platform, machetes dangling from their belts. Still garbed in his headdress and robe, the old man gazed stoically at Okimbo as though clinging to the remnants of his dignity. Okimbo pointed to the church. "Take him to the altar," he told the soldiers. "Make of him a sacrifice as in the Old Testament, when man truly feared his God."

At this, Bobby's father slumped. The two men dragged him toward the church, his feet barely touching the ground, then disappeared inside. An army captain approached the platform. "Sanitize the rest," Okimbo ordered, and then pointed toward Omo and Marissa, adding softly, "But not those two."

Arms folded, Okimbo presided over the execution of those who survived—to Marissa all the more terrible because the soldiers carried out their orders with such deliberation, each act of murder carrying a weight it could not have had in the slaughter that had gone before. Amid this tableau, soldiers with wheelbarrows carted away corpses, while others searched the burning rubble for anything of value. Through the door of the one remaining house came a corpulent sergeant, Bobby's fax machine tucked under his arm. Seeing an old woman sitting nearby, he pulled the pistol from his belt and shot her in the eye.

Through it all, Omo lay still.

Numbed by shock, Marissa watched. Okimbo stood on the platform, arms still folded, observing the horrors in front of him without expression. Absently, Marissa stroked the girl's hair.

Two soldiers hauled a youth to the platform, hands manacled behind him. "He was trying to escape," one told Okimbo.

"Then let him try the creek."

With his hands still shackled, they bore him to the creek, its surface slick with oil. Dully, Marissa watched as they held him upside down, lowering him face-first into the oily water until his head vanished. His torso writhed helplessly. Then bubbles appeared amid the oil, and his body stilled.

Only then did Marissa hear Okimbo's footsteps. "When I was a child," he told her in conversational tones, "we, too, practiced total-immersion baptism." For Marissa, meeting his eyes required an act of will. Staring down at her, he asked, "Do you wonder why I saved you?"

Steeling herself, Marissa felt Omo stiffen beneath her fingertips. Laughing softly, Okimbo said, "Perhaps you can sacrifice this girl in your place."

"She's dead."

"And yet she breathes," Okimbo said softly.

"No." Marissa's mouth felt dry. "Take me."

Okimbo paused, as though pondering her offer, then knelt beside Omo. "You can awaken now," he whispered into her ear. "Do not be afraid."

Omo stirred. Almost gently, Okimbo took both her hands and drew her up to face him. She stood before him, her thin shoulder blades moving with each ragged breath. Okimbo smiled at the girl, then turned to Marissa. "My bride and I must borrow your home. To my regret, your village lacks accommodations."

Reflexively, Omo looked up at Marissa, her lips trembling. Marissa felt herself swallow. Then, slowly, she nodded.

Okimbo took Omo's hand. As she followed him to Marissa's home, Omo gazed back at her older friend, eyes moist and frightened. Marissa forced herself to watch until they disappeared inside.

The silence that followed was, for Marissa, more terrible than the sounds that had gone before.

She sat alone among the dead, her senses absorbing what had happened, her conscious mind struggling to accept it. She measured her life in minutes.

At last Okimbo emerged from what once had been her home.

He stopped and gazed up at the sky, now a light blue from which all evidence of the eclipse had vanished. Then he came to Marissa.

"They are all dead now," he told her. "There is no one left to be your witness."

Marissa forced herself to stand. In an ashen voice, she asked, "Where is my husband?"

Okimbo shrugged. "He's here somewhere, I suppose. Why don't we look for him together?"

Marissa could not speak. He took her hand as he had taken Omo's. "A man's own house," he said, "is the logical place to start."

Like an automaton, Marissa took one step, then another, picking her way through the dead. At the door of the house, Okimbo stood aside, waving her inside with an air of courtesy. Staring through the doorway, Marissa could see nothing but Bobby's ruined desk.

Swallowing her dread, she stepped inside.

At once she gasped, covering her mouth.

Omo lay on the carpet, her dress around her waist. Her open eyes were sightless. A ribbon of blood came from her throat.

Marissa reeled. As she stared down, a moving shadow seemed to merge with Omo's body. Marissa started, then looked to her side.

Bobby hung by his wrists, shirtless, lashed to the ceiling fan by a rope. Eyes filled with pain and horror, he held the neck of a beer bottle clamped between his teeth. His pants were spotted with urine. As the fan slowly rotated, exposing his back, Marissa saw the bloody welts of a whipping. From behind her, Okimbo said, "He understands that if he drops the bottle, the lashes will redouble. So far he's doing admirably. Though watching your young friend's last moments seemed to have upset him."

Marissa fought to keep her sanity. Focusing on the tenuous fact that Bobby was still alive, she waited to see his face. The fan, groaning, strained with his weight. "No worries," Okimbo said. "He'll come around again."

A stocky soldier leaned against the wall, eyes glazed, a heavy, blood-streaked chain dangling from his hand. "Bring Okari his father," Okimbo told the soldier.

Instinctively, Marissa stepped forward, reaching to touch her husband's bare ankle. When Bobby's face appeared again, he gazed at her in mute suffering. Suddenly his eyes widened and the bottle dropped from his mouth.

Flinching, Marissa turned to see. The soldier stood in the doorway, Chief Okari's severed head tucked in the crook of his arm. The chief's headdress, nailed to his skull, was slightly askew.

"No matter," Okimbo said to Bobby. "It is said you never listened to him."

Bobby's eyes closed. Kneeling, Okimbo retrieved the bottle.

"No," Marissa cried out.

"No?"

"You can't do this to him," she said in desperation. "I'm an American citizen . . ."

Okimbo laughed aloud. "Oh," he responded, his voice a parody of awe. Turning to the soldier, he said, "Mrs. Okari has become American again. We must cut her husband down."

The soldier stared, as though stupefied by what he held. "For God's sake," Okimbo snapped. "Drop the head."

The man blinked, then laid Chief Okari's head on the carpet and drew the machete from his belt. As he advanced toward Bobby, passing close to Marissa, she smelled the gin and marijuana. She was terrified that Okimbo wanted the soldier to sever Bobby's head.

She shut her eyes as the soldier's blade whirred; the next sound was the thud of her husband's body hitting the floor. Her eyes opened only when she heard him moan.

Bobby lay curled in the fetal position. Standing over him, Okimbo solemnly declaimed, "I arrest you on charges of vandalism and sedition, and for the murder of three employees of PetroGlobal Luandia. Further charges will be added stemming from the villagers' resistance to your detention."

Bobby gave no sign of hearing. Okimbo turned to Marissa, a mocking glint in his eye. "He will face our system of impartial justice. Do not expect to travel; nor will it be in your husband's interests for you to speak ill of your adopted country to the foreign press. But as an American citizen—not to mention a Luandian—you will be treated with due respect. In fact, I will personally escort you to your husband's compound in Port George."

Overcome by fear, Marissa was barely able to comprehend the scene around her: the dead ravaged girl, so precious to her; the head of Bobby's father bleeding on their carpet. Her husband had at last passed out, a mercy.

She knelt by his side. Roughly, Okimbo wrenched her arm. "Let us go," he said.

10

PIERCE WAS STILL AWAKE WHEN DAWN CAST ITS thin yellow light on the grass, the cypresses, the white-capped ocean. He sipped coffee as he read the latest report from the BBC, posted just minutes ago.

"Luandian president Savior Karama," the bulletin read, "has announced the arrest of the dissident Bobby Okari on charges of murder and sedition. While there are fragmentary reports of military activity in the vicinity of Goro, none are confirmed, and the government states only that 'appropriate measures have been taken to quarantine resistance.'

"A spokesman for the principal oil exploration company in the Luandian Delta, PetroGlobal

97

Luandia, says that it has removed all personnel from the affected area and has no knowledge of conditions on the ground."

Filled with worry, Pierce typed out an e-mail, hoping that a quick message to Marissa might draw some response. "Are you safe?" he asked. "If you can, answer ASAP."

Hours passed. Fretful, Pierce checked his e-mail every fifteen minutes or so. The only message was from Amy, requesting that he forward his keys to the house.

His reaction was a spasm of anger. As he sat down, mentally composing a response, a second e-mail appeared on the screen.

"They've killed hundreds of us," her message said, "and taken Bobby. We need help from America. Please come."

PART

The Twilit Maze

1

WAITING AT LONDON HEATHROW FOR HIS FLIGHT
to Luandia, Damon Pierce felt as if he were
about to leave his life behind.

Upon landing he could be a target for kidnapping or robbery by those who would see only an affluent white man, perhaps an oil company executive. On the advice of his security firm—retained at the insistence of experts—Pierce had concealed ten thousand dollars in a waistband, a leg strap, and a sock with a hidden compartment. In his briefcase was an alarm that, when wedged against a hotel door, would emit a piercing shriek were someone to break in; in the prior month there had been seventeen hotel robberies in Waro, Luandia's commercial center and most populous city, where armed gangs had gone door to door unimpeded by police. He would have bodyguards in Waro and Savior City, the capital. But in the Luandian Delta this was pointless; even were his protectors not hopelessly outgunned by the militia groups pervading the delta, such a force would defeat his purpose. One could not search out witnesses to a government-ordered massacre accompanied by a private army.

"The delta's one of the most dangerous places on the planet," the chief of his security team had advised him. "People die there without knowing why."

That was seven days ago. Since then, the State Department had warned Americans in Waro about bombings by Islamic terrorists, then evacuated all diplomatic personnel from the delta and admonished civilians not to go there, citing militia attacks anticipated in reprisal for the arrest of Bobby Okari. Setting aside Karama's assertion that the massacre had not occurred at all, the irony of Goro, Pierce's security adviser noted, was that the Asari were the only dissident group Okimbo could slaughter at will. Their movement was, after all, nonviolent.

Now Pierce scanned his fellow passengers. Some wore bright African clothes, others Muslim garb. Many of the women were round, and their smooth faces reminded him of Marissa's quip that only white women required plastic surgery. One little boy shot Pierce glances of curiosity from behind his mother, reminding him that he was about to become an oddity.

Pierce had never been to Africa. Even those friends who had gone there avoided the Luandian Delta. It was, Bryce Martel had told him with a smile, "a place so paranoid that it makes Beirut look like Cincinnati."

THEIR MEETING HAD been central to Pierce's preparation. Martel was a former highly placed CIA officer now dedicated to strategic planning in the post-9/11 world: Luandia, as Martel explained, had become an obsession among those fixated on sources of oil beyond a Middle East beset by hostile forces. "Luandia's like a criminal syndicate that peddles oil instead of heroin," Martel said. "The world needs what Karama has. Okari and the delta are caught up in our addiction."

They were dining at Aqua, an elegant seafood restaurant in San Francisco. A sybarite, Martel had chosen a particularly prized Meursault. Savoring the wine, Pierce said, "Tell me about conditions in the delta."

Martel pondered the question. In his late sixties, he remained slim, with salt-and-pepper hair, a weathered visage, and bright green eyes too sharp to require glasses. His manner was crisp and wholly unsentimental. "They're deteriorating," he said bluntly.

"The delta's principal city, Port George, is dangerous in the extreme. Like the delta as a whole, it's riddled with militia groups who live off oil theft and kidnappings. In the last two weeks nine people were killed in street fighting between rival gangs. A third gang kidnapped a project engineer for PGL; a fourth snatched the state governor's three-year-old daughter. In that environment, some bad guy may think you're an oil executive or a spy. Worse, the bad guys include the army and police, both of which are capable of killing you unless they'd prefer to shake you down."

"Terrific."

"No help for that. But you can reduce the risk. Hide your cash. Don't bring information about your finances that you don't need. Observe all police and military checkpoints; they may rob you if you do, but they'll shoot you if you don't. Don't take pictures of anything—the police may jail you for espionage. Never travel after dark. Take no trips to remote areas. Don't ride in an open boat. Refuse strangers who offer you assistance. Don't meet with militia groups. Avoid the creeklands where they hide—even if you're lucky enough not to meet them, you're certain to get lost. Sensible rules," Martel concluded with a sigh. "But given what Marissa Okari wants, you'll break them all if you live that long.

"It's not enough to visit Okari in prison. What he needs are facts compelling enough to make his death embarrassing to Karama and Luandia's customers in the West. Your experience equips you to do two things: prove that what happened in that village was a massacre, and build Okari a defense. You can't do either hiding out in a hotel. In effect, Damon, your friends are asking you to risk your life."

"They've risked their lives for years," Pierce answered. "I've got no wife or kids or anyone who depends on me. All I am is a lawyer with skills they may need, and that I haven't used lately in the service of anything more than becoming richer.

What might help me function better is to understand how Luandia got so screwed up."

An observer by nature, Martel paused to scan the people around them. The restaurant and its bar were jammed with people in their thirties and forties: lawyers, investment bankers, venture capitalists, providers of arcane financial services, and others riding out the collapse of a real estate market some had done their best to overheat. The more curious trio sitting at the next table—a fat sixty-year-old man with two underdressed and suspiciously pneumatic Asian women young enough to be his granddaughters but who obviously were not—drew from Martel a wintry smile before he said, "We can start with our friends the British.

"In the colonial era, the Europeans busied themselves carving Africa into nonsensical so-called countries composed of warring tribes who despised one another. But it was the Brits' particular genius to design Luandia out of two hundred and fifty different ethnic groups, many with their own distinct languages. The stated mission was to bring these benighted races the civilizing benefits of Christianity and economic progress. In truth, the economic progress included a lively slave trade, and the ranks of civilizers combined the enterprising but greedy with the worthless younger sons of aristocratic families—licentious in the extreme, arrogant in their privilege, and hostile to the native people they didn't sell or kill.

"Their legacy was chaos. In 1960, by which time this enterprise had become an embarrassment, the British left behind a self-governing 'country' with no sense of community, scant infrastructure, and wild disparities in education. Little has changed in the first fifty years. Of particular concern since 9/11 is the Muslim north, where until recently there was literally one college graduate and few resources of any kind, creating a population—at least in the minds of some—ripe for Islamic terrorism. That's another reason we want Karama to like us."

"What accounts for *him*?"

Briefly, Martel scanned the menu. "An extreme form of social Darwinism," he answered. "In theory, Luandia's federal system looks pretty much like ours—there's a president, a congress, a supreme court, and thirty states with governors. In reality, the government is inefficient, hopelessly corrupt, and outright brutal, with a history of stolen elections, military coups, and assassinations among competing factions. The result is a monster like Karama. He's been in power for seven years now and shows no sign of leaving."

Pierce frowned. "I'm trying to square that with the potential Marissa saw."

"Oh, it's *there*. Taken as a whole, Luandians are assertive, brash, funny, and smart. To see all that human capital mired in poverty, criminality, oppression, and disease is tragic. In the last half century they've gone backward. Their life expectancy is falling; Luandians' sole statistical boomlet is in AIDS. And the biggest reason is the one Okari complains about: Luandia is wallowing in oil."

"That makes no sense to me."

"Start with the law. Under British law, natural resources belong to the state. That's the system in Luandia. The land you walk on may be rich in oil, but the government owns it." Martel's smile was bleak. "That's why Karama wanted to be president. Our president makes four hundred thousand dollars a year; for Karama that's fifteen minutes of income from institutionalized corruption.

"Because the state owns the oil, Karama forces companies like PGL to give sixty percent of all oil revenue to the government. That means three things. First, the government is free to ignore its people—with multibillions in oil revenues, they don't need to collect taxes or build schools or hospitals or roads. Second, kleptocrats like Karama can steal tens of millions every year to help keep themselves in power." Martel leaned forward, looking at Pierce intently. "Third—and for your purposes the most important—the world needs Karama's oil too much to criticize his corruption and brutality."

"That may have been true," Pierce countered. "But Bobby's gotten the attention of the U.N. and a raft of human rights groups."

Martel shook his head. "Perhaps. But September 11 focused the world's voracity for oil on the Luandian Delta. The industrialized world uses ninety million barrels a day. In ten years that figure will reach a hundred twenty; in thirty years, some experts think, the world may run out of oil altogether."

Pierce was mildly astonished. "Can that be right?"

"Conceivably. In the last fifteen years, Americans' demands for SUVs and McMansions has raised our consumption by twenty-five percent. And in ten more years India and China will import more oil than the U.S. and Japan combined." Martel's eyes glinted with chilly amusement. "So everybody needs to corner the market—the U.S., the Europeans, India, Japan, and, most venal, the Chinese. But God put most of the world's reserves in some of the world's worst places: Russia, Venezuela, and the Middle East—"

"Made *that* worse, didn't we."

Martel gave a short laugh. "We've become vulnerable everywhere there's oil. The Venezuelans hate us. The Gulf of Mexico is subject to hurricanes. Aside from our disaster in Iraq, the Middle East is shadowed by bin Laden, Sunni-Shiite rivalries, and the threat of a nuclear Iran empowering terrorists. And we've got no real program to wean us from foreign oil.

"In other words, we've become the equivalent of

a crack-addicted whore, ready to turn tricks for anyone who can give us a fix. Including Savior Karama." Martel's tone was grim. "Karama's sitting on some of the best oil in the world—light sweet crude, plentiful and easy to refine. In the minds of many of our geopolitical strategists, Luandia's the make-good on the neocon fiasco in Iraq. Within ten years, they project, a quarter of our oil will be Luandian. The problem is that the Europeans, Indians, and Chinese need it as much as we do."

The cacophony of diners had reached its peak, Pierce noticed, and more customers awaited tables. After he and Martel paused to order dinner, he said, "So it's Karama's oil, and everyone wants it."

"True. But our problem's even more complicated than that. Instability in Luandia could throw us into a recession." Martel spoke in a clipped, emphatic tone. "The competition between oil gluttons means there's no spare capacity—any interruption in supply causes the world price per barrel to spike. In the last ten years the price has risen four hundred percent; September 11 plus Iraq drove it from thirty bucks to seventy. Now a hundred dollars per barrel is the floor, and the vultures who speculate on oil futures are betting that it will keep going higher."

A sudden thought struck Pierce. "What happened to the price when PGL shut down Asariland after those oil workers were murdered?"

Martel smiled grimly. "Up six bucks a barrel. If I were speculating in oil prices, and had known about those murders in advance, I'd have made a killing." At once the smile vanished. "No matter who did it, the murder of PGL employees is a very serious matter. In the minds of our security strategists, we need all the Luandian oil we can get, and PGL is central to maintaining our national defense."

"PGL is not performing a public service," Pierce objected. "They're making billions."

"Granted. But the delta's already violent and unstable. It's become easier for the State Department to get volunteers for Iraq, and now the execs from oil companies are hiding out in compounds. Karama won't allow PGL to hire its own Blackwater for protection, which means it has to pay Karama's army. Never mind that officers like Okimbo are murderers in uniform. PGL's got ninety oil fields, eighty flow stations, and four thousand miles of above-ground pipeline to protect from the armed militias who tap the company's pipelines and kidnap its people. Now there's been these murders. The new neocon nightmare is a wave of violence that drives PetroGlobal out of Luandia altogether."

"Is that likely?"

"It's possible." Martel took another sip of Meursault. "Suppose Luandia goes off-line. The price of oil could shoot up twenty-five dollars a barrel, helping to trigger a worldwide recession. Suddenly our military, which runs on oil, will have to pay for gas instead of troops. Less fortunate Americans can't drive a car; retirees on fixed incomes can't heat their homes; more companies can't sell their products overseas. Freight haulers raise prices; their customers transport fewer goods to fewer buyers. Pretty soon the stock market crashes, wiping out the baby boomers' retirement plans. In the bleakest scenario, our recession becomes the economic version of nuclear winter."

"All because of Luandia," Pierce said in a skeptical tone.

"Sometimes our worst fears turn real. Imagine a shutdown in Luandia at the same time Al Qaeda sets off a WMD in Saudi Arabia." Martel's voice softened. "My point is that there are people at the Defense Department, the NSA, *and* my former agency for whom Karama equals stability equals supply."

Dinner arrived—poached lobster for Martel, rare ahi tuna for Pierce. "There *are* Americans in Luandia who could help you," Martel added. "Our ambassador, Grayson Caraway, has good contacts and good judgment. There's also an ex-colleague of mine, Dave Rubin, who gives strategic advice to multinationals trying to navigate the Luandian murk. I'll put you in touch with both."

Thanking him, Pierce decided to let Martel enjoy his meal without interrogation. At its end, Martel ordered Armagnac for both of them. Though he swirled his snifter before sipping, savoring its aroma, his look of abstraction suggested that his thoughts were elsewhere. "There's something more," he said at length. "Did you know that Karama and Okari once were friends?"

Pierce was startled. "That's hard to imagine."

"Nevertheless, it's true. A few of my former colleagues speculate that the two had some sort of corrupt relationship, followed by a falling out, and that Okari is either more or less than he seems."

Pierce put down his snifter. "From what Marissa describes, the events in Goro suggest more than a 'falling out.'"

Martel shrugged. "I don't know Okari. But neither, I expect, do you—after all, you haven't seen him for twelve years. For all you know, he's capable of murder." His tone became philosophical. "Luandia's a hard environment, Damon. The absence of moral restraint can warp people in terrible ways. In that sense corruption and murder arise from the same conditions—no one has to account for what they do." He paused to drain his Armagnac. "The age-old question is whether men refrain from evil out of a higher morality, or only when they fear the consequences. Luandia supports the skeptics' answer."

2

FLYING INTO PORT GEORGE AS NIGHT FELL, PIERCE gazed out at the twilit maze of creeks at the heart of the Luandian Delta.

Somewhere in this web of palms and mangroves and polluted water was Asariland and Bobby Okari's ruined village; concealed throughout were the armed militia that preyed on PGL. As the skies darkened, the flames of a hundred gas flares appeared like torches, turning the maze into a surreal replica of Dante's inferno. In the distance appeared the lights of Port George.

Shuddering, the plane swooped toward the runway. The woman beside him gasped; the lights of the descending plane captured the rusted skeleton of an airliner that had crashed several years before. "Maintenance error," Martel had told him wryly. "They left it there as a metaphor for the country." Pierce was almost glad to land.

An hour later he had passed through a customs station guarded by armed Luandian soldiers and into the chaos of a cavernous but shabby airport where Africans pushed in all directions. In the press of bodies and babel of dialects, a bulky man grasped the handle of Pierce's suitcase and offered a ride in English so rapid that Pierce found it less comprehensible than threatening. Wrenching back the suitcase, Pierce said, *"No,"* and kept weaving through the crowd, absorbing the strangeness of being a white man surrounded by blacks in such an alien place. A quick glance at a newspaper rack revealed the headline "Three Killed in Cult Attack."

As someone grabbed his arm, Pierce started. The firm grip belonged to a short, intense-looking man in his early thirties wearing a blue sport shirt and gold-rimmed glasses. Perceiving Pierce's anxiety, he looked both impatient and amused. "I'm Atiku Bara," he said, "Bobby's lawyer. Keep moving."

Though Pierce complied, his sole reason to trust the man clutching his elbow was that he had named the man Marissa was sending. Bryce Martel's last injunction echoed in his brain: "Trust no one—not Okari, not even Marissa Brand."

"This way," his guide directed sharply.

They rushed through an exit door to a sidewalk crammed with shouting cabbies and double-parked cars and taxis until they reached a beat-up sedan. After opening the passenger door for Pierce, his new guide scurried into the driver's seat, turned the key in the ignition, and floored the accelerator. The car lurched into a space in traffic Pierce had not perceived, joining a disorderly scrum of cars and cabs and trucks hurtling toward Port George on what would have been, were any rules obeyed, a two-lane road. "The trick is not to stop," said Pierce's supposed escort. "Or be followed. Welcome to Luandia."

Still apprehensive, Pierce decided he had no

choice but to trust this man until he could get his bearings. He hesitated, then asked baldly, "How's Bobby?"

Bara—if indeed he *was* Bara—glanced at him, his eyes narrowed. "A week after his arrest there are still no charges, at least not formally. Nonetheless his punishment proceeds. They took him to a military compound in Port George. He is often chained, sometimes beaten, fed very little, and forced to shit in a bucket they seldom remove from the cell he shares with rats. Even as his lawyer I cannot see him outside the presence of the butcher Okimbo."

Beneath his rapid speech—a rhythmic patois that evoked Jamaica—Pierce heard both fatalism and anger. Before Pierce could respond, the headlights in the opposite lane revealed a gap into which Bara accelerated, throwing Pierce back into his seat as they passed a doorless van crowded with Luandians. "A necessity," Bara said coolly. "There are those who wait by the road for oilmen to kidnap. Driving with a strange white man is not my favorite thing.

"As for Bobby, physically he was never strong. He has suffered greatly. But his spirit remains unbroken. He will not speak of the horrors he endured, only those he saw."

"According to the government," Pierce said, "Bobby saw no horrors. All Okimbo's soldiers did was overcome armed resistance."

"Yes. From chickens, goats, children, and headless old men. For which our grateful women showered them with sexual favors before dying from the pleasure of it." Bara's voice softened. "I'm alive because I came too late to die. I was returning from a trip to England; on the road to Goro that day, I saw a mother and daughter who had managed to escape. They tried to tell me what was happening, though the words came hard. Then they vanished into the forest—perhaps the only witnesses save for Bobby and Marissa. I decided to turn around."

"Had you expected a massacre?"

"After the traitors abandoned Bobby? Yes." Eyes fixed on the road, Bara added quietly, "Perhaps I was late on purpose. I did not wish to die."

He fell silent. Captured by the headlights, Pierce spotted what could have been, had his mind accepted it, a charred corpse protruding from the bushes at the shoulder of the road. As Pierce turned, staring back, the phantom disappeared.

"Yes," Bara said matter-of-factly. "I saw him driving out."

The car struck a pothole, lifting Pierce from his seat and shooting a spasm of pain through his spine. "Do you know what happened?"

Bara shrugged his shoulders, both hands still grasping the wheel. "Perhaps he was a robber, perhaps worse. If the would-be victims overwhelm an attacker, they will sometimes beat him to the ground, put a flat tire around his neck, douse the tire in gasoline, and immolate the wrongdoer." He spoke with weary resignation. "It's a form of citizen justice—the police do nothing they aren't paid to do. The rule of law in Luandia is rhetorical."

"So it seems."

Bara glanced sideways. "African savagery, a Westerner might say. But before the English came, our communities were self-policing. It was from the British we learned that the police could be tools of violence and repression, indifferent to all crimes but dissent. Our police have simply jacked up the violence and corruption."

Above the darkened wetlands the scattered lights of Port George appeared closer and brighter. "The police we fear most," Bara went on, "are those we can't detect. The state security services are everywhere, spies waiting for us to commit whatever crime Karama chooses to invent. Imagine the forces of law in the hands of someone who can make an opponent vanish in the middle of the night, or order police to assassinate him and disguise it as a murder-robbery. One can die for taking pictures of something Karama wants to erase from public knowledge. Like the rubble of a village full of mutilated bodies."

"By now I assume the bodies have vanished."

"Yes. They have gone to a better place—a mass grave."

Pierce stared into the darkness. At length, he turned back to Bara. "How is Marissa?"

"As well as can be expected. You will see, tonight."

Imagining Marissa, Pierce realized that the car felt hot and stuffy. "Can I open a window?"

Bara shook his head. "Best not to. We're approaching the outskirts of Port George."

Abruptly, they reached the edge of a shantytown, an enveloping web of garbage-strewn alleys between wooden structures with corrugated roofs. The streets were dirt and rutted with potholes.

Bara's eyes darted from one side to the other. "Keep watching," he instructed Pierce.

"For what?"

"Anyone. Even though the soldiers have come, the gangs may suddenly appear. They fight one another for territory, the right to kidnap people or tap pipelines, and their tentacles reach deep into the creeklands. They are what happens when impoverished people see their leaders getting rich." As the road widened, cars passed in the opposite direction, weaving to avoid ruts. "For you," Bara continued, "what I fear most is kidnapping. But if warfare breaks out in the street, we could get caught in the cross fire. Thirteen people died from gunshots last week, one inside her home when a bullet shattered a window."

The city closed around them. They passed between two-story buildings and beneath tangled phone lines stretching from crooked poles. Dense smoke from what seemed to be a slaughterhouse fouled the air. On a corner Pierce saw a dimly lit gas station from which projected a line of perhaps twenty cars, surrounded by beggars or peddlers.

Bara followed Pierce's gaze. "Ironic, isn't it? We ship billions of dollars of our oil to America, while Luandians wait in line for gasoline. Port George is our nightmare."

Pierce was gripped by the strangeness of it. "Who lives here?"

"The deluded. People who thought there was work here, and discovered that the work was violence, robbery, and prostitution." He pointed ahead. "Look there."

From the haze and darkness materialized a massive garbage dump, amid which raggedly dressed scavengers, their faces masked against the fumes, appeared and disappeared like ghosts. "That is their profession," Bara said. "Grubbing through our offal."

Beyond the garbage dump, Pierce realized, must be the Gulf of Luandia. Outlined in the torchlight of a gas flare was a massive complex of steel railings and satellite dishes seemingly suspended above the water—an oil platform no doubt owned by PGL. "Let's find dinner," Pierce requested. "I need to talk with you before I see Marissa."

Stalled behind two cars, Bara accelerated past them. "Once you're spotted with me," he answered, "the police will mark you. But they camp outside the Okari compound, so I suppose it doesn't matter. The real problem is that our dinner might end before dessert. The kidnappers know where white men go."

Pierce strove for a certain fatalism. "Whatever I do, it seems the outcome is pretty random. Why be kidnapped hungry?"

Bara's glance suggested disapproval of Pierce's careless manner. In an arid tone, he said, "Then we'll go where you'll fit in."

Abruptly making a U-turn, he sped down one side street and swerved onto another. "It's best to reach our destination quickly," he said. "The neighborhood draws trouble like flies. Even the locals are careful." As they turned onto a thorough-fare dense with cars and Luandians hurrying on foot, Bara added, "They are going home. They fear the gangs and soldiers."

Ahead Pierce saw the spire of what appeared to be a mosque. "Are there Muslims here?" he asked.

"Some. Not so many as in the north."

The wail of a siren split the air. The taxicab in front of them screeched to a halt, Bara braking with a jolt to stop inches from its bumper. Feeling a spurt of nausea, Pierce saw an SUV convoyed by two police trucks speeding through a cross street, nearly hitting a pedestrian. Then the flashing lights disappeared, and the wails receded into the night. "Most likely an oilman," Bara said tightly, "arriving on a business trip—they pay the police as though hiring their own militia. If this one's smart, he won't leave his hotel."

At the side of the road Pierce saw a watery trench. "Is that an open sewer?"

"Yes. But then the shantytown we just drove through is a sewer of its own—no electricity or running water. Even here you have four or five or six people living in a room, sharing a toilet with thirty or forty others. Potable water's hard to come by. So people get malaria, TB, diphtheria, typhoid, cholera, and, of course, HIV/AIDS."

The traffic began moving again. "How many people live here?" Pierce asked.

Bara's brow furrowed. "Two million or so—no one knows for sure. After the oil boom, it grew without the government or the oil companies caring how. So Port George became the desperate place you see." He pointed to the wall of a brick dwelling on which was painted, in white, THIS HOUSE NOT FOR SALE. "The latest fraud is selling houses that don't belong to you. Home owners are wise not to go on vacation."

Pierce sat back. "Hard to believe."

"Why? Do you think a man can move here and start up a business? One needs money to buy a generator; or bribe our officials for a business license; or pay the police for the protection they won't give." He turned to Pierce, anger etched in his youthful face. "Our people lack what you Americans call a 'social safety net.' They are not criminals—they're resourceful, intelligent, industrious, and determined to survive. So they do what they must. But all Westerners see, if anything, is oil and corruption . . ."

Bara braked abruptly. Pierce saw the police van speeding from an alley a split second before it sideswiped Bara's car. Together they skidded to a stop, the van looming in their front window.

Bara froze behind the wheel. Two policemen with semiautomatic weapons jumped from the van. The taller one strode swiftly to the driver's side, staring in at Bara as the second man stood with his gun aimed at the windshield. "Get out," the first man ordered in English. "Both of you."

When Bara cracked open the door, the policeman jerked him upright. Pierce got out, approaching them with the reflexive confidence of an American accustomed to having rights. Then he felt the second policeman put a gun to his temple.

Bara's eyes widened, a warning to Pierce. All Pierce could do was breathe.

The first man grasped Bara's collar. "You damaged our car," he said. "You should go to prison."

Bara slumped. "I was careless. Truly, I am sorry." He hesitated. "Can we help with your repairs?"

Still clutching Bara's shirt, the policeman studied him with rheumy, bloodshot eyes. Turning to Pierce, he demanded, "Who are you, *oyibo*?"

Pierce felt the gun pressed harder against his

temple. He forced himself to stay calm. "I'm a businessman."

"American or English?"

Pierce hesitated. "American."

Cars inched around them, their drivers' eyes averted. At once Pierce understood that the policeman could shoot him in the middle of the street, and those near them would turn blind. Sweat glistened on Bara's forehead.

"Five hundred dollars American," the first man told Pierce. "Or your driver goes to jail. You can walk these streets alone."

Slowly, Pierce reached into the back pocket of his khakis for the decoy wallet with some cash and a credit card, calculated to keep the police or robbers from searching him for more. Mouth dry, he counted out five one-hundred-dollar bills.

Releasing Bara, the policeman took them. "Disappear," he said.

To disappear was Pierce's most fervent wish. He waited with Bara as the two men drove away.

Bara expelled a breath. "By the way," he said, "*oyibo* means 'white man.' You're likely to be hearing it again, and seldom as a compliment."

3

THE RHINO BAR, BARA TOLD PIERCE, WAS A HANG-out for expatriate oil workers.

They sat at a table near the back, Pierce registering his companion's distaste at the atmosphere around them. The floors were wooden and worn; the walls featured framed rugby shirts, beer signs, and a flat-screen TV broadcasting a soccer match; the sound system blared throbbing American dance music that drowned out the cacophony of talk and laughter and shouts from partisans of one team or the other. The men were white; the women black. Two of the women were dancing and grinding against white guys twice their age. Nearby a tall and stunningly beautiful Luandian woman in a shiny short skirt danced provocatively in front of a doughy man who sat at a table drinking and smoking and watching her as though appraising merchandise.

"They're trolling for money," Bara said. "Or, if one hits the jackpot, some man to take care of her. This place reeks of the corruption oil brings. But here no white men complain about the cost; here money buys what their absent wives won't give them."

"Seems like there *is* a price, though—the risk of kidnapping."

"These are the addicted ones," Bara answered in

a sardonic tone. "High on the exotic strangeness of Luandia, the absence of rules. The saner ones now hide in walled compounds." His voice went flat. "Luandian men do not come here. To see the women with these swine offends them."

Bara signaled a waitress for two beers. Though the light was dim, Pierce could study him more closely: he had the look of a scholar—thoughtful and sober, yet careworn by a constant anxiety that Pierce had begun absorbing. "That policeman," he asked. "What were the odds he'd put a bullet through my brain?"

Bara's look of abstraction was so deep that Pierce did not know if he had heard. "Hard to say," Bara responded slowly. "The army and police are jumpier than before. Port George and the creeklands are spinning out of Karama's control. He still seems to believe that fear and death will pacify the delta."

"And it won't?"

"It's made the problem worse. Last week one of our radio stations gave a 'shooting forecast,' predicting the next week's toll of death and injuries from warfare in the streets. Okimbo arrested the disc jockeys at once." Bara began peeling the label off his beer bottle. "What Karama has done to the Asari and to Bobby will strengthen those who steal his ideas to justify their violence. You have heard of FREE?"

"No."

"It's an acronym for Force to Reclaim Our Economy and Environment—the most powerful militia group. FREE hides in the creeklands, arming itself with money from kidnapping and stolen oil. When it's opportune, they raid Port George. You will hear more of them, believe it." With a fractional smile, Bara added, "I assume that you're still hungry."

Without awaiting an answer, Bara ordered snails in red sauce as Pierce watched the crowd and drank from his long-necked beer. All around them the music pulsed; the liquor flowed; women focused on the men so intensely that Pierce could almost smell their desperation. When one approached him, smiling, he slowly shook his head. Bara watched this interchange without comment or expression.

"What do you think Karama will do with Bobby?" Pierce asked.

Frown lines creased Bara's forehead. "That depends on many things—some unknowable, most beyond our control—and, to some extent, on Bobby. I know him well enough to guess how little he will kowtow to Karama."

"When did you meet him?"

"Six years ago. It was kismet, of a kind—my wife curses the day. I was still at Cambridge, about to become its first Asari graduate in law, when Bobby came to see me and Maryam." Bara's smile was reflective. "He was giving speeches, raising money and support anywhere he could. I knew who he was, of course—they already called him the Asari Mandela. But I was not prepared for him to sit down on my couch, look deeply into my eyes, and say that the Asari movement required more of me than a glittering degree. They needed my brains and my heart.

" 'On a platter?' my wife could not help but ask.

"At first Bobby ignored this. 'You have written well about injustice,' he told me. 'Someone of your abilities can help me build a grassroots movement that turns your words into action. I cannot do this work alone.' Then he turned to Maryam, his voice gentle yet impassioned. 'Yes, there will be the risk of imprisonment, or worse. But unless we who are privileged seize this moment, our only success will be in stealing enough but not too much; biting our tongues as our neighbors disappear; leading lives so innocuous in the face of evil that, should we survive, our legacy will be the contempt of those not moved to imitate our cowardice. Can you wish for yourselves such quiet misery?'

" 'I wish to sleep at night.'

" 'A vain hope,' Bobby told her. 'All you can choose is the reason to be sleepless.' Turning to me, he said, 'Sleep is the thief of enterprise. There will be time enough to sleep once we free Asariland.' "

Bara shook his head. "That night I did not sleep

at all. The next morning I told Maryam that history had walked into our living room."

Pierce struggled to imagine choosing a course so risky and profound. "Do you regret it?"

Bara contemplated the droplets of condensation running down his beer. "It has not been easy, and not just because of fear." He turned to Pierce with an air of curiosity. "There was a time when you must have known Bobby Okari well."

Pierce weighed his answer. "I was closer to Marissa. What I saw in Bobby was the sense of destiny you describe."

Something in Pierce's response made Bara study him more closely. "Bobby," he said after a moment, "has the defects of his strengths. If you resist him with a well-considered argument, he will listen. But once he chooses a course, his mind is difficult to change." Bara took a quick swallow of beer. "A man too convinced of his own selfless-ness too easily attributes opposition to baser motives. And for vanity or pride of place, so preva-lent among our chiefs, he has little patience. Less so irresolve."

"In a leader whose movement needs friends, turning potential allies into enemies is a weakness. We saw that on Asari Day—and after."

"At the time, did you think Asari Day a mis-take?"

The swiftness of Bara's answer suggested how deeply he had considered this. "I was in England, trying to rally international support—Karama had already restricted Bobby's movements. But when I heard that Bobby had ordered PGL facilities to be seized, I believed there would be trouble." Bara's voice grew soft. "Then I heard about those workers, and was certain."

The pause that followed caused Pierce to wonder what Bara knew, or suspected, about the hangings. Before he could form a question, Bara continued, "Maryam and I have two young girls. My first thought was of their safety; next of my own. So I delayed my return to avoid the airport and made the last leg by boat."

"And yet you came back."

"My family is here—and Bobby. It was too late for me to turn away." Looking at Pierce, he said, "I suppose you understand the risk you're taking."

Lurking in the comment, Pierce thought, was curiosity about his motives. "I'm learning." He paused, then said, "When I knew Bobby, his embrace of nonviolence was unwavering. Is it still?"

Bara seemed to parse the question, including the latent inquiry at its core. "The Asari are few in number," he responded. "To model himself on Dr. King instead of Yasser Arafat, Bobby argued, was not only practical but the surest route to international support. And I never doubted his commitment to nonviolence. But then FREE arose, promising deliverance and riches at the end of a gun." Bara picked up his beer, then put it down without drinking. "Our young men grew more restive. Bobby was always a provocateur who understood the uses of controversy. Now, to compete, his rhetoric grew edgier. The intellectuals among our leadership worried that his words and actions might persuade Karama that he wished to foster a secessionist movement throughout the delta, and that nonviolence was a transitory veneer.

"Bobby did not see this. Even as those closest to him became fearful, he seemed to believe that his international reputation insulated us from the worst."

"And so he went too far."

Bara smiled slightly. "Now I grasp why you wished to speak to me without Marissa. Yes, many among the Asari elite came to fear that Bobby was marching us toward disaster. As their worries grew, so did Bobby's intransigence and, perhaps, his desperation to keep our young from gravitating toward FREE." Bara paused. "Revolutionaries are not easy people. The fierce purpose that drives men to take on causes that frighten others does not admit of flexibility. Perhaps Bobby became too fixated on his dream.

"Had I been here, I would have counseled him against seizing PGL facilities. But even now, the fact that Okimbo spared him may feed that 'sense of destiny' you noticed. *I* fear that Bobby's destiny may be to die at Karama's pleasure."

Pierce met his gaze and held it. Bluntly, he asked, "Who ordered those workers killed?"

Bara did not flinch. "We may never know. A favorite trick in Luandia is to kill one man and blame another. Sometimes the man who orders the killing has the murderer killed for his own protection. About *these* murders, there is nothing I can tell you. But for Bobby to inspire them would have been suicide. As we have seen."

What struck Pierce about the answer was its lack of an insistence on Bobby's innocence. Bara was a sophisticated man, he sensed, whose admiration of Bobby was mingled with an undercurrent of unease deeper than he acknowledged. Given the pressures on Bara and his family, Pierce recalled Martel's admonition: trust no one. "About the massacre," Pierce said, "it seems that PGL's boats and helicopters were used. What do we know about that?"

Bara shrugged. "Only that PGL was involved. The depth of the involvement is known only to PGL and the government. This much I'll say— PGL runs to the army whenever it feels inconvenienced. For me, the only question is how much Okimbo may have exceeded their expectations."

At last their dinner arrived, snails drenched in sauce and accompanied by two more beers. "Take my advice," Bara said. "Alternate bites with a swig of beer."

Within three bites, the fiery red pepper sauce brought beads of sweat to Pierce's forehead. He started to remark on it when he noticed Bara eyeing the crowd gathered at the bar.

A tall young Luandian, conspicuous among the throng, sipped a beer as he looked casually around him. Bara stood, touching Pierce's shoulder, and then edged through the white men and black women as he headed for the bar.

Bara tapped the Luandian on the shoulder. Surprised, the man turned. He seemed to recognize Bara: the two men exchanged words, their faces close as the Luandian bartender, noting them, drifted to the other end of the bar. After Bara spoke again, the man nodded. Then Bara turned abruptly and returned to the table. As Pierce watched him, the Luandian took a last sip of beer and left without paying. "What was that?" he asked.

In a low voice, Bara answered, "He's a member of FREE. No doubt he's scouting for PGL executives to kidnap. FREE gets pictures of the important ones from Luandian employees at the company."

"How do you know him?"

"He was with us before he decided that nonviolence equaled weakness. Perhaps it was also FREE's promise of money for his work. But we remain friends. You will find this a place of odd relationships, shifting alliances, and mixed motives—it is useful to keep communications open. In this case, I told him you were not PGL, but a journalist. I also suggested that this was not a good night to work the Rhino."

"So what will he do?"

"There are other bars. Still, it would be best to leave."

Though they were halfway through dinner, Bara signaled for the check. When the waiter appeared, Pierce produced a sheaf of Luandian bills from his spare wallet. Together they angled through the dance floor thick with bodies and cigarette smoke. As they stepped out the door, Pierce heard what sounded like gunshots from an indeterminate distance and direction.

"Hurry," Bara ordered tersely.

They rushed to Bara's car. He started the engine and drove cautiously down a thoroughfare that seemed oddly bare of traffic. Then, perhaps thirty yards ahead, Pierce saw three Luandians pull a struggling white man out of another bar.

Bara braked abruptly. At the sound, one of the kidnappers pointed his pistol at the car.

Bara worked the clutch, backing up. Suddenly a black van appeared from a side street near the bar, squealing to a halt. The kidnapper put away his gun and helped his companions shove their terrified captive into the van. Only as it drove away did Pierce notice the body of a Luandian soldier lying in the entrance to the bar. Then he saw another man standing in the doorway—the Luandian from the Rhino. The man stepped across the body, glancing swiftly to each side, and vanished down the alley.

4

Vigilant, Bara resumed driving down the empty street. "FREE never kills its hostages," he said phlegmatically. "No profit in that, and it's bad PR. But someone will pay for that soldier." After that, the two men said nothing until they reached Bobby's compound.

Surrounded by walls and a garden, the two-story house was backlit by a gibbous moon and the orange glow of oil flaring on the beach. The only other illumination came from an upstairs window and a light beside a wrought-iron gate that blocked the driveway. Parked across the rutted street was a black car, the two heads of its occupants briefly caught in Bara's headlights. "She wishes to see you alone," Bara said without inflection. "There's a buzzer by the gate—press it, and she'll come. Tomorrow, if we can manage, you'll see what is left of Goro."

Pierce thanked him and got out.

His footsteps crunched gravel at the mouth of the gate. Pressing the button, he saw a circular drive shadowed by palms whose fronds caught the light of the burning oil. A faint breeze touched his face, reminding him that in San Francisco, spring was just beginning. He heard the whisper of footsteps crossing gravel, then saw a slight form moving toward him on the other side of the bars. The mechanical gate parted, and Marissa Okari stepped forward.

In the half-light, Pierce could not see her face. He put down his suitcase. "Nice place."

She managed to laugh, then glanced past him at the men parked across the street. "State security services," she told him. "Come inside."

She pressed a button, and the gate slowly closed behind them. Briefly, she leaned against his chest, hugging him tightly. Then she drew back to look up at him, and he saw her face more clearly. It was the same, yet not—still beautiful but subtly older, a woman's face on which hard experience was written. Quietly, she said, "I can hardly believe you've come."

He looked deeply into her face, even more lovely than he had imagined. "I'm glad I did."

"I'm grateful, Damon. More than you can ever know."

For a moment they were silent. She took his hand, the touch of a guide, and led him toward the house.

She wore a simple Luandian dress; though her movements lacked the kinetic energy he recalled from their past, her posture remained erect and proud. She opened the door, nodding to a slender houseboy with watchful eyes, whom she introduced to Pierce as Edo. Then she ushered Pierce up a central flight of stairs to a patio luxuriant with flowers. "It's better we talk here," she said under her breath. "I can see who listens."

They sat at a wooden table overlooking the Gulf of Luandia. A mile or so offshore, the lights from an armada of oil tankers sparkled like a floating city. The source of the unnatural glow, visible now, was a black pipe whose flame lit a quadrant of debris-strewn sand. To the far right were scattered lights demarking what Pierce knew to be Petrol Island, an offshore compound chosen by PGL for its relative safety from militia attacks. Quietly, Marissa said, "I can't imagine what you're thinking."

"The trivial and profound. I was wondering how you and Bobby managed to come by such a place. Far more important, how you are."

Marissa seemed to study his face, as though discovering him anew. "As to how we live, Bobby's writing paid well. His second novel, *Delta Boy,* became an international bestseller. He was also the son of a wealthy chief, one of the traditional elite—he never pretended not to be privileged." Her voice lowered. "As for me . . ." She stopped and looked down. "When I saw him hanging there, I entered a world without limits. Maybe we've always lived this way and I refused to see it. But now I live with horrors I literally can't express: isolated, under constant surveillance, threatened with further harm to Bobby if I speak to the foreign press. I can't even see him, and they've taken my passport. Other than that, the government seems content to keep me here, as though pretending that the massacre is something I imagined. For the world at large it may become that: anyone who survived by hiding in the forest knows better than to be a witness." Pausing, she seemed to shiver, murmuring in a husky voice, "Last night I dreamed about his father's head. But this time the head was Bobby's."

Pierce groped for a way to comfort her. "I'm here for a while," he promised. "Until I can figure out how an American lawyer can best help you and Bobby. Once I find a way, the next step is to persuade my law firm to support it. In the meantime, this is my vacation."

Marissa ignored his attempt at lightness. "Vacation? Before I interrupted your life, you were in the midst of a divorce. There must be better ways to heal."

"I can't think of any. Perhaps you did me a favor—before your e-mail I had too much time to think."

Marissa looked at him again, her face softening. "You must be so tired. Do you need to sleep?"

"Only if you do." When she shook her head, Pierce added, "I wouldn't mind some coffee."

Marissa stood, opened the glass door, and called out a few words in Asari. Within moments, the houseboy brought a carafe of coffee. Smiling, he said, "You're welcome," and left before Pierce could thank him.

" 'You're welcome,' " Marissa explained, "is a

universal greeting—don't ask me why. And don't misread his smile. Edo is deeply scared; warmth and kindness is his reflex. As a whole, Luandians are quite wonderful—humorous, emotive, and patient in a way that completely eludes Bobby. There's a favorite saying that always drives him crazy: 'The clock did not invent man.' But they're also incredibly enterprising. Even their scams are inventive."

"Like selling other people's houses?"

Marissa shook her head. "They're just *so* poor. They look at those tankers out there and see the money Karama and his people haven't stolen flowing to PetroGlobal. What can they do? E-mail their congressman? Sue someone? There's no outlet for them—no civic culture or means of protest or sense of solidarity—only an obsession with hierarchy and who's got what *they* need. So their only recourse is scraping by or attaching themselves to a 'big man,' like Chief Okari, who'll give them crumbs from his table." Her speech softened again. "That's one reason Bobby and his father were estranged. Bobby was trying to change the consciousness of a people, replacing the reliance on big men with a belief in social justice. That made the big men angrier than you can imagine. In Luandia, Karama's the biggest man of all."

"And Karama rules through his own network of big men, whose loyalty he buys with oil money."

Marissa nodded. "That means every level—the army, navy, police, security services, the governors of states, even local leaders. Their only job is to keep the lid on in return for stealing public funds. The people get nothing but ruined land and the right to bribe officials with money they don't have. No wonder teenagers take to the creeks with guns." She leaned forward, speaking with quiet sadness. "What Bobby offers the Asari is unique in Luandian history. That's why Okimbo came to our village."

Pierce realized he had forgotten his coffee. He took a lukewarm sip, then said, "Only after scaring or bribing most of Bobby's lieutenants."

Marissa stared at her folded hands. "They were brave for so long," she answered. "Once you see Goro, maybe you'll understand."

"But who does that leave for you to trust? Atiku Bara?"

Marissa tilted her head, as though listening for sounds only she could hear. "There's a path from here to the beach," she told him. "Why don't we walk for a while."

THOUGH IT WAS dark, the glow of flaring gas illuminated the oil-slick beach like a movie set at night, its distant roar carrying on the wind. Ahead a stray dog limped in and out of shadows, veering aimlessly toward the silver outline of an oil derrick. Stopping, Marissa gazed at the torchlike flame. "In Goro, the children never knew a dark night."

Though she spoke aloud, she seemed solitary. Pierce tried to imagine the will it had taken for Marissa to adapt to Luandia and then to embrace her husband's struggle against such odds, and the terrible aloneness she must feel now. "You asked about Atiku," she continued. "The truth is, I can't know.

"Oil poisons souls. People know there's a lot of money; how to get some becomes an obsession. People are frightened; they fear for themselves and can't protect their children. They master deceit because they don't know who to trust. You never know whether you're speaking to an enemy or a friend, or what might have changed that overnight." She turned to Pierce. "For years Atiku Bara was one of the best men I've ever known. But now Bobby's in prison, his home village slaughtered. Men they both counted on have fallen away. Atiku knows too well that Karama and Okimbo have no limits. What's to keep them from making his wife and children disappear? What's to keep Atiku from taking money to make them safe? What does it mean that Atiku's managed to survive?

"That's what happens, Damon. You don't know who to trust. So you trust people you shouldn't and don't trust those you should, knowing their psychic equation could alter in a heartbeat." She folded her arms, looking out at the flotilla of tankers. "In his way, I believe Atiku loves Bobby as much as I do. But he doubts Bobby in other ways he never acknowledges. I think that's why he managed to be in England on Asari Day, and elsewhere when the soldiers came to Goro.

"I'm not saying that he knew. But I know how afraid he was. Who can blame him? In Luandia, children become hostages."

Pierce shoved his hands in his pockets. "Is that why you never had them?"

Marissa was quiet for a time. "That was one reason," she answered. "After Karama came to power, one of his rivals, another general, went underground. Karama sent his troops to the man's house. A soldier put a gun to his wife's head and asked his seven-year-old son where his father was. When the boy couldn't tell him, they took away the mother. No one's seen her since. Bobby was afraid to have his children used against him."

"And you?"

Marissa drew a breath. "We all know couples who stop flying together once their kids are born. In that sense Bobby and I are flying together. We didn't want to crash and leave a child." She closed her eyes. "Even being married makes us vulnerable. Right now I wonder what they're doing to him while we're walking on the beach. All I know is that he's just as afraid for me."

Pierce reached out, gently resting a hand on her

shoulder. As though remembering his presence, she opened her eyes. She grasped both of his hands in hers, the tightness of her fingers expressing what she did not say.

"Bobby needs a story," Pierce told her. "Who else could have hung those men?"

"Anyone. FREE or another militia. Someone acting on Karama's orders."

"And the motive?"

"A pretext for getting rid of Bobby. The motive's always the same—oil. Karama wants to control it. The militia groups want to steal it. Bobby wants to redistribute the money it brings." Marissa released Pierce's hands. "If the Asari movement spread across the delta, the people's lives would change. But that would eliminate the rationale for FREE, as well as the basis of Karama's power. If Bobby dies, so does his movement."

Pierce watched her face. "Another possibility is that someone in the movement hung them. Maybe out of frustration, or for money. Or because they imagined Bobby wanted that."

"No one sane could think that," Marissa said emphatically. "It would endanger everything we've worked for. Including international support for the Asari cause."

"True. But Bara worries that Bobby overrates that. Especially now."

The change of subject caused Marissa to pause. She took a few steps toward the water, staring out at its seeming infinity. "So do I. Praise from Greenpeace or the London *Times* won't be enough to save him. Even before this, foreign reporters were afraid to come here. Now they can't. And in America, few people care—it's just Africa, they think."

"Maybe not PetroGlobal." Pierce moved beside her. "Suppose we could prove that PGL's equipment was involved in the massacre and even put its people on the ground. Making Okimbo the face of PGL would be a considerable embarrassment. Bobby's death would make PGL's position that much worse.

"I don't know how much pull PGL has with Karama. But it's got to have some—he makes billions off it every year. And I'm certain PetroGlobal has friends in the White House. There may be a way, if we can find it, to use forces more powerful than the Asari to keep Bobby alive."

" 'We'?" Marissa repeated.

Pierce nodded. "I'm an American lawyer. I've got more freedom of action than you do. I'll try to get a meeting with PetroGlobal. What I need from you—and, for better or worse, Atiku Bara—is help in trying to establish that there *was* a massacre and, with luck, who actually hung those workers."

Even as he said this, Pierce felt uncertain of what course he was committing himself to follow; what unknown circumstances might intrude; what hard choices he might face; how deeply he wished to involve himself with lives as dangerous as the Okaris' in a country as deadly as Luandia. He knew only that, now that he had seen Marissa in this place, his conscience was too uneasy to let him simply wish her luck before resuming what had become his all-too-comfortable life.

Marissa seemed to read this on his face. In a quiet tone, she said, "After Goro, I had no one else to turn to. Somehow, after all this time, I believed you'd care. I also know you've got experience we need." She touched his sleeve again. "But this has nothing to do with you, Damon. After all, if it had been up to you, I would never have come here."

Pierce managed to smile. "But then you wouldn't be you. So here I am."

"Then at least tell me you know how dangerous this is. Even for you."

It was better, Pierce sensed, to pass over what he had already experienced. "It's certainly interesting," he answered. "Can't say I like Port George."

She gave him a questioning look. "It's not just the kidnappings—people die for nothing. I'm sure Karama's people saw you tonight. Pretty soon they'll know who you are. The only help for that is to leave and not come back."

She realized, Pierce saw at once, that the thought had already occurred to him. "Not before I see Goro for myself. After that, we'll figure out what else I can and need to do. But there's one thing I need to know from you."

144

"What's that?"

"Whether Bobby ordered those murders. Or allowed them."

Marissa stiffened. "How can you even ask me that?"

Pierce steeled himself. "Because you're desperate enough not to tell me. From what you say, Luandia breeds dissembling. Even among friends."

Marissa stared at him. "You *have* changed, haven't you? You're harder."

"So it seems. But then twelve years is a long time."

"All right, Damon." Marissa's voice was strained. "I saw Bobby's face when we found those men. He couldn't have known. I wouldn't have asked you to come if I wasn't sure." She hesitated, then spoke more softly. "There's another reason. I know you're not here for Bobby, but for me. I wouldn't put you in danger for a lie."

Watching her eyes, Pierce saw nothing but her desire that he believe her. Summoning a smile, he said, "I've got the luck of the Irish, remember? Mine and Robert Kennedy's, as well."

Marissa did not return his smile. "Robert Kennedy's brother, the president, said that life is unfair. His own death proved that. But I never thought you really believed it.

"Until now, your own experience suggests that life *is* fair—that most people end up getting what they deserve. Faith like that is alien to Luandia. It's not just people who die here—it's illusions."

For a moment Pierce wondered if Marissa was also speaking of herself. "I *have* changed, Marissa. My illusions died at The Hague."

Almost imperceptibly, Marissa shook her head. "Did they, Damon? After all, you won that case. So you still believe in the rule of law." She took his hand and looked at him, her eyes searching his. "Luandia changes people—there's so much cruelty and caprice. It's not just Bobby and me I worry for, Damon. It's you."

5

A T DAWN, MARISSA, BARA, AND PIERCE DROVE TO a boat launch outside the city. The air was dense, the heat already searing. Though the black car outside the compound followed, no one stopped them. By the time they reached the launch, the car had vanished.

"It's good they don't know where we're going," Pierce observed to Bara.

Bara shrugged. "Maybe they don't care—Asariland is still a military zone. Unless we're lucky, the army will stop us from reaching Goro. But the route we're taking, however circuitous, is the only way to avoid Okimbo's soldiers."

Marissa said nothing. Her gaze was abstracted: though, as a witness to a massacre, her presence

146

was necessary, Pierce knew that she dreaded returning.

They climbed into a Boston Whaler piloted by a thick-waisted Luandian who took five hundred dollars of Pierce's money. Then he started the motor and eased the boat through an inlet, toward the polluted brown waters of Port George Harbor. "Thus begins a tour of corruption," Bara remarked dryly. "This port is a haven for diamond smuggling, the drug trade, and oil stolen from the creeks we're heading toward. Nothing leaves here without the fingerprints of crooks in government."

Bara and Pierce sat at the rear of the boat. Alone, Marissa stood near the front, bracing herself against the metal railing, the breeze rippling her hair as the boat picked up speed. Above the mouth where the inlet met the harbor was a bridge groaning with stalled cars. Marissa gazed up at it as they passed beneath and then, as though drawn by something she had noticed, turned back to look. Beneath the deep thrum of the motor, Bara told Pierce, "She and Bobby lost a friend on that bridge—a man who dared to run for state governor against Karama's handpicked minion. He was driving to a rally when his opponent's hired gunmen tried to intercept him. He managed to stay ahead of them until he reached the bridge.

"There was a traffic jam, of course. So his pursuers left their car and pumped a hundred or so bullets into his SUV. There was hardly enough of him left to bury. Why bother to stuff a ballot box when you can easily kill a candidate?"

Hands in the pockets of her jeans, Marissa turned from the bridge.

At one edge of the broad harbor a garbage-strewn beach with tin-roofed shacks gave way to a cluster of stilts holding up a ragged expanse of cloth, creating patches of shade that, Bara explained, Luandians rented for an outing. The boat veered to avoid the rusted hull of a capsized barge. Turning, Pierce saw three gray warships of the Luandian navy at anchor beside an oil tanker longer than two football fields. Bara pointed to the mouth of the harbor. "We'll be passing close to Petrol Island."

The pilot accelerated, throwing Pierce and Bara back in their seats. Marissa, still standing, bent her knees to ride out the boat's erratic jolts. At close range, Petrol Island appeared surprisingly barren: from the water, Pierce saw only the steel structures of an oil refinery and the walls of a compound. "PGL's employees feel safe here," Bara remarked. "There's even a village of prostitutes to service the residents. Too bad for all of us that most of the oil is still onshore." He did not need to mention the three dead workers for whom Bobby might pay with his life.

Still Marissa had not spoken. Nor had she an hour later when the boat docked near a rutted road leading to the heart of the delta.

A YOUNG MAN in a beat-up van waited at the isolated landing, looking about with an air of apprehension. "Have you seen soldiers?" Bara asked as they got in.

"Not yet."

Bara fell into a pensive silence. Pierce surrendered himself to fate; anxious inquiries would only add to the tension he felt building in his companions. Sitting in the van's passenger seat, Marissa stared straight ahead.

The road was marked by craters and rivulets of open sewage. They saw few cars. A kaleidoscope of dystopic images appeared in Pierce's window: a heap of burning garbage; a leper begging; a poster that showed the governor whose thugs had killed the Okaris' friend grinning insanely at the empty road; two boys selling jars of stolen oil as though at a lemonade stand; PGL access roads marked by signs that warned against trespassing. Beneath the seat, Pierce noticed, the driver had concealed a gun.

"Shit," Pierce heard Bara say.

Ahead, a makeshift checkpoint of mangrove branches and rubber tires was flanked by two policemen. Marissa sat rigid, staring fixedly out her side window as though she had seen nothing. The only sign of emotion in Bara was the rapid movement of his eyes. Slowing the van, their driver muttered, "Don't look at them."

Pierce understood the stakes. They could be arrested for espionage, and the presence of a white man only increased the risk. Even in times of lesser tension the police used their power at will, and rape was common. Pierce's deepest hope was that these men would not recognize Marissa. It was bad enough that she was beautiful.

When the car stopped, a tall policeman in sunglasses sauntered to the driver's side, his companion behind him. He leaned inside, one arm resting on the open window, and looked into the front and back. "Who are you?" he snapped at Pierce.

Pierce saw Bara tense. "A visitor from America," Pierce answered.

The man peered closely at the others, his gaze lingering on Marissa. "This road leads to a military zone," he told Pierce. "Only spies have business there."

Pierce's mouth felt dry. "I'm no spy."

Scowling, the policeman motioned Pierce outside. When Pierce complied, the man grasped his shoulder in a viselike grip. "To spy carries penalties for anyone who helps the spy. Do you understand?"

"Yes."

"Yes. And I am a man with children whose boss pays him next to nothing."

Pierce hesitated. "I understand."

"The price for a spy is five hundred dollars American. A spy's friends cost one hundred each." The man glanced at his companion. "Passing into the military zone will cost two hundred more. How much will a spy pay for the privilege of risking death?"

Swiftly, Pierce tried to sift his thoughts. He needed to see Goro. Yet to turn back might be safer: this offer might be a trap, and to accept it might trigger their arrest. All he felt was astonishment at the instincts required for survival. In a tentative voice, he said, "I'd like to see more of Luandia."

The ambiguous answer caused his questioner to remove his sunglasses, staring hard at Pierce. With stiff fingers, Pierce produced his wallet and counted out sixteen thousand in inflated Luandian currency, then four thousand more. The man kept staring until Pierce's gaze broke. Then he took the money, nodding curtly.

Pierce got back in the car. As they drove past the barriers, no one spoke. He felt as though his nerve ends were rubbed raw.

THE SILENCE STRETCHED for minutes. Sulfurous smoke from gas flaring drifted through the sweltering air; there were fewer birds; the palms and mangroves appeared scrofulous and stunted. At times Pierce could hear the distant roar of another flare. Now and then a Luandian man or woman trod along the road as though on a treadmill to eternity, their slow, repeated movements bespeaking weariness in the bone and brain, days endlessly the same. Near a nexus of aboveground pipelines was the shell of a two-story building identified by a faded sign as the Awala Hospital. The sight prompted Bara's first words in a half hour. "A Potemkin project," he told Pierce. "PGL builds things like this to pacify an angry community. But they've got no way to maintain them. You can't run an MRI machine without electricity or training."

Pierce kept gazing out the window. As they reached a red dirt path at the side of the road, Bara instructed their driver to stop. To Pierce he said, "There's something I must show you."

AT THE END of the path a pool of oil was spreading from a ruptured pipe that bisected what once had been a field of maize. "A pipeline leak," Bara said, "maybe from corrosion, maybe because someone tapped it. The result is the same—fishing and farming erased, kids with distended bellies." Pierce followed him to the edge of the pool, Marissa and the driver trailing behind. "A common sight," Bara continued. "The oil spills; the government does nothing. So a local gang springs up to demand a 'clean-up contract' or to provide 'security' against more oil theft. Then PGL pays them off.

"But this one caught on fire—some idiot with a cigarette joined a group of people scooping up oil in buckets. Fifty or so died when he lit up." He walked a few steps to a patch of crusted oil at the edge of the spill. Stuck like a fossil in the crust was a small flip-flop and what Pierce realized was the charred face of a child who, when alive, might have been its owner. Almost conversationally, Bara remarked, "King Tut looks somewhat better, don't you think? A month ago, Bobby spoke at this very spot. After all he had seen, it was this child who moved him to tears."

Behind them, the driver called to Bara.

Beside him a teenager in a T-shirt and shorts had materialized with a semiautomatic weapon. As the youth walked toward them, Bara murmured wearily, "Another parasite with a gun."

The young man looked from Bara to Pierce. "This is our land," he said harshly. "PGL pays us to clean it up."

"Then perhaps you should remove the bodies," Bara said.

The youth raised his weapon, pointing it at Pierce. "You from the oil company, *oyibo*?"

"No."

"Then go back where you came from. We don't want strangers here."

Twice in as many days, Pierce thought, a man had aimed a gun at his head, not even knowing who he was. "Let's go," he told Bara.

THEY DROVE A few miles more, fearful of encountering soldiers. Abruptly, their driver turned down a dirt road barely wider than the van and stopped beside the grassy banks of a creek. Waiting there with an open speedboat was a young Asari man. "This route is safest," Bara told Pierce. "They can block roads, but not these waters. You'll see."

Pierce and Marissa followed him to the boat. Their new pilot started the outboard motor, breaking the near silence to ease the craft forward into a maze of creeks bounded by thick groves of palms and mangroves. Within minutes Pierce had lost all sense of direction: they were specks in a vast alluvial plain barely above sea level, covered by so many creeks and swamps that it defied cartography. With each turn from one creek to another, the channel grew narrower, until the trees and vegetation seemed to close around them. Their pilot steered past the spectral branches of half-submerged trees, seemingly attuned to other perils below the water's surface. He must have spent years, Pierce guessed, mastering this labyrinth; it was little wonder that armed militias chose to conceal themselves in such a trackless maze. The thought struck him that an enemy could make them vanish without a trace.

Their pilot turned into another creek, and suddenly environmental ruin was all around them. The trees were bare and stunted, the water's surface slick with oil. Pipelines appeared among the mangroves; the malodorous stink of flaring gas reentered Pierce's nostrils. Save for a tree monkey, he saw no birds or animals. On the shore, some Asari had hacked a clearing for a village; half-naked children and sullen-looking adults sat idly on the muddy bank. Standing near the front, Marissa seemed not to notice them.

Ahead the creek forked. The pilot slowed further, taking the narrower course.

At once he stood straight, staring ahead at a rusty barge almost as wide as the creek itself. Armed men appeared at the front of the barge; Pierce saw what appeared to be a makeshift hose connecting an onshore pipeline to the barge's hull.

He turned to Bara. "What's this?"

"Militia," Bara said tautly. "They siphon the oil from PGL's pipelines to sell on the black market—bunkering, it's called. Then they arm themselves with the proceeds."

As they neared the barge, one of the armed men signaled for them to stop. Another man threw a rope to the pilot. When the pilot grabbed it, the same man towed the boat to the side of the barge as his comrades aimed their weapons.

The leader stared down at them. "What's your business here?"

Bara gestured to Pierce and Marissa. "This man is a journalist. This is Marissa Okari."

The leader's face showed contempt. "Okari's

people died like fools. We are FREE, and ready to kill our enemies."

A muted anger appeared in Marissa's eyes. Calmly, Bara replied, "We came to see Goro, not to report you. Let us go."

The leader weighed this. As Pierce stared up at him, he noticed the young man at his shoulder. With a jolt of recognition followed by uncertainty, he recalled the man at the Rhino Bar, talking to Bara, then saw him stepping across the murdered soldier in the doorway of the second bar. The man stared back, impassive. In a flat tone, the leader said to Bara, "Goro? I wish you the joy of it."

Arms folded, Marissa turned away.

The man from FREE waved them forward. Carefully, the pilot slid their boat past the corroded hull of the barge. Above them, someone laughed.

WITHIN MINUTES, THEY had slipped into another creek. "That encounter was lucky," Bara said. "The odds are good now that there will be no military at Goro. When FREE is bunkering oil, often the commander in the area makes his soldiers disappear. It's one thing to destroy an unarmed village. It's quite another to take on a force better armed than yours, such as FREE, which pays you to leave it alone while it steals PGL's oil."

"Does FREE pay Okimbo?"

Bara shrugged. "PGL does. But no one knows who else may."

Marissa did not seem to hear them. Pierce did not ask Bara about the man from the Rhino Bar.

ANOTHER HALF HOUR passed. The sun, now at its apogee, beat down on their heads. "We're getting close," Bara said.

As the creek widened, Pierce saw its mouth meet the white-capped ocean. Turning, he followed Marissa's gaze.

Along the banks of the creek were the charred remnants of wooden huts. Their pilot nudged the boat against a muddy patch of earth on which, hauntingly preserved, rested three canoes whose owners had no need of them.

Marissa stood, stepped from the boat, and walked alone toward what used to be Goro. She stopped at the edge of the ruins.

Getting out, Pierce and Bara stayed at the canoes. They watched Marissa slowly approach an open area at the center of the village, its red earth now sprinkled with ash.

Pierce followed her, stopping a few feet back. Marissa did not look at him. "We had a well," she said softly. "Somehow the Asari found fresh water below sea level. No one knew how this could be, only that we were blessed."

Pierce moved beside her. In the rubble lay a tin cross, its shape distorted by heat. "That was the church?" he asked.

"It's where they took Bobby's father. Before,

when a chief died, he would lie in state at the center of the village."

When she began walking again, Pierce understood that he was meant to follow.

They stopped beside a charred cart with stone wheels. In the same distant tone, she said, "This was the marketplace. They sold what mangoes and pineapples and papayas still grew here. A few fish." She pointed to a cantilevered tin roof that had settled on chunks of half-burned wood. "That was the school. The children's books were so old the pages fell out."

For a while she was still. Then she was drawn to a metal pot now blackened by fire. "This was Omo's house. Her mother would sit in front, cooking. And that was her parents' bed."

Looking up, Pierce saw a melted bed frame sagging amid the charred ruins. Then Marissa turned toward the only home still standing. For an instant her eyes closed. Her body was still, her face rigid.

Pierce left her there. Crossing the rubble, he felt the whisper of death.

Every few feet he stopped, forcing himself to study the grounds with care. He found a woman's pink plastic purse, intact amid the ashes; a headless chicken; charred bones that might once have been a human forearm. Spotting several bullet casings, he put them in his pocket.

The casings, he knew, would be from the kind of ammunition used by the Luandian military.

Everything about the scene bespoke a massacre, not armed resistance. In the Balkans—in another life—his forensics team would have combed the rubble; searched for a mass grave; dug up skeletons with missing limbs and bullet holes in the backs of their heads; ferreted out survivors. His evidence, as it had before the tribunal at The Hague, might have included the testimony of civilian underlings Pierce had turned against the butcher who'd caused so many deaths. There would be none of that here. Aside from Marissa and Bobby, the only surviving witnesses might well be Okimbo's soldiers. Though there was little doubt of what those men had done, actual proof would be harder to come by.

When he returned to Marissa, she remained frozen by the sight of the home she had shared with Bobby, the memory of what she had last seen there. A shadow crossed the space between them. Looking up, Pierce saw that the sky had turned a dense gray-yellow. Quietly, Marissa said, "It's going to rain."

"Tell me what happened here, Marissa. Everything."

For a long while, she looked directly into his eyes. Then she gazed into the distance and, speaking slowly and succinctly, told him all she could. For minutes, her face and voice were expressionless, as though she were subduing the pain of memory with all the resources she possessed. "When Okimbo and his men took me away," she finished, "I could still hear gunshots."

"They were killing the last witnesses." Pierce paused for a moment. "Did you see who piloted PGL's boats and helicopters?"

Marissa shook her head. "It was dark. Once the eclipse passed, all I saw was soldiers."

"Were the sea trucks still on the beach?"

She stared at the ground. "I don't think I looked there."

A drop of rain stirred the ashes at their feet. When Pierce glanced up, another struck his face, and suddenly the skies unleashed a torrent of hard rain.

Bara and the pilot scrambled beneath a grove of palms. At the center of the village, Pierce and Marissa had no shelter.

As though by instinct, she took his hand and began pulling him toward the house. She stopped at its threshold, shrinking back, then stepped inside.

Pierce followed. The room was shadowy, the ruins of Bobby's desk half visible. The ceiling fan was still. Arms folded tightly, Marissa paused to study it. Then, inexorably, her gaze moved to a dark stain on the carpet where, Pierce was certain, a girl had bled to death from a throat wound after Paul Okimbo raped her. Above them a fresh assault of rain struck the zinc roof like a fusillade of bullets.

Marissa began to shiver. Pierce pulled her close, feeling the ragged rhythm of her breaths until, at last, they slowed. Her arms stayed tight around him.

6

BY MIDMORNING OF THE FOLLOWING DAY, LUAN-dian soldiers were streaming into Port George. Trapped at an intersection, Pierce and Bara gazed through the windshield at the jeeps and trucks filled with armed men. "A reprisal for the dead soldier we saw in the doorway of that bar," Bara speculated. "Easier to root out FREE's supporters in Port George, real or imagined, than to set off a firefight in the delta."

"Especially if you've been bribed?"

"As I said, who knows about Okimbo. But at least he'll be too busy to keep you from visiting Bobby."

Pierce watched the soldiers. "You still think I'll get in?"

"You should. I gave the authorities a letter telling them you're an American lawyer who may help represent Bobby Okari. For the moment, they're trying to tamp things down by honoring the form, if hardly the substance, of our so-called human rights. Still, you're lucky that Okimbo isn't at the prison today."

Once again, Pierce pondered the fluidity with

which Bara navigated between ostensibly opposing forces. At last the army passed and Pierce and Bara drove to the barracks at Port George.

SURROUNDED BY A high stone wall, the barracks had but one entrance, a steel gate guarded by two soldiers. After Pierce showed his passport, a mustached young officer appeared. Stone-faced, he introduced himself as Major Bangida, and permitted Pierce to enter.

They crossed a courtyard surrounded by soldiers' quarters. To one side, a two-story stone prison with barred windows looked down upon a platform that appeared to be a gallows. Bangida led Pierce to a metal door to the prison and told the soldier guarding it to direct him to Okari's cell. But for the gallows, Pierce could have been visiting a prisoner in America, until he climbed the stone steps to the second floor, dark and dank and fetid with the odor of human waste.

At the end of the corridor was a cell without windows, illuminated only by a bare bulb in the ceiling. As Pierce came closer, a form rose from the shadows with the painful slowness of an old man, gripping the bars for balance. Then Pierce saw Bobby Okari peering through the bars.

Bobby's bloodshot eyes betrayed hope and apprehension. His chin was flecked with gray stubble, and the lines graven in his gaunt face seemed more than the years could account for. "Bobby," Pierce said. "It's Damon Pierce."

Bobby studied Pierce's face as though examining every feature. "Damon," he replied softly. "This I never expected."

"Marissa e-mailed me," Pierce answered. "How *are* you?"

"As you see me. A bottle to piss in; a bucket to shit in; rats and roaches for company. They don't let her come—a kindness perhaps. Since we last met, I have learned much about how men can subvert the essence of what it is to be human."

Pierce nodded. "I want to help you," he said quickly. "I'm trying to figure out how to develop some legal leverage—I've got the background for it. But we may not have much time, and there's a lot I need to understand. Starting with your relationship to Karama. *Everything,* from the beginning until now."

Bobby's teeth showed in a brief smile, a ghost of his former animation. "You've made inquiries, I see."

"A necessity. Your fate's in Karama's hands."

Bobby's gaze turned inward. "I first met him fifteen years ago," he said at length, "when I was a novelist and sometime journalist in Port George. He was Captain Karama then—like many young officers, he saw the army as a path to power. *I* saw him as an interesting person, most of all for how he listened to others: attentive, watching their eyes and weighing their words, asking questions to deepen his understanding. Without quite saying so, he implied that he wished for the army to secure the democracy we'd never truly had." A weary irony crept into Bobby's voice. "I had my own ambitions for Luandia and needed friends who might someday have the power to help. During that time, Karama and I spent several long evenings together. Only later did I discover his gifts for deception."

"How so?"

Bobby seemed to wince. "One night, after many drinks, we discovered that we shared a woman. Ela was also a journalist, beautiful and ambitious— that she'd be using us both was unsurprising. But as drunk as I was, I saw the change in Karama's eyes.

"When I next saw Ela, she was a shell. It seemed that she'd learned things about Karama's tastes she would not speak aloud. Soon after, she vanished. No one knows where." Bobby looked directly at Pierce. "Marissa knows nothing about this. When I brought her here, Karama was not in power. The best thing you can do is remove her from this place."

"Karama has taken her passport, Bobby." Pierce paused, waiting for Bobby to absorb this. "You haven't finished the story."

Bobby touched his eyes. "While I was in America, to my further surprise, Karama immersed himself in army politics. Fairly soon after I returned, a general close to him decided to depose the corrupt civilian president, who, nevertheless, was preferable to a military ruler.

"The general's plan was to assault the presidential palace at night. To his surprise, Karama ordered his soldiers to slaughter the troops who were to carry out the coup, and personally dispatched his former patron with a bullet to his head. When dawn broke, the president had survived and General Savior Karama, now the army's chief of staff, was the most powerful man in Luandia." Bobby's tone remained soft. "Two years later he went to the palace, put a gun to the president's head, and reminded him how easily he could pull the trigger. The president chose to resign. The quiet officer of my acquaintance had become Luandia's nightmare."

"Not forever," Pierce said. "Presidents don't last here."

"So I hoped. But Karama became a prodigy of paranoia. He built a new capital city meant to be so impregnable that no usurper would dare a coup. He began sleeping by day and governing at night, so that enemies could not use the dark against him. Even those closest to him learned to fear for their families. Distrust your foreign minister? Take his thirteen-year-old daughter as your mistress and dare him to complain. The man *wished* that Karama had killed her . . ."

His voice trailed off. "Are you all right?" Pierce asked.

Bobby closed his eyes, leaning his forehead against the bars. "Karama likes group sex. His partners were screened, of course. One night the procurer in chief flew in three prostitutes from Paris. After Karama had the first two, the third claimed that she wanted him at once, and offered him what she said was Viagra.

"Karama asked her to take it first. When she began to cry, he explained the alternatives to her in detail. After that she took the pill. Karama gave her two companions to his men; the girl who died foaming at the mouth was lucky." Bobby stared at the chains around his ankles. "Their deaths are the first movie of a double feature Karama shows to those who servility he questions. The second film records the death of the general who recruited them. During the viewing, it is said, Karama serves champagne . . ."

Abruptly Bobby sagged. Reaching through the bars, Pierce kept him from collapsing. "Just brace me for a minute," Bobby murmured.

He took one deep breath, then another, and gripped the bars again. "After this attempt at assassination failed, Karama decided to hold an election—"

"Which you called on the Asari to boycott."

"Yes—Karama wanted a 'mandate' for all the world to see. He left little to chance. Candidates opposing his slate were jailed or killed. His thugs drove off voters and stole their ballots—I saw soldiers cruising through Port George with ballot boxes in their jeep. When a poll watcher complained, Okimbo's soldiers dropped him at his home with both Achilles tendons cut. The only flaw in Karama's plan was the Asari."

Pierce heard something scurry in Bobby's cell, perhaps a rat. Bobby seemed not to notice. "After the election, Karama summoned me to his palace in Savior City . . ."

His voice breaking, Bobby struggled to remain upright.

"Rest," Pierce urged him.

"You must hear this." Straightening himself, Bobby began speaking, his memory so precise and vivid that Pierce imagined himself there.

IT WAS PAST midnight. A minion in resplendent dress led a frightened Bobby through a marble sitting room with fifty-foot ceilings and sumptuous French decor. Karama stood in a spotlit garden, hands clasped behind his back, staring through iron bars into the darkened void of what Bobby understood was his personal zoo. The uniform that fit him so precisely had been tailored on Savile Row.

Gazing at the president's back, Bobby waited until he turned.

Even at night, Karama now wore aviator sunglasses; his face showed no emotion, as though seeing Bobby after fifteen years was unremark-able. From the darkness came the growl of what Bobby guessed to be a lion. "You have heard of my zoo?" Karama asked.

"Yes."

"One side houses zebras and giraffes; the other, lions. At first I wondered about their inherent natures before their parents taught them. So I took a lion cub and fed him vegetables in the sitting room, hoping he'd become a house cat." Karama laughed softly. "He *ate* the house cat. That ended my experiment with turning lions into vegetarians. Predators will always be predators."

Bobby could think of nothing to say. Karama placed a hand on his shoulder. "It is one thing to share a woman, my old friend. Two men cannot share a country."

Bobby shook his head. "I care only that my people share what oil brings."

"And yet you asked them not to vote." An under-current of anger crept into Karama's speech. "For this, you demand the attention of the United Nations. What do you imagine—that you will win the Nobel Peace Prize by preening like a peacock on the world stage? Or do you simply enjoy holding me up to ridicule?"

At once, Bobby knew that Karama still resented his "betrayal" with Ela. "You can end my people's suffering," he answered as calmly as he could. "Then they won't need the world's help."

Suddenly, Karama smiled broadly. "So those who tell me you're a secessionist have given me false information. This is good news, old friend."

"Then let me tell you how to help us—"

"All in good time," Karama interrupted with sudden heartiness. "Once you move to Savior City and become my oil minister, we can talk at leisure."

Grasping Karama's purpose, Bobby felt a chill: Karama meant to hold him captive to fear until he became a stranger to his people, forced to mouth Karama's words. "I'm honored," Bobby answered slowly. "But my ambitions are for the Asari."

Karama's face became stone. "There's only one way to achieve them. Join me."

"In time, perhaps—"

"If I manage to win your approval, you mean. Then you will intercede with the world on my behalf."

Unsure of how to answer, Bobby remained silent.

"In time you will let me know your judgment," Karama said with an eerie smile. "Then I'll make mine. In the meanwhile, I will have my private jet fly you to Port George."

Apprehension flooded Bobby's mind. Karama had once ordered a rival pushed from a cargo plane at twenty thousand feet. At the least, Karama not only had the power to imprison Bobby in his own fear but, by flying Bobby home so ostentatiously, to spread the rumor that Karama had corrupted him. "Travel safely," Karama told him softly. "If only for your wife's sake. They tell me she's as beautiful as Ela."

PIERCE STILL HELD Bobby upright. Through his cloth shirt, Bobby's ribs felt too close to the skin. His account of Karama's parting words lingered in the silence.

"Besides Karama," Pierce asked, "who wants you out of the way?"

"PGL. Their manager in the delta, Trevor Hill, seems a decent man. But he doesn't decide how his bosses deal with us. If the Asari movement manages to spread across the delta, Hill's superiors may feel that they have too much to lose."

"Who else?"

"Local chiefs paid off by PGL, men like my father." Briefly, Bobby's eyes shut again. "The gangs and militias, FREE most of all. They use the goals of the Asari movement to cover their own criminality and greed . . ."

Bobby's knees gave way. "Rest," Pierce urged again.

"Just hold me up," Bobby answered fiercely. "I will not face another man sitting in my own filth."

Their faces were inches apart. After a moment,

Pierce asked, "What about the leaders closest to you, the ones who backed away?"

Bobby's eyes clouded. In a softer voice, he answered, "Eric Aboh and the others feared that our movement would disintegrate, leaving them alone. A lone man is frail; only a mass movement can sustain him. Without this, the best of men—even those like Atiku Bara—crumble under the weight of fear and temptation."

"But did they conspire with Okimbo?"

"To frame me? That I do not wish to believe."

"No?"

"No," Bobby said with sudden force. "You cannot help me by blaming the Asari. What we need now is for Americans to understand how Karama and the oilmen force our people to live, and how your country has become a part of it.

"It is not just filling your tanks with our petrol. It is a new imperialism where the government cares only that petrotyrants like Karama deliver you from the threat of Osama bin Laden and your disasters in the Middle East." Anger sustained the strength in Bobby's voice. "When your military strategists look at Luandia, they don't see the Asari or others in the delta. All they see is the Muslims in the north, worried they'll become 'Islamofascists' or whatever buzzword they're using to frighten Americans and ignore the rights of others.

"Long ago your government should have been

shamed by its own arrogance. Instead you continue to blunder through the world pursuing policies you misconceive as clever, and end up with one brutal mess after another—from Vietnam to Iraq—which you then try to correct by creating yet another mess in another country. So now it is Luandia's turn."

Though their perspective was very different, Pierce was struck by how closely Bobby's vision hewed to Martel's warning that Luandia was becoming a pawn in the fight for oil. "What do you need me to do?"

"Help your country *see* us. My people need the very things America says it stands for: transparency, fair elections, a civil society that nourishes and protects us." Reaching through the bars, Bobby gripped the front of Pierce's shirt, eyes glinting with almost feverish passion and, Pierce guessed, exhaustion. "We need schools, roads, water, programs that persuade a new generation of leaders that violence is not the answer. More than that, we need hope. Without hope, the violence of Karama and FREE will create a conflagration that consumes Luandia *and* companies like PGL." Bobby's fingers tightened. "*That* is my message to America. If the United States cares nothing about what happens here, my people—and yours—will reap what you sow: a delta so savage and so criminal that not even Karama can contain it.

"*That* is why I cannot die. I alone can deliver all

of us from this nightmare. Without me, there will be no one left who can negotiate a peace."

Pierce looked into Bobby's eyes. Perhaps sleeplessness and hunger had stripped the veneer of humility from Bobby's self-belief, exposing its molten core; perhaps his anguish at the massacre cut so deep that to insist on his own transcendence was his only defense against the fear of failure and death. Pierce looked at Bobby's hands and then into his face, attempting to fathom how this man must feel now. Quietly, he asked, "Do you know anything about who hung those workers?"

Bobby's eyes dimmed. "No."

"Not followers who might have believed they were acting in your name?"

"That is not what I believe."

"What *do* you believe?"

Bobby inhaled, releasing Pierce's shirt. "That it was Okimbo."

"What reason would he have?"

"If Okimbo fails to crush the Asari movement, he loses what matters most to him, power and money—whether from Karama, PGL, or militia groups like FREE. Maybe he even imagines himself as Karama's successor." Bobby spoke more softly. "When I found those men, Okimbo was already there. And yet they were not protected from death."

Pierce smiled a little. "I've wondered about that myself."

Taking Pierce's hand in both of his, Bobby finished with quiet urgency, "Then do not doubt me, Damon. Help us. Help Marissa."

Meeting Bobby's eyes, Pierce felt the weight of his helplessness. Slowly, he nodded.

Footsteps sounded behind them, and then the soldier who had taken Pierce to Bobby's cell led him away again.

BARA WAS PARKED outside. Above the shantytown Pierce saw a thick cloud of smoke split by tongues of flame. Gunfire sounded in the distance.

Drained by his encounter with Bobby, Pierce slid into the passenger seat. Bara's face was grim. "Okimbo?" Pierce asked.

"Yes. The army's decimating the so-called neighborhood where they claim the killers of that soldier came from. Unless Bobby lives, that is the face of our future."

"So he believes." Pierce reflected for a moment, then took out his cell phone and asked his security team to book a flight to Waro.

7

PIERCE LANDED IN A COCOON OF PROTECTION. As soon as he got off the plane, his chief security adviser, Hank Vorster, shepherded him to a private corner of the airport, cordoned off from the sea of Luandians departing and arriving. Though they had never met, Pierce had seen Vorster's photograph, a safeguard against kidnapping by an impostor. Vorster was a veteran of the South African special forces; the second member of the team—Dennis Clellan, formerly a British marine—awaited them. Though Vorster was taller and sported a beard, both men wore close-cropped hair, looked remarkably fit, and had the same expression of tensile alertness. Their mission, honed by protecting visiting businessmen, was to keep Pierce safe. Their briefing was to the point.

"It's forty kilometers to Waro," Vorster told Pierce. "The traffic is stop-and-go at best, especially on the bridges. That's where criminals can break into the van and take you away—or, in your case, worse guys pretending to be criminals who work for God knows who.

"The goal is not to stop between here and our destination. There'll be a police truck in front and in back of our vehicle, both with a trained driver and an armed guard." Vorster looked at Pierce intently. "Your job is to follow a few simple rules. If we have to slow down, or there's trouble, we'll handle it. Don't open a window. Don't make eye contact. Keep your hands where anyone can see them. Some of these guys are twitchy—reach for your cell phone and they'll shoot you. That we don't want—a stupid death is unforgivable. Any questions?"

"Yeah. You just hire Luandian police like they're security guards?"

Vorster shrugged. "Everything's for sale here. These guys don't make squat."

"But don't they know why I'm here?"

Vorster grinned. "They think you're an oil company executive. We'll wait for someone else to disabuse them."

He nodded to Clellan. Looking around warily, they shepherded Pierce through the chaos, one at each elbow.

THE WHITE SUV was double-parked between two police trucks watched over by Luandian policemen with semiautomatic weapons. Vorster and Clellan hustled Pierce inside it.

The dark, hawk-faced man in the back, Bryce Martel's former CIA colleague, extended his hand. "Dave Rubin," he said. "Welcome to the wonderful world of Waro. Hope we can tell you enough to make the trip worthwhile."

Vorster got in front, Clellan behind the wheel. Abruptly, the lead police truck turned on its siren and flashing lights, and the three-vehicle caravan pushed into the six-lane road amid the worst traffic Pierce had ever seen—not only congested but without discernible rules. There were no sidewalks: in the sweltering late-afternoon smog, pedestrians scurried along the edge of the road, inches from being struck; men on mopeds sliced through narrow spaces between cars and trucks; vehicles stopped so abruptly that bumpers often collided. Their caravan careened through traffic, forcing aside other cars and herding pedestrians to the side, the reflexes of each driver so remarkable that Pierce began to laugh. "Is it always like this?"

Vorster turned to answer. "Unless it's worse. Traffic governs the life of everyone here—all movement can stop for hours, and you sit there in a catatonic trance, afraid of being snatched or robbed." He pointed to an adolescent tapping on the window of a stalled car. "He's selling SIM cards for cell phones. Waro runs on them—it's the only way you can tell someone you're suffering from vehicular paralysis."

"It's a metaphor," Rubin interjected. "You'll see when we get closer to Waro. Someday soon the traffic will stop, the sewage will back up, the power grid will give out; bands of armed criminals will occupy the hotels, and the whole place will cease to function. No wonder Karama left."

"I thought this was a police state," Pierce said.

Rubin shook his head. "It's a kleptocratic autocracy. Karama doesn't care if Waro is an urban jungle. He doesn't worry about criminals unless they're stealing from him. The only 'law breakers' he cracks down on are people like Okari.

"The result is the slow disintegration of civil order—or, in places like the delta, the entire fabric of society. Young men either join a militia or find some other way to extract money from PGL. A teenager who doesn't like those choices can leave for the city." His voice filled with disgust. "You saw Port George."

The SUV squealed to a stop. Briefly, Pierce was distracted by the sight of a New York Yankees cap passing, as though suspended on air. Peering out, he saw that it belonged to a man without legs, his torso balanced on a skateboard he propelled with his arms. Then the caravan started forward again, sirens screeching. "In the creeks," Pierce said, "we saw militia men bunkering oil, and no military in sight. That can't work without graft."

From the front seat, Vorster smiled, the corners of his blue eyes crinkling. "Ah," he said amiably, "the dawn of wisdom."

"Aside from Karama," Rubin told Pierce, "the criminal militias have been Okari's greatest challenge. But who's to say that Karama and the militias are strangers to each other? In the grand kleptocracy of Savior Karama, corruption is the sole ideology that can unify opposing forces."

"In other words," Pierce said, "illegal bunkering needs—or feeds—corrupt officials."

"Assuredly. But don't forget the element of competition." Rubin sat back. "Hank and I make a dime or two advising folks in the oil business about security issues in the delta. So I've distilled militia predation to its essence.

"Start with the raw materials—a pool of youth

who are undereducated, unemployed, and pissed off that their standard of living is *worse* because of oil. They go three places: armed gangs with names like 'Blood Suckers' and 'Creek Vipers,' ethnic militias, or FREE—"

"What's the difference?"

The SUV lurched, bouncing the three men in their seats as Clellan braked to avoid a boy in a wheelchair who was begging amid heavy traffic. "The gangs are local," Rubin answered, "the ethnic militias, tribal. FREE is delta-wide, and spouts high-sounding principles it swiped from Okari. But most of these guys originated as election enforcers for rival politicians; all depend on oil theft and kidnapping. The upshot is a proliferation of nonstate rival armies—maybe fifteen thousand men with twice that many weapons—engaged in a Darwinian battle for territory and control.

"One's always attacking another. Often the boys are high on confidence builders like pot or cocaine, which don't do a lot for their judgment—lucky one of the guys you ran into didn't use your head for target practice. Whatever the inspiration, they kill one another indiscriminately. The more enterprising among them pay the heads of local army units to help eliminate their rivals."

Vorster laughed at this. "When I see news about the army battling some gang, I always wonder what other gang paid them."

"Unless it's a local politician," Rubin amended. "The governor of Asariland uses state oil money to finance a militia group that steals *more* oil, which in turn funnels him a share of the profits. That also assures him of a standing gang of enforcers available to rig the next election—"

"Behold," Vorster announced to Pierce, gesturing toward the windshield. "Beautiful Waro Harbor."

The city, Pierce saw, was built on islands connected by a network of bridges, one of which was choking the traffic ahead. As they reached the bridge, Vorster scanned the pedestrians on both sides, alert for danger. Pierce focused on the water. In the foreground was a floating slum, thousands of wooden houses perched on stilts above their own bobbing refuse, their rusted tin roofs wreathed in the haze of cooking fires. A few fishermen in canoes skimmed the surface of the water, as sludgy as an oil slick. The walls of the public housing on the adjacent island had turned a leprous gray-black. In the sooty air, the high-rises beyond looked like a mirage.

"Eighteen million people," Vorster remarked. "The world's largest slum. Those of us who love Africa find this a sorry sight."

Rubin's gaunt face, as he stared out the window, took on a melancholy cast. "So let us return to FREE. It has a fascination unique among the militias, and it's essential to understanding the forces that bear on Okari's fate.

"To FREE, as much as to Karama, Bobby Okari is the enemy. FREE has cynically embraced his stated goals: resource control, redistribution of oil revenues, and rebuilding the delta. But if nonviolence succeeds, FREE's whole rationale for 'armed resistance'—that is, kidnapping and bunkering—evanesces."

"In other words," Pierce said, "FREE could have killed those oil workers and hung the murders around Bobby's neck."

"Or paid someone to do it. But here's another thing about FREE: no one knows for sure who runs it, or what their motives are."

"The other gangs are merely killers," Vorster put in. "But FREE has a highly sophisticated command structure, and their military operations are so effective that Dave and I are convinced their leaders were trained abroad—my own guess being the Middle East. They're also way better armed than their rivals *or* the army—including grenade and rocket launchers—which means they're connected with the most serious arms dealers on the planet."

"Politically, FREE is as shapeless as an amoeba," Rubin explained. "Their field commander is a Luandian who calls himself General Freedom. But their head is a man known only as Jomo." Rubin smiled wryly. "The fascinating thing about *him* is that no one knows if he exists. Jomo communicates with the world only through a series of highly articulate e-mails. No one outside FREE claims to have met him, and the man who reports to him, General Freedom, claims he's sworn to secrecy.

"Theories abound. Some believe Jomo doesn't exist; others, that he's General Freedom. Still others argue that he's a South African arms dealer, a Luandian general, an American financier, or even someone close to Karama himself." Rubin's look of amusement faded. "Whoever's calling the shots, FREE's attempting to absorb or destroy the other militias. If it succeeds, whoever controls FREE will control a multibillion-dollar business—oil theft."

The convoy reached the end of the bridge, still weaving through dense traffic. Above its sirens, Pierce heard horns blasting, drivers shouting, radios blaring. Vendors dodged cars, hawking T-shirts or candy or magazines. A boy of ten or eleven with a hideously burned arm waved a basket at Pierce's window, begging for money. Ignoring him, Rubin continued: "It doesn't end with stealing oil. Luandia is a transit hub for drug smuggling, illegal arms trading, and money laundering—all interrelated with oil theft, all generating payoffs for people in government. FREE's tentacles now reach into every one of them."

Pierce absorbed this. "Only as long as the delta remains unstable," he ventured. "FREE still depends on oil theft, right?"

182

"FREE," Vorster responded, "depends on PGL. The trick is to steal enough but not too much. That way PGL remains in business, Karama stays in power, and America gets the lion's share of Luandian oil."

Pierce considered that. "To help Bobby Okari, I need to put pressure on PGL. A huge missing piece is how deeply PGL was involved in the destruction of Goro."

Rubin glanced at Vorster, who raised his eyebrows and shrugged. "We have no idea," Vorster said. "PGL's security guy in the delta, Roos Van Daan, is a blight on my fellow Afrikaners—a racist for hire who's been on the worst side of some of the dirtiest wars in Africa. But it's hard to say what Van Daan knew or did, or how clearly anyone at PGL anticipated Okimbo's methods. In an environment like the delta, PGL doesn't call the shots, and things have a way of spinning out of control."

The convoy entered a street flooded with a sewage overflow. Traffic slowed to a halt. "We should catch some dinner," Rubin told Pierce, "sit out this mess. After that you've got some attractive entertainment options."

"Which are?"

"Going to your hotel to meet the hookers at the bar. Or my recommendation—an evening with Savior Karama." Rubin's face turned somber. "He's scheduled a speech tonight in the soccer stadium in Waro, where he can harangue a hundred thousand fellow citizens. His subject is the threat to national security posed by the Asari movement. This speech should pretty much tell us what Okari is up against."

Pierce felt numb. "What does it tell you that he's making this an event?"

"Nothing good." Rubin glanced toward Vorster. "You'll remember the last public speech he gave there."

"The one about subversion by the press?"

"Yup." Rubin turned to Pierce again. "Karama delivered that one at midnight. The next morning the state security services kicked down the door of Waro's last independent newspaper, smashed the desks, destroyed the computers, and beat up the reporters. They were the lucky ones. Their editor—the only 'enemy' Karama had mentioned by name—was kidnapped, tortured, and left dead by the side of the road."

"His name was Peter Agbo," Vorster added softly. "Some of us admired him quite a lot. We'll drink to him tonight."

8

THE YES CLUB, PIERCE DISCOVERED, HAD TWO floors: an upper level on which privileged expats could eat and drink in peace, and a first floor packed with young Luandian women in heavy makeup and provocative dress whose means of survival was hustling white men. As Vorster and Clellan steered Pierce and Rubin inside, their armed police escorts stationed themselves at the door, prepared to stop anyone who might be carrying a weapon. Then Vorster guided Pierce through the throng of desperate, eager women toward the stairway to the second floor. "They're like eels," Vorster said. "A new man doesn't pass without getting touched."

As he said this, the women closed around Pierce in a claustrophobic press of bodies, putting their hands on his wrist, arm, back, legs, and buttocks as they murmured presumably seductive phrases. One pushed between Vorster and Pierce. She was caked in makeup; though her face was covered with festive silver sprinkles, her smile was forced, her eyes anxious and sad. "Do you need a woman?" she asked.

"Thank you," Pierce answered gently, "but I have one."

Her lips formed a wistful smile as Pierce moved past her. "Sad," Pierce murmured to Vorster.

"Common," he said. "Before oil she might have been a village woman—a circumscribed life but, one can argue, far better. It certainly beats dying of AIDS or getting brutalized by a sadistic stranger. Most of these stories don't end well."

Rubin and Clellan followed them to the second floor, a large room with wooden tables, a bar, and a couple of televisions tuned to CNN and a soccer match. Rubin, Vorster, and Pierce sat at one table, ordering drinks: Clellan sat apart, watching the entrance. Both Vorster and Clellan, Pierce noted, asked for soft drinks.

Rubin touched his beer glass to Pierce's. "Your e-mail asked about how bunkering works. So fire away."

Pierce marshaled his thoughts. "I'm still figuring out how many people profit from crushing the Asari movement. Bunkering seems like a road map—selling billions in stolen oil requires more than the thieves and crooked army officers."

"True enough. Bunkering is like a hydra, with tentacles into every segment of the Luandian elite. The CIA has made a study of it: our people worry that the proceeds could be used to finance terrorists, or that theft and violence will eliminate the delta as a reliable source of oil." Rubin spread his hands in a gesture of helplessness. "Problem is, it's nearly impossible to stop, given that everyone gets a cut of the profits."

" 'Everyone' being?"

"Start with what you saw," Vorster suggested. "A rust-bucket tanker loaded to the gunnels with stolen oil. Already you need PGL engineers to open a pipeline, the militia to tap it, the barge's crew and its owner to take the oil away, and army officers to ignore them. But that's just the beginning.

"The next stage is to move the tanker through the

creeks to an oil freighter in international waters. For the purpose of this exercise, you're FREE. Who do you need for that?"

Briefly, Pierce considered this. "For openers, the village chiefs along the creeks."

"Yup. Also local officials and state governors, admirals and generals to keep the navy and army away, customs officials to let the tanker cruise right through Port George Harbor into the Atlantic, a freighter no one bothers that takes the oil to refineries in Guinea or Angola—"

"All of which requires," Rubin added, "federal officials at the highest levels. No thievery so lucrative and blatant occurs without them taking a piece."

"In short," Pierce said, "no one who can stop PGL from bleeding wants to."

"Right. Analogies abound: you can say that PGL's the semivoluntary host to a swarm of parasites; or that bunkering is a cancer that's metastasized; or that the entire governmental structure of Luandia is a Mafia operation in the form of a West African state. As one example, FREE has already bought the Luandian navy: the biggest incentive to being an officer is the chance to retire on dirty money. It's also believed that most of the tankers and freighters are owned by those close to Karama, including his national security adviser, Ugwo Ajukwa—who may well play a behind-the-scenes role in deciding Okari's fate. But Ajukwa's merely one among the many crooks knee-deep in bunkering who'd be happy to see Okari and his movement eradicated."

Listening, Vorster put down his club soda. "When Okimbo destroyed that village, he benefited FREE and its corrupt legion of stakeholders—all in the name of law and order. Pinning the murders on Bobby would finish the job."

Rubin nodded to Vorster, then turned back to Pierce. "Bunkering is embedded in Luandian corruption. Luandia's most corrupt institutions—the military, police, and customs—produce its future presidents. Shutting down the Asari serves them all. But it's foolish to assume that Karama wants to shut down FREE—"

"So wiping out that shantytown in Port George was all for show?"

"Sure," Vorster said. "Maybe a couple of residents hid the guys who shot that soldier. But I guarantee that whoever planned that PGL man's kidnapping isn't living in a shack without water or electricity. Okimbo's raid was a symbolic gesture to PGL, sacrificing a few hundred feckless victims on the altar of hypocrisy."

Rubin drained his beer. Sardonically, he said, "Let's focus on more cosmic issues than the slaughter of incidental victims. Like the world price of oil."

"Yeah," Pierce said. "Martel mentioned that."

"Well he might. OPEC's far from the only

player. Four years ago, FREE's first wave of theft and kidnapping pushed the price of oil to fifty bucks a barrel. Now it's twice that and rising fast, in some part due to what's happening in Luandia.

"FREE's operations help drive up the world price of oil per barrel, and every price rise makes FREE's bunkering business more profitable in an oil-hungry world. FREE's getting richer, more powerful, and better armed. Pretty soon it could have the power to shut down the Port George airport, kidnap hundreds of PGL workers, and sabotage a quarter of PGL's operations."

Vorster nodded vigorously. "And what's after that?" he asked rhetorically. "FREE could buy the next 'free election' for its chosen candidate, bankroll insurrections in West African countries rich in oil or diamonds, even finance terrorists abroad. Whatever else they do, our oil security strategists worry that FREE could completely destabilize Luandia. Makes the fate of Bobby Okari seem like pretty small potatoes."

This disheartening litany aroused Pierce's resistance. "Not to me," he said. "Certainly not to Bobby. He believes that his movement can bring stability to the delta."

Rubin gave Pierce a crooked smile. "That's the problem, isn't it. Too many people with power don't want that. The only 'good' thing is that these same people know better than to make PGL's existence totally intolerable. For everyone's sake—the crooks and ours—PGL has to keep pumping oil. A two-year shutdown in the delta could cut America's oil supply by twenty percent, perhaps leaving the Chinese to pick up the pieces."

A waiter appeared, a polite young Luandian who stood at a respectful distance. Looking up, Vorster ordered more drinks and several dishes for the table. "You'll have to trust me," he told Pierce with a smile. "Whatever we'll have you'll never have eaten before."

Pierce waited for the young man to depart. "In the car," he said to Rubin, "Hank theorized that FREE's military leaders were trained in the Middle East."

Rubin placed a finger to his lips, as though pondering how much to say. "In Libya," he finally answered. "At least General Freedom was. Though the delta's Christian, he's a Muslim convert. That means nothing in itself—the world's full of Muslims who aren't obsessed with fucking us over." Pausing, he looked from Pierce to Vorster. "We know that two years ago a Saudi-backed group affiliated with bin Laden sent an emissary to General Freedom. Our information is that Freedom sent him back—FREE is making too much money bleeding PGL to get mixed up with jihadists.

"Still, a clever terrorist could use FREE's bunkering network to pull off a one-shot operation worse than anything we've seen. The Pentagon has come up with scenarios that make 9/11 look like nothing."

"Such as?"

Rubin's gaze settled on Pierce. "FREE transfers a load of stolen oil down the creeks to a freighter offshore. But *this* freighter is owned by Islamic jihadists. Instead of heading for an African refinery, the jihadists fill the freighter with explosives and ram it into New York Harbor.

"That would blow up the entire port and destroy New York City for blocks. There's nothing to stop it from happening—despite all the rhetoric about homeland security, our ports still aren't secure, and there's no way of tracking down an anonymous oil freighter in the middle of the Atlantic." Rubin's tone was clipped. "Right now the *only* force, if any, that can stop FREE from doing that is Karama and the military—"

"Which is riddled with corruption," Pierce objected, "and maybe in bed with FREE in any case."

"Unless FREE goes too far. But Karama's all we've got. That's another reason why the White House won't be eager to pressure him about Okari." His voice lowered. "The president *knows* Karama's a murderer and a crook—our intelligence reports have left him with no illusions. But Okari's caught up in the geopolitics of oil and the global war on terror. Right now, we need Karama."

Pierce felt another surge of anger. "Which is precisely what Okari told me. No matter that Karama has jailed Bobby and wiped out an Asari village. Because Karama and FREE are empowered by oil, we're afraid to save the one man who might stop them from oppressing the delta, destabilizing the country, pushing America toward an oil-driven recession, and maybe helping Osama blow us up. We don't even know who in Luandia's doing what with whom, or on whose behalf, except that all of them want Bobby gone."

Vorster gave him a look of sympathy. "Assuming it wasn't Okari himself, who does *he* say killed those men?"

"He thinks Okimbo. The question is why."

Rubin raised his eyebrows. "Other than that Okimbo killed them on Karama's orders? A story, then. Two years ago, when General Freedom was foolish enough to show his face in Port George, he was arrested by an overzealous army captain.

"They threw him in the jail where they're keeping Okari. Strike you as easy to break out of?"

"Hardly."

"Me neither. But somehow the general managed. Then, as now, Okimbo was in charge."

Dinner arrived, steaming dishes of rice, peppers, snails, and chicken. Pierce gazed at it without appetite.

"Eat up," Rubin said mildly. "Soon enough, we're off to see Karama. That should give us some enlightenment."

9

THOUGH IT WAS CLOSE TO MIDNIGHT, THE SOCCER stadium at Waro was besieged by Luandians waiting in lines that crept forward a foot at a time. By prearrangement, Pierce, Rubin, and Vorster went to the head of a line, passing money to a policeman at the entrance. As they went inside, Pierce stopped, transfixed.

Illuminated by banks of klieg lights, the grass of the soccer field shone. Giant television screens were stationed at all sides of the field; at its center was the focus of the cameras, an elevated speaker's platform. Of the stadium's one hundred thousand seats, only those farthest from the field remained empty. The faces Pierce saw reflected conflicting emotions—excitement, anticipation, resignation, restiveness, boredom, and apprehension. "Why are they here?" Pierce asked Vorster.

Vorster looked around. "Soldiers and government workers are 'encouraged' to bring their families. Companies with government contracts bus in their employees. Some of these folks may even like Karama, not that it's relevant. What matters is that *he* likes a crowd."

They found three seats with a clear view of the field. The klieg lights captured smudged wisps of air; Pierce's eyes stung, and his lungs began burning from the smoke and exhaust. The stadium continued to fill, the cacophony rose, and groups of Luandians began chanting, *"Karama, Karama, Karama . . ."*

A deputation of Chinese filed in two rows below them, their expressions somber and dutiful. "They're used to this kind of thing," Vorster observed.

Minutes passed. The stadium filled to capacity; suddenly the noise swelled, spreading through the crowd as two jeeps carrying armed soldiers emerged from a tunnel. Behind them, a black convertible bore Savior Karama.

Flanked by two soldiers with rifles, Karama stood where the rear seat would be, his posture still and imperious. Behind his black aviator sunglasses, he did not acknowledge the crowd; it was as though he were offering himself as an object of veneration. Pierce found his appearance chilling: the man's dissociation seemed complete.

The jeep arrived at the speaker's platform, surrounded by armed soldiers. A young officer opened the door for Karama. He stepped from the jeep and mounted the steps, eyes straight ahead, his expressionless face and glass-covered eyes magnified by the massive screens. He could have been walking in his sleep.

He was tall, and his features were coarse. On both sides of his face were three symmetrical grooves, tribal scars inflicted in childhood. The gold braid on his red officer's cap set off the perfectly tailored green uniform arrayed with combat ribbons. At last he raised a pristine white glove, inducing silence, sudden yet complete.

"Greetings, my people," he began.

Carried by loudspeakers, his resonant voice seemed to hover above the crowd. "Nineteen days ago, three employees of PetroGlobal Oil—a guest in our country—were lynched in Asariland. On that very day, I swore to bring the murderers to justice. One week later, our military arrested the author of this brutal act: the would-be dictator of his imagined secessionist state, Bobby Okari."

The implacable rhythm of Karama's words did not invite applause. "The crimes of which Okari stands accused are many. Kidnapping and murder. Plotting to overthrow a democratically elected government. Incitement of sedition. Sabotage against the economic interests of the state." On the screen, Karama's blank gaze moved across the stadium, as though his senses could discern the traitors in its midst. "These are the acts of a would-be tyrant who, in his egotism, imagines himself a colossus in the eyes of the world. And so the Asari became his soldiers."

The loudspeakers crackled with a sarcastic laugh that startled his audience. "How foolish. Did they imagine marching on Savior City and hanging *me,* as well?

"If so, they are as deluded as Okari. Until Asariland is pacified, it will remain a military zone under the command of Colonel Paul Okimbo, closed to outside agents of sedition . . ."

"That means CNN," Rubin murmured to Pierce. "And you."

"Certain allies of Okari," Karama said with muted anger, "have depicted our response to homicide and treason as genocide. So I tell you—and them—that the only violence was launched by the terrorist Okari against the protectors of the state."

Pierce saw Vorster grimace. Issuing from his expressionless face, Karama's voice carried above them. "We will tap the telephone lines, monitor the bank accounts, intercept the mail, and access the computers of all those who may have conspired with him." Karama paused, speaking slowly and emphatically. "Anyone who writes or utters words destructive of the unity of Luandia is guilty of treason. Anyone who impedes the production of oil is guilty of sabotage. Anyone who makes false charges against the state is guilty of sedition.

"*All* are punishable by death. Anyone suspected of these crimes will be detained." Karama's tone became flat. "They will have no right to ask our reasons. They will have no right to seek an end to their confinement. They will have no access to lawyers or the courts."

Rubin arched an eyebrow. "Sound familiar?"

"For those charged with crimes against the state," Karama continued in the same unvarying monotone, "our justice will be swift and sure.

"In thirty days, Bobby Okari will be tried for his crimes by a special tribunal." Karama paused to let the weight of these words permeate the crowd. "The tribunal will be composed of two senior judges and a member of the army. There will be no appeal of its rulings or its judgment. I alone will determine whether, when, and how its sentence will be executed."

"A telling choice of words," Rubin murmured.

Pierce said nothing. He was remembering the gallows in Port George.

Once more, Karama's mirrored gaze swept the silent crowd. "Justice will be served, my people. God's will for Luandia *will* be done."

Uncertain how to respond, his listeners waited for cues; some around Pierce simply stared at the giant face on the screen. Karama raised his hand— half salute, half benediction. A claque began chanting, "Karama, Karama, Karama . . ."

Suddenly the stadium was plunged into darkness. "Uh-oh," Pierce heard Vorster say. "Whoever's running the power grid is getting it in the neck."

Confused, the people around them milled and chattered. Unlike in Goro, Pierce reflected, there were no flares to illuminate the dark.

When the klieg lights came back on, Karama was gone.

OUTSIDE, THEIR POLICE escort had vanished. "Let's get in," Vorster snapped, and the three men joined

Clellan in the SUV. A weapon rested on the console beside him. "Our friends suddenly took off," Clellan said.

As Clellan started the SUV, Rubin surveyed the throng. "Guess someone knows you're with us," he said to Pierce. "The punishment for lawyers is driving through Waro unescorted."

As they drove, Pierce imagined Marissa listening to the speech. "What did you think?" Vorster asked.

"As Okari's would-be lawyer? Luandia has signed six different international agreements on political, legal, and human rights. This speech violates every one. The kangaroo court for Bobby rips due process to shreds. Karama picks the court, reviews its verdict, and passes sentence. Why not just shoot him in the head—Karama's done it before."

"So what can you do?"

"About Karama, nothing. Whoever represents Bobby will have to find some other way to stop this."

Rubin gave him a dubious look. "Ah, yes," he said finally. "The court of world opinion. In thirty days, they'll have pretty well cleaned up Darfur."

Pierce ignored the mordancy of Rubin's tone. "Too little time," he said.

THEY WENT SILENT as the car crept through the crowd. Vorster looked from side to side, waiting for some threat to emerge. Abruptly, Clellan turned down a darkened side road bounded by squat concrete houses behind barbed-wire fences.

"Bad choice," Vorster said.

Clellan kept driving. "Didn't like the crowd back there. Too many people to watch."

Captured in their light beams, a group of young Luandians spread across the road. "Area boys," Vorster told Pierce with a fair show of calm. "They pick out a neighborhood and rip people off. At least that's what I hope they are."

"Shall I run them over?" Clellan asked.

"No. Considering Damon's with us, the authorities might decide to care."

Clellan kept driving toward the line of men, then braked abruptly with less than a foot to spare. Several men jumped back; another sauntered to the driver's window. Clellan rolled it down.

"You were driving too fast," the bulky young man said harshly. "Unless you pay us, we'll call the police."

Clellan seemed to consider this, then to reach for his wallet. Pierce watched his hand reappear with a gun aimed at the man's face. "If your friends don't evaporate," Clellan told him, "your head will."

The man froze as if hypnotized, then turned to his companions, waving them away. They disappeared like shadows in the night.

Clellan accelerated. "About your hotel," Vorster told Pierce. "It's pretty secure." No one mentioned the area boys.

THE HOTEL WARO was a five-story building surrounded by high stucco walls; its management, Vorster said, paid the police well for the privilege of making foreigners feel safe. Pierce thanked his companions, checked in, then stopped at the outdoor bar.

It was situated near a swimming pool surrounded by palms. At a table nearby a fat German business type fondled a young Luandian woman; intent on their conversation, the four Chinese at the next table ignored this. Pierce sat at the bar and ordered a brandy.

He sipped the warm amber liquid, waiting for his thoughts to overtake his emotions. Then he put down some money and went to his room.

The rug was dirty, the sink and bathtub mottled by rust. Pierce thought of a trip he had taken with his college girlfriend, staying at cheap hotels in shabby southwestern towns. He took out his cell phone to call Marissa.

Three times the call didn't go through; Pierce feared that they had cut her lines. When he tried her cell phone, she answered. "It's Damon," he told her. "Are you okay?"

"They haven't come for me yet." He could hear her breathe. "I watched Karama on television. He means it, Damon."

Her voice carried the echo of fear. "I've got some ideas," Pierce said. "But we should talk in person—"

The connection went dead.

Pierce sat on the edge of the bed. Now that he was alone, these unfamiliar surroundings felt surreal, as though he was caught in a dream he feared would end badly. He wondered how Marissa's dream—a life of meaning in Luandia—seemed to her now.

At length he checked his e-mail. The American ambassador, Grayson Caraway, had taken note of Karama's speech. He could see Pierce tomorrow in Savior City.

10

SAVIOR CITY WAS THE OPPOSITE OF WARO: THE road from the airport was smooth, and the outer environs—green lawns and sleek high-rises—reminded Pierce of those of an affluent southern city in America. As they entered the capital's heart, Vorster pointed out the Ministry of Defense, built in the shape of an enormous battleship; a new soccer stadium; and the headquarters of the Luandian National Petroleum Corporation, PGL's partner, a marble tower whose smoke-colored windows seemed appropriately opaque. If Pierce had not seen Waro and the delta, he might have imagined that Luandia was prospering under the firm but farsighted guidance of President Savior Karama. Then Vorster pointed out the entrance to Savior Rock, the presidential redoubt, and Pierce recalled Karama's true purpose in building his own capital.

The barred fence was guarded by a line of soldiers and flanked by two armored personnel carriers. Within the high walls were Luandia's Congress and high court, making their members, in effect, Karama's prisoners. In the distance, Karama's fortified palace was set against a sheer natural edifice of black volcanic rock. The site was immune to surprise attacks: the only path for soldiers mounting a coup would be to convoy for hours to the city, break through these barriers, and proceed to the palace in a frontal attack. "Eleven A.M.," said Vorster, checking his watch. "The president's no doubt asleep. For Karama, vampires and enemies come out at night."

Silent, Pierce wondered how to persuade such a man to release Bobby Okari.

IN ITS DESIGN, the embassy captured post-9/11 America: a walled concrete bunker bristling with security devices, seemingly designed to withstand explosive devices. After a security check, a young diplomat escorted Pierce to the office of Grayson Caraway.

The ambassador rose from his couch, greeting Pierce with a firm handshake and the offer of coffee and a comfortable chair. He was tall and spare, perhaps in his late fifties, with graying brown hair, glasses, and a thoughtful, somewhat professorial demeanor. Caraway was an able man, Martel had assured Pierce—representing America in such a complex place was no job for the dilettantes who purchased ambassadorial posts by raising campaign money for whoever won the presidency. Caraway got to the point at once: "Like you, I found Karama's pronouncement disturbing."

Pierce smiled faintly. "That's a diplomatic way of putting it."

"Diplomacy," Caraway rejoined, "is my business. I've already spoken to Karama's foreign minister, also a professional. It's clear to me that he wasn't consulted before Karama decided to spit in the world's face."

"So who can make Karama listen?"

Caraway sat back on the couch, his fingers steepled, his expression penetrant and serious. "A few rules of the road, Mr. Pierce. First, be assured that I consider Okari's fate a serious matter. It's also my job to represent the interests of our government, and it's not up to me to define what they are. With that caveat, and assuming your good faith, I'll be as helpful as I can.

"Let's define good faith. Because of the defects in our intelligence about Karama, my job involves a good deal of guesswork. I don't want to guess about you." Though even, Caraway's tone conveyed a steel practicality. "I need to know where you're going, and the tactics you're using to get there. I also need to understand your relationship to the Okaris. I don't expect you to tell me confidential information. But I want to know that whatever you *do* tell me is reliable—and, above all, that you won't try to use me to save a man you know ordered the murder of three employees of an American company deemed critical to our security."

Pierce held up his hand. "I don't know who had those men killed. But I know Okari well enough to doubt that it was him. I've also been to Goro. The one thing I'm sure of is that the army slaughtered hundreds of unarmed civilians. So Karama and Okimbo *are* murderers—it's logical to suppose they planned the first murders to justify this massacre. One of my expectations is that our government will do its damnedest to keep Karama from murdering Bobby Okari."

Caraway rested his chin on folded hands, contemplating Pierce. "I'd hope for the same. But remember that America has many interests, and State, Defense, and our intelligence agencies often disagree on what the priorities are. If you attack us publicly it will help neither your country nor Okari.

"Assuming that he's innocent, I think America's interests are best served by keeping him alive. But if I find out he's guilty, or that you're trying to mislead me, we're done. Fair?"

"Fair."

"All right." Caraway's long frame seemed to relax a bit, and he spoke in a milder tone. "Let me give you a primer on Luandia and geopolitics. Start with two rules. The first is that 9/11 trumps everything: our preeminent concern is oil supply and the fear that Islamic terrorists will infiltrate the Muslim north. Second, like Putin, Hugo Chávez, and the Saudi royal family, Karama knows that oil empowers him to disdain world opinion. Hence last night's speech."

Pierce nodded. "The way Martel put it is that 9/11 started the new cold war: all that matters is that you're on our side."

"That's part of the problem. Then there's the nature of Luandia itself. It has all the elements of instability—right now, Karama's what we've got." Caraway turned, pointing out the window to a high-rise in the middle distance. "That building's a gift from China. They're spending billions to buy influence, which translates into oil. The Chinese are tailor-made for Karama: they crave oil, they believe in graft, and they don't give a damn about human rights." Caraway's face turned grim. "If I advocate standing up for Okari, someone in Washington will say I'm bringing Karama and the Chinese closer."

Pierce tried to envision the geopolitics enveloping Bobby Okari. "How real is the threat of Islamic terrorists in the north?"

Caraway got up, pouring more coffee for them

both. "The basis for *imagining* a threat's real enough. The north's borders are porous, and its expanses of desert are so vast and ungoverned that some envision it as 'Afghanistan 2020': a base for terrorist operations no one can control. It doesn't help that bin Laden made a tape calling northern Luandia 'ripe for liberation.' My personal theory is that he's stoking our paranoia, hoping to draw in a visible contingent of U.S. troops whose presence will offend Luandian Muslims. But there's a large pool of unemployed men in the north who despise the Karama government *and* our invasion of Iraq. It's not uncommon to find infants named Osama."

"Is there any hard evidence of jihadists in Luandia?"

"Some. Our satellites have located what they believe may be a terrorist training base in the north, and our intelligence people snared a guy with ten million dollars and a cell phone programmed to call jihadists in Saudi Arabia. But Luandia's Muslims are Africans, not Arabs. They're also Sufi—a decidedly gentler sect scorned by Islamic militants." Caraway's slight smile had an ironic cast. "Still, Karama knows how to play the terrorist card. His story is that he, and only he, is America's bulwark against Islamic terrorists infesting the north."

"What about in the delta?"

Caraway looked at him shrewdly. "Against an Islamic alliance with FREE, you mean? That's not a natural fit. But some fear that Al Qaeda could become a shipper and refiner of bunkered Luandian oil, dramatically expanding its ability to finance expanded terrorist operations against the West.

"There's precedent for that. Ninety percent of the drugs derived from poppies grown in Afghanistan are sold in Europe and come back as arms for the Taliban. The Iranians funnel petrodollars to Hezbollah. That's led to another factor that strengthens Karama—our nascent military presence in Luandia."

Pierce was genuinely startled. "I didn't know we had one."

"It's not large yet. But we have military personnel in the north, training Luandian soldiers in counterinsurgency tactics. They're potential targets for kidnappings or killings—God knows what we'll do if *that* occurs. Nevertheless, the Pentagon wants to increase our military beachhead here. Even, some propose, in the delta." Caraway checked his watch. "I'm about to get on a conference call with the State Department about Karama's speech. Someone's going to ask how pressing Karama about Okari helps us put more soldiers here."

Pierce felt discouragement become anger. "They've got it backward," he said. "To stabilize the delta you need the kind of social justice Bobby stands for. Kill him, and all the troops in the world won't buy your nervous friends a good night's sleep."

"As it happens, I agree." The ambassador seemed to reach a decision. "Come to my house for dinner tonight. There may be more for us to discuss, including what—if anything—*you* intend to do. I'm still not quite clear on your purpose here." He raised his eyebrows. "By the way, what did you put on your visa application?"

Pierce smiled. "Vacation."

"Oh, dear. That may have helped get you into Luandia, but it may also keep you here. The last intermeddlers in the delta who claimed to be tourists, three documentary filmmakers from Germany, were jailed by the state security services on charges of espionage. My friend the German ambassador can't seem to spring them." Caraway stood, offering his hand. "Make this trip a short one, Mr. Pierce. You don't want the cell next to Okari's."

11

OUTSIDE HIS HOTEL, A LUXURIOUS HIGH-RISE, Pierce encountered a row of limousines guarded by armed soldiers. As he and Vorster entered, the lobby buzzed with blacks and whites on cell phones, the elite classes whose dealings with one another, so profitable for themselves, did nothing for Luandia or its people. A tall and imposing Luandian man in traditional dress swept past them, accompanied by a fawning deputation of Chinese. "That's Ugwo Ajukwa," Vorster explained, "Karama's national security adviser. The man's knee-deep in the oil business—legal and otherwise. The sight of him with the Chinese is not a happy one."

Pierce went upstairs and left a detailed voice mail for the managing partner of his law firm, Larry Kahan, outlining his preliminary thoughts on how to save Bobby Okari. Then he scribbled notes for hours, assessing all he had heard through the prism of law until, exhausted, he prepared for dinner by napping.

CARAWAY'S ONE-STORY HOME fronted a lagoon shaded by palm trees. They sat beside the water at twilight, on a patio illuminated by torches. "My own version of flaring," Caraway said. "Keeps the mosquitoes at bay."

The two men sipped glasses of single-malt scotch. After a time, Pierce asked, "How was your conference call with State?"

Caraway considered his answer. "Much as you'd expect. The self-styled 'realists' consider Okari a luxury on whom we should expend—at most—pious words. Others see Karama as the luxury. To them, our obsession with this 'global war on terror' could lead to a disaster similar in kind, if not scale, to Iraq—the descent of a strategically important region into chaos. Imagine the choice between military intervention in the delta and letting the oil go." Pausing, Caraway took a careful sip of scotch. "There's only one principle agreed to by all: no one wants to back Okari if he's a murderer.

"As Martel surely told you, some of the skeptics believe that Okari cares more for power than principle." He held up a hand. "To begin, do you really think Okari was as naive about Karama's character as he now suggests? There are those who argue that Karama was Okari's ticket to ride, and only when that failed to work out did he turn to the Asari—that his ultimate aim is to become the 'big man' of all Luandia, its president. If Okari's ambition is for himself, then nonviolence may be just another stratagem, as disposable as the rest."

Pierce set his drink down. "I don't believe that."

"And I'm disinclined to. But FREE was cutting into his support, especially among the youth. Okari's a man completely certain of his own rightness. In a place like Luandia, with all its tests and temptations, that can have a dark side."

"He's not stupid," Pierce said. "Those lynchings were a disaster."

"True. But Okari needed to hang on to his militants. He wouldn't be the first revolutionary who told himself, 'Just this once, for the greater good.'" Caraway's tone became forceful. "You suggest that Karama arranged the hangings to justify a massacre. Ask yourself why Karama would perpetrate a lynching that makes him look bad *and* intimidates his cash cow, PGL. As for the massacre itself, I suspect it happened the way Okari says. But as long as Karama's in power, it's beyond our capacity to prove that and, some would say, against our interests to try."

"Everyone knows who Karama is," Pierce answered in disgust.

Glancing up, the ambassador gestured to a young American soldier who doubled as a messboy, suggesting that a first course would be welcome. "*We* know who he is," he replied. "Karama sits at the top of a very slippery pole. To stay there he's used surveillance, rape, torture, economic blackmail, secret prisons, and mass murder. He's subverted the military chain of command by enlisting junior officers as spies. He's mastered the art of whom to bribe and whom to kill." The rhythm of Caraway's speech slowed, as though to emphasize an important moment. "When I first met Karama as ambassador, it was at three A.M., and we were watched by North Korean bodyguards—the worst of the worst, recruited because they have no connection to Luandia. Karama was smart, articulate, even amusing. But by the end of the meeting I understood that he had no interest in me *or* my country. All that mattered was how he could use us to ensure his own survival."

Pierce felt gloom settle around them like the

night. "Suppose we're both right," Caraway continued. "That Okari didn't order those men lynched, and neither did Karama. What then? One possibility is that someone's playing Karama for reasons of their own, certain that he'd proceed against Okari precisely as he has. I think Karama's genuinely afraid that the Asari movement might spell the beginning of a secessionist uprising that sweeps the delta." Caraway propped both elbows on the table, his expression reflective. "Without oil, the game's over for Karama. That's more than enough reason to justify dispensing with Okari."

Pierce finished his scotch. "So who would kill those oil workers to set Karama off?"

Caraway grimaced. "Luandia's far too byzantine to know. But if Karama's innocently proceeding against an innocent man, he'll be that much harder to persuade."

The first course arrived, a fruit salad featuring pineapples grown in Luandia. His appetite diminished, Pierce sampled the salad, then put down his fork. "For the sake of argument, suppose the U.S. made saving Okari a priority. What would we do?"

Caraway pondered this. "Try to figure out some sticks and carrots. But there's no way we'd cut off military aid. And cutting off humanitarian aid would be pointless—there's too little of it, and Karama wouldn't care."

"Suppose America were to boycott Luandian oil?"

Caraway emitted a mirthless laugh. "We *are* talking theory. We wouldn't do it alone—the oil would just go elsewhere, maybe to China. The Europeans wouldn't join us; they're as addicted to oil as we are. As for other African countries, they don't like helping whites push other blacks around, and several of their leaders resemble Karama more than Okari." Fastidiously, Caraway wiped his mouth with a white napkin. "You'd also be surprised by Karama's support in Washington. He's got a small army of lobbyists trumpeting all the good he does for his people, headed by a former black congressman who, before he discovered Karama's money, pushed human rights in Africa. If you take on Okari's cause, I'm certain he'll try to stymie you.

"That brings me to Okari's ultimate problem: time." Caraway shook his head in bemusement. "I assume thirty days isn't nearly enough for a lawyer to prepare his defense, even if the trial court wasn't a joke. I can assure you that it's not enough time for a mechanism as cumbersome as our government, faced with a country as complex as Luandia, to focus on saving the life of just one man."

"You're suggesting that it's hopeless," Pierce said in a toneless voice.

"Difficult." As the messboy approached, Caraway fell silent, waiting until the man had filled their wine glasses. "You may wonder why I've asked you to dinner. You're a lawyer and a free agent. You may be able to say and do things in America that a mere ambassador can't.'"

Pierce looked at him fixedly. "So could Marissa Okari. She'd be far more effective on TV or working Congress than I'd be. What can you do to get her out?"

"I took that up with the foreign minister. Karama won't let her leave." Caraway puffed his cheeks, expelling a long silent breath. "Though she's an American, she's also become a citizen of Luandia. An admirable gesture, and extremely shortsighted. Luandia won't recognize dual citizenship. It's more difficult to pry her loose, no matter how dangerous things get for her here."

Glum, Pierce sampled the wine, considering his next remarks. "We're leaving out PGL," he said at last. "They have leverage with Karama *and* the White House."

Caraway gave him a quizzical smile. "Why would PGL expend its capital on Okari's behalf? Or, for that matter, his wife's?"

"Because the army came to Goro in PGL's helicopters and boats." Pierce spoke quietly but coolly. "Bad enough to destroy a people's way of life; worse to give them nothing for it in return. But it's truly special to help a murderous autocrat and a psychopathic army colonel commit a mass atrocity against civilians. People like that get convicted of war crimes."

Caraway put down his wine glass, staring at

Pierce. In a measured voice, he said, "That's a serious charge. Of one thing I'm certain: if PGL's equipment was used, its people will claim they were unable to anticipate—let alone control—what Okimbo did with it."

"They're not virgins," Pierce snapped. "Most likely Okimbo and his soldiers were on PGL's pay-roll; no doubt PGL asked Karama for 'protection.' They know damn well who these men are, and what kind of 'protection' they were likely to get."

"So all that's left for you is the small matter of proof." Caraway's voice held quiet irony. "When I first moved here, I bought a boat with an outboard motor for puttering around in this lagoon. One day someone stole it. When I went to the police, they said, 'We have no gas. If you give us money to fill our boat, then we will find *your* boat.'

"So I did. And they *did*. Otherwise I'd have no boat." Caraway poured each of them another half glass of wine. "I won't belabor the analogy. Perhaps they stole my boat; perhaps they murdered the person who did. All I know is they brought it back."

"In this case," Pierce retorted, "they murdered Okari's father. That means he can sue PGL in an American court. If they prove to be complicit in a massacre, I doubt they'll enjoy the consequences."

Caraway considered him. "Results take time. Law, like diplomacy, moves at glacial speed."

Pierce smiled a little. "Yes. I've thought of that."

"What you're asking is whether I'd facilitate a meeting with the head of PGL."

"That would be nice. Preferably before Karama throws me in jail."

For a time, Caraway gazed out at the lagoon. "Let's enjoy our dinner," he replied. "For the moment, I think we've done sufficient business."

The waiter served the main course, then dessert. It was only over coffee that Caraway returned to the subject of Pierce's mission. "I'll do what I can," he promised. "In turn, will you accept a last piece of advice?"

"Of course."

"You'd be better off leaving here and never coming back. But as long as you're here, don't assume that because Americans and Luandians share a common language, words share a common meaning. They don't. Listen not only to what is said but to what the speaker may be trying to convey. If someone lies to you, don't waste your time on outrage. The only useful question is whether he's really trying to mislead you, or whether the lie's so obvious that it's meant to express a deeper truth. The most critical thing about anyone you meet is not their words, but their motives." He smiled briefly. "That applies not only to Luandians, by the way."

Politely, Pierce thanked him.

12

THE NEXT EVENING, BACK IN WARO, PIERCE RODE with Vorster and Clellan to the home of PGL's managing director. As they drove, Pierce observed the street life of the city: a brightly dressed woman bearing a basket of fruit on her head; a gaunt bicyclist carrying a satellite dish; an urban marketplace with tin shacks and a muddy parking lot. Then Clellan cut across a sandy field to avoid an intractable traffic jam, and Pierce saw on the waterfront the expensive homes of Waro's elite, protected by concrete walls with jagged shards of glass inserted at the top, a disincentive to intruders. "An opulent prison," he observed.

"Everyone's in prison here," Vorster responded. "But some prisons are nicer than others—as you'll soon see."

An hour later, they arrived at a compound with fifteen-foot walls, its entrance a marble archway so massive that Pierce thought at once of the Arc de Triomphe. Stationed by its metal gate were mobile policemen wearing green fatigues and flak jackets, carrying AK-47s. "Luandians call them 'kill and go,'" Vorster said. "They're law enforcement's equivalent of Okimbo."

Stopping at the gate, Clellan gave Pierce's name to a security guard. The man placed a telephone call; after a moment the massive steel gate slowly opened, and they entered a rarefied world of palms and manicured gardens and enormous villas. They parked in front of the largest, a sprawling terra-cotta residence that, Pierce guessed, was close to thirty thousand square feet. "Remind you of Goro?" Vorster murmured to Pierce.

"No oil slicks. This must be where the money goes."

Leaving the car, Pierce followed a winding stone path to a sturdy iron door monitored by a security camera that protruded from the wall beside it. Pierce pushed the intercom button and, when questioned, announced himself. A servant in a white coat and dark trousers opened the door and led him to a sitting room. "Mr. Gladstone will be with you presently," the houseboy advised.

Alone, Pierce gazed out the deep glass windows at a capacious lawn and garden sloping to the water's edge. In the distance, the office towers of Waro looked pristine. Absorbed by the view, he barely heard the footsteps behind him. When he turned, an elegant Luandian man in a cashmere sport jacket extended his hand. "I'm Michael Gladstone."

As Pierce returned the man's languid handshake, Gladstone smiled at his quizzical expression. "You were expecting someone lighter."

"In a word, yes. No one told me you were Luandian."

"That's progress, I suppose. My predecessor was

British; now he's my landlord, safely ensconced in Dubai. May I arrange a drink?"

"Thank you, no."

Gladstone waved at two chairs near the window. "Come, sit."

The executive glided to a chair opposite Pierce. He was roughly forty, Pierce guessed, with close-cropped hair, smooth skin, keen eyes, and an expression that suggested watchfulness and habitual caution. "So," he said, "you're Okari's friend, perhaps his lawyer. What is it you want from us?"

"For the moment, mutual understanding. I assume you saw Karama's speech. This farce of a tribunal can't be good for PGL."

A troubled look briefly surfaced in Gladstone's eyes. "Not good," he parried, "is three Luandian employees hanging from a tree in Asariland."

"Or having your helicopters and boats used in a massacre?"

Gladstone placed a graceful finger to his lips. "This is not a deposition, Mr. Pierce. Our conversation is private; I'm seeing you at Grayson Caraway's request, to learn what you want. As to Goro, the government denies a massacre. Whatever may have occurred, no one from PGL was present."

"Then who flew the helicopters?"

"Again, Mr. Pierce, we are not in court. Were we, all that I could tell you is that my people inform me that our equipment was, quite literally, borrowed."

Pierce kept his tone mild. "Your 'people' being Roos Van Daan, ex-mercenary soldier in Angola, now PGL's chief of security in the delta. He seems to have a certain reputation.

"Let me tell you about Goro, Mr. Gladstone. PGL helicopters and sea trucks transported Okimbo and his soldiers. They proceeded to burn the village and slaughter all the residents except the Okaris. Soldiers beheaded Bobby's father; like the hundreds of bodies, his head's gone missing. Okimbo himself raped a fifteen-year-old girl before he slit her throat. Okari was forced to watch." Pierce paused a moment. "Granted, you weren't there. But please don't tell me you're surprised."

Gladstone stared at him. "My job is to protect our employees and operations. Okari's followers seized our oil platform and blocked access to our facilities; for all I know, he ordered those lynchings. I am left to hope that Okimbo responded reasonably, and that Okari's trial will fairly ascertain his guilt—both matters beyond our control." Gladstone's speech gained quickness and force. "In fact, we control almost nothing. Your friend has helped make us a hostage in a war between the government and the people of the delta. And for what? We, too, are victims of corruption. We do not dictate how oil revenues are spent. We can only make one very stark choice: stay or leave—"

"You could also stop turning the delta into a toxic-waste dump."

Gladstone spread his hands. "When PetroGlobal came here, the government expected nothing. For my predecessors, oil and corruption were the apple Adam bit. I will concede that in earlier days PGL screwed the natives, took the oil, and enjoyed the profits. The results were as you see them: yet more corruption, violence, and human and environmental misery.

"All I can alleviate is the latter. As soon as possible, we'll stop flaring and repair our antiquated pipelines. But it's late in the day, and there's no one to help us. Certainly not Savior Karama. Nor," Gladstone continued with palpable anger, "Bobby Okari. It's not pleasant to be the scapegoat for a demagogue with a Messiah complex whose self-serving rhetoric inflames the militias he claims to deplore. Nonetheless, I hope Karama spares him, or the first Easter after Okari's death will disappoint him hugely."

"You're free to hope," Pierce shot back. "This tribunal is his death warrant, and the delta once he's gone will disappoint *you* hugely. The change Okari wants will help PGL survive."

Gladstone shook his head in demurral. "All Okari brings to our door is trouble. Does he truly think making our corporate life miserable will transform Karama? Corruption is not an incident of government policy—it *is* the government's policy.

221

"Do they help clean up the environment? Do they tend to the poor who are so outraged at us? Do they fight the militias, or end the bunkering so many of them profit from? Do they maintain the community projects they harass us to build? No. They blame us, and encourage *others* to blame us, for failing to do the things for our people only they can do." Gladstone softened his tone. "We both know what those are, Mr. Pierce. Democracy. Infrastructure. An end to corruption. Stewardship of land and water. Are you laughing yet? Well, you should be. Because to say such things in Luandia is a joke."

"Poor PGL," Pierce said with equal quiet. "Such good intentions; so little love in return. And even less influence. I'm sorry if you're not enjoying your job. But you can't take the money, then wash your hands of what happened in Goro. I assume you've met Okimbo."

"Yes."

"How'd you like him?"

"I didn't. Nor did I appoint him Karama's chief enforcer. So imagine for a moment that you're our manager in the delta, Trevor Hill. So many of our executives get kidnapped that he's taken out hostage insurance. But that only gets FREE more excited about kidnapping. So Hill's people start to develop post-traumatic stress disorder." Gladstone's voice became quiet, uninflected. "A kidnapper from FREE raided a compound and killed the daughter of Hill's closest friend in her front yard. To protect the survivors, her father slammed the iron door to the house, cutting off the shooter's hand. All the police did was stick it in an evidence drawer. Somewhere in the delta is a murderer with a missing hand.

"So we hired Roos Van Daan. But all Van Daan can do about Asariland is accede to Okimbo's demands for money and arms, leaving us to hope—if not expect—that the army will honor PGL's very explicit policies on human rights." Gladstone's tone became sardonic. "When three people were hung from a tree, were we not to call Okimbo? Were we to wait for Okari to do what he did not—condemn the murderers in no uncertain terms? If so, we might as well pack our bags and leave Luandia's oil to our competitors from Europe and the oh-so-scrupulous Chinese."

Pierce stared at him fixedly. "You asked Okimbo to 'restore order.' If Bobby Okari sues PGL, you can explain to someone else why you thought that meant a decorous inquiry replete with Miranda warnings."

Gladstone stood, hands jammed in his pockets. "So you came to threaten me."

"I came to ask you to use your influence, instead of denying that you have any."

Gladstone walked to the window, gazing out at the garden. "You have no idea what you're playing with—none. To be held responsible for the acts of this government *could* drive us from Luandia. Never mind the impact on our share price. Never mind the impact on Luandia: that at the margins, we operate as a check on Karama's excesses, and that whoever replaces PGL would be far worse. Consider the potential impact on America's oil supply, or the price your fellow citizens might pay to heat their homes and fill their cars." His voice rose. "Do you think the American public, or the present administration, would countenance whatever bogus lawsuit you imagine—"

"I don't think it's up to them, and I don't give a damn. That's what federal judges are for." Pierce joined Gladstone by the window, looking him in the face. "I assume you've been in touch with headquarters. Will they 'countenance' you inviting this 'bogus lawsuit' by refusing to help prevent an execution that can only make the delta worse? I doubt that. In fact, I imagine they've already set PGL's price for approaching Karama."

To Pierce's surprise, the trace of a smile surfaced in Gladstone's eyes. "For whatever good that would do. But tell Okari this: if he asks you to drop this potential lawsuit, and ends his campaign against PGL, and agrees to leave Luandia, we'll appeal to the better angels of Karama's nature— perhaps to provide Okari with safe passage to the country of his choice."

"That's quite a lot to ask."

Gladstone shrugged. "If Okari prefers to take a run at martyrdom, that's his concern. Mine is to safeguard PGL and its people."

Holding Gladstone's eyes, Pierce absorbed the ambiguity of the moment. He did not know how complicit Gladstone was in Okimbo's crimes; perhaps Gladstone believed Bobby was complicit in the lynching, and even that Pierce might know it. Whatever the case, they both had business to transact. "I'll tell him," Pierce answered.

"Then we're done here, Mr. Pierce. You know the way out."

Pierce began to leave, then turned back. "I'm curious. Did you bother to vote in the last election?"

Gladstone considered whether to respond. "I tried. But Karama's soldiers had already closed the polls. So I suppose I must have voted for him."

"As a Luandian, how did that make you feel?"

Again, Gladstone hesitated. "Unsurprised," he answered with a trace of weariness. "Whatever else I felt hardly matters. The next day, as before, my job was the same."

13

AFTER MEETING PIERCE AT THE AIRPORT IN PORT George, Atiku Bara drove him directly to the prison as Pierce explained his mission. Sounding dubious, Bara said, "Good luck with him."

"Assuming I get in." Pierce reached for the door handle, then turned back. "If you were Bobby, how would you respond to Gladstone's offer?"

Bara's brow knit in a complex look of introspection and worry. "By choosing to live," he answered. "In exile, he can someday return; he can do no good buried in Luandia. Tell him that."

Nodding, Pierce got out and presented himself to the sentries at the steel gate. In moments, the inscrutable Major Bangida led him past the empty gallows toward the prison. Curtly, he said, "Colonel Okimbo wishes to see you."

Pierce felt the flesh tingle on the back of his neck. He followed Bangida inside the prison to an office on the ground floor.

Bangida knocked on its door. "Yes," a deep voice said brusquely, and Bangida let Pierce in.

The man at the desk was massive in every dimension. He examined Pierce in silence, his visible eye conveying an indifference of feeling so profound that Pierce could have been looking into the eye of a bird. The one other man in whom Pierce had seen this quality, a Serbian now condemned to life in prison, had ordered the slaughter of thousands; Pierce, his prosecutor, had wished he could seek the death penalty. Staring back at Okimbo, Pierce envisioned this man slitting the throat of a girl whose usefulness to him was done. "You wish to see Okari," Okimbo said. "Have you smelled him?"

"Yes," Pierce said with an edge in his voice. "Have you?"

Okimbo stood abruptly, his large fingers splayed on the desk as he pushed himself up. He stared at Pierce as though ready to close the space between them. "There are those who wish you to speak with Okari. That would seem to require the retention of your tongue."

At once Pierce felt Michael Gladstone's unseen hand. "How fortunate."

Okimbo's smile was no smile at all. "Should your luck continue, you'll return to America intact. But Marissa Okari will remain with us. Remember that."

Anger overcame Pierce's fear. "Marissa Okari," he said succinctly, "will remain an American citizen. She's not as defenseless as a fifteen-year-old girl. You remember *that*."

Okimbo's dark eye became opaque, as though Pierce's words had driven him to a place beyond human reach. Every instinct in Pierce urged him to escape. Turning, he went out the door, expecting to hear Okimbo behind him. But the only sound besides his footsteps was their echo off the stone walls of the prison.

THE NEXT SOUND Pierce heard was the rattle of chains. Stiffly, Bobby Okari rose from the filth around him, gripping the bars for leverage. "Damon?" he said feebly.

Pierce was filled with pity. "Do you know about Karama's speech?"

"Yes. They play it for me every night, again and again."

Pierce placed his hand over Bobby's. "I don't have much time. But for whatever it's worth, Michael Gladstone's offered to intercede."

"Karama's handmaiden." Bobby shook his head. "Does he require me to go deaf, blind, and dumb?"

"Merely silent. And in some other country." Though quiet, Pierce's tone was urgent. "Once in America or England, you can say what you like. Your only alternative, as Gladstone knows, is to hope that my firm and I can somehow get you out of this."

Bobby's face hardened. "Gladstone must think a lot of me. And very little."

"Gladstone claims to doubt your innocence. He wonders, as I do, why you didn't condemn those lynchings. Nonetheless, he seems to prefer that you not die."

"As well he might." Bobby drew himself up. "This is my message to him: help free me, and things will be better for PGL. Help me salvage our land and waters, and things will be better for PGL. But don't ask me to become a stranger to my people."

Pierce could feel his own pulse. "Even for Marissa?"

"Even so." Audibly, Bobby inhaled. "You're

afraid for her, as am I. But neither your fear for her nor mine can outweigh what you've seen here."

"I've seen many things," Pierce said tightly. "Including Okimbo."

Briefly, Bobby's eyes shut. "Two favors, then. At whatever cost to me, try to keep Marissa safe. But do not tell her of my refusal. It will cause her great pain and accomplish nothing."

"Not nothing. If they ever let her see you, she might be more persuasive than I've been."

Bobby grasped Pierce's wrist. "Are you so willing to break a confidence, Damon? Do you wish to come between Marissa and me? That is not the act of a lawyer."

Caught in his own conflicted feelings, Pierce could not respond. The shadow of a memory surfaced in his mind: that, on meeting Bobby Okari, he had sensed that this man's life might not be long. But then martyrs, like believers, envision an afterlife. Damon Pierce was neither.

"Give Gladstone my answer," Bobby told him. "And Marissa my love."

SITTING ON THEIR patio, Marissa took Pierce's hands in hers. Her face was drawn, her eyes haunted, as though what she had experienced was beyond the power of time to heal. It struck Pierce that he had never seen her cry.

"I'm leaving tomorrow," he said gently. "There's nothing more I can do here. But even in America I may accomplish very little. My law firm may not let me take this case. The courts might not listen if I do. I have no legal right to return here, any more than you have the right to leave. Whatever I might wish, I may never see Luandia again."

Marissa tried to muster a smile. "Think of all you'd miss." For a moment, her throat worked, and then she spoke with fresh resolve. "I've already made a list for you of people I'd like you to call: human rights groups, media contacts, Luandian exiles, friends. Anyone in America who can help."

Pierce felt the weight of all he had not told her, and of what might happen once he left. "I'll do all I can," he promised.

For a time, she looked at him intently, as if committing his every feature to memory. As though on impulse, she brushed her lips against his. "Then go now," she said softly. "At least I'll know you're safe."

PART

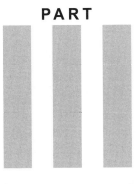

The Amber Night

1

IT WAS LIKE AWAKENING IN ANOTHER DIMENSION.

Pierce sat in Larry Kahan's corner office. Night had fallen; through the tall windows the lights of scattered boats blinked on the darkened bay between the city and the glittering hills of Marin County. The Asian decor around them befitted the managing partner of a fifteen-hundred-lawyer firm whose offices girded the globe, from San Francisco to London to Shanghai to Tokyo. Kahan, whose demeanor Pierce had once described as "Jewish-mandarin," appraised him with a look of sympathy and skepticism. Pierce was in no mood for either; he had come directly from the airport after twenty-seven hours in transit. "You look like hell," Kahan told him.

"This couldn't wait," Pierce answered. "Any day now Okari may be dead."

Kahan's eyes, almond slits in the broad planes of his Slavic face, narrowed further. "Executed by the Luandian government," he amended. "What do you propose we do about that?"

"Two things. Let me defend Okari before this joke of a tribunal, and file a suit in federal court for the wrongful death of his father—"

"Against whom?" Kahan cut in. "This may not be my area, but I do know that you can't sue

Karama and his regime in an American court for violating international law."

Pierce looked at him more closely. "Why do I sense, Larry, that someone got to you before me?"

"The chairman of PetroGlobal Oil," Kahan answered bluntly. "John Colson himself. He claims you threatened the managing director of PGL with a lawsuit this firm hasn't authorized."

Pierce's anxiety quickened with anger. "To get them to use their leverage with Karama—"

"In return for which Okari is unwilling to back off an inch." The last trace of sympathy vanished from Kahan's manner. "PGL says that any lawsuit would be slander in the guise of a pleading. Even to me, blaming PGL for the Luandian military's actions in that village is a reach. What can you allege with any confidence?"

"Several things. PGL pays and equips the Luandian army. PGL asked it to 'restore order,' knowing full well that might mean a massacre—"

"Who else were they supposed to call? The Red Cross?"

"The army works for PGL like hired mercenaries." Pierce's voice rose in frustration. "Okimbo committed an earlier atrocity in the town of Lana, and PGL damn well knew that. Before *this* atrocity, its helicopters were used to reconnoiter Goro. The army invaded in PGL's choppers and boats, and no doubt slaughtered the villagers with guns the company paid for. For all I know

PGL's personnel flew the copters, piloted the boats, and helped plan the operation in advance."

Kahan shook his head. "For all you know, Damon, PGL knows nothing except that Okimbo hijacked their equipment. What does Gladstone say?"

"Exactly that—as I'm sure you already know. Did you expect him to take credit for a massacre? To state the obvious, Luandia's not America—"

"And yet you propose suing in an American court. You're perilously close to asking Kenyon & Walker to put its name on a lawsuit against one of this country's most powerful corporate citizens without any basis in fact. If some jackal of a plaintiff's lawyer did that to one of your Wall Street clients, you'd ask the judge to sanction him—"

"Wait a fucking minute," Pierce said with real heat. "Let's break this down.

"First, jurisdiction: under the Alien Tort Statute, a foreign national like Bobby Okari can sue an American corporation like PetroGlobal in federal court. Next, substance: the ATS allows suits for violation of international human rights norms under statutes like the Torture Victim Protection Act—which, by the way, covers murder."

Kahan held up his hand. "According to PetroGlobal's general counsel, PGL is exempt from suit under something called the Act of State Doctrine—"

"Jesus, Larry—how many phone calls did it

take for them to feed you all this bullshit?" Pierce lowered his voice. "I know international law inside and out. On your better days, you also wouldn't accuse me of wanting this firm to file a bogus suit. PetroGlobal is desperate to save its own ass."

Leaning back in his chair, Kahan crossed his arms. "So they're not objective? Neither are you, Damon. By your own admission you're close to Okari and his wife, and the only leverage you have on Karama is through PGL. Aside from the connections you've already mentioned—payments, use of equipment, maybe some awareness of Okimbo's proclivities—what do you think you'll find to nail PGL?"

Pierce thought quickly. "Ideally? Direct payments to Okimbo before *and* after the massacre. Direct involvement in its planning. Direct involvement of PGL employees in the operation itself: reconnaissance, staging, and carrying it out—on Asari Day, Marissa says, she saw a white man's face when PGL helicopters hovered overhead." Sitting back in his chair, Pierce spoke more slowly. "Going back in time, I'd want communications between PetroGlobal, Karama, and Okimbo establishing that Okimbo can be considered an agent of PGL. In Luandia nothing gets done without someone getting paid. I'm betting there are documents that breach the supposed wall between PGL and the Luandian government."

"Even assuming that, PGL knows all the delaying tactics you do. In what decade do you expect their lawyers to hand you the smoking gun?" Kahan's tone became clipped. "We're meeting here tonight because Karama can try, sentence, and execute Okari within weeks. In that time, you won't see a single document from PGL—let alone a single witness. You'd be lucky to get a trial on the tenth anniversary of his death."

For the first time, Pierce smiled. "That's why I propose to ask for injunctive relief and accelerated discovery. Within days, not years, I mean to depose Gladstone and PGL's chief of security in the delta, Roos Van Daan."

"Injunctive relief," Kahan repeated with real astonishment. "To prevent what actions, and by whom? You can't undo a massacre and put Dad's head back on."

"True. But I can enjoin PGL from fomenting further acts of violence."

"For God's sake—"

Pierce spoke over him: "*And* from collaborating in a drumhead tribunal that—on its face—violates Okari's due process rights under international law. Stopping an unlawful execution is certainly grounds for injunctive relief. Executing Bobby without due process is an 'extrajudicial killing' under the Torture Victims Protection Act. There's no unbiased tribunal, right of appeal, or rational process for amnesty, pardon, or commutation of sentence. Even if there were, a trial in thirty days denies him the time for an adequate defense.

"Karama's created a mutation outside any recognized system of law. It's a pretext for murder dressed in a black robe. Henry the Eighth's decapitated wives had more rights than this."

Kahan shook his head. "No American court has the power to enjoin Karama, or to bar PGL from cooperating in a foreign legal proceeding—especially one arising from the murder of its own employees. Why are any flaws the fault of PGL?"

"Because PGL is completely entwined with Karama. In fact, I'm almost certain that it could stop this trial altogether."

Kahan pressed his lips together. "What if the evidence shows that Okari planned these murders?"

Pierce shot him a look of incredulity. "What 'evidence' would *you* believe in a tribunal like this? There's every chance any 'proof' against Bobby will be trumped up. And if PGL gets drawn into its fabrication, that's another violation of due process.

"Look, every rogue regime uses show trials to help perpetrate its crimes. The Nazis did it; the Soviets did it; the Russians and Chinese still do it. And every one of them requires the cooperation of outsiders. Somewhere in the process PGL will get drawn into the sewage."

Kahan settled back in his chair, as though to consider Pierce from a different angle. "PGL will claim it's only doing what it has to."

"Too bad. Okimbo is effectively PGL's man in Asariland. If it's legally responsible for *his* acts or Karama's, it'll have to do business some other way. Fuck it if that's unfair. What's really unfair is profiting from legalized murder."

Kahan turned, gazing out the window. At length, he said, "You'll need more than a judge with an unusual sense of urgency, or the usual human rights advocates picketing the Luandian embassy, or even a few damning documents. You'll need someone inside PGL to help you weave it all together. That's not likely." He turned to Pierce again. "PetroGlobal's chairman was fierce. To Colson, you're trying to drive a stake through its heart. PetroGlobal's instinct will be to fight *you,* not Karama. It won't acknowledge fault for doing business with him—it can't open itself to lawsuits or admit complicity in the acts of a murderous regime.

"In PetroGlobal's eyes, remaining in Luandia is an act of corporate patriotism. It's supplying the lifeblood of America—oil—and it has powerful friends in this administration. They won't just go after you in court, but in every way they can."

Pierce shrugged. "So who deserves our sympathy? Regardless of what we do, PGL will survive. Bobby may not."

Kahan folded his hands. "This is too serious for our Pro Bono Committee to decide," he said at last. "I'll have to go to the Executive Committee. Until they vote, anything you do will be as a private citizen, *not* a member of this firm."

Pierce fought back his weariness. "Then tell ExCom this: That PGL's displeasure is nothing compared to a good man's life, and the safety of his American wife. That this case won't last nearly as long or cost nearly as much as the death penalty appeals we take on as a matter of principle. That if Karama executes Bobby, he'll do it in record time. And that if we don't try to stop him, I'll resign."

Kahan stared at him. "You're serious, aren't you?"

"Completely. If Nelson Mandela had been facing execution and this firm had been presented with a chance to save him, would we have taken it? The firm *I* joined would have—no matter who opposed us or who we had to sue. This case is the closest Kenyon & Walker will ever come to that."

Kahan gave him a thin smile. "I'll be sure to mention that."

2

BEFORE DAWN THE NEXT DAY, PIERCE HAD CONtacted Amnesty International and Human Rights Watch; engaged a publicity consultant to help coordinate a public relations campaign; e-mailed Bobby's celebrity contacts in England and the United States; strategized by telephone with Joshua Kano, an exiled Luandian journalist who was the Asari people's spokesman in Washington; and, through Grayson Caraway, requested meetings with key officials at the State Department and the United Nations. Then, at Kano's suggestion, he opened his copy of the *New York Times.*

On page 6 was a full-page ad featuring photographs of what Atiku Bara had called PGL's "Potemkin projects"—a clinic, a school, a water purification plant. PctroGlobal, the text assured readers, was "committed to the future of Luandia and its people." The bold letters above the text read: "PGL: Energy for a Better World." The oil company, Kano assured him, meant to create its own reality before Pierce could.

Pierce put down the *Times* and watched morning sunlight spread across the bay. The beauty and safety of his surroundings felt comfortable yet strange, as though if San Francisco were real, Luandia could not be. His apartment was more sparsely furnished now; in his absence, Amy had taken her last possessions. Suddenly Pierce felt suspended between a past that had left him without a family and a future he could not envision. He could only imagine Marissa's isolation, so much greater than his own.

He went back to work. By eight that night he had submitted a memo to the Executive Committee and, with Kano's help, drafted a petition to be signed by celebrities and human rights groups, reprinted in the *New York Times,* and presented to

PetroGlobal, the State Department, the United Nations, and the media. Its demands were simple: the recipients should urge Karama to open Asariland to the press and human rights groups; allow an independent inquiry into the destruction of Goro; and grant Bobby Okari the legal rights afforded him under international law. Until then, the petition concluded, it was PetroGlobal's moral and legal obligation to suspend all oil production in Luandia.

Pierce e-mailed Marissa, packed, and caught a night flight to Washington.

JOSHUA KANO MET him for breakfast at the Madison Hotel.

Amid the lobbyists and political consultants, Kano looked out of place, a lean, plainly dressed man whose soft speech and gentle aura were belied by a twitchiness that meant that some part of his body—drumming fingers or jiggling knees—was always in motion. "Hampton Sizemore," Kano said, "is already at work."

Pierce knew Sizemore by reputation: a former civil rights leader turned outspoken member of the Congressional Black Caucus until, in his fifties, he started a consulting firm that lobbied for African governments while soliciting them for American business clients. "His passion for justice," Kano explained with quiet distaste, "has been replaced by a passion for money. Not only does he front for

Karama but they're partners in two apartment complexes on the East Side of Manhattan. Even his town house in Georgetown belongs to Karama."

"Then how does Sizemore have any credibility?"

Kano's chuckle was mirthless. "Are you asking how someone who's such an obvious whore for Karama nonetheless has so much access to Congress, the White House, editorial boards, and talk shows? Sizemore claims he's still a 'change agent,' dedicated to justice for all, but that now he works for change from the inside." Kano's smile flashed and vanished. "Not 'small change,' either—millions in fees as a middleman and in profits from crooked Luandian businesses. It doesn't hurt that Sizemore also funnels money, it's rumored, from Luandians like Ugwo Ajukwa into the campaign coffers of American politicians. I cannot tell you how it incenses me to see this pious phony use his credibility to call Karama, the Hitler of West Africa, a beacon of hope." He snatched that morning's *Washington Post* from his brief-case, folded to a page in the middle of section 1. "And now this."

Pierce first saw a three-paragraph article headed "U.N. Official Addresses Unrest in Luandian Delta," the gist of which was that the man had expressed concern about reports of violence against "Asari-populated areas." Then Kano gestured for him to unfold the paper; the entire opposite page, labeled "The Truth About Bobby Okari," had been purchased by the "Committee for Luandian-American Relations." The "truth," Pierce discovered, was that the Asari movement was a "secessionist front group that traffics in terror." As to the most egregious example of such terror—the "lynching of three Luandian family men"—the "world community should allow justice to take its course."

Pierce stared at the newspaper. "It's only Africa," Kano said quietly. "No one who reads this will ever see Goro. Nor can they hear from the dead. On a blank canvas, Karama and Sizemore can paint any portrait they like."

"Not quite blank," Pierce responded. "There must be other exiles who've seen Karama's atrocities at first hand."

"True. But most of them have loved ones within Karama's reach."

Pierce struggled to suppress his fear. "Like Marissa, you mean."

Kano looked up at him. "Yes," he responded quietly. "But that is her wish."

FOR THE NEXT two days, Pierce anxiously awaited his firm's decision; though his threat to resign was real, he could not mount such a complex lawsuit without the resources only a major law firm could provide. The only salve for his anxiety was activity—meetings, pressing for an audience at

State, giving one media interview after another. His message was simple: he had seen the delta, the ruins of Goro, the misery of Bobby's confinement—no one who had seen these things could doubt that the tribunal was another instrument of tyranny. On the evening of the second day, when he took his message to the PBS *NewsHour,* Hampton Sizemore appeared to provide balance.

Sizemore breezed into the green room three minutes before the interview. Seeing Pierce, he introduced himself, flashing his whitened teeth in a smile that did not match his look of shrewd appraisal. How was Pierce's stay so far? he asked, as though Pierce had come to see the sights. Swiftly, Pierce perceived a man spoiled by a soft living made from retailing cynical nonsense—a comfortable paunch, rheumy eyes, dyed black hair at odds with a face that reflected the gravitational pull of age, the faint whiff of cologne. Pierce had seen versions of this man a hundred times before: glib, lazy, and morally hollow. And yet Sizemore's mellifluous voice once had spoken hard truths in the harshest precincts of the South, sometimes at the risk of his life. That man, Pierce reflected as they entered the studio, would have seen Bobby Okari as a brother.

Two days of interviews had honed Pierce's presentation. Grasping this, the well-coiffed interlocutor, Margaret Ames, gave him a full minute before asking Hampton Sizemore to respond. At once Sizemore's air of condescension vanished, and his voice and manner became calm, measured, and a bit mournful, that of an advocate for an emerging African nation now wrongly disparaged.

"It is well to remember," he told Ames, "that Mr. Okari's arrest arises from the tragic deaths of three Luandian employees of PetroGlobal Oil. Our own experience in America tells us that, all too often, the victims of violence are forgotten. And the government of Luandia has a duty, as does ours, to protect the lives of its own people—including those who work for American companies that provide resources essential to our lives—"

"What about Goro?" Ames cut in. "Mr. Pierce claims that what he saw could only be the aftermath of an atrocity committed by the Luandian military."

Sizemore pursed his lips, his expression judicious. "The Luandian government says the sole violence occurred when the Asari movement, which advocates secession, opened fire on the soldiers who had come to detain Bobby Okari. The only people who claim otherwise are Okari and his wife."

"According to Mr. Pierce, that's because all the villagers are dead."

Sizemore shook his head. "Mr. Pierce wasn't there. With all respect, all he can do is repeat the Okaris' account." His tone filled with regret. "The only murders we *know* occurred precipitated Mr.

Okari's arrest—the lynchings for which he stands accused. Lynching is a crime, whether in the Old South or the new Luandia. The Karama government is proceeding publicly and expeditiously—I can only wish that, when my colleagues in the civil rights movement were brutally murdered, the local authorities of that time had done the same. The community of nations should allow the Luandian justice system to proceed without condescension or prejudgment."

Ames turned to Pierce. "How do you answer, Mr. Pierce?"

"With questions." Pierce turned to Sizemore. "Will Karama readmit reporters and investigators to Asariland? Will he allow Bobby Okari a cell with a toilet and without rats? Will he let Marissa Okari come to America? And will he conform to the human rights standards agreed to by the president he overthrew?"

Ames nodded. "Go ahead, Congressman Sizemore."

"Margaret," he began, "I can't speak for the Luandian government—"

"And yet they sent you here."

"So they did. But they also must safeguard their own internal security—"

"With rats?" Pierce interrupted.

Ames held up her hand to silence him. "President Karama faces great challenges," Sizemore temporized, "including ethnic divisions and a threat of Islamic terrorism even more dangerous than that which threatens us. His government should be given a certain leeway as it works toward the optimal methods of ensuring security for the Luandian people and defeating the forces of national division."

Ames raised her eyebrows. "Mr. Pierce?"

"The congressman evokes the civil rights era to defend the torture of an advocate for civil rights. He evokes lynchings to justify a trial no better than a legalized lynching. He evokes the war on terror to defend a regime that terrorizes its own people. He answers no questions and deploys every weapon but the facts." Pierce faced Sizemore again. "Will the Luandian government allow me to represent Bobby Okari at his trial? Or does Karama want to pick Bobby's lawyers as well as his judges?"

Sizemore paused. "I don't issue visas—"

"The autocrat who pays you does," Pierce snapped. "So tell *him* to give Okari the same rights you once stood for. Still have it in you, Congressman?"

Sizemore drew himself up. "I was fighting injustice before you were born."

"And stopped shortly after," Pierce shot back. "At least go visit Bobby in prison. Then you'll recall what injustice looks like."

The briefest glimmer of amusement showed in Ames's eyes. "We'll have to leave it there," she said. But Pierce had done what he had come to do: embarrass the Luandian government, perhaps sufficiently to help protect Bobby and Marissa. The other result, for better or worse, was to increase his own chances of returning to Luandia.

Without a word, Sizemore left.

THE NEXT MORNING Pierce got his meeting at the State Department.

The senior officer on the West Africa desk, Anthony Gersh, was a slender man with russet hair, pale blue eyes, and the amiable but jaded air of someone whose job it was to monitor an insane asylum. The experience inclined him to candor.

"Yesterday," he told Pierce, "my guests were PetroGlobal, the Luandian ambassador, and your sparring partner Hampton Sizemore, lobbying for a 'statement of interest.' In case you don't know, that's a letter from the secretary of state informing whatever judge you might draw that Okari's presumptive lawsuit would impair America's relations with Luandia."

"I assume the word 'oil' was mentioned."

"Most often 'constructive engagement,' a phrase calculated to make a State Department bureaucrat drool like one of Pavlov's dogs. That's our policy toward China: the more business you do, the more influence you have. Though not enough to keep the Chinese from using any backlash you cause to eat our lunch in Luandia."

"What about the massacre at Goro?"

Absently, Gersh straightened some papers. "The 'alleged massacre,' you mean? The problem is using it to drag PGL into an American court. A lot of us think that's like suing a crime victim for calling the sheriff."

"So PGL says," Pierce responded pointedly.

"And so we believe. The second problem for us is that countries like Luandia believe that the president can control what happens in our courts."

"Karama controls his," Pierce rejoined. "This tribunal is an excuse for murder."

Gersh rearranged more papers. "There's another problem," he acknowledged. "We've become leery of American courts adjudicating human rights violations by foreign governments. Look at the reverse: the Chileans would love to put Henry Kissinger on trial for the murder of President Allende; the Nicaraguans would equally enjoy trying the CIA for atrocities carried out by our proxies the contras—"

"In other words," Pierce interjected, "you can't save Okari because we're busy protecting whatever we're doing at Guantánamo."

Gersh shrugged. "There's a grain of truth in that. In fact, our department has stated a number of reservations about the very human rights agreements you rely on."

Pierce felt a growing despair. "Okari's trial starts in twenty days. The U.N. will never move in that short a time. All I can hope for is this lawsuit and whatever help you'll give me."

Gersh looked him in the eye. "Then I'll give it to you straight. *If* we don't oppose you in court, it's because someone has decided that this lawsuit advances our interest in saving Okari without us slapping Karama in the face. If it helps, several of us thought you made Sizemore look like a hypocrite. The more sensitive among us don't enjoy hypocrisy." Pausing, Gersh regarded him askance. "We *also* wondered whether you've considered your own situation."

"How so?"

"For one thing, we've read the CIA's psychological profile of Savior Karama. To put it mildly, he's not subject to the usual social incentives. And the Luandian Delta's such a horror these days that people even die by accident. You might not be so lucky."

It was a thought that had caught up to Pierce in the hours when sleep eluded him. "There's also Okari and his wife," he answered. "I made them a promise I can't lightly break."

"Marissa Okari," Gersh said at length, "is an American citizen. It could be easier for us to extract her from Luandia than to do anything for her husband. She might do more good advocating for Okari from here than you could by returning to Luandia. You should tell her that, Mr. Pierce. I'm sure her husband would agree."

• • •

PIERCE BENT OVER his laptop, calling Marissa on Skype from his room at the Madison. "Are you all right?" he asked.

"The same." Her tone was so clear that Pierce could feel her worry. "Atiku thinks Bobby's still alive."

Pierce hurt for her. Swiftly, he explained Gersh's implied offer.

"No," she said at once, and then her voice softened. "If you decide to stay in America, I understand. But I can't leave."

"Why not? Maybe Gersh is right."

"For you." A moment's silence was punctuated by the crackle of static. "When I married Bobby, I married his cause. Now I'm more valuable to Bobby as Karama's hostage—if I return, the American government will have one less reason to care about what happens to Bobby." Her speech slowed, as though she was trying to reach out to him. "Please hear me, Damon. This isn't your commitment. It's mine."

But it was not so simple. Bobby would not leave, even to save her; Marissa would not leave without him. Only Pierce, caught between them, knew the truth.

"I understand," Pierce answered.

A HALF HOUR later, Pierce had not moved. Outside, the leaden skies of late afternoon seeped rain that streaked his windows. The room felt like a prison.

Pierce's cell phone rang.

It was Larry Kahan. "I heard from Hampton Sizemore," the managing partner said. "He tells me Okari is not what he seems."

"Neither is Sizemore."

Kahan gave a short laugh. "No, he's exactly what you showed him to be. Congratulations, Damon. You've got your lawsuit, and the legal team to see it through. Assuming some right-thinking judge doesn't throw you out on your ass."

Pierce did not know what to feel. "Thanks, Larry," he said. "Whatever comes, I promise not to embarrass you."

3

WITHIN THREE DAYS, PIERCE HAD FILED SUIT against PetroGlobal in San Francisco. Two days later, at nine A.M., he faced United States District Judge Caitlin Taylor.

Her courtroom was modern and commodious, its high ceilings meant to evoke a temple of the law, and Caitlin Taylor ran it crisply, conscious of both the crowd of human rights advocates who had come to support Bobby Okari and the sprinkling of reporters. Slender and patrician, Taylor had long, dark hair and a pale, sculpted face accented by wire-rimmed glasses, and she leavened her keen mind and decisive manner with the occasional shaft of arid wit. Though Taylor was no easy mark, that she had drawn the Okari case fed Pierce's sense of hope—cool-headed and gifted with a steady internal compass, Taylor cared less about other people's opinions than her own. Pierce's arguments—and Bobby's plight—would get their day from Caitlin Taylor.

This was fortunate, given PetroGlobal's shrewd choice of counsel. A quick-thinking African-American, Clark Hamilton was a former Stanford basketball hero whose professed concern for civil rights endowed his legal skills with the appearance of moral weight. But Pierce shared the minority view that Hamilton was a calculating man who understood the uses of public piety. That Hampton Sizemore sat behind them in this courtroom reinforced Pierce's skepticism.

Sitting next to Pierce was his junior partner Rachel Rahv. Pierce was glad for her presence—in her mid-thirties but already seasoned, Rachel was tough, smart, and cared enough about human rights to have insisted on helping with Bobby Okari. This morning she looked bleary with fatigue; like Pierce, she had pulled two all-nighters to assemble their complaint. Should Taylor not dismiss the case outright, Rachel would lead a team of lawyers to Luandia to cull whatever documents were pried loose from PGL.

"We face a series of complex issues," Taylor told the lawyers, "not the least of which is Mr. Okari's request for injunctive relief. So I'll take them one at a time."

Hamilton stood. "Thank you, Your Honor. But before we proceed, I ask that former congressman Hampton Sizemore be heard on behalf of the Luandian government."

"Mr. Pierce?" Taylor said.

"Luandia is not a party in this lawsuit, Your Honor. Its government has no standing here."

"True enough. Still, the congressman represents a sovereign country whose actions are at the core of your complaint. The court will hear him."

With a satisfied glance toward Pierce, Sizemore stepped into the well of the court as Camilla Vasquez, Hamilton's associate, handed a one-page letter to the judge and a copy to Rachel Rahv. "As you'll see," Sizemore told Taylor, "the foreign minister of Luandia spells out the damage that would emanate from this unwarranted lawsuit." He gazed down at the copy in his hands. "Let me quote Minister Adu: 'This lawsuit challenges our ability to combat the civil unrest that plagues the oil-bearing region of Luandia, and to protect our citizens and the employees of foreign companies. It offends the sovereign interests of the Luandian government. It impedes our efforts to attract the foreign investment essential to the prosperity of our people . . . ' "

"At least Savior Karama," Rachel whispered to Pierce.

In his orotund voice, Sizemore finished reading: "'I am sure that the United States would object to a Luandian court passing judgment on its official conduct in curbing violent activities within its own borders.'" He looked up. "I can only add that America's ability to prevent another 9/11 would be seriously compromised if foreign courts reviewed our treatment of foreign terrorists at their relatives' request."

This was the ploy Pierce had expected. "Thank you," Judge Taylor said. "Any comment, Mr. Pierce?"

"Yes, Your Honor. This is a delaying action dressed up as diplomacy and gift-wrapped in fear. Our complaint alleges that the Luandian government—abetted by PetroGlobal—protected its 'sovereign interests' by slaughtering several hundred civilians and beheading Bobby Okari's father. Unless the court acts, the next victim may be Mr. Okari himself." Pierce briefly glanced at his notes. "I can only hope that Karama's treatment of my client, reminiscent of Stalin or Mao Tse-tung, is unimaginable in America no matter what the crisis. Whether Karama's kangaroo court passes muster is governed by international law, not irrational fear."

Taylor turned to Hamilton. "Is the State Department taking a position?"

Hamilton stood with an air of reluctance. "Not at this time."

"No? Then we'll just have to stumble along, won't we." Nodding toward Sizemore, Taylor said, "Thank you, Congressman."

Pierce repressed a smile. "All right," Taylor said. "We'll hear PetroGlobal's contention that this lawsuit should be filed in Luandia. Mr. Hamilton?"

"Luandia is the only logical forum, Your Honor," Hamilton responded smoothly. "The facts occurred there; the witnesses and documents remain there. Furthermore, Luandian courts and Luandian law are best equipped to adjudicate matters inherent to Luandia. This court should not decide a matter foreign to it in every possible way."

"Mr. Pierce?"

Once more Pierce stood, glancing at Hamilton. "My impulse is to ask if Mr. Hamilton is joking. How can we bring a lawsuit for torture and extrajudicial murder in a country whose government survives by those means? The 'special tribunal' decreed by Karama shows just how little we can rely on 'Luandian courts and Luandian law.' *What* law, when Karama can change it at will? Counsel's plea is a euphemism for 'summary execution'— death for this lawsuit, and for Mr. Okari."

Taylor gazed briefly at Pierce, then turned to Hamilton. "A central question," she said, "is whether there's *any* lawsuit here that an American court can entertain. Tell me why I should dismiss Okari's complaint forthwith."

Sitting beside Pierce, Rachel Rahv tensed—this,

they both knew, was where PetroGlobal might prevail. "The Act of State Doctrine," Hamilton began, "precludes a United States court from inquiring into the official acts of a duly recognized government within its own territory. The color with which Mr. Pierce characterizes events should not obscure that he asks this court to judge the conduct of a foreign government in a distant place, under ambiguous circumstances, where it cannot compel that government to respond.

"When it comes to PetroGlobal itself, Mr. Pierce is caught in a fatal contradiction. He can't argue that PGL knew, or should have known, that the army would perpetrate the alleged slaughter without asserting that such a massacre is the *official policy* of Luandia and, therefore, immune from adjudication by an American court."

Pierce rose to answer and then, on instinct, turned to Hamilton Sizemore. "Help me here, Congressman. Are rape, torture, mass slaughter, and extrajudicial murder the 'official policy' of the Luandian regime? If so, we can all go home."

An anonymous snicker issued from the packed gallery of observers, stifled before Taylor could react. Glaring at Pierce, Sizemore answered, "I refuse to become a prop in your performance, Mr. Pierce."

"No letter for *this* one? Oh, well." Turning to Taylor, Pierce said, "For the record, the international agreements we rely on—signed by

Luandia's government—reject such conduct. As to Goro, General Karama denies any intention to murder anyone. Does PetroGlobal now accuse its business partner of lying? Or will Karama now come forward to embrace the Act of State Doctrine by admitting that he routinely orders the slaughter of unruly citizens?" Pierce briefly smiled at Hamilton. "In which case, Your Honor, the fatal contradiction is Mr. Hamilton's.

"In truth, the Karama government disdains such massacres *in theory*—placing the tragedy at Goro outside the Act of State Doctrine—while commonly perpetuating massacres in fact. PGL was well aware of both—"

"Hold on," Taylor interjected sharply. "Even assuming that alleged atrocities by the Luandian government can form a basis for your lawsuit, how can this court hold PetroGlobal liable for the acts of Colonel Okimbo's soldiers? Let me hear from Mr. Hamilton on this."

Standing, Hamilton looked relieved. "Consider PetroGlobal's dilemma, Your Honor. Three of its Luandian employees were murdered in parallel with acts against PGL facilities ordered by Bobby Okari. *This* court, and *this* government, could do nothing to prevent the murder of still more. PGL's sole recourse was to the Luandian military." Hamilton's voice became stern. "If the court holds PGL responsible for the army's purported actions, *no* American corporation will be able to seek the protection of any foreign government for fear that the response might not meet the standards of an American court. It would be impossible for America to conduct a foreign policy that includes doing business as part of influencing other governments for the better. It would be impossible for PetroGlobal to exist in the majority of oil-producing states—like Russia, Saudi Arabia, and, yes, Luandia—where the government is, or may become, less than exemplary in the treatment of its citizens. In short, it would require America to abandon its sources of foreign oil and any effort to improve conditions where oil may be found."

"It's the conditions in Luandia," Taylor said, "that face us now. Mr. Pierce?"

"We're not trying to confine American business to Canada, Your Honor. We assert that PGL was intertwined with a military predictable in its bru-tality. PGL hired them, paid them, and asked them to restore order. What Okimbo did in Goro—using PGL's boats, helicopters, guns, and bullets—PGL had every reason to expect."

"Your Honor," Hamilton protested. "There was no one else to call, and PGL had no reason to expect anything other than the restoration of order. For all it knows, this 'massacre' never happened."

"Then let PGL prove it," Pierce rejoined. " 'Take my word for it' is not grounds for dismissing a lawsuit."

Taylor adjusted her glasses, as though to see

Pierce from another angle. "What evidence do *you* intend to offer? Mr. Hamilton is correct in noting that we can't order the Luandians to give you anything at all."

Pierce nodded. "That leaves PGL. We want the access to their documents and employees that only this court can provide, and that PGL is so desperate to prevent. If the court dismisses this lawsuit, only PGL and Bobby Okari will ever know the truth, and only PGL will survive Okari's trial."

"Which raises the most vexing issue of all," Taylor replied. "Your request that we enjoin PGL from its alleged 'wrongful participation' in the legal proceeding of a foreign state. Which proceeding, in itself, is beyond our power to affect."

"Precisely," Hamilton put in. "No court has ever presumed to intrude in the conduct of a criminal proceeding in a foreign country. No court has ever restrained an American corporation from responding to a legal process in a nation where it does business and where, as here, refusal to participate would itself be a crime.

"But Mr. Pierce's evocation of Alice in Wonderland transcends even that. He now asks the court to rule on the fairness of a legal proceeding that has yet to occur. He would make this court not only the Luandian Court of Appeals but the World Court of Judicial Divination—all with unseemly haste. Absurd."

Pierce saw Rachel Rahv wince involuntarily.

Covering his own concerns, Pierce stood to answer. "Mr. Hamilton need not worry," he began. "Under the rules Karama designed for Bobby Okari, there is no 'Luandian Court of Appeals' to replace. Nor need the trial commence for this court to 'divine' that the tribunal selected by Karama—one of them a soldier under his command—violates due process on its face. Nor should it ignore the regime's record of private trials, summary executions, and mysterious deaths in prisons like the hellhole to which they've consigned Bobby Okari, now supervised by Okimbo. As for 'unseemly haste,' Mr. Okari's trial commences in roughly two weeks." Pierce let his anger show. "What's absurd is for Mr. Hamilton to pretend that the polite atmosphere of this courtroom has anything to do with what happens once Karama's handpicked judges take Okari's life in their hands—"

"Even granting that," Taylor interrupted, "what does PGL have to do with Karama's tribunal, and how in the world can *this* court make the slightest difference?"

"In several ways. First, the court can order PGL to provide Mr. Okari with any documents and witnesses helpful to his defense. Second, given our belief that Colonel Okimbo is on its payroll, this court can direct PGL to withhold his compensation should he impede our access to Okari. Third, this court can instruct PGL not to cooperate with the prosecution in concocting perjured testimony and falsified documents."

"I must protest," Hamilton objected. "There's no basis for such a claim."

"Luandia is the basis," Pierce responded. "Counsel resents the implication that a company that knows Okimbo, pays Okimbo, and equips Okimbo could actually 'divine' what Okimbo might do. Okimbo needed bullets; now he needs 'evidence.' It's reasonable to ask that PGL not respond when those needs overstep the truth." Pierce inhaled, and his voice became quietly urgent. "Very soon the Karama regime may execute Bobby Okari. This court may not be able to stop that, but it is reasonable to try. What we ask of PetroGlobal is nothing more than law and decency requires."

Taylor considered him with a look of gravity and doubt. "I know that time is of the essence," she told Pierce, "and that your client needs a ruling. The court will reconvene at eleven-thirty, and you will have it."

For over an hour, Pierce and Rachel Rahv sat across the courtroom from Hamilton and Vasquez. Neither side spoke to the other—the waiting was too tense, feelings too raw. "I wonder if we'll get there," Rachel murmured. "Luandia, I mean."

Pierce could feel her misgivings. Once or twice he caught himself hoping that he would lose;

unlike Rachel, he had seen Luandia. Then he imagined Marissa waiting for news, and despised himself for his own fears.

Now and again he looked at Hamilton. Though his opponent was expressionless, Pierce sensed that Hamilton, like himself, had no idea what Taylor would do. The buzz from the spectators was jittery and muted.

At eleven-thirty, Taylor reappeared. "Remain seated," she said, her voice and manner so subdued that she seemed, for once, shaken by what she had to do.

For a moment she stared at the notes she spread before her. "I'll address the issues one by one," she began, "mindful that to rule for PetroGlobal on any one of them would terminate Mr. Okari's lawsuit.

"To begin, PGL urges that this lawsuit should be filed in Luandia. We note that Mr. Okari charges the government with rape, torture, mass murder, and establishing a tribunal that clearly violates international laws. It seems contradictory to compel Mr. Okari to seek redress from a regime for practices that may violate our government's stated policy of upholding human rights." She briefly glanced at Sizemore. "If the State Department felt otherwise, it could have said so."

This much Pierce had expected; the rest worried him far more. "PGL," Taylor read, "next argues that the wrongs alleged in the complaint are acts of state, and therefore not subject to review in the

United States." Looking up, Taylor spoke to Hamilton. "Unlike PGL, we will take Luandia at its word that murder, rape, and torture are not official policy. Oh, yes, and beheadings."

As Hamilton frowned, Pierce saw Rachel's mouth twitch briefly. "PGL next argues that the Alien Tort Statute does not allow Bobby Okari to sue for its alleged participation in such crimes. But PetroGlobal's reading of the law would emasculate the law."

The cadence of Taylor's voice, swifter now, conveyed the sense of an inexorable force. "PetroGlobal contends further that the specific allegations of the complaint, even if true, are insufficient to establish its complicity. We find this a close question. We agree that payments to the army and the use of PGL equipment do not themselves make PGL liable for the alleged massacre at Goro. But given that so many of the facts are known only to PGL, this court will allow Mr. Okari access to those facts."

"We're going to win," Rachel whispered. But Pierce could not relax. On the bench, Taylor paused, surveying the crowded courtroom. "Finally, PGL claims that the facts alleged are insufficient to justify issuance of a temporary restraining order. We agree. As to its further contention—that the court lacks any basis for enjoining its alleged wrongful complicity in a tribunal that violates due process—we need not rule today." She looked from Hamilton to Pierce. "The day before the scheduled commencement of Okari's trial, this court will hold a hearing to address that very question."

Pierce felt the tension seeping from his body. "Now the rest," Taylor told the lawyers crisply. "There's not much time here. You'll be proceeding in a foreign country with no tradition of discovery and different cultural understandings of truth where fear may well be a factor. This court has no power to compel the cooperation of Luandian citizens not employed by PetroGlobal. All the parties can do is ask Luandians to volunteer for depositions. As to that," she added tersely, "good luck."

Taylor now addressed Hamilton. "A final word for PetroGlobal. As you say, Luandia is where the proof is. That's why I'm ordering discovery to proceed there, through PGL's offices in Waro. I expect you to make your witnesses and documents available to Mr. Pierce on an expedited basis. But if the government of Luandia keeps him from returning, it becomes your obligation to provide them here." She smiled faintly. "Expensive fun, I know. So I hope that you and Mr. Sizemore use whatever influence you have with the Luandian government to see that Mr. Pierce is able to go back."

Pierce felt the prospect of returning to Luandia seep into his consciousness. "A final word," Taylor told the lawyers. "It seems we're in a race with a very special branch of the Luandian justice system.

This is *not* a race an American court is well equipped to win. Do your best to help us.

"Thank you."

"All rise," the courtroom deputy called out, and a cacophony of sound filled the courtroom. Only Pierce remained still.

ALONE IN HIS office, Pierce called Marissa. "We're still alive—" he began.

To his surprise, she laughed. "That's a funny way of putting it," she answered, and then relief suffused her voice. "I can't believe you're coming back."

"Neither can I," Pierce answered. "But I worried that you'd miss me."

He meant it as a light remark. But now Marissa did not laugh. "I have, Damon. You've no idea how much."

4

ON THE LONG FLIGHT TO PORT GEORGE, PIERCE dreamed.

It was Christmas, and he was with his parents in their three-decker in Dorchester. In the dream, Pierce still believed in God; the crucifix on the wall did not seem alien to him. And yet he was the same age as his parents, successful beyond their imaginings. Sean Pierce wore his Christmas sweater; he gave his crinkly smile as Pierce's mother handed Damon a brightly wrapped gift box. "Open this when it's time," she told him, "and then you'll find her. Everything will change."

Pierce jolted himself awake. Fragments of the dream were indeed a gift; his parents' faces were vivid, and he still had time to say, in spite of all their differences, how much their love had meant to him, how much he loved them in return. The rest was obscure. In life, his mother was not given to mystical pronouncements: the concrete world of his parents had been bounded by the known, and Pierce could test its limits without fear. Now he was returning to Luandia.

He shut his eyes again and imagined Marissa's face.

As PIERCE CLEARED customs, the official looked up from his passport, staring wordlessly into his eyes. Then he passed Pierce through, and two Luandians on the other side began walking a few feet behind him.

Waiting in the crowded airport, Atiku Bara extended his hand, glancing over Pierce's shoulder. "I know," Pierce said. "Let's go."

They were silent until they reached Bara's car. Inserting his key into the ignition, Bara smiled a little. "You're back after all."

"You're surprised?"

The smile vanished. "Perhaps it's me. Every night I imagine leaving."

Bara steered into the traffic. Almost three weeks

ago they had first taken this road to Port George. Since then Pierce had seen things he had never imagined; though he could not yet define how, he felt changed. "How is Bobby holding up?"

"No one knows; Okimbo is keeping him incommunicado." Bara's voice softened. "It seems you made him angry."

Pierce felt the vise of fear tightening again. He had spent much of the flight cultivating fatalism; fear, he had told himself, was better than self-contempt. Now he was here. "I'll go to the prison tomorrow," he told Bara.

IT WAS DUSK when they reached the Okaris' compound. As before, two agents of the state security services watched from across the street.

Marissa waited on the patio. Seeing Damon, she ran to him, heedless of Bara's presence. She held him so tightly that for a moment he thought of his sister's red-haired child, Bridget, jumping into his arms after awakening from a nightmare. But when Marissa leaned back to look at him, her eyes held a craving for hope so deep that it cut through him like a knife. Though he had seen Goro, he could not imagine Marissa's dreams.

She managed to smile. "Twelve days," she told him. "Forever."

Pierce felt Bara watching them. Releasing Marissa, Pierce turned to him. "And fourteen days until Bobby's trial. Let's get started."

They sat around the table. "We've got two different cases," Pierce began. "Bobby's suit against PGL, and his defense in Karama's show trial. One feeds the other: even if the tribunal won't admit evidence from the civil suit, we can use it to embarrass PGL—perhaps so badly that it will try to salvage Bobby.

"For that we'll need witnesses and documents showing that PGL knew Okimbo was a murderer in uniform; that managers were involved in planning the attack on Goro; and maybe that its employees piloted the boats and helicopters used in the attack." He looked from Bara to Marissa. "There's also the matter of proving that there *was* a massacre. You're Bobby's wife; some confirmation would help."

"From whom?" Bara demanded.

"Soldiers involved in the attack. Survivors hiding in the forest. Personnel from PGL—if there *are* any—who witnessed the massacre."

"And are eager to tell the truth?" Skepticism bled from Bara's voice. "More likely, I suppose, than that soldiers would speak against Okimbo *and* themselves, or that those who fled the soldiers would put their lives at risk. But how much chance is there that the tribunal would hear such witnesses? None. They will say that what happened in Goro is irrelevant—that it came *after* the lynchings Bobby's charged with."

"Not before I make an offer of proof—brutally

270

specific—and force them to try to cover up the massacre. There's no way they can hold Bobby's trial in secret now."

Bara shook his head. Quietly, Marissa said, "Tell Damon what you've learned."

Bara looked somber. "I have a relationship with the prosecutor, Patric Ngara. He tells me that two Asari youths claim to have heard Bobby order the lynchings."

Though he should not have been surprised, Pierce felt dismay. The stories could be fabricated; they could also be true. "Do we have names?" he asked.

"Not yet." Bara glanced at Marissa. "No doubt they were threatened, or bribed."

Pierce heard a sliver of doubt, perhaps undetectable to Marissa. "Can you try to find out?"

Bara shrugged. "In theory. But who admits to lying in a country where to tell the truth is death?"

The remark, Pierce realized, could also apply to Bobby Okari. For a time he looked at the moonlit water; the glow of flaring gas; the lights of the oil freighters awaiting their loads, stolen or not. "*Someone* ordered those men killed."

"Okimbo," Marissa said. "Or FREE. Or Asari acting on their own. Whoever did it wanted to frame Bobby. Now they need to conceal who they are."

Pierce nodded. "True. But in order to convict Bobby, the prosecution needs these supposed witnesses. If we can find out who told them to lie, then we know who ordered the lynchings."

Bara shrugged again, as though to acknowledge the conundrum. "The immediate problem," Pierce told him, "is who does what.

"I'm keeping my four associates in Waro—hopefully, they'll be safe at the hotel and at PGL's headquarters. The only member of my team I'll put at risk in the delta is me. I'll help you look for witnesses."

Marissa shook her head. "State security will follow you wherever you go. White men are easy to spot."

"So is Atiku, and so are you. We'll have to do what we can." Facing Bara, Pierce said, "You must still have a network of people who tell you things."

"Only a few. But more people than I trust."

Pierce saw Marissa look away. Whether in distrust or despair, he could not guess. "Even lies," he answered, "may tell us something."

Bara studied the table. "We'll start in the morning," Pierce suggested. "Your family will be glad to see you."

"Yes," Bara answered softly. "Assuming they're still at home."

Once again Pierce reflected that Bara, like Marissa, was a hostage—at least until the moment of betrayal. Pierce hoped the moment would never come.

• • •

"So," Marissa inquired in the darkness. "Do *you* trust Atiku?"

They sat at the table, their faces half visible to each other, the remains of dinner between them. Briefly Pierce thought of other dinners, long ago, where their talk was of stories, and the quickening urgency he had felt to keep her from going to Luandia. Then the future was unknown, and much was possible; now they were here. "I have to," Pierce answered.

Reaching across the table, she touched his hand, gazing intently into his face. "I say things like that to myself, all the time. It makes me sad to hear *you* say them. Because I know why you came back."

Pierce stared at her hand on his. "For you, of course. For Bobby, too. But also for myself."

"How so?"

"I'm a romantic—you told me years ago. Cowardice is not romantic. Causes are." He looked up at her again. "I'm more than a little serious. It's true I wouldn't be here if you hadn't asked. But you asked because I'd prosecuted war crimes. My need to do that wasn't about anyone but me.

"I believe the world is the sum of who's in it— that in some way what we do makes other lives better, or worse. So do you; so does Bobby. The two of you are the greatest romantics of all—you risked your own lives for a cause. For one brief moment, it's my turn. Like you and Bobby, I've got no kids to consider if I crash. Except that I'm flying alone."

Marissa's gaze deepened. Her lips parted, as though to speak. A moment passed, and then she squeezed his hand. "You must be tired, Damon. Let me show you where your room is."

SHORTLY AFTER DAWN, Pierce and Bara reached the prison. They waited for an hour. Then Major Bangida appeared, curtly telling Pierce, "The colonel wishes to see you. Alone."

Like an automaton, Pierce followed him past the gallows to the open door of Okimbo's office. Catlike in his chair, Okimbo stared at Pierce, the look in his eye glassy and abstracted. On the desk was a half-empty glass of a liquid that looked like whiskey. "Close the door behind you," he told Bangida.

As the door shut, Pierce saw the truncheon in Okimbo's lap. "So," Okimbo said softly, "you come here again, having blackened my name in your country."

Pierce watched him caress the truncheon with the fingers of one hand. "I'm here to see Okari, not you."

Okimbo kept stroking the truncheon. "What if I start with your genitals. From that, I can gauge your tolerance of pain."

Pierce tried to detach himself. The voice issuing from his throat was a fair semblance of his own.

274

"That would anger my government and embarrass Karama. As you say, I've made you known far beyond the delta."

Okimbo's fingers on the truncheon tightened, as though he were weighing the benefits and risks of sating his desires. Pierce was quite certain that Okimbo imagined killing him, but not before stripping him of humanness. "You wish to visit Okari?" Okimbo said. "Then I wish you to experience his life. Within fifteen minutes you'll be screaming to get out, with no one but Okari to hear you."

Pierce filled with apprehension. "Just take me there," he said. "My friend is waiting."

Okimbo's laugh was grating. "This is Luandia. You have no friends."

He stood, circled his desk, and walked up to Pierce. Pierce could smell his sweat and the liquor on his breath. Then Okimbo strode to the door and beckoned Pierce with a waggle of one finger. "Okari's lonely. Perhaps, at leisure, you can describe for him your evenings with his wife."

Deeply unsettled, Pierce followed him up the steps, Okimbo's broad shoulders brushing the walls. Halfway to Bobby's cell Okimbo stopped, studying a bloodstain on the stone. When Okimbo looked up at him, Pierce sensed that the wrong word or gesture would alter the connections in the man's synapses, sending him to a place where violence was his sole release. Coldly, Okimbo said, "Have Okari tell you of the amusement I arranged for him. However briefly, he enjoyed the company of his people."

Okimbo led Pierce to Bobby's cell. There was no light there; Pierce could detect no sign of movement. He was hit by a stench of feces and urine so strong that he stopped abruptly, his throat working as he suppressed the urge to gag. Laughing harshly, Okimbo fished the keys from his pocket. "The law is a hard mistress," he said. "Serve her well."

Before Pierce could respond, Okimbo shoved him into the pitch-dark cell. Staggering, he stumbled over a bucket of waste, then braced himself against the wall. Okimbo locked the door. His footsteps echoed off the stone, diminishing until there was only silence. Pierce fought against panic.

A soft voice said, "They took the light away."

Staring down, Pierce saw the fetal shape of a man sitting in the corner, arms resting on his knees. "That must be you, Damon. Forgive me if I don't stand."

In a dispirited way, Bobby sounded as mad as Okimbo. Leaning against the wall, Pierce tried to steel himself against the smell. "What have they done to you?"

"Aside from what you see? No visitors, little food, dark always." Bobby spoke with precision, as though practicing how to match words with meaning. "They keep me from sleep. Or they chain me in positions so painful I pass out. When I awake, darkness closes around me."

Pierce crouched in front of him, touching Bobby's shoulder with his hand. "One night," Bobby continued in a hollow voice, "they put an Asari man and woman in the nearest cells, and left them alone with soldiers. As they screamed in agony, Okimbo told me what each sound signified—the insertion of a cattle prod in the woman's vagina; a man with a razor wire tightening around his penis. 'This,' Okimbo told me, 'is your legacy among the Asari.' Then the screaming stopped."

Pierce forced himself to believe that he remained a lawyer, free to go. Finding Bobby's wrists, he gripped them tightly. "Before I left, Gladstone made you an offer. I've got way more leverage now that there's a lawsuit. Let me try to get you out of Luandia—for your sake *and* Marissa's."

And mine, Pierce thought but did not say. Curling forward, Bobby rested his face on his knees. "If I leave the Asari," he whispered, "our sacrifice means nothing. Imagine me in London, begging for alms at cocktail parties until no one cares to come. I'd sooner die or go insane."

A fresh wave of odors made Pierce swallow. Softly, he said, "Maybe you already are. Dying brings you nothing but a martyr's grave. For the Asari and Marissa, less than that."

"I'm not insane." Suddenly Bobby's head snapped up, and there was a hard edge in his voice. "I can embody courage for my people, or take it from them."

"You face Karama's tribunal. *If* you live."

Bobby drew a breath. "How long until my trial?"

"Thirteen days."

"Thirteen days. At least there I can speak for the Asari. Surely I can last till then."

His tone was at once weary and determined. Despite his misgivings, Pierce felt an unfathomable pull that compelled him to respond. "If you do," he said at last, "I'll be there."

Bobby's torso sagged again. "In Berkeley," he murmured, "how little I understood you."

Pierce waited for a moment. "About the trial: there's something I must tell you."

"Yes?"

"There are two witnesses against you. They claim to have heard you order those workers lynched."

"To whom did I give these orders?" Bobby asked with quiet despair.

"We don't know." Pierce hesitated. "Do you know who might have said this?"

"Yes." Bobby raised his face. "Someone who wishes me to die."

Footsteps echoed on the cobblestones. At once, Pierce felt both fear and hope. Head turning at the sound, Bobby said quickly, "Tell me about Marissa."

"She's scared for you. But safe—at least for now."

"Then she *must* stay strong. Please, do not tell her how you've found me."

Okimbo's massive frame loomed above them. When Pierce stood to face him, he could smell

Okimbo's whiskey breath between the bars. "Do you wish to go?" Okimbo asked. "Okari doesn't."

Relief flooded Pierce's mind. He touched Bobby's shoulder. Then Okimbo opened the door, and Pierce stepped onto the stone path outside the cell. He heard the click of the passkey as Okimbo secured the lock.

Pierce began walking. Behind him, the measured thud of Okimbo's footsteps echoed as before. Only when they reached the prison's metal door did Pierce trust himself to speak.

"Feed him," Pierce said. "Let him sleep. It'll mean less trouble for you, trust me. He's not alone anymore."

Okimbo's smile was a ghastly stretch of lips. "What trouble? What you just experienced never happened. The lies Okari told you are a symptom of insanity."

Pierce stared at him. But he could not risk saying more—he had to catch a flight to Waro. Tomorrow, across the table, Michael Gladstone would take an oath to tell the truth.

5

LESS THAN TWENTY-FOUR HOURS LATER, PIERCE studied Michael Gladstone.

In that time, Pierce had barely slept. His first task had been to contact Grayson Caraway, human rights groups, Joshua Kano, and their publicist in

Washington, detailing Okimbo's treatment of Bobby Okari. Then, cloistered with Rachel Rahv and their team at a hotel in Waro, he had reviewed the documents they had culled from PGL, preparing for his cross-examination of Gladstone and, on the following day, Roos Van Daan. Then he had briefly called Marissa, telling her a semblance of the truth that omitted only the worst of Bobby's ordeal; in the back of his mind, he worried that Okimbo imagined her as his prisoner. The thought shadowed his consciousness: sitting across from Gladstone and his lawyer, Clark Hamilton, Pierce felt as though his last two days did not belong to the same life.

PGL's headquarters was like a corporate compound transported from America to Waro, gated and walled, with a golf course, gym, meeting center, dining room, and executive housing. The sole difference—elaborate security apparatus and an armed complement of Luandian police—completed its isolation from the city. Across the lacquered conference table, Pierce contemplated Gladstone in his handmade suit and silk tie, the human embodiment of these contradictions—a man of superior intelligence, caught between his American overseers and his appreciation, however reluctant, of PetroGlobal's entanglement in the tragedy of his native country. Pierce hoped that this complex psychology had left cracks he could exploit.

"As happy as I am to see Mr. Gladstone," Pierce told Hamilton, "our request was to first depose Trevor Hill, PGL's principal supervisor in the delta."

"As we told you previously Hill has business in Saudi Arabia—"

"Which has airplanes," Pierce cut in. "Hill is closest to the facts on the ground. He supervises Van Daan, and reports to Mr. Gladstone. Questioning Hill is a necessary predicate to deposing the next two witnesses."

"In due course," Hamilton said calmly, "we'll produce him. PGL has turned itself inside out to give you everything. Including its managing director." He pointed to the telephone. "If you think we're not cooperating, call Judge Taylor. We can reschedule Mr. Gladstone to follow Trevor Hill."

Pierce felt certain that there was a tactical reason for Hill's nonappearance. But Hamilton had him trapped in the press of time. "I want Hill within three days," Pierce said.

"Duly noted," Hamilton answered with affected boredom.

Pierce sat back, briefly taking in the setting—the court reporter, the witness and his two lawyers, framed by a glass wall through which Pierce could see the high-rises of Waro. Facing Gladstone, he asked, "The Luandian National Petroleum Corporation and PGL are business partners, correct?"

Gladstone nodded. "The government has a sixty percent interest, PGL forty."

"And those profits emanate almost entirely from the Luandian Delta."

"That's also true."

Sitting next to Hamilton, his associate Camilla Vasquez began scribbling notes. Idly, Pierce wondered how long it would take him to make her change expressions. "With respect to security matters in the delta," he asked, "who was principally responsible for your liaison with the Luandian military?"

For an instant, the question made Gladstone freeze. "Mr. Van Daan."

"What is his background?"

Gladstone steepled his fingers. "I believe his original career was in the South African military. Later as a hired soldier in various conflicts in West Africa."

"How did Mr. Van Daan's particular talents come to your attention?"

Gladstone hesitated. "We had a recommendation from Ugwo Ajukwa, national security adviser to General Karama."

Surprised, Pierce sifted this answer with what he knew about Ajukwa: that he was well connected in Washington and, according to Rubin, rumored to be involved in illegal bunkering and, perhaps, with FREE. "Did you discuss your concerns about security with Mr. Ajukwa?"

"Yes."

"What did he say?"

"That as our business partner, the Luandian government considered it essential that we have a capable and experienced man to interact with the Luandian military. And that, from personal acquaintance, he knew that man to be Roos Van Daan."

"Did you take that to be a suggestion, a request, or a demand?"

Gladstone smiled faintly. "I considered it a strong suggestion."

Sitting back in his chair, Pierce stretched, adopting a position of relaxation. "After you hired Mr. Van Daan, did you have another meeting with Mr. Ajukwa regarding PGL's security?"

"Yes. In London. Perhaps four months ago."

"Who else was present?"

"General Karama," he said at length. "Also Colonel Okimbo. From PGL, Hill and Van Daan. And me."

"Who suggested London, by the way?"

"Karama," Gladstone answered with palpable irony. "He likes London."

Hamilton, Pierce saw, watched the witness closely. With an air of mild curiosity, Pierce said, "How did that meeting come about?"

"Our executives had been kidnapped, our pipelines tapped, our facilities vandalized. We also faced an organized campaign in Asariland led by

Bobby Okari. Our message was clear: our ability to continue to operate in the Luandian Delta depended on the *government's* ability to protect our personnel and facilities."

"Of the problems you faced, Mr. Gladstone, which did you consider the worst?"

"Kidnappings. There had also been a murder at one of our compounds, the daughter of an executive. As far as facilities go, bunkering was a real problem—it affects production, and the ancillary damage to the environment from leakage was considerable. FREE and the like aren't big on cleanup."

Still watching Gladstone, Pierce reached for a document. "On the subject of bunkering, how did Karama and Ajukwa respond?"

"Ajukwa said that bunkering was difficult to control. And that the worst potential problem was the Asari movement."

Gladstone, Pierce sensed, had not believed this answer. "And Karama?"

"He was vehement about the Asari—that Okari was building a secessionist movement that would finish Luandia as a nation."

"Did you share that fear?"

"Karama stated the worst case. But did the Asari movement concern us? Yes."

"How did Karama respond to your concerns?"

"By assigning Colonel Okimbo to oversee our security needs in the delta."

"Did you know Colonel Okimbo?"

"No."

"Did anyone from PGL?"

Across the table, Vasquez stopped writing. "Perhaps Van Daan," Gladstone ventured. "At the meeting, Okimbo requested that he work directly with Van Daan."

"Did anyone discuss the particulars of that work?"

"No. That was to be arranged between Okimbo and Van Daan." Gladstone sat straighter. "But our policy toward security matters was clear: to encourage the military to respect human rights; to discourage the use of unnecessary force; and to shun rape, torture, and wanton destruction of property."

"And who was responsible for helping the military implement that policy?"

"Trevor Hill." Watching Pierce's eyes, Gladstone added, "Also Van Daan."

"Prior to this meeting, did you know anything about Colonel Okimbo's record with respect to human rights?"

"No."

Pierce feigned surprise. "No one told you that Okimbo had on occasion been accused of perpetrating murder and rape?"

"No."

"More recently, did you hear about Okimbo's involvement in a massacre in the village of Lana?"

"I heard vague stories about Lana, but not that Okimbo was involved." As though unsettled, Gladstone glanced at Hamilton. "Mr. Hill, however, did relate rumors to that effect. I asked Van Daan to investigate."

"What did he report?"

Pierce saw Hamilton's eyes narrow. "That Okimbo denied it," Gladstone answered. "Van Daan's opinion was that the entire story was propaganda spread by the Asari."

"At the London meeting, did *you* form an impression of Colonel Okimbo?"

As if in warning, Hamilton looked sharply at the witness. Gladstone gazed at the table, less concerned with the impression his silence made than with the formulation of his answer. "What I thought was that Okimbo would pursue the Asari problem with determination. I had no basis for assessing precisely what that might involve."

For a moment, Pierce simply watched him. Then he slid a document across the table. "Can you identify the document marked as Gladstone Exhibit 1?"

Gladstone stared at it. Tonelessly, he answered, "It's the memo I wrote to the chairman of PetroGlobal, reporting on the London meeting."

Pierce nodded. "Let me quote a passage: 'I emphasized that the Okaris' activities should be closely monitored and, if possible, discouraged.'" Looking up, Pierce asked, "What on earth did you have in mind?"

Gladstone glanced at his lawyer. "In general terms," he said with care, "that the military maintain sound intelligence about Okari's activities. And that he and the Asari movement be dissuaded from actions that threatened our operations."

"How did you suppose Okimbo would 'dissuade' the Asari?"

Gladstone crossed his arms. "That was a matter for Okimbo and Van Daan."

"Prior to Asari Day, did PGL make payments to the Luandian military?"

"Yes. But only for protection."

"How, and by whom, were those payments negotiated?"

Gladstone tented his long fingers in front of him, contemplating them as if concerned with his manicure. "Mr. Van Daan was given a budget for security operations. Within that budget, he had discretion to make payments as needed, fully accounted for, to those rendering services related to PGL's security."

"Did Van Daan make payments directly to Colonel Okimbo?"

"Yes." Gladstone straightened his tie. "To augment his salary, in recognition of his critical role in protecting PGL."

"Who decided the amount and timing of these payments?"

"Okimbo and Van Daan, I assume."

"And they, too, are 'fully accounted for'?"

Gladstone hesitated. "They should be, yes."

"According to your records, you paid Okimbo every month for six months, up to the month before Asari Day. Did the payments stop?"

Fleetingly, Gladstone looked perplexed. "I can't answer that."

"Nor can I." To Hamilton, Pierce said, "Please double-check your records of payments to Okimbo. I'd hate to think there's something missing."

Hamilton shot him a look of annoyance. "I've got no reason to think that."

"Check anyhow." Pierce slid another document across the table. "I show you what has been marked as Gladstone Exhibit 2. Do you recognize this document?"

"It's a memo regarding the purchase of weaponry for Colonel Okimbo."

"Including bullets, grenades, rocket launchers, AK-47s, and tear gas?"

Gladstone glanced from the document to Pierce, a troubled expression passing through his eyes. "Again, this was within Mr. Van Daan's authority."

"Did you notice that this memo is dated two weeks before Asari Day?"

Gladstone shrugged. "I don't know what one can make of that."

"Then let's flash forward to Asari Day. Were you aware of Okari's plans?"

"What I *knew*," Gladstone said, "is that he planned a mass protest against PGL's operations, involving three hundred thousand Asari. Among the things I *feared* was what happened: the Asari seizure of a pumping station and an offshore oil platform. What followed that was the lynching of three PGL employees."

"Did the Asari commit any acts of violence at the pumping station or platform?"

"They did not."

"I guess that leaves the oil workers. Who killed *them*?"

Gladstone frowned. "Obviously, I can't know."

"On Asari Day, did PGL assist Okimbo and the military in 'monitoring the activities' of the Asari gathered in the village of Goro?"

"I don't know."

Pierce's questions came quicker now. "Who could authorize such activities?"

"Mr. Hill. Or Mr. Van Daan."

"After the lynchings, you shut down PGL's operations in Asariland. Did you discuss these measures with anyone in the government?"

"General Karama." Gladstone paused. "I told him we couldn't continue unless the government protected our facilities and—especially—our employees."

"How did he respond?"

"That Colonel Okimbo would see to it that Asariland was peaceful."

"Did you discuss how to facilitate that effort with anyone at PGL?"

"With Mr. Van Daan and Mr. Hill. By conference call."

"What measures were discussed?"

"Among other things, Mr. Van Daan suggested that he and Colonel Okimbo approach the more reasonable leaders of the Asari movement."

"Did that approach involve cash payments to specific leaders?"

"Not explicitly." Gladstone stretched his arms in front of him, flexing his fingers as though to ward off stiffness. "He mentioned what he called 'personal concessions.'"

Pierce handed him a document. "I show you Gladstone Exhibit 3. Do you know what it is?"

Gladstone's brow knit. "It's a PGL form showing cash disbursements."

"I point out the line that records 'payments to Asari community leaders for security advice.' What does that mean?"

"Just that, I assume. The particulars were up to Van Daan."

"Did you, Hill, and Van Daan discuss other methods of 'bringing peace' to Asariland?"

"Van Daan suggested the imposition of martial law and the arrest of Bobby Okari." Gladstone paused. "According to Van Daan, Okimbo believed that Okari had ordered the murder of our employees."

"At that point, Mr. Gladstone, did you have any experience with the Asari movement practicing violence against PGL employees?"

"We did not. But Okari's rhetoric was becoming increasingly heated, including assertions that violence would follow if we did not meet his demands."

"During this call, did Hill express any view about the possibility of violence?"

Gladstone glanced at the memo in front of Pierce. "He expressed concern that Okari would not back down, and that the situation might become inflamed."

Pierce gave him the memo. "I assume you've seen Exhibit 4."

Gladstone paused, then answered in a subdued tone. "It's a memo Trevor Hill faxed to me an hour or so after our conference call."

"May I ask you to read its second-to-last paragraph aloud?"

Eyes fixed on the document, Gladstone fished into his pocket for a pair of gold-rimmed reading glasses, then softly repeated Hill's words as if from memory: " 'I must reemphasize the concerns expressed in our call. The murder of our employees is a tragedy, and steps to prevent any further loss of life are imperative. But I worry that the army may take violent measures in response to further civil disobedience by the Asari. Therefore PGL should encourage the use of tear gas and rubber bullets, so as to minimize any possible loss of life.' "

Pierce cocked his head. "In your conference call,

did Mr. Hill express any reason for his concerns *not* contained in this memo?"

Camilla Vasquez stopped taking notes. Hamilton's face went blank. "Yes," Gladstone said at length. "Despite Van Daan, he restated his belief that Okimbo had ordered an atrocity at Lana."

"I take it Van Daan was a bit more sanguine."

"Van Daan still insisted that the stories about Lana were an Asari fabrication. He also argued that it was impossible for Okimbo to limit his men to rubber bullets without knowing what dangers they might face."

"From whom? Were the Asari known to have supplies of weapons?"

Gladstone looked up at Pierce. Softly, he answered, "I don't know."

"So how did you respond?"

"By telling Van Daan to advise Okimbo, once again, of our policy on human rights."

Pierce raised his eyebrows. "You also confined PGL employees in Asariland to their homes. Did that include Van Daan?"

Briefly, Gladstone's gaze broke. "No. He and others, at his discretion, had latitude to work in concert with military and civil authorities."

"Do you know the specifics of that work?"

"No."

"In other words," Pierce snapped, "you don't know *where* Van Daan was when Okimbo's soldiers came to Goro. Or who *else* from PGL might have been there."

Gladstone crossed his arms. "According to Van Daan, no one."

"Really? Then PGL's helicopters and sea trucks arrived by magic?"

Gladstone winced, as though contemplating the degree to which the deposition had slipped beyond his control. "*If* they were there, Van Daan assures me, the army borrowed them without anyone knowing *how* they might be used."

"Someone did know," Pierce rejoined. "When did you first hear of the 'special tribunal' Karama designed for Bobby Okari?"

"Karama's speech," Gladstone said firmly. "All I knew before that is that he meant to take 'stern measures.'"

"Which, in the event, involves violating every human rights agreement your country ever signed." Pierce leaned forward. "Who from PGL is responsible for communicating with the government regarding Okari's prosecution?"

Hamilton's lips compressed. "Mr. Van Daan," Gladstone answered.

"Do you know the specifics of their communications?"

"I do not." Gladstone's speech became tight and precise. "My instructions to Van Daan were clear: monitor the proceedings and cooperate with the authorities when asked. The dead were our employees, Mr. Pierce. We can do no less." His voice hardened. "So let me be plain. I know *nothing* about Goro. And I know nothing that undermines the charge of murder that led to Okari's arrest."

Pierce smiled faintly. "Or anything about Van Daan or his activities, it seems."

"Enough." Hamilton's voice pulsed with anger. "Now you can apologize."

Pierce ignored him. "Tell me, Mr. Gladstone, do you at least know something about the conditions of Okari's imprisonment?"

A shadow crossed Gladstone's face. "No."

"Then let me tell you. Okimbo is his jailer. He's forced to shit and piss in buckets until they over-flow. Sometimes Okimbo's soldiers chain him to walls; at other times they torture his fellow Asari so Bobby can hear them scream. They've barred all visitors; they barely feed him; they've taken the light from his cell. That's the pastime of the 'authority' with whom Van Daan's working. So I suggest that you remind them of your 'human rights standards' one last time." Turning to Hamilton, Pierce said, "Look harder for those doc-uments, Clark. And do get me Trevor Hill."

6

THAT NIGHT, PIERCE AND RACHEL RAHV SAT ON
the patio of the hotel bar, sipping brandy and
gazing at the empty pool. They had spent several
hours preparing for Van Daan; now it was eleven
o'clock and, except for the palm trees, humid air,
and desperate lack of sleep, they could have been
two lawyers in America.

"Sounds like you did pretty well with
Gladstone," Rachel said. "Van Daan wasn't his
hire but Ajukwa's. Together, Okimbo and Van
Daan cut Hill out of the loop. From there on—
assuming you believe Gladstone—Van Daan controlled the relationship with Okimbo. He paid
Okimbo, helped Okimbo bribe Okari's lieutenants,
and bought Okimbo's soldiers the weapons used to
wipe out Goro." She took a quick hit of brandy.
"PGL's in trouble. By Gladstone's own account, he
knew zip about what was going on. He ignored
Hill's warning about Lana. He doesn't even know
if Van Daan was at Goro. Now Van Daan is 'monitoring' Okari's prosecution. Pathetic."

Pierce contemplated the yellow half-moon.
"Unless Gladstone is lying. He's surely guessed
more than he's saying; I'd say he's pretty sure
about what happened in Goro. But he doesn't want
to know, and probably couldn't. From PGL's
standpoint, that's not good, but it's a hell of a lot

better than knowing about the massacre." Pierce put down his brandy. "Here's the problem, Rache—according to Gladstone, Van Daan is maybe the only man who does know. Think *he's* going to help us?"

"Nope. Right now, Hamilton's got him in a room, going over exactly what Gladstone said. Without expressly saying so, Hamilton is telling him what we know, what we don't know, and what it's safe to lie about." Rachel paused, flicking back her raven hair. "About Hill, seems like Hamilton is jerking us around."

"Of course. My guess is that he'd be just as happy if Hill's plane crashed on the way back from Saudi Arabia. Though it's not clear how much Hill could know."

"What about the payments to Okimbo? It's funny to me that Van Daan ships Okimbo weapons before Asari Day but doesn't make his monthly payment. Seems like Okimbo would double-bill for a massacre."

Briefly, Pierce laughed. "That's why I love you, Rachel—you've got a lawyer's view of human nature. Of course, your *kids* are screwed."

"Warped for life. What do you make of Ajukwa's role as Van Daan's godfather?"

Pierce shrugged. "Maybe it's nothing, another piece of Luandian weirdness. But it's interesting that Ajukwa may own freighters used to transport bunkered oil, and then tells Hill that bunkering is hard to get at. Kind of makes you wonder about Van Daan. But we'll probably never know how that relates to Bobby."

Rachel finished her drink. "Oh, well," she said. "Bedtime in Luandia."

"How are you liking it?"

"The drive from the airport was memorable," she answered dryly. "Other than that, all I've seen is this fucking hotel."

Once again, Pierce thought of Marissa. "Safer that way," he answered.

BEFORE GOING TO bed, Pierce checked his e-mail. He opened the one from Bara, expecting to find an account of his and Marissa's efforts to turn up leads for Bobby's defense. Instead, Bara wrote, "I'm forwarding an e-mail from 'Jomo.' The man no one knows—General Freedom's phantom superior, the supposed leader of FREE."

Unsettled, Pierce scrolled through Bara's attachment. "Mr. Pierce," it began. "No one who matters wants Okari to live. You come here with a lawyer's paper sword, prating about 'due process.' But Luandia is a Gordian knot—you need a machete to cut it."

At once, Pierce e-mailed Bara: "What the hell is this?"

Within moments, Bara responded: "It's what he does. Don't know what he knows, or how he got my e-mail address. Should I send him yours?"

Pierce considered this. "Yes," he typed. "And tell him my name is God."

Pierce sat back, enveloped by a feeling of disquiet. Then he e-mailed Dave Rubin: "What do you know about Roos Van Daan and Ugwo Ajukwa?"

BY THE NEXT morning, Pierce had heard from Rubin.

Pierce, Hamilton, Vasquez, and the court reporter had reassembled around the table in PGL's glass-walled conference room, mugs of coffee in front of them. The only new presence was Roos Van Daan.

Van Daan placed both arms on the table, as though to establish his territory. He was a fleshy Afrikaner in his forties, with gray-blond hair and a creased young-old face from which shrewd eyes, a startling light blue, regarded Pierce with indifference. Answering Pierce's preliminary questions in a monotone, Van Daan allowed that he had been a major in the South African military; had left once Mandela ended apartheid; and since had served as a "military adviser" in numerous African wars. Sitting on either side of the witness, Hamilton and Vasquez had the alert but contented look of lawyers who expected no harm.

"In Angola," Pierce said, "you served with the anti-communist forces?"

"Yes," Van Daan answered. "Those are my principles."

"At that time, were you also under contract to the CIA?"

Hamilton's eyes froze—the question, obviously a surprise, warned him against complacency. Van Daan's eyes changed as well, indifference vanishing in a look of reappraisal. "Yes," he said at last.

"Is Angola where you first met Ugwo Ajukwa?"

Touching the witness's arm, Hamilton intervened. "Mr. Van Daan is barred from answering by certain confidentiality agreements unrelated to his service with PGL. If you want an answer, you'll have to go to Judge Taylor."

"I'll do that." Turning to Van Daan, Pierce said, "Did you meet Ajukwa in connection with your employment by the CIA?"

"Yes. And that is all I can tell you."

For the moment, Pierce knew this to be a dead end. "Did Ajukwa recommend you for your current job as PGL's director of security?"

"Yes."

From Van Daan's monosyllabic answers, Pierce already knew what was to come: indifferent to Pierce and the impression he made, Van Daan would volunteer nothing. "For what reason did Ajukwa suggest you to Gladstone?"

Van Daan took a swallow of coffee, then moved his heavy shoulders in a shrug. "Perhaps he thought my skills were suited to the delta. Ask *him*."

Van Daan's faint smile betrayed his knowledge that no Luandian official would submit to questioning. "How did you first meet Okimbo?" Pierce asked.

"I don't recall."

"Was it before or after your employment by PGL?"

Eyes veiled, Van Daan seemed to consider the implications of the question. "After, I believe."

"But before the London meeting with Ajukwa and Karama?"

The slits of Van Daan's eyes opened slightly. "I believe so, yes."

"Did you meet through Ajukwa?"

The smile had vanished. "I recall nothing of the circumstances."

"Yet, at that meeting, Okimbo asked to work with you directly."

"Yes."

"For what reason?"

"Again, ask him." A trace of sarcasm entered Van Daan's voice. "Perhaps he would say that, as I was director of security, he wished to work with me on matters of security."

"Were you familiar with Okimbo's reputation?"

"Only what he said," Van Daan answered dismissively. "It is plainly for effect, an African thing. Not even I know two hundred ways to kill a man."

Pierce kept watching his face. "According to Mr. Hill, Okimbo was reported to have ordered the murder of unarmed civilians in Lana. In fact, Gladstone asked you to investigate that matter."

Van Daan shrugged again, eyes focused on Pierce. "West Africa is full of such stories. Some are true, some are not. Okimbo denied this one."

"Surprising. What other inquiries did you make?"

"I really don't recall."

Pierce stared at the witness. "What importance did you attach to the prospect that PGL's chief military protector might have butchered civilians?"

"I thought the reputation helpful," Van Daan said with indifference. "My job was to find means of protecting PGL's employees in a dangerous place. Hanging is not a pretty death, and those who did it meant to frighten our people. If Okimbo frightened them in return—or *anyone* who threatened us— that was good."

"Did Okimbo frighten FREE, Mr. Van Daan?"

"How would *I* know? Ask FREE."

"How did you and Okimbo plan to control them?"

As Van Daan contemplated the question, Pierce had the familiar impression of a witness fabricating an answer. "We had plans, which I decline to broadcast." His tone became flinty. "Our first priority was dealing with Okari and the Asari who overran our facility and murdered three workers. FREE could wait."

"Did 'dealing' with the Asari include providing Okimbo with guns, armaments, tear gas, and grenades—two weeks *before* Asari Day?"

"We supplied the army," Van Daan responded coolly. "We did not specify its targets. That was Okimbo's department."

"Did you discuss with Okimbo PGL's policy on human rights?"

"Yes. I even gave Okimbo his own copy." Van Daan's voice was flat. "In Africa, what exists on paper often stops there. Our only influence was in trying to engage the military to protect PGL in an appropriate way."

Pausing, Pierce decided to shift gears. "Did that involve paying them?"

Disdain stole back into Van Daan's ice-blue eyes. "They lacked funding," he answered. "You speak of bullets. There was also food, medical care, payments to the soldiers who guard our compound or PGL executives, and payments to officers like Okimbo. Anything required to make us less than wholly defenseless."

"Did you also pay Okimbo in advance of specific operations?"

Van Daan was momentarily silent. "I could have."

"Did you ever pay him for an operation *after* it occurred?"

Van Daan's eyes narrowed. "I don't recall that."

With the trace of a smile, Pierce asked, "Do you have some rule against it?"

Van Daan's eyes locked on Pierce's. "About payments, there were no rules."

"Then let's take a specific example—the so-called arrest of Bobby Okari. Did you discuss that with Okimbo in advance?"

Van Daan settled back in his chair, putting more distance between himself and Pierce. "In general terms. He assured me that he would only use such force as necessary."

"Did you ask what that might mean?"

"How could I know? I was more concerned that the Asari stop killing our people."

"When Okimbo told you of his plan to arrest Okari, did he solicit payment?"

Van Daan's face closed. "I don't recall."

"Did you pay him for the Goro operation after it occurred?"

"I may have paid him after it occurred. That's different than paying *for* something. As I told you, I don't recall having made such payments."

Pierce glanced at Hamilton. "But if you did, you kept scrupulous records."

Van Daan delayed answering. "Sometimes. My practices aren't consistent."

Pierce turned to Hamilton. "*Are* there records of such payments to Okimbo?"

Hamilton glanced at Vasquez. "We haven't had time to look further," she said.

"Please do." Turning to Van Daan, Pierce asked, "You *did* keep records of payments to Bobby's lieutenants—Eric Aboh, Ubuke Odola, John Kipari, and Ala Sisune?"

"Yes. They each received fifty thousand dollars U.S."

"For what purpose?"

"Okimbo hoped to persuade them to abandon Okari." Van Daan's tone became pointed. "After Okari murdered our workers, that was not difficult."

"Still, you paid them. And then they signed an agreement calling for an end to demonstrations against PGL."

Van Daan leaned forward. "Yes. Isolating Okari was an effort to save lives—theirs and ours. Better cash than bullets."

"And yet two days later, the operation at Goro occurred. Where were you?"

"Somewhere in the field, on the way to Port George. I can't be more specific."

"What was the purpose of the trip?"

"To check some broken pipeline, near the village of Olala."

"Were you alone?"

"No. I travel with at least two officers from the mobile police."

"What were their names?"

Van Daan's eyes glinted. "I forget. They were new."

Pierce kept firing questions. "When did you first hear of Okari's arrest?"

"When I reached our compound at Port George. Okimbo called me. He said that his people had been shot at, but they'd arrested Okari."

Pierce gave him an incredulous look. "According to your intelligence, were the villagers of Goro armed?"

Van Daan crossed his arms. "I had no way of knowing."

"Did Okimbo mention civilian casualties?"

"He said there were a few, at most. The rest fled into the creeklands."

"You've seen many wars, Mr. Van Daan. Did you believe that?"

"Why is it my business to believe or disbelieve?"

"Oh, I don't know," Pierce said sharply. "Maybe because PGL personnel were involved in the operation."

Van Daan stared at him. "I don't believe that."

"Then how did it happen that PGL's equipment was used?"

"After the murders, Okimbo requisitioned helicopters and sea trucks. The Asari had occupied our platform and pumping station. The colonel said our equipment might be useful."

"Did he also mention Goro?"

"I don't recall."

Stymied, Pierce searched for his next question, and then a sudden instinct yielded one. Carefully watching Van Daan's eyes, he asked, "On the night of Asari Day, when Okari spoke at the rally in Goro, did you fly a helicopter over the village?"

Van Daan hesitated, lips parted, as though trying to discover the source of Pierce's question. "Do you need the question read back?" Pierce asked.

"No." Van Daan's voice lowered. "Yes, I flew the helicopter."

"For what reason?"

"Intimidation." Van Daan's smile was sour. "Apparently it didn't work."

"When did you find out about those workers?"

"That they were dead? From Okimbo. I first knew they were missing an hour or so before." Van Daan's tone dripped irony. "One of the men hadn't shown up at his son's soccer game. So his wife called."

"Where were you?"

"Near Goro. Preparing to fly the helicopter."

"Who was with you?"

"A couple of Okimbo's soldiers. And, no, I *don't* know who they were."

Van Daan's anxiety, faint but palpable, suggested that this area of questioning unsettled him. "Did you go to see the corpses?" Pierce asked.

"No. I returned to Port George."

Pierce cocked his head. "How do you know Okimbo didn't kill the three workers?"

"Why in hell would he do that?"

"You tell me, Mr. Van Daan."

"I can't."

"Then what's the evidence against Okari?"

Van Daan seemed preternaturally watchful now. "I don't know the specifics. All Okimbo has told me is that there are witnesses."

"Who are they?"

"I don't know."

Pierce sat back, looking from Hamilton to Vasquez and back to Van Daan. "In connection with the prosecution of Bobby Okari, have you given Okimbo money?"

A brief silence ensued, in which Hamilton glanced sharply at the witness. "Any payments to Okimbo," Van Daan said, "were for the usual security services."

"Not for witnesses?"

"No."

"How do you know that?"

"Objection," Hamilton cut in. "No foundation. Once Van Daan pays Colonel Okimbo, he can't know where the money goes."

Pierce turned to Van Daan. "You may answer."

Van Daan shrugged. "My counsel just did. I know nothing about Okimbo paying witnesses."

There was something wrong here, Pierce felt certain. But there was no way to probe it. "After I depose Hill," he told Hamilton, "I want Mr. Van Daan back again."

"Not without a reason," Hamilton snapped. "If you ever get one, let me know."

BACK AT THE hotel, Pierce hastily checked his e-mail. "Eleven days to trial," Jomo had noted, "and no defense. Would you like one?"

Staring at the screen, Pierce felt paranoia overwhelm him. His correspondent knew too much, and his inquiry smelled of deception—or, worse, entrapment. What might follow could destroy Bobby's hopes and, quite possibly, Pierce's career.

For a long time Pierce sat there. Then he typed a response: "Truth is the only defense. So you tell me: do you have one?"

It was the question Pierce kept asking himself.

7

BY MIDMORNING, WHEN CLELLAN AND VORSTER drove him to the airport, Pierce still had no reply from Jomo—or from Dave Rubin, of whom he had requested, "Tell me what else you know about Ugwo Ajukwa." When they arrived, Vorster passed Pierce a duffel bag. "I suggest you take this."

"What's inside?" Pierce asked.

"A handgun. Know how to use one?"

In the delta, Vorster was reminding Pierce, no one could protect him. "My cousin's a cop," he answered. "He taught me how to miss my foot."

Vorster nodded. "Then put it in your suitcase."

Reluctantly, Pierce took the bag.

• • •

As before, Bara met him in Port George. Driving to the Okaris' compound, the lawyer seemed preoccupied. "What's wrong?" Pierce asked bluntly.

Intently watching the road, Bara answered, "To begin, Marissa's at the jail. She's sick of being passive, she says—the reason she hasn't defied them sooner was fear of reprisal against Bobby." His voice was somber. "Now her greatest fear is that he'll die in prison. The only way to live is do everything she can."

Pierce felt anxiety fray his temper. "Okimbo is there, for God's sake."

"She's Bobby's wife," Bara said in the same quiet tone. "Caraway is using your report to try to alleviate Bobby's suffering. That probably means she'll be safe."

Unable to voice his fears, Pierce stared out the window. After a time, he asked with weary asperity, "What else is there? More e-mails from Jomo?"

"It's about the massacre." Bara paused. "There may be a witness. We still have a network—hidden, but they're working."

Surprised, Pierce turned in his seat. "On what?"

"On things best undescribed until they ripen." Bara's face closed. "You're a stranger here," he admonished. "You'll learn only what Bobby's lawyer can use."

More completely than before, Pierce felt like a

man in a metaphoric version of the creeklands where, three weeks before, he had placed himself in the hands of a pilot whose name he'd never asked. When they reached the compound, it was late afternoon, and Marissa had not returned.

He sat on the patio, scribbling notes to pull together the threads of Bobby's defense. At odd moments he found his pen stopping, his thoughts preempted by worry for Marissa. In the last few hours he had faced the core truth: above everything else, he had came back to Luandia because Marissa Okari was still here.

SHORTLY BEFORE SUNSET, she appeared.

Pierce turned at the sound of her footsteps, caught between relief and anger. "You're an idiot," he said.

She stopped there, two feet away, and slowly shook her head. "Please, don't."

She did not look at him. He went to her, placing his hand under her chin. When she met his eyes, it was as though her pupils had been exposed to too much light.

Pierce felt his stomach clutch. "Okimbo," he said.

When Marissa could not speak, Pierce took both her hands in his. Then, in a monotone, she told him what had happened.

SHE HAD GONE to the prison with three Luandian friends, a woman and two men, members of the human rights community brave enough to join in an act of defiance that, however small, made them more vulnerable to those whose whims could end their lives. When Major Bangida appeared, he refused to let the others come with her.

As the gate closed behind her, Bangida took Marissa's arm, saying, "Colonel Okimbo wishes to see you."

For an instant, her legs felt disconnected from her brain; she remembered Omo looking back as Okimbo led her away. Then she saw the gallows and stopped, staring up at it. "Come," Bangida said.

The young officer seemed emotionless. But when he led her to Okimbo's office, opening the door for her, his voice was gentle. "Please step inside."

When the door shut, she forced herself to look at the man who waited.

Okimbo sat on the front edge of his desk, his massive legs splayed, his single eye examining her. "Did you come to apologize?" he inquired with disquieting calm. "Since we last met, your lawyer said much about me in America. And yet I retain the power of life and death."

Marissa fought against the images of Goro. "I want to see my husband."

Her voice sounded parched. She watched the calculation surface in his eye. "What if you have weapons?"

She held out her empty hands, a gesture of entreaty for which she despised herself at once. "I meant beneath your dress," he said.

Slowly, he stood, his body uncoiling like a cat's. Anger and alarm made her voice defiant. *"No."*

"No? Then you must show me."

Marissa could not answer. "Do you want to see him?" Okimbo demanded. "Alive, that is."

Numb, Marissa touched the top button of her dress. She chose a place on the wall to stare at. After seconds that seemed like minutes, she felt and heard her dress whisper to the floor. All that concealed her were her bra and panties. "Everything," Okimbo directed.

Mechanically, Marissa unhooked her bra. For some reason she clung to it, dangling it from the fingertips of one hand. "Look at me," he ordered.

When she did, she was staring at the lens of a camera. She heard one click, and then the only sound was Okimbo's breathing. A smile curved his lips.

As though in a trance, Marissa slid her panties to the floor. The camera clicked twice. Evenly, Okimbo said, "I will tell you what else to do. Then you will do it."

The instructions that followed were soft, explicit. Willing her mind to leave her body, she complied. The clicking of his camera marked each stage of her humiliation.

Okimbo never touched her. "Cover yourself," he

ordered with faint contempt. "Before Bangida comes."

As she bent to retrieve her dress, Okimbo turned his back. When the door opened, the only evidence of what had happened was inside Okimbo's camera.

SEEING HER ANGUISH, Pierce asked only, "Did you tell Bobby?"

"I couldn't." Her throat worked. "He's better now. He has light in his cell, and food."

The dissociation in her voice left Pierce uncertain of what to do. "And you?"

"It was frightening and degrading." Her voice filled with shame. "Worse than that. It's been so long since any man . . ."

She could not continue. Overcome by confusion, Pierce reached out for her. Wordless, she came to him. He could feel the softness of her breathing.

At the sound of footsteps, Pierce turned an instant before Marissa did. Watching them, Bara's face was studiously blank. "There's someone we have to meet," he told Pierce.

IN THE DANK, dark basement of the Okaris' house, Bara knelt, a flashlight in one hand, reaching for a heavy barrel lid that sat on the stone floor. When Bara wrestled the lid aside, Pierce saw that the stone beneath it was not mortared. "Help me lift this," Bara said.

Pierce and Bara pried loose the stone, exposing an open shaft in which Pierce saw the first few steps of a ladder. "It's a tunnel," Bara said. "One of Bobby's precautions. The only others who know are the Asari who dug it. And now you."

Pierce disliked darkness and confinement. After Bara disappeared, he made himself follow, straining not to show his apprehension.

Bara stood at the bottom of the ladder, roughly ten feet down. When Pierce reached the last step, Bara shone his flashlight into a passageway beneath the earth, propped up by makeshift carpentry. This close to sea level, the trapped air felt damp; when Pierce touched an earthen wall, moist dirt crumbled in his hand.

"It's held so far," Bara said phlegmatically, and Pierce felt his assessment of this lawyer rotate like the needle of a compass.

Bent from the waist, Bara began moving. Pierce followed, Bara's body a dark form that half-blocked the light emanating from his hand. The walls felt closer. Enveloped by claustrophobia, Pierce thought that at any moment their hurried footsteps would cause the earth, collapsing, to swallow them alive. Still they moved deeper into the tunnel; for countless minutes, Pierce imagined himself vanishing without a trace. At last Bara stopped, his hand touching a ladder at the tunnel's end.

At the top of the ladder, Bara pushed against a

piece of wood. The shaft admitted a glimmer of moonlight, into which Bara vanished. When Pierce surfaced, inhaling deeply, he found Bara crouching in an abandoned shack barely big enough to hold them. Bara doused the flashlight. Peering out an empty window frame, Pierce saw, then smelled, the bleak terrain of a garbage dump at night: rotting food, scraps of metal, the rusted carcasses of automobiles. Hunching to avoid detection, Bara began scrambling across heaps of garbage. Stumbling behind, Pierce saw rats skittering between them.

Bara veered toward the corroding shell of a doorless jeep. Pierce slid beside him onto the rotting cloth of its back seat, the palm of one hand resting on an exposed spring. "What's *this* about?" Pierce whispered.

From the seat in front of them a silent head rose. "Beke Femu is a soldier," Bara murmured.

Bizarrely, the man extended his hand across the car seat. When Pierce briefly took it, Femu said simply, "I was at Goro."

At once Pierce's reflexes kicked in. "You saw it?"

Femu's head inclined in a nod. In the same undertone he answered, "We committed murders."

"Tell us," Bara urged.

The soldier seemed to gather himself. "The eclipse was coming. We were going to Goro, Captain Igina told us, to arrest Bobby Okari. Our platoon was chosen because none of us were Asari." Femu's voice faltered. "We were waiting for the eclipse to fall when a helicopter landed, flown by an *oyibo*. The colonel who came with him I knew only by his eye patch."

Pierce's nerve ends tingled. "What did the white man look like?"

Femu looked from Bara to Pierce. "The man was big. With blond hair."

"How old?"

"No longer young. His hair seemed also gray."

"When you say big . . ."

"Tall. Not fat, but big in his body, too. Maybe with a belly beginning. They stayed there, talking, too far away to hear. Then the *oyibo* flew away." Femu's voice remained flat and quiet. "Colonel Okimbo ordered Captain Igina to form us up. Our orders had changed, he said. There was resistance from the Asari—we were to kill everyone in our path and burn Goro to the ground. Then the colonel laughed like a man insane."

In Pierce's mind, Femu's voice merged with the landscape of waste and metal in a haunting coda to what Pierce had seen in Goro. Femu continued in his uninflected tone. "Before they died, Okimbo said, the women could be ours. Then he led us to the helicopters and gave us weed and gin.

"All this time, the moon drew closer to the sun. I smoked until only the space of a hand seemed to separate the moon and sun. Then Okimbo ordered us into the helicopters—"

"Who flew them?" Bara interrupted. "Men from PGL?"

Femu shook his head. "All I remember was darkness coming. When we landed, the sun was gone."

For the next minutes, Pierce listened. The horror was much as Marissa had described it, except that the soldier, seized by trauma and memory, had lapsed into the present tense. "I am shooting," he concluded, "until there is no one left to shoot. Then we are taking the bodies and throwing them in a ditch. Some are pouring gasoline and lighting the dead on fire." He paused. "I'm still smelling this."

"Why are you telling us?" Pierce asked.

Femu shook his head, as though bewitched. "My village was like Goro," he said at last. "One day an oil spill turned our fields black and drowned our chickens. My father came in the house with legs black from the curse that swallowed his crops. But there was no Okari to speak for him."

"So you want to help Bobby now."

Femu hesitated. "Maybe yes. But how do I do this?"

"Come to Waro and let us record your story. Perhaps after that, they'll be afraid to harm you. Then you can testify at Bobby's trial."

Femu looked around them. "For travel, I would need money."

"We'll cover your expenses. Helping us will cost you nothing."

Femu slid toward the door. "Do not come for me. If I decide yes, I'll come to you."

Pierce had no choice; he had no ability to compel a witness. Without saying more, Femu slipped from the jeep. Pierce saw his shadow scurrying across a mound of refuse, too visible in the moonlight.

When Femu vanished, Bara touched Pierce's shoulder. Looking around them, they left the corroding vehicle and hurried toward the shack, the only sound the crunch of their shoes on rusted metal. Then they retraced their silent journey beneath the earth. In the darkness, Pierce said, "It was Van Daan."

"So it seems," Bara answered. "But can we ever prove it?"

When at last they reached the Okaris' basement, Bara went to Marissa, Pierce to check his e-mail. Rubin had written that he would be in Port George tomorrow to speak with Pierce in person. Jomo's response said simply, "If you want the truth, you must meet with General Freedom. Yes or no?"

Sitting down, Pierce thought for a moment, then typed, "Yes."

8

SHORTLY AFTER MIDNIGHT, PIERCE STIRRED FROM a restless sleep, conscious of a presence in his room.

When he reached out in the darkness, he felt her cotton nightgown. She sat on the edge of the bed, silent, her slender back to Pierce. Her fingers curled around his.

"What is it?" he asked.

"Everything."

She sounded utterly bereft. Shirtless, Pierce sat up, his chest grazing her arm. "Do you want to stay?" he asked.

He felt her body half-turn to him. "If you understand."

"I do."

Pierce drew aside the sheets. Marissa slid in next to him, her back against his chest. He felt a tenderness for which he had no words.

They lay there, quiet in the dark. He could feel the rhythm of her breathing, at first even, then slower and deeper until, at last, she slept. At some point in the night, Pierce followed.

He awoke just before first light. Her lips were grazing his forehead in a silent thanks. Then she slipped from the bedroom, softly closing the door. When next he saw her, eating breakfast with Atiku Bara, the only sign that their night was not a dream was the faintest smile in her deep brown eyes.

AT TEN O'CLOCK, Dave Rubin appeared at the gate of the compound in a black Mercedes-Benz. Parked across the street were the omnipresent men from state security. Pierce climbed into the Mercedes. Inclining his head toward their minders, Rubin said, "I thought it would be better to have this conversation in person."

Pierce nodded. "You safe here?"

"Think so. FREE knows who to kidnap; their spies at PGL give them descriptions of executives who'll fetch the highest price." Rubin shifted into drive. "You've developed an interest in helicopters. Ever fly in one?"

"Never wanted to."

"Too bad," Rubin answered. "For privacy, you can't beat it."

THE STATE SECURITY men followed them to the airstrip, a patch of cement near the harbor. Waiting was a gray helicopter marked only by numbers. "Thought I'd show you Petrol Island," Rubin explained.

This was better than a tunnel or a prison cell, Pierce consoled himself. He clambered up into the passenger seat. Rubin pushed some buttons; above them the blades rotated with a thud that caused the helicopter to vibrate. Both men put on headphones, enabling them to communicate above the deafening noise. Then, as though lifted by a hydraulic force, the helicopter jumped straight up. After a vertiginous dip that made Pierce queasy, the chopper stabilized, rising high above the harbor. Pierce looked down at the dirty water, the rusted hulls, the fleets of oil freighters. "Tell me about Ugwo Ajukwa," he said.

Rubin adjusted his sunglasses. "He met Van Daan through the agency, when both were on our payroll. Ajukwa had a piece of the diamond-smuggling business in Angola and needed someone lacking scruples to help him on the ground. Hence Van Daan.

"Later, we think, Van Daan may have helped Ajukwa move bunkered oil to a refining facility in Angola—"

"That's a funny qualification for becoming PGL's security guy."

"Not really. Van Daan surely understands the problem." Rubin adjusted the controls. "Put it this way: Ajukwa knows Van Daan's abilities, and Van Daan has enough leverage with Ajukwa to use him as a reference. The question becomes whose interests Van Daan serves—Ajukwa's or PGL's. Or both."

Pierce gazed out at the blue horizon. "Can't be both. If Ajukwa's involved with FREE in moving oil bunkered from PGL, then Van Daan may be. Does Gladstone know?"

"He suspects. As you may have observed, doing business in Luandia requires a degree of willful blindness."

"And Okimbo?"

"Has historic ties to Karama, of course. More recently, to Ajukwa. So it's possible to imagine an Ajukwa–Van Daan–Okimbo axis." Rubin grinned. "But that's the problem with Luandia, isn't it? You can imagine so many things that your chances of being wrong are almost perfect."

"Still," Pierce said, "it's logical to wonder why Karama, as paranoid as he is, makes a man with ties as complex as Ajukwa's his national security adviser."

"*Because* of those ties, in part. We'll get to that in a moment." Rubin pointed out the windshield toward Petrol Island. "Take a look."

The island was flat and grassy. Down its center a well-paved four-lane road ran from one end to the other, connecting a refining facility that featured enormous storage cylinders with a residential compound that, from Pierce's vantage point, looked like a gated community in Houston or Miami bordered by an airstrip, two soccer fields, and a golf course. At the water's edge was an oil platform, resembling a squat stationary ship with steel railings, along with, Rubin explained, a storage tank for volatile liquid gas. In a curvature on the opposite shore nestled a harbor that housed speedboats, the principal transport to the mainland for residents and workers. The one unexpected feature seemed lifted from Port George: a shantytown near the harbor.

Rubin slowed the chopper, causing it to glide downward so that it hovered closer to the ground. "Let me give you a brief review on General Freedom," he said. "His true name's Soboma Henry. You already know he's a Muslim convert who received military training in Libya through the largesse of Colonel Qaddafi. Beyond the fact that Freedom acquired a certain tactical ability, State, Defense, and the CIA are still debating about precisely what that means. Politically, the general advocates a program drawn from Bobby Okari's, but in the service of a criminal enterprise he justifies as his only financial recourse. Some believe that he's at least marginally sincere. For sure, he's clever and articulate. So is Jomo: as I told you, one theory is that they're the same guy."

"You never quite said what *you* think."

Rubin lowered the chopper still farther, his sharp features in profile as he gazed keenly at the harbor. "I rather like the idea that Jomo is an arms merchant or a shady financier with ties to an international criminal cartel. But in Luandia, he could even be someone like Ajukwa."

Surprised, Pierce turned to him. "Are you serious?"

"Semi. But I could never work out all the implications." Rubin nodded toward the windshield. "Look down at the harbor. Notice anything?"

"No traffic?"

"Exactly. Those who live here almost never leave now. Petrol Island is safer, they believe, and it has all the comforts of home—a health club, a movie theater, and plenty of security fences."

"Do you think it's safe?"

"No. Neither does someone like Van Daan, I imagine. Though raiding Petrol Island would be more brazen than seems reasonable. The militias have easier pickings on the mainland."

Pierce gazed out at the refinery. "How critical are the facilities?"

"They're significant. One plant processes crude oil into petroleum; another takes raw gas—the stuff PGL flares elsewhere—and processes, cools, and liquefies it, then ships it off to Europe for use in power stations. Gladstone's idea is that Petrol Island provides an alternative to gas flaring with benefits for all, if only because acid rainfall won't be eating through the tin roofs of the impoverished." Caught in a downdraft, the chopper dipped sharply, taking Pierce's stomach with it until Rubin reasserted his control. "That shantytown you see is the island's greatest amenity, Hooker Village."

Inhaling deeply, Pierce gazed down at the floating slum. "Named for its residents, I assume."

"Yup. They're an essential part of the ecology,

conveniently located. See the side road from the highway to the shacks?"

"Uh-huh."

"The common practice is for a man to leave work, stop at Hooker Village like he's picking up a video, and take a woman to the compound for the night." Rubin glanced at Pierce. "At the gate to the compound, George or Buster checks her in at the security gate, taking responsibility for her actions until he drops her off again. Very corporate. PGL even keeps a registry of names."

Beneath them, Pierce saw a thin woman in a bandanna hang a dress on the sill of a broken window. Then Rubin accelerated the chopper sharply upward, veering back toward Port George. "There's one subject you haven't raised," he told Pierce. "Ever think about the market in oil futures?"

"Not since Bryce Martel mentioned that at dinner. I thought it was a throwaway line."

"Maybe not. You know how oil futures work?"

"Sure," Pierce answered. "Today the world price of oil is a hundred bucks a barrel. For a fraction of the cost, I can buy the right to purchase a million barrels at a hundred and five in two weeks' time. If it's over a hundred and five on the date I've got to exercise my option—say, a hundred and ten—I make five dollars for each barrel I sell. That's a five-million-dollar profit."

"Exactly. And if the world price rises, say, thirty

dollars instead of ten, the profits are that much bigger. So let me ask you this: what's the futures play on Okari's execution?"

Pierce was startled. "If you're asking about the effect on the world price of oil, I'd guess that if Bobby dies, it goes up."

"*Way* up, given the fear of further instability in the delta. Which brings me back to Ugwo Ajukwa.

"You asked why Karama trusts him. Karama trusts no one. But Ajukwa has ties to America— power brokers, moneymen, *and* the CIA—that makes him useful to Karama. A prudent autocrat would want to keep a man like Ajukwa close enough to watch."

"Why the ties to Washington?"

"One of the reasons Ajukwa signed up with the CIA for a while was to help him amass political power—which, in Luandia, also means financial power. That's why he was in diamonds; that's why—or so we believe—he's involved with FREE in bunkering oil. Some within the Agency also believe that Ajukwa is now connected to a Swiss arms dealer, Alois Shue, who's begun supplying FREE with advanced weapons, like surface-to-air missiles, paid for by the Russian government."

Astonished, Pierce asked, "What's the point of that?"

"Power. For example, if FREE can shoot down any helicopters—for instance, those used by PGL to repair facilities—that could affect oil supply.

Which, in turn, makes Russia more important in the world oil market. Problem is that Shue is also helping the CIA supply anti-Taliban forces in Afghanistan, so no one wants to push this theory too hard. It all gets pretty diabolical." Throttling down, Rubin lowered the chopper to scan Port George Harbor. "For your purposes, the most interesting rumor is that Ajukwa's partners may also include financial types with ties to the current American administration, whose political influence, in turn, helps them make more money. One of these men, Henry Karlin, is unusually successful at trading in oil futures."

Staring at Rubin, Pierce processed this. "Which brings us back to Luandia."

"Sure. Consider what crises might affect the world price of oil. The most obvious are Iran going nuclear and a total meltdown in Iraq. But our oil strategists have placed a huge bet on Luandia, which magnifies the price effect of any event that signals volatility. When PGL shut down in Asariland, the world price per barrel shot up six dollars in a day. All you needed to know was exactly when someone would hang those workers."

Pierce shook his head. "Hard to imagine that as a futures play."

"Is it?" Rubin turned to Pierce, his expression as serious as his tone. "In the last year, three acts of sabotage by FREE drove the price of oil sharply higher. Suppose FREE blows up a couple of facilities, or seizes an offshore oil platform and kills whoever's there. Or maybe Jomo announces that all oil workers must leave or die, or some act of sabotage creates a massive oil spill in the Gulf of Luandia. If you were speculating in oil futures, wouldn't you like to know about events like these before they happened?"

Pierce rubbed his eyes; the constant pounding of the chopper blades had caused a throbbing in his temples. At length, he said, "Including the fact and timing of Bobby's execution."

Rubin nodded. "At some point, Karama will decide whether and when Bobby Okari will die. The word I have is that Ajukwa is pressing for his execution on the grounds that Bobby is a secessionist threat. In addition to the patriotic virtue of putting a bullet through Okari's brain, there just might be some money in it."

Pierce watched his face. Though Rubin had come to him through Martel, Pierce's paid consultant, that did not preclude one or both from having other interests. But what those might be, Pierce did not know and could not ask. Finally, he said, "What are you telling me, Dave?"

Rubin seemed to weigh his answer. "Just to think about the futures market. It may be part of what, in the end, helps you make sense of the senseless. Like Okari says, oil kills."

Abruptly, Rubin dropped the helicopter toward

the airstrip. When they landed, the men from the state security services were parked near Rubin's Mercedes.

REACHING THE OKARIS' compound, Pierce went upstairs to check his e-mail.

A message from Rachel Rahv was marked "urgent": "PGL is finally giving up Trevor Hill tomorrow. Will you depose him, or should I?"

Without responding, Pierce checked the next e-mail. "Good," Jomo had answered. "Your friend will help lead you to my friend."

Gazing at the screen, Pierce felt Atiku Bara behind him. Slowly turning, he said, "Are *you* my friend, Bara?"

The lawyer was expressionless. "I'm known to them," he answered. "You recall the man I spoke with in the Rhino Bar, the night FREE killed that soldier?"

"Of course."

"We're on different sides, but he knows I won't betray him. That's why Jomo contacted me, I'm sure. I've become your character reference."

Pierce turned back to the screen. When Bara had gone, he replied to Rachel Rahv: "Hill is yours. For now, I'm staying in the delta."

9

J OMO'S REPLY INSTRUCTED PIERCE TO MEET A stranger in Port George.

Sitting on the patio, he repeated this to Marissa and Bara. Marissa shook her head. "To meet openly in a city? Why is FREE so confident you both won't be arrested?"

Pierce glanced at Bara. Leaning forward, Marissa gazed at Pierce with new intensity. "Suppose FREE and their friends in government are looking to get rid of you. You agree to go, and then vanish in the swamps. It's perfect for them: there'd be no one's fingerprints on your disappearance, no lawyers to take your place. I don't like the way this feels."

Her words struck Pierce hard; by stating his own fears so concisely, Marissa deepened them. Bara still watched Marissa. "Why murder Damon?" he asked her.

"Because they can." Her voice was raw with anger. "Because Damon has brought his law firm's resources to bear. Because he's trouble. Why would whoever lynched those oil workers stop there?"

"Perhaps they wouldn't," Bara answered calmly. "But we don't even know who 'they' are. That's what Damon's hoping to find out." He turned to Pierce. "The man you're meeting is the one I encountered in Port George. He wouldn't knowingly betray me."

Pierce's mind flooded with distrust and doubt—of Jomo, of FREE, of Bara himself. But in the half-formed pattern growing in his mind, General Freedom might know why, and by whom, the workers had been killed. In this place where motives were impossible to guess and so many ways existed to get rid of him, for Pierce to shun this invitation made no more sense than to accept it. With nine days until the tribunal convened, he still had no defense for Marissa's husband. "I have to go," he told her.

Abruptly, she stood and walked to the edge of the patio, her back to Pierce and Bara. Quietly, Bara said, "I'll leave you two alone."

For an instant, Pierce wondered what Bara might imagine. Still watching Marissa, he nodded.

She gazed out at the South Atlantic as the evening sun, falling, blurred the far horizon. Standing beside her, Pierce placed his hands on the railing. Softly, she said, "I never should have asked you here."

"Too late," he answered. "All that's left to decide is how I live this out."

She turned to him, the pain in her eyes so tangible he could feel it. "I've had enough of martyrdom. I don't want that from you, Damon."

Once again, it struck Pierce that Bobby, without her knowing it, had placed Marissa in great danger.

Bobby had refused exile: the result, a lethal irony, was that Pierce would risk himself to save her. "The idea," he told her, "is not two martyrs. It's none."

To Pierce, it seemed Marissa could no longer look at him. "Then please come back," she said.

THE NEXT MORNING, Bara dropped Pierce at the mouth of an alley in Port George.

Following instructions, Pierce turned down a second alley, then a third, finding a restaurant that resembled an abandoned shack. Though the sign in its dirty window read closed, the door was not locked. Glancing over his shoulder, Pierce stepped inside.

Alone at a table was the man from the Rhino. He stood, motioning to Pierce, and led him out a rear exit. In still another alley waited a Land Rover with three Luandians inside. Pierce's guide opened the front passenger door.

Pierce got in. The driver wore sunglasses and a black T-shirt that hugged his muscled body. Of the two men in the rear seat, the fleshy one held an English-language paperback of *Quotations from Chairman Mao;* the other smoked a joint, his eyes half-shut beneath the visor of a Boston Red Sox cap. Each wore a cartridge belt; two AK-47s lay between them. The sheer weirdness of this moment left Pierce caught between instinctive dread and the reflex to laugh aloud. The driver stomped the accelerator, and the car, spitting mud, sped from the alley.

They took dirt roads out of town, passing homes and shops barely better than hovels. After a time Pierce kept his eyes on the road, accepting his destiny with as much fatalism as he could muster. Then they reached the landing where, accompanied by Marissa and Bara, Pierce had begun the haunting trip to Goro.

Everything else was different. A waiting sea truck was occupied by five armed men, all in black hoods. Around each man's shoulders were draped two leather belts from which tipped bullets protruded like sharks' teeth in a dull gold necklace. Stepping into the boat, the driver indicated a seat in the back for Pierce.

He sat between the reader of Mao and the marijuana smoker. Both covered their heads with black cloth hoods, the latter carefully placing his Red Sox cap beside him. Pierce tried to imagine them as his friends—in less than an hour, he had grasped the essence of Stockholm syndrome.

Wondering at the absence of uniformed military, Pierce took stock of the boat. White cloth banners flew from poles bolted to the deck, on which lay boxes holding weapons. The boat itself was new, powered by two gleaming outboard motors; when the pilot pulled the throttle, the boat accelerated so swiftly that it threw Pierce back. The hooded men, standing but bent at the knees, absorbed the jolting movement without much effort.

The boat skidded across the harbor, still gaining speed. Suddenly the Red Sox cap was captured by a gust of wind; it fluttered in the air like a wounded bird before dropping behind them into the churning wake. Standing, its owner shouted something guttural in a language unknown to Pierce. Spinning the wheel as he cut the motors, the pilot turned the boat in a slow trajectory aimed for the floating cap. As they passed it, the marijuana smoker leaned gracefully from the boat and grasped the visor. Then the pilot turned again, heading toward the creeklands as the man wrung filthy water from his cap.

WITHIN ANOTHER HOUR'S time, Pierce experienced again the sense of being swallowed by a trackless netherworld. He could have been here before, or not. Banks thick with palms and mangrove closed around them; the pilot made unfathomable decisions, choosing one tributary in the watery maze, then another. The occasional village seemed to have imbued its inhabitants with the same weary lassitude Pierce had observed before, their boats and fish nets lying unused on the muddy banks. The spray of water on his face was slick with the oil that moved sinuously across the surface like a formless black amoeba.

A third hour passed, the creeklands becoming

narrower, the foliage thicker. Suddenly a helicopter appeared above the trees. For the first time, the heavyset reader of Mao spoke. "Perhaps the army," he told Pierce. "If they drop a grenade, maybe our boat will sink, and they'll shoot anyone swimming in the water." But he said this with a curious unconcern. After a time, the helicopter vanished.

THE SUN WAS straight above them now, radiating a muggy heat that dampened Pierce's shirt. Still they took one creek, then another, seemingly without direction. Every so often the pilot, studying the terrain, spoke in an unknown dialect to a hooded man beside him. Then the pilot pointed to a landmark Pierce could not discern, and the man next to him replaced the white cloth flags with red ones. They took a hairpin turn into another creek, so sharp that their new course was hidden from view.

When they completed the turn, another boat was waiting there, its bow pointing directly at them.

The pilot shouted out. The other craft began speeding toward them, its armed occupants kneeling as bullets ripped the hull of Pierce's boat.

Stunned, Pierce froze. As the men around him hit the deck, he followed, sprawling forward. Beside him the owner of the Red Sox cap crumpled and was still.

The militiamen grasped their weapons, all sense of randomness vanishing in the discipline with which they returned fire. Crouching, the pilot whipped the wheel; the boat swerved, barely missing their enemy as it sped past them in the narrow creek. Then he spun the boat again, and suddenly they were in pursuit.

The other boat was twenty yards away. Moving to the front, Pierce's companions laid down a barrage of bullets. Ahead, two of their attackers fell, one pitching headfirst into the water. Then the man who read Mao stood, shouldering a grenade launcher. With a percussive whir, the launcher recoiled.

Reflexively, Pierce half-stood as the dark sphere arced toward its target. The enemy boat shuddered, bursting into flames. As Pierce heard a scream of agony, a second grenade struck.

Tongues of blue-orange flames burst from the broken hull. A gas tank exploded. Pieces of fiberglass flew in all directions, and then the water was ablaze.

Standing, the pilot throttled back abruptly. As their boat slowed, gliding past the wreckage, a man screamed in anguish amid a burning oil slick. Next to Pierce, the reader of Mao stared down at his dead companion, pink-white brains seeping from the man's shattered skull. With calm deliberation his friend raised his AK-47, turned, and launched a fusillade of bullets at the survivor, which caused him to twitch as though a metal clothesline was holding him above the surface. Then he sank amid a red-black skein of blood and oil, and the reader of Mao resumed his contemplation of the dead man.

At length he took out a cell phone and called someone. The softness of his tone required no translation.

MOMENTS AFTER THE pilot continued their journey, the reader of Mao returned to his vigil beside the corpse. Numb, Pierce sat alone.

Slowing, the boat glided into a shallow creek. In a clearing along the shore stood a group of hooded men, their chests bare except for ammunition belts. Red and white cloths were knotted on their arms. In front of them lay a white wooden casket.

Stepping from the boat, Pierce's companions dipped their hands in the oily water. To Pierce, the reader of Mao said, "You also."

Uncomprehending, Pierce complied. Two men stepped from the shore and bore the dead man to the casket.

Gently, they placed him inside. Then four men lifted the wooden box, taking a path through the palms and mangroves as the others followed in a single file, Pierce trailing behind. When the path opened again, he saw them in another clearing, gathering around a shallow grave dug from the red-orange clay.

The coffin lay beside it, the man inside gazing sightlessly at a patch of blue sky. The reader of

Mao knelt again, shutting the man's eyes with a forefinger. The militiamen crowded around the casket, chanting what to Pierce sounded like an anthem of battle. Then they removed their hoods.

They were startlingly young. Most could not be twenty; some struggled to mask their grief. Tears in his eyes, the reader of Mao placed the Red Sox cap inside the casket, then closed its lid.

Standing apart, Pierce saw the men pick up wooden shovels. They each took turns covering the casket with dirt. When they were through, someone planted a makeshift wooden cross above the grave.

The reader of Mao approached Pierce, his eyes still red. "Come with me."

Pierce glanced at the grave. Quietly, he asked, "Who killed him?"

For a moment, the man gave no sign of hearing. In a flat tone, he answered, "Who knows. Perhaps they came for you."

ONCE MORE THEY climbed into the boat. As before, the militiamen donned hoods. No one spoke at all.

For another hour, they navigated the maze of creeks. Then they beached the boat again, this time on a patch of mud. A narrow path, not visible from the water, led into a sunless growth of palms and mangroves so dense that Pierce had no sense that it could end. Finally light appeared, and then an encampment of armed men.

Astonished, Pierce took in the concrete barracks, the shirts and pants hanging from clotheslines, the men loitering or smoking joints or clustered around iron cooking pots. The reader of Mao led him to a hooded man sitting apart from the others on a bench carved from the trunk of a palm tree. Lithe and well muscled, this man seemed taller than the rest, and the impassivity created by his hood was deepened by the intense stare he fixed on Pierce. In a commanding voice, preternaturally deep, he said, "I am General Freedom. I'm told you think I had three men hung."

Pierce weighed his answer. This man could kill him in an instant; but then he could have ended Pierce's life without extracting him from Port George. The instincts he possessed, those of a trial lawyer, were to be direct and nondeferential. "It's occurred to me," he said.

Freedom's eyes became slits in a black mask. "Why would I do that?"

"To discredit Okari, and give Karama an excuse to execute him."

To Pierce's surprise, Freedom emitted a contemptuous laugh. "No great loss. Okari became so infatuated with his own celebrity that he mistook his people's defenselessness for immunity from death. Okimbo shattered their illusions."

"Leaving the field to you, Okari's rival."

"Okari's rival," Freedom repeated with disdain. "It is true that, by arousing fear, we make Okari more attractive to cowards. But his downfall was inevitable: only a fool imitates Martin Luther King when his opposition is Savior Karama." Beneath his contempt, Freedom's tone was imperative. "We did not scheme to give Karama a pretext, and he did not require one. I want you to understand that."

Hearing this, Pierce relaxed a little; whatever else was at stake in this conversation, it was not Pierce's life. "Why does it matter?" he asked.

"Because of the Western press. When you returned to America, you caused a considerable stir. If Okari becomes a martyr, I do not want FREE to share the blame that should be Karama's alone. So listen well." Leaning forward on the log, Freedom spoke intensely. "There's the genuine FREE, and then there are groups that cloak their actions in our name. But we do *nothing* in the delta that I would be embarrassed to claim.

"We do not lynch defenseless oil workers; we kidnap their masters. Kidnapping is profitable. Murder is bad for our business in every sense." Freedom's voice became stern. "Nor are we the cat's-paw of Islamists. I've converted to Islam— that much is true. I share Al Qaeda's aspiration to fight those who would perpetuate our slavery by stealing our oil. But bin Laden's struggle in the Middle East has refocused America's avarice on us. Our sole concern is gaining control of the only asset that can end our misery and oppression."

As Freedom spoke, some of his followers came

closer, listening intently. Pierce took stock of his own impressions: this was a man of blunt charisma and, he guessed, considerable intelligence. But in the service of what or whom, he could not guess. "Control?" he asked. "How does kidnapping and extortion profit anyone but you?" *Or whoever gives your orders,* Pierce thought but did not say.

Freedom's eyes lit with contempt. "As opposed to speeches, slogans, and marching unarmed Asaris to the slaughter? Okari's day is done; I do not need him dead. With every act of 'kidnapping and extortion' we recruit more men and buy more arms. Soon we, not Karama, will effectively control the delta; soon he will understand that Okimbo cannot save him."

"I thought Okimbo was your friend."

Freedom stopped abruptly, his body tensing as he seemed to measure Pierce anew. "We have many friends," he answered. "Friendship follows fear. Someday Karama will give us what we want, or he will lose his country. If you ever meet our president, tell him that."

"Tell him yourself," Pierce answered. "You didn't bring me here to say that, and I didn't come to hear it."

Freedom's eyes drilled into Pierce's. "We did not hang those workers," he said succinctly.

"Then who did?"

Freedom leaned closer. "There is a witness. Follow instructions, and he will come to you."

Abruptly, the man stood. "In the meanwhile, you will stay here for the night. I have another message, this one for Karama. I do not wish for you to spoil it."

10

PIERCE SPENT THE NIGHT ON A WOVEN MAT SPREAD across the floor of a mud hut. He did not sleep; his thoughts were shadowed by the image of a dead man, brains seeping from his skull, and the burial that followed. Outside he heard footsteps and voices giving orders—the sounds, novel to Pierce but unmistakable, of a military operation unfolding in the dead of night. When morning came, Freedom was gone, the encampment virtually deserted.

The reader of Mao stuck his head through the door. "Come with me," he said with quiet disgust. "On this day of days, my contribution is returning you to Okari's wife unharmed."

THE TRIP THROUGH the delta, ominous but uneventful, culminated with two militiamen—unhooded and innocuous in appearance—dropping Pierce at the landing where his journey had begun.

Bara waited in the car. "So," he said dryly. "You're alive after all."

"By accident," Pierce retorted, and outlined what had happened. "FREE's up to something," he concluded. "That's all I know for sure. We're left with Freedom's version of the truth, waiting for a 'witness' about whom we know nothing."

IT WAS DUSK when Pierce reached the Okaris' compound.

Marissa was on the patio. She turned at the sound of his footsteps; for a moment she simply looked at him, and then her smile became the grin Pierce had not seen for twelve years. She stood there, shaking her head. "It's just so strange," she told him. "Everything's terrible. Suddenly I'm smiling like a madwoman because you're still alive."

Pierce put his hands on his hips. "You set the bar pretty low."

"In a minute, I'll go back to being miserable." Her voice softened. "While you were gone, I couldn't sleep or eat. For weeks now, every time the phone rings or someone knocks on a door, my first instinct is that Bobby's dead. For the last twenty-four hours I've included you."

"Well, I'm back," Pierce said gently. Neither of them, he realized, had made any move to touch the other.

SHORTLY MARISSA BROUGHT out two candles, a bowl of pasta primavera, and a bottle of passable red wine. "Bobby stopped drinking," she explained. "He called alcohol 'the waste of a clear-headed hour.'"

343

Pierce sipped the wine. "I have less far to fall," he said, and told her about General Freedom. "It bothers me," he finished, "how much he seems to know about what I'm thinking."

Gazing at the candles, Marissa did not comment. "Whatever he tells you to do," she said finally, "I'm doing it with you."

"Too dangerous," Pierce objected.

"Luandia is dangerous," she replied. "I understand it far better than you can. Whatever you hear from whoever this is, I want to hear it too."

For the moment, Pierce chose not to argue. As they began eating, he realized that he was ravenous.

After dinner, they stood gazing out at the ocean—the tankers waiting offshore, the distant lights of Petrol Island. Their conversation turned to Pierce's life in America, and then to his parents. "They're both dead now," he told her. "But after my dad died, I actually got to know my mother."

"Because she was free to speak?"

"It was more subtle than that. I'm sure she always had opinions; it was just that no one but my father knew them. Once he was gone, I realized that—within the limits imposed by religion and her natural antipathy toward psychological analysis—she was an acute observer of her children and their lives." He remembered his own bemusement. "Know what she said about Amy? 'I knew she'd never want children—Amy's her own

344

creation, and perfecting that is all she cares about.' That the remark encapsulates Mom's anti-feminist bias didn't keep it from being true."

Marissa glanced at him. "Do you still want children?"

"Yes. Even more now that I'm older and feel a little less likely to commit malpractice. Parenting means you have to look hard at yourself to keep from screwing up a child. But whatever my parents' flaws, I know they loved us unreservedly. What a joy it must be to feel that for another human being."

They fell silent for a time. In the light of flaring gas, Pierce saw—or thought he saw—the outlines of several powerboats moving across the water with unusual swiftness. Then Marissa said, "You'd be a good father, Damon."

Pierce turned to her. "Why do you say that?"

"Part of it is the capacity to love, which I know you have. But another part is detachment: the ability to see another person—in this case, your child—as someone whose needs are separate from your own. I saw that in you a long time ago."

To his surprise, Pierce felt touched. "Thanks," he said lightly. "Amy's greatest compliment was that I excelled at trial tactics."

After a time they turned to Marissa's life: her mother, shadowed by ill health; her final break with her father, less a dramatic rupture than the last expression of his vast, incurable indifference; then, briefly and touchingly, Omo—for whom, though Marissa did not say this, her feelings had become maternal. They did not speak of Bobby; it was plain she did not wish to. It came to Pierce that in some recess of her soul Marissa was alone. Even when they were quiet, she made no move to leave. "It's getting late," he finally said. "Time to check my e-mail."

A muffled explosion made Pierce start an instant before he heard Marissa's brief cry of astonishment. Rising above Petrol Island, an enormous ball of flame transformed the night to amber. "Liquid gas," she said tightly. "Oil can't blow up like that."

For moments they watched the inferno light up Petrol Island. Pierce thought of the fleeting image of speedboats on the water, and then his cell phone rang.

It was Bara. "Tell Marissa to turn on the radio," he said quickly. "FREE is broadcasting on the government station."

Pierce repeated this to Marissa. She led him to her bedroom and turned on the sound system. "FREE has blown up PGL's liquid gas facilities," the voice of General Freedom was announcing, "and kidnapped three engineers, using female loyalists pretending to be prostitutes." Freedom laughed. "PGL hoped to screw Luandians, and instead Luandians screwed them. Now our fighters have 'borrowed' Karama's radio station to explain to PGL that its workers will not be safe anywhere in the delta or at sea until the government meets our just demands: reparations, restoration, and rebuilding." His voice rose. "Free the people," he cried out, and then the station went dead.

Taking Marissa's hand, Pierce returned to the patio.

The ball had receded to a low flickering fire, the embers of Michael Gladstone's prototype for the elimination of flaring. Pierce considered many things: this irony in FREE's chosen target; the boldness of its tactics; the failure of Okimbo and the army to protect critical facilities; the impact on Karama. Then another thought struck Pierce so forcibly that he hurried to his laptop, Marissa following.

"What is it?" she asked.

Swiftly, he read an e-mail from Rachel Rahv: during his deposition, Trevor Hill had professed to know very little, conceding his stated doubts about Okimbo but adding nothing Pierce and Rachel did not already know. Then Pierce clamped on earphones and Skyped his law school roommate, Jeff Schlosser. Waiting, Pierce told Marissa, "My pal is chief of enforcement for the Commodities Futures Trading Commission."

Schlosser, it transpired, still answered his own phone. "Jeff? It's Damon."

"You sound harassed," Schlosser answered. "Where are you?"

"Back in Luandia. I'd like you to look at some-thing."

"What?"

"Unusual trading patterns in oil futures, someone placing big bets on a price rise. Key it to two events bound to drive up the price of crude oil per barrel. The first is the lynching of three PGL oil workers in Asariland about six weeks ago. I just witnessed the second: the explosion of a PGL facility on an island off the delta. I'd particularly like to know if someone positioned themselves to make a killing on both."

Schlosser sounded perplexed. "Got anything more?"

"Maybe a name. See if whatever entity bought the futures is tied to an American named Henry Karlin."

"What's this about, Damon?"

"Maybe nothing. Or maybe a particularly ambi-tious form of insider trading: someone who knows in advance about disasters that affect the world price of oil."

Schlosser paused. "Even if there's something there, I may not be able to tell you much."

"Whatever you can, Jeff—as soon as you can. Someone's life may ride on this."

Schlosser did not ask. When Pierce signed off, he saw another e-mail.

"Enjoy the show?" Jomo said. "Instructions to follow."

DEEP IN THE NIGHT, PIERCE SAT ALONE ON THE patio, absorbing all that had happened since he had first come to Luandia.

His sense of respite with Marissa—a brief flight to "normality"—had vanished with the explosion on Petrol Island. Now images disturbed his consciousness like the aftershocks of a nightmare: the wasted wilderness of the delta; the ruins of Goro; the horrors of Bobby's imprisonment; Karama's expressionless image on an enormous screen; Okimbo's abuse of Marissa; meeting a frightened soldier in a waste dump; the murder of a stranger by unknown militiamen; e-mails from a phantom whose intentions were as obscure as what might happen the next day. Yesterday, Pierce could have died. This was the reality he had chosen.

Jomo's last e-mail had said only that Pierce must travel to a town called Raha and wait in a hotel for more instructions. Marissa was insisting on going with him. "I understand the people," she had told him tautly. "I know the Asari dialect. I'm tired of waiting for other people to save my husband, or to kill him. My role now is to help you."

"How?" he had asked.

"By giving you second sight." She grasped his hands. "You're functioning on instinct without any basis for your instincts. God knows who General

Freedom is allied with. You think maybe Okimbo or Ajukwa or even Roos Van Daan; I think he's had tentacles into the Asari movement long before Goro. Together both of us may be less blind."

"Remember your airplane metaphor?" Pierce answered. "Go with me to Raha, and we're flying in the same plane. If the worst happens, who'd be left for Bobby?"

Marissa's eyes met his. "Yesterday, waiting for you, the worst happened to me a thousand times."

For a moment, Pierce was silent. "And the state security services?" he asked.

"Will follow you with or without me. Unless this is a trap, FREE will have a plan." Her tone was level and determined. "Except for Bara, our Luandian friends are underground now—all we can do is send each other e-mails we delete before we dare to answer. You still have the freedom to act. If I don't go with you, I'm in prison, too."

Pierce grasped Marissa's misery. Only action kept the darkness he felt at bay; when it was impossible to know the right course from the wrong one, all that remained was fatalism. Then there was this: he did not wish to be alone.

"All right," he said at last. "Get some sleep."

Now it was two o'clock. Perhaps she had succeeded; Pierce had not. This lack of sleep was troublesome—it made him question whatever judgment he still possessed. Not that it seemed to matter.

He went to bed, trying to remember his life

before Luandia. At last he slept. When he awakened, dawn had broken, and Marissa was touching his shoulder. "It's time," she said.

THEY DROVE TOWARD Raha, Marissa taking a rutted road that tested her nerves and reflexes. In profile, her sculpted face was intent, her keen eyes alert to difficulty. Movement seemed to help her: she seemed a mature version of the woman he had met at Berkeley, tempered by time and trouble.

Now and then she glanced in the rearview mirror. No one seemed to follow them. Perhaps they did not need to; Pierce no longer knew what anything meant.

Four hours later, with little said between them, Pierce and Marissa crossed the bridge to Raha.

If this had been frontier Oklahoma, Raha might have qualified as a boomtown. Since a recent oil strike, shacks and a ramshackle hotel had sprung up; on the outer limits of town, PGL had built a compound for its executives, crammed with modular housing. But the creeklands surrounded it and therefore danger. Though jeeps filled with soldiers patrolled the town, Pierce saw no white men on the streets.

They checked into adjacent rooms, making plans to meet for dinner. Pierce gave Marissa the shriek alarm to wedge beneath her door. He kept the handgun, Vorster's gift, in the duffel bag he carried with him.

• • •

Shortly before eight, they met in a sparsely populated dining room with woven mats on lacquered tables. "Any messages?" she asked with muted anxiety.

"Only an e-mail from Grayson Caraway: State is letting him ask to visit Bobby, and he's met with Karama's foreign minister. What's embarrassing to the U.S. and PGL, Caraway argues, is also bad for Karama. Like torture—"

"Or kangaroo courts?" she interjected tartly. "I thought they were merely weapons in the global war on terror."

Pierce frowned. "It's a problem," he acknowledged. "Karama is taunting Caraway with the secret prisons and special courts we've used since 9/11. But the ambassador's real problem is three dead men. It's hard for State to campaign for Bobby's release when we can't prove he's innocent."

Marissa picked at her food. "So where are we?"

Pierce considered his answer. Though they had sorted through all the pieces, in her anxiety Marissa kept trying to fit them together in her mind, as though obsessive reexamination would yield a new pattern. "My overall thinking," Pierce began, "is that the murders were a pretext for the massacre, and that therefore the same person—or people—planned them both. The obvious motive is eliminating Bobby and crushing the Asari movement. The obvious unanswered question is, Who wanted that the most?"

"Karama," she said tightly. "And Okimbo."

"Also FREE, which scorns nonviolence. Maybe Van Daan, or even others from PGL—"

"They'd hang their own people?"

Pierce glanced around: their nearest neighbors, two white men, were absorbed in conversation. "But who *are* Van Daan's people?" he inquired. "Does he work for PGL, Ajukwa, or both? I still don't know.

"That's the problem—we know nothing about the lynchings, and all we know about the massacre is that it happened. Except for you and Bobby, our only witness is a soldier whose testimony we can't compel. And he's the only one who places Van Daan—or at least someone who looks like him—anywhere near Goro."

This summary, though no surprise, seemed to distress Marissa. She looked down at the table, her eyes half shut. Pierce tried to console her. "There's also public relations," he said. "Your friends in America's human rights community are trying to pressure the U.S. and PGL. That's the purpose of our lawsuit: PGL doesn't want to be found liable for Karama's and Okimbo's crimes. If it looks to PGL like we can prove that they knew—or should have known—what would happen at Goro, it may try to salvage Bobby before the case gets any worse. Trevor Hill's deposition takes us closer: he warned Gladstone about Okimbo before the massacre. What we need is concrete proof tying Van Daan to Goro."

"And the thing about oil futures?"

"Is a flier. We know that Ajukwa is tied to Van Daan; that Van Daan may be tied to Okimbo; and that Okimbo may have ties to General Freedom. If someone linked to Ajukwa knew that those oil workers would be lynched, and then that FREE would raid Petrol Island, who told him? All I know for sure is that it could *not* be Bobby Okari."

Marissa's shoulders turned in, as though to ward off a chill. "When we were at Berkeley," she said at last, "I never imagined anything like this."

"That's life," Pierce responded gently. "It happens a little at a time, until you can't go back. No point in regretting what no one could foresee."

Though casually made, the remark seemed to trigger fresh pain. For an instant, Marissa struggled for composure, then covered Pierce's hand with hers. "I need to sleep," she said. But what Pierce heard was that she wished to be alone.

"Do that," Pierce said. "I'll wake you if something happens."

When they went upstairs and Marissa closed the door, Pierce waited until he heard the click of her locks.

• • •

HE HAD RECEIVED no e-mails.

The room was depressing—at once shabby and stark, with the desk light burned out and broken window blinds that obscured Pierce's view of the darkening creeklands. He had never felt so alone.

Shirtless and in jeans, he lay across the bed waiting for something to happen. The minutes on his wristwatch, becoming hours, passed with excruciating slowness. He began checking his e-mail at fifteen-minute intervals.

He thought of Marissa. What he had last seen on her face, he sensed, transcended fear for Bobby: it was a sadness so profound that she could not bear to speak it. But he had no way to touch her and sensed it would be cruel to try.

The shrillness of a shriek alarm jolted him upright.

For an instant he was transported to America, imagining a parked car gone berserk. Then he knew that the sound came from Marissa's room.

Heading for the door, he stopped abruptly and unzipped the duffel bag with clumsy fingers. Then he burst into the hallway with the gun in hand.

Marissa's door was open. Through the crack he saw her bare leg on the carpet, the rest of her blocked from view by a man bending over her. Pierce hesitated, then softly pushed the door open.

The man was dressed as a soldier. Though Marissa wore only a bra and panties, he appeared to be pulling her upward. Her face was filled with terror. A second soldier, in glasses, backed away, staring wide-eyed at Pierce as he reached for his holstered gun. *"Stop!"* Pierce shouted, and the second soldier froze.

The first man, turning, looked at Pierce in surprise. Marissa was breathing hard; Pierce fought to keep his gun steady, aiming at the soldier with glasses. They were both young; suddenly Pierce remembered Clellan and the area boys. "Get out," he ordered them. "Both of you. Or I'll make your heads disappear."

Pierce had never imagined killing a man before. For Marissa, he could: his voice was surprisingly calm. Standing aside from the door, Pierce glanced from one man to the other.

Slowly, the man holding Marissa released her.

More speech was superfluous, instinct told Pierce; what mattered was an air of certainty. He angled his head toward the door.

The man in glasses let his arm drop to his side. Cautiously eyeing Pierce, he walked to the first man and pushed him toward the door. Briefly glancing at Pierce, the soldier in glasses followed. Pierce heard their footsteps in the dim hallway, not hurrying, as though they were guests themselves.

Still watching the door, Pierce extended his left hand to Marissa. Pulling herself up, she half-leaned against him, seemingly aware that she should not block his view. "Bring your stuff," he said.

Briefly, she pressed her face against his shoulder. Then she went to her suitcase and retrieved a cotton nightshirt. Hurriedly, she closed her bag. Taking her hand, Pierce led her into the hallway, holding his gun as she rolled the suitcase behind her.

Despite the shriek alarm, the hall was empty. There was no sign that anyone at the hotel cared about what had happened. Pierce glanced through his open door. Seeing no one, he said, "You first."

She complied. Backing in, Pierce closed and locked the door, replacing the shriek alarm. Then he began wrestling the chest of drawers over to block it. Marissa came to help him. When they had finished, he asked, "Was that a kidnapping?"

Marissa shook her head in confusion; it struck him that she had yet to speak. When he sat on the edge of the bed, placing the gun beside him, he realized the safety was still on.

Bending forward, Pierce touched the bridge of his nose.

His stomach felt empty. Marissa began to speak, and then could not. A single tear ran down her face.

Softly, Pierce said, "I've never seen you cry before."

Marissa shook her head. In a muffled voice, she said, "It's not because of them."

Pierce waited. When she spoke again, she did not

look at him, and her voice was flat but clear. "Before Asari Day, I told Bobby how afraid for him I was. What a wife would say to a husband.

"'Then promise me,' he answered. 'If I die, make sure the world does not forget me or the Asari—what we have suffered, why we tried to fight. Please, Marissa, make them remember.'" Briefly, Marissa's eyes shut. "That was what we'd become. The movement had consumed us—our marriage, as a marriage, had ceased to exist. But I was still his wife. So I promised."

Her last few words, Pierce realized, explained everything.

After a time, he pulled the covers back, placing the gun on the nightstand. Marissa slipped in beside him.

Turning out the light, he kissed her on the forehead. "I was born lucky, remember? So maybe you can sleep."

Time passed in the darkness. Pierce listened for sounds; Marissa, he thought, slept. Then he felt her stirring.

"Are you okay?" he asked.

Silently she touched his face, then brought her mouth to his.

She kissed him softly, her lips still closed, as though this were an experiment. Pierce felt himself respond, and then their lips opened.

At last she drew back. By unspoken consent, tender but urgent, they helped each other undress.

Then their bodies came together, overcome by a craving that felt years deep. Without hesitance or prompting, their mouths found the places they both desired.

When at last Pierce slipped inside her, Marissa's arms went tight around him. "Damon," she murmured with a kind of wonder.

Then neither one could speak. Only after she cried out again, this time from the depths of her, did Marissa repeat his name. "Now you, Damon. Now you."

Afterward, they held each other close. "In the morning," she said softly, "I'll still be his wife."

And I'll still be his lawyer, Pierce thought. "I know," he answered, and then his cell phone rang.

12

SITTING UP IN THE DARKNESS, PIERCE FLIPPED open his cell phone. "Yes?"

"Damon? It's Jeff Schlosser."

Pierce hesitated; intent on FREE, he had not thought of his call to Schlosser. He felt Marissa behind him, her face on his shoulder. "What time is it in D.C.?" he asked.

"Ten at night—I just got home." There was a brief silence. "We need an understanding, pal. We can't make CFTC investigative files public until we either file a case or close one. What I'm about to tell you didn't come from us."

"All right."

"I personally looked at our tracking data. Your guy Henry Karlin turns out to be a *very* major fund-raiser for our incumbent president and a frequent White House guest. But he's also, one might say, extremely lucky."

Pierce stood and began to pace. "In oil futures?"

"Yup. He bought a slew of futures two days before those lynchings, then cashed in the morning after, to the tune of seven million dollars. He also bought futures four days before the raid on Petrol Island. Yesterday, when the world price per barrel spiked another six bucks a barrel, he exercised his futures contract to buy two and a half million barrels for six dollars less. Then he sold at the new market price. For the math challenged, that's another fifteen million dollars in profit."

"Were there any developments outside Luandia that would lead a speculator like Karlin to buy up oil futures when he did?"

"Not that I can see. And there's something else: three months ago, Karlin made his initial killing. You familiar with a group called FREE?"

In the darkness, Pierce sat again, taking Marissa's hand. "That's the group that raided Petrol Island."

"Thought so. A week after Karlin's first big bet on futures, FREE blew up two of PGL's pumping stations and kidnapped its chief petroleum engineer." Schlosser's voice was edgy with excitement. "You've got three crisis-type events in Luandia, two clearly tied to FREE. The other—those lynchings—allegedly involves your client Okari. But Karlin cashed in after every one."

The implications of this struck Pierce so forcefully that he was silent.

"So what do you make of it?" Schlosser prodded.

"The same thing you do. It looks like someone told Karlin in advance of militia actions against PGL, maybe someone with ties to FREE. It couldn't be Okari—when Petrol Island blew up, Bobby was in prison. Which leaves this question: who knew before it happened that those workers would be lynched?"

"Maybe whoever lynched them," Schlosser said impassively. "Good luck."

Shutting his phone, Pierce faced Marissa. "What is it?" she asked.

Pierce told her. "The most benign assumption," he concluded, "is that someone within FREE is part of a chain of informants that leads to Henry Karlin. The darkest is that FREE planned the lynchings in advance."

Though he could not clearly see her face, Pierce sensed Marissa reflecting. "Maybe," she said. "Or maybe the person passing information to Karlin has ties to FREE *and* whoever hung the men we saw at the end of Asari Day."

The last phrase reminded Pierce of all that she

had suffered in six weeks' time. "Yes," he quietly agreed. "It could work like that."

In their silence, his cell phone rang again. When he flipped it open, a man asked in Luandian-accented English, "Do you not read your e-mail?" Then the line went dead.

Quickly, Pierce switched on his laptop. Marissa stood beside him, her naked body illuminated by the glow from Pierce's screen. When he turned to her, a reflex, she gazed back at him, neither proud nor shy. Then he summoned Jomo's e-mail.

Its instructions were terse: Pierce was to leave the hotel at once and walk to a bar with a neon Heineken beer sign in its window. "Are you still going?" Marissa asked.

Pierce turned to her. "I have to."

"Then so do I."

They dressed together. The strangeness of the moment, with its semblance of domesticity, went unremarked. Only when Pierce put the handgun in his duffel bag did Marissa say softly, "Thank you for saving my life. Or at least from something terrible."

Pierce managed a smile. "As I said, I'm lucky."

Briefly, Marissa kissed him. When she drew away, still looking at his face, Pierce knew it to be a valedictory. They had acknowledged a desire that, whatever else occurred, could not be satisfied again. "Leave the suitcase," Pierce said. "Hopefully we'll be back."

IT WAS PAST four o'clock in the morning. The hallway was empty, the hotel lobby quiet. Once again, Pierce wondered if the uniformed intruders were truly soldiers, and how many hotel employees they had paid off to ignore them. Then he and Marissa walked outside.

There was no one on the pitch-dark street. The only light, perhaps a hundred feet to the right, was a beer sign glowing in the window of an empty bar.

Pierce turned toward it, duffel bag in one hand, Marissa's fingers in the other.

Suddenly, from around a corner, the headlights of a jeep appeared, moving toward them like the eyes of a malevolent bug. As the jeep passed the beer sign, Pierce saw the outlines of raised weapons brandished by four soldiers. He and Marissa froze.

The jeep kept coming, impaling them on its headlights. Three feet away, brakes squeaking, it skidded to a stop.

The soldier in the front passenger seat was drinking from a whiskey bottle. The driver, young but cadaverous, leapt from the jeep and walked toward Pierce and Marissa with suspicion burning in his eyes. Stepping in front of Marissa, Pierce faced him.

The man's voice was harsh. "So, *oyibo,* what is your business at this hour? Nothing good, I think."

Pierce thought of the gun in his duffel bag, so

easily a pretext for their arrest. "Nothing at all," he answered.

"This does not impress me. Show what's in your bag."

Pierce knew it would be foolish to resist. Then a deep voice from behind them said, "These are my friends."

As the speaker stepped into the headlights, Pierce recognized the man from the Rhino Bar. Calmly, he took a wad of Luandian bills from his back pocket, holding it out to the soldier. "They are also visitors from America."

The soldier looked from the man to Pierce, a series of calculations showing in his eyes. Seconds passed. Then he took the money from the stranger's outstretched hand. "And for *her*?" he pressed.

The man from the Rhino produced a few more bills. Counting them, the soldier inquired, "That's all?"

"She's smaller," the stranger replied with quiet authority.

Turning, the soldier said something to his companions. Then he got in the jeep and drove away, the soldier in the passenger seat again tipping the whiskey bottle to his lips.

"Come with me," the man from the Rhino directed.

A nondescript Honda was parked near the bar. Edgy, Marissa got in the back seat, glancing up at

Pierce. He shut her door and slid in front beside their guide.

The man from the Rhino drove for minutes in the direction from which the soldiers had come. Just before the road ended, he swerved right, toward a grove of trees, so sharply that Marissa cried out before the car slipped through the foliage onto a concealed path. They went deeper into the palms and mangroves, perhaps two hundred yards. Then the headlights captured a dilapidated shack beneath a corrugated roof. Stopping the car, the man abruptly told Pierce, "Go inside."

Bara trusted this man, Pierce thought, and it was too late to wonder whether he should trust Bara. Nodding toward Marissa, Pierce said, "She comes with me."

Together, they left the car and walked toward the shed, Pierce holding the duffel bag. The door was ajar, emitting a soft glow. Pierce entered before Marissa.

In a chair to one side sat a man holding a gas lantern in one hand and a gun in the other. The man raised his gun, aiming at Pierce's head, and Pierce suddenly knew he would die in Luandia. He almost said, "Don't shoot," then realized how pointless this would be.

"I *know* you," Marissa told the man.

Eyes still on Pierce, he lowered his gun. "Yes, madam."

"Do you have something for us?"

Slowly, the man placed the weapon in his lap, putting the lamp on the floor beside him. In its light, Pierce saw that he, too, was young, with liquid brown eyes in a sensitive face. "My name is Sunday Opuba," he told Marissa. "My loyalty is to FREE. I joined the Asari movement to learn whatever I could. So I made it my business to cultivate friendships, smoking weed and hanging out in bars. Two guys I spent time with were Moses Tulu and Lucky Joba—"

"From Ela," Marissa said.

"Yes. Three weeks ago we were in the bar there. Your husband had been arrested; there were many rumors about Goro. We drank much gin. But Joba kept watching me, more keenly than before. Finally, he said, 'We all know Okari's finished.'

" 'Yes?' I asked.

" 'Yes,' Joba said, like it was settled. 'But there may be a way for us to profit from it.' When I asked him how, he said, 'You should meet the one-eyed colonel.' "

Pierce glanced at Marissa. Calmly, she said, "Go on."

"Two nights later Joba and Tulu drove me to the barracks at Port George. I was frightened—when the soldiers let us in, everything was dark, and I could hear a prisoner screaming." Briefly, Sunday could not look at Marissa. "The officer with us laughed and said it sounded like your husband. But I do not think it was."

Marissa's face showed nothing. "What happened then?" she prodded.

"We went inside the prison to an office. At once I knew Okimbo by his eye patch. The *oyibo* with him was a stranger who did not give his name."

Pierce felt the tingle of anticipation. "What did he look like?"

"He was big—not fat, but broad. His hair was blond with gray. But mostly it was the colonel who spoke to us." Sunday looked somberly at Marissa. "They needed witnesses against your husband, he said, to prove what they already knew.

"I was scared, wishing to get out. Then Okimbo turns to Joba, saying, 'Tell him.'

"Before Asari Day, Joba says, he was waiting outside Bobby's home in Goro. He heard Bobby on his cell phone. 'There must be deaths now,' he tells me Bobby said. 'There are repair crews in the field—who dies doesn't matter, only that it's done.'" Pausing, Sunday told Marissa, "It's like he's telling a story. But then Tulu says he heard this, too."

In the yellow light of the lamp, Marissa's expression did not change. "So then Okimbo asked you to become a witness."

"Yes, madam."

"What exactly did he say?"

"That now I knew your husband was guilty as charged. But his lawyers would call Tulu and Joba liars. That was why they needed me to corroborate their story."

"How did you answer?"

"That my fellow Asari would see me as a traitor." Sunday glanced at Pierce. "The white man said there'd be money for me—fifteen thousand American, five before the trial, ten after. Then he laughed and said, 'Why fear the Asari? They do not believe in violence.'"

Anger surfaced briefly in Marissa's eyes. "Did you agree?"

"No. I told them I was in my village all the days before Asari Day. Too many people would remember." Sunday bit his lip. "When I saw Okimbo's face I promised to say nothing.

"'You *will* say nothing,' he told me. 'That much I can promise you.' When he picked up the phone, I felt like I would piss my pants. 'Take him away,' Okimbo says.

"The soldiers came for me. When they took me toward the gallows, I was sure that I would die. Then they took me to the front gate and pushed me into the street."

"And your friends?" Marissa asked.

Sunday shook his head. "I stayed away from them. Instead I came to General Freedom."

Pierce stepped forward. "Is this the truth?"

"Yes." Slowly the man looked up at Marissa. "I will swear to it in court. You may find me through the man who drove you."

Without saying more, he stood, nodding to Marissa, and walked out the door. Quiet, they watched until the light of his lantern vanished in the foliage.

"Van Daan," Pierce murmured.

"Yes." Marissa's voice was etched with doubt. "Unless he's lying."

It was five days until the trial.

The Last Dawn

1

O N THE MORNING OKARI'S TRIAL COMMENCED, Atiku Bara drove Pierce and Marissa to the courthouse in Port George.

The building was a remnant of British rule, a staid Edwardian structure surrounded by Okimbo's soldiers. The few demonstrators who'd braved the government's disapproval were thwarted by a system of military roadblocks that controlled access to the courthouse, admitting only a trickle of foreign journalists, human rights workers, diplomatic personnel, and, observing for PGL, Clark Hamilton. Pierce's mood was grim. In the past five days, little had changed: Beke Femu—the soldier-witness to Goro—had vanished, as had Sunday Opuba, the spy for FREE, and Pierce had been forced to seek a week's delay in asking Judge Taylor to enjoin PGL from allegedly colluding in Bobby's prosecution. Nor had Caraway's diplomatic efforts, as far as Pierce could tell, succeeded in blunting Karama's resolve to rid himself of Bobby. And so, as Rachel and their associates had labored in Waro, Pierce had prepared for a grotesque distortion of the judicial process, certain only that whatever happened would be as Karama ordained. In only days or weeks, Bobby might be dead.

That knowledge shadowed Pierce's interactions

with Marissa. Though they treated each other with kindness, an unspoken sense of betrayal seemed to haunt them both: the knowledge that Bobby's lawyer and his wife desired each other was, in light of his prospective fate, painful beyond words. Pierce's fear that his judgment was compromised, his motives tangled, caused him to ruthlessly censor any thought of his relationship with Marissa outside or beyond the trial. Now, with Bara, they passed through the checkpoints and barricades in silence.

Arriving at the courthouse, they saw a Black Maria waiting, a steel truck with darkened windows evocative of a hearse. As they exited Bara's sedan, two soldiers opened the door of the Black Maria. Stiffly, Bobby Okari stepped out, his hands manacled, his movements resembling those of an old man no longer certain of his balance. Seeing Marissa on the other side of the barricade, he gave her a smile so bright and brave that it seared Pierce just to see it. Then the soldiers took both his arms, half-dragging him up the courthouse steps before his wife could reach him. He turned his head to see her; Marissa smiled back at him until he vanished inside, and then briefly closed her eyes. Pierce had never entered a courtroom with such foreboding.

THE WORLD OF a trial, Pierce had long ago learned, is hermetic, its ruthless imperatives consuming every resource he possessed. But every trial has its own peculiar character. The trial of Bobby Okari, Pierce knew at once, would be as bleak as it was unjust.

One factor was the courtroom itself: once a temple of the law—with tall windows, wooden floors, and a judge's mahogany bench—it had fallen into disrepair, the floors worn, the air-conditioning groaning, the lights flickering at random. Worse was the presence of soldiers stationed on all sides; worst was that Okimbo sprawled in the jury box with an air of command, like the silent impresario of a drama with its end already written. Sitting beside Pierce, Bobby murmured, "Okimbo's the jury. These judges are on trial, too."

They seemed to know this. In the moments before the trial commenced, the presiding judge, George Orta, glanced at Okimbo with an apprehension at odds with his air of gravity. In another setting, Pierce would have found his appearance laughable: a sour-faced man in a three-piece suit topped by a black bowler, he reminded Pierce uncomfortably of an undertaker from an era long since past. The judge to Orta's left, Sidney Uza, was an elderly man so thin that he appeared in the grip of a wasting disease. The more robust member of the tribunal, Colonel Yakubu Nubola—a man without legal training who served to represent Karama's interests—wore a purple beret, combat fatigues, and a seemingly permanent scowl.

Eyeing them, Bobby murmured, "The faces of justice," and began scribbling on a notepad.

Rising from the jury box, Okimbo held up his hand to Orta, signaling that matters would be held in abeyance. He paused in the well of the courtroom, giving Marissa a look that bespoke a lascivious remembrance. Then he walked to the prosecutor, Patric Ngara, placing both hands on the table and speaking so that only Ngara could hear. Ngara, a lean, mustached man whose air of professionalism could not conceal the anxiety of a functionary who could not afford to err, listened intently. Pierce suspected that this conference was less important for its substance than its reminder that Karama, through Okimbo, controlled the fate of everyone involved.

Nodding curtly to Orta, Okimbo went back to the jury box. For an instant, humiliation surfaced in the presiding judge's eyes; by reputation a once distinguished jurist, he had been recast as Karama's puppet in a procedure that mocked every tenet of the system of justice, founded in English law, in which he had risen. The genius of an autocracy, Pierce supposed, was that fear reduced most men to a cowardly commonality. But not the man Pierce was defending.

He placed his hand on Bobby's arm, a gesture of support. A court reporter entered with a stenotype machine, and then a courtroom deputy intoned, "The special tribunal in the matter of Robert Okari is now in session. God bless this tribunal and the sovereign nation of Luandia."

Expressionless, Orta spoke; only his lips, seeming barely to move, marred Pierce's impression of a waxworks dummy. In a deep voice, he said, "You may enter your appearances."

Ngara stood. "Patric Ngara, Your Honor, on behalf of the people of Luandia."

Orta turned to Pierce and Bara. "Atiku Bara on behalf of the defendant," Bara said. "With me is Damon Pierce, an eminent trial lawyer from the United States. I ask that the court admit him to practice before it for the sole purpose of representing Mr. Okari."

Orta inspected Pierce like a frog contemplating a bug. "Can you assure this court that you will conduct yourself in a manner consistent with its dignity?"

In its perhaps unintended irony, the question tempted Pierce to suggest that it was impossible to answer. Instead he responded smoothly, "Of course, Your Honor. Beginning with the appropriate devotion to the rights of my client."

Though Orta's lips opened, it was a moment before they emitted a sound. "Very well, Mr. Pierce. But the nature of those rights will be determined by this tribunal."

"I would like to address that now," Pierce responded promptly. "To protect those rights, I ask that the tribunal postpone this trial for six months' time."

Orta remained impassive. "On what grounds?"

"Several. We have no witness list from Mr. Ngara, nor a summary of the evidence against Mr. Okari. We've been denied adequate access to our client, as well as sufficient time to prepare a defense." Pausing, Pierce concluded emphatically: "These are the rudiments of a fair trial, Your Honor. We cannot proceed without them."

As Ngara stood, Orta said, "Do you wish to be heard, Mr. Ngara?"

"I do. Counsel's argument is disingenuous. He is utterly aware of the charges against Bobby Okari. We have not impeded him from investigating. And if he wants to know our witnesses, we will tell him. As for the delay he seeks, an expeditious trial preserves the national security of Luandia. In perilous times, the justice system must preserve the right of a nation to defend itself against secession and sedition."

Orta nodded. To Pierce, he said, "Motion denied. The trial will proceed."

Pierce did not sit. However hopeless matters appeared, he would make his record for the world press. "There are other grounds, Your Honor." After turning briefly toward the gallery, he gathered himself, speaking quietly but clearly. "There are observers in this courtroom from around the globe. And what they are about to see, unless this trial is adjourned, is a proceeding so lacking in the basic elements of due process that it is unrecognizable as justice.

"This tribunal is empowered to take Mr. Okari's life. Yet there is no appeal from its rulings, or its verdict. Equally fatal, the tribunal is not independent of President Karama: one of its members, Colonel Nubola, is under the president's direct authority as commander in chief. *All* of its members were selected by the president himself." Seeing Orta's look of outrage, Pierce spoke to him directly. "I am aware, Justice Orta, of your distinguished career. So I know that *you* are well aware that this proceeding violates the constitution of Luandia, every human rights agreement this country has ever signed, and the basic tenets of justice that we, as lawyers, swear to uphold. The only way this court can stop these abuses is to cease to exist."

The courtroom was completely still. As Pierce sat, Bara looked apprehensive, while Bobby eyed Justice Orta with an expression of bemusement. Orta pursed his lips, his expression conveying anger and humiliation as Ngara rose to speak. "This tribunal," Ngara said firmly, "is an expression of our national sovereignty in the face of terrorism. What is the lynching of three men, if not an act of terror." He glanced at Pierce with scorn. "Mr. Pierce comes to us from America, prating about due process. On what platform of moral superiority does he propose to stand? Surely not his government's. *This* is not a secret court. *We* did not dispatch Bobby Okari to a secret prison in a foreign country. *We* did not consign him to a Guantánamo specifically designed to deprive him of rights written into the U.S. Constitution. When *we*, like America, protect our national security, we do not conceal our methods in shame." Ngara slammed his fist on the table. "*We* act here, in the open, for all to see. This tribunal is *our* answer to acts of terrorism. Let Mr. Pierce reform America."

Pierce looked at Okimbo, watching from the jury box, then snapped to a decision. "A final word, Your Honor. Mr. Ngara argues that you are proceeding 'in the open.' He might have added, 'as virtual captives, surrounded by armed soldiers and supervised by Colonel Okimbo.' The colonel is my client's sadistic jailer, the military oppressor of the delta, a central figure in this case, and, as Mr. Okari witnessed, the perpetrator of a brutal massacre. He has no business in this courtroom. He's here for one reason only: to ensure, through silent intimidation, that this court denies my client's rights and covers up his own crimes." Pierce softened his voice again. "There is only one alternative, Your Honor. To adjourn."

Okimbo stared at Pierce and then, with great deliberation, trained his gaze on Orta. "Mr. Pierce," the judge said reprovingly, "your security, and that of everyone here, is in the hands of Colonel Okimbo. Not two weeks ago, militiamen raided Port George and Petrol Island. And yet you cite the colonel's presence to sully our integrity.

"You begin poorly, Mr. Pierce. Is contempt of court among the rights you claim?"

Contempt of *this* court, Pierce wanted to say, would be impossible. Instead, he responded with a calm he did not feel. "If anything I've said suggests a lack of respect, Your Honor, let me apologize. My intention was otherwise: by asking this tribunal to uphold Mr. Okari's rights, I am expressing my respect for those among its members sworn as judges to do so. Please separate any offense I've given from your moral and legal obligation to adjourn."

With deep unhappiness, Orta studied him. Then he turned to his colleagues, asking them to confer. The three men huddled, Orta whispering to the others. Pierce was aware of witnessing a small tragedy. Orta and Uza, surely ashamed of their role, could reclaim their dignity only by adjourning. But such defiance could have great cost to them or their families and little benefit to Okari: Karama would find more compliant judges, and the only lasting consequence would be to the men they replaced. Still, from Pierce's point of view, any adjournment would buy time, and the embarrassment to Karama might, in some small way, facilitate the efforts to save Bobby. As though immune to what was happening around him, Bobby continued writing.

On the bench, Orta finished whispering. Judge Uza, the jaundiced skin of his face resembling parchment, briefly answered. With apparent vehemence, Colonel Nubola interrupted, and the conference broke up.

Facing the courtroom, Judge Orta spoke without inflection. "The motion is denied. Counsel for Mr. Okari may be assured that this proceeding will be conducted with full awareness of his client's rights."

Bobby, Pierce noted, had stopped writing and was peering intently downward; following his gaze, Pierce saw a cockroach crossing the floor between them. "Let him live," Bobby whispered. "Someone should survive this."

"The defendant will rise," Judge Orta intoned.

Bobby looked up. Sighing, he stood, not without difficulty. Though he was pitifully thin, his eyes were bright, his posture straight. "How do you plead?" Orta asked him.

"Does it matter?"

The first sound of his voice, quiet but ironic, induced utter stillness before Orta instructed, "You must answer."

"Very well." Picking up his notepad, Bobby read:

> "The judge in black clothing
> Presiding over murder disguised as farce
> His moral decrepitude
> And legal ineptitude
> Dressing a tyrant in platitudes
> Cowardice masked as law."

Bobby sat abruptly, resuming his look of emotional distance. Angrily, Orta demanded, "Do you wish to remain here? Or shall we conduct this trial without you?"

Apprehensive, Pierce stood. "My client wishes to remain, Your Honor. I ask that you enter his remarks as an elaborate plea of not guilty."

Orta scrutinized Bobby. "The defendant pleads not guilty," he pronounced at length, and the trial of Bobby Okari got under way.

2

IN THE RECESS BEFORE THE PROSECUTION BEGAN, Patric Ngara approached Pierce and Bara. "You asked for the names of witnesses. Today's are Lucky Joba and Moses Tulu."

Bara and Pierce attempted to look puzzled; it was plain Ngara knew nothing about Sunday Opuba. "Who are they?" Pierce inquired.

"Asari youths," Ngara answered with a satisfied expression. "They tie Okari to the lynchings."

Instinctively, Pierce glanced toward Bobby. But his client did not hear; he was standing close to Marissa, their foreheads touching, a portrait of tenderness and restraint. Turning away, Pierce nodded to Ngara and began scribbling.

LUCKY JOBA WAS a thin, crafty-looking man in his early twenties, with close-cropped hair and a certain twitchiness of manner—as Ngara questioned him, he kept shifting in the witness stand, as though unable to find a comfortable position. Methodically, Ngara extracted his account: that he had waited outside Bobby Okari's home in Goro, overhearing Bobby on his cell phone as he directed the murder of PGL repair workers. His climactic testimony was an almost verbatim rendition of the story Sunday Opuba had described to Pierce and Marissa. " 'We must kill them now,' " he quoted Bobby as saying. " 'There are repair crews working near us. It doesn't matter who you choose as long as it is done.' "

"He's lying," Bobby murmured to Pierce. Stone-faced, Bara scribbled notes; in the jury box, Okimbo rested his folded hands on his belly, his eye half shut, his expression satisfied and complacent.

Standing, Pierce walked toward Lucky Joba, conscious of the troubled expression on Justice Orta's face. He stopped a few feet from the witness. "When this supposed conversation happened, was anyone else with Bobby?"

Joba shifted in his chair. "I saw no one."

"What was Bobby wearing?"

Joba crossed his legs. "Why would I remember such a thing?"

"Oh, I don't know," Pierce said carelessly. "Maybe because someone told you to. Let me ask you this: who else did you tell about this conversation?"

Joba glanced at the prosecutor. "Mr. Ngara."

Pierce smiled a little. "I meant before that."

Joba gave Okimbo a surreptitious glance. "Colonel Okimbo," he said at length.

"Where did that meeting occur?"

"At the barracks in Port George."

Pierce hesitated, then decided to take a chance. "You'd seen the colonel before, hadn't you?"

Joba looked around himself, seemingly disoriented. "He came to Elu," he said at last. "To meet with Eric Aboh about peace with the Asari."

"There was also a white man with Okimbo, correct?"

"Yes."

"How would you describe him?"

Joba shrugged. "I don't know. Big, I guess."

Pierce moved closer. "With gray-blond hair?"

Joba stopped fidgeting. "Yes."

"Were you present when these men met with Eric Aboh?"

"Objection," Ngara called out. "Irrelevant. Whether the colonel met with Eric Aboh after the lynchings has nothing to do with who ordered them."

This, Pierce knew, was the first test of Judge Orta. "Your Honor, the witness's relationship with Colonel Okimbo, to whom he first told his story, has everything to do with its credibility. My client's life is at stake. So is the credibility of this proceeding. I ask the court's indulgence while I establish relevance."

For Orta to refuse, Pierce knew, would expose him as a puppet. After glancing at Okimbo, Orta instructed Joba, "You will answer."

"No," the witness said finally. "I wasn't present."

"But you heard that Okimbo and the *oyibo* gave Eric Aboh money, yes?"

Joba hesitated. "Yes."

Pierce felt another piece fall into place. "Aboh distributed some of that money among the Asari youth, didn't he."

"Eric paid us, yes."

"And told you not to follow Bobby's leadership."

"Yes."

Pierce smiled. With an air of curiosity, he asked, "How much did you make?"

Joba frowned. "I don't remember. Maybe fifty U.S."

"A pittance. By the way, did Eric Aboh pay you before or after you supposedly heard Bobby Okari order up a lynching?"

Joba seemed to examine the question for traps. "After."

"And before Aboh paid you, you hadn't told anyone at all about overhearing Mr. Okari direct the murder of PGL employees."

Joba turned to Okimbo, as if for help. With no intervention forthcoming, he answered, "No."

"Not even Mr. Aboh or any other Asari leader."

"No."

Pierce stared at him in disbelief. "Then what made you tell Okimbo rather than a fellow Asari?"

Joba fidgeted with his wristwatch. "I don't know."

"Let's return to the meeting between you, Moses Tulu, and Colonel Okimbo regarding Bobby Okari. Where did it occur?"

"The barracks in Port George. In the colonel's office."

"Who initiated the meeting—the colonel or you?"

"I did."

Pierce skipped a beat. "There was also an *oyibo* with Okimbo this time as well, true?"

Joba's eyes widened, and he looked toward Okimbo again. "The colonel can't help you," Pierce said calmly. "You'll have to pick an answer."

"Yes," Joba snapped with open hostility. "There was an *oyibo*."

"The same man who had come with Okimbo and paid Eric Aboh money?"

"Yes."

"Is his name Roos Van Daan?"

Joba crossed his arms. "I don't know his name."

"But you *do* know that he works for PGL."

Joba hesitated. "I think so, yes. This is what I heard in Elu."

"Okay. What happened at this meeting with Okimbo and this white man?"

Joba's shrug resembled a tic. Cautiously, he said, "I told them what I overheard Bobby saying."

Half-turning, Pierce glanced at the prosecutor. From the intentness of Ngara's scrutiny of the witness, Pierce guessed that the involvement of a white man, with its whiff of bribery, was an unhappy surprise. Facing the witness, he asked, "Did the *oyibo* offer to pay *you* for this testimony?"

Joba paused, then said carefully, "Expenses only."

Pierce smiled. "Fifteen thousand U.S. dollars' worth of expenses?"

Joba became still, as though impaled by the question. In a muted voice, he said, "I don't remember."

"Come off it," Pierce snapped. "The question is whether, less than a month ago, this white man offered you fifteen thousand dollars in Okimbo's office. Yes or no."

"It was expenses for traveling to Port George."

"Did the round-trip to and from Okimbo's office cost you fifteen thousand?"

Pierce heard a quiet chuckle, Bobby Okari's. With an expression of deep unhappiness, Orta looked from Bobby to the witness. "No," Joba murmured.

"No?" Pierce repeated softly. "And yet the white man has already paid you five thousand U.S. dollars."

Startled, the witness stared at Pierce, lips slightly parted. "I did not count it."

Pierce thought swiftly. Ngara would use Moses Tulu to rehabilitate this witness; it would be best to hold back some surprises. "When you get the last ten thousand," Pierce advised Joba, "count it. I'd hate for this *oyibo* to cheat you."

ON REDIRECT, NGARA compelled the witness to affirm his accusation. Pierce contented himself with observing the participants: Ngara seemed punctilious but dispirited; the two jurists, Orta and Uza, listened with looks of weary skepticism; Okimbo inspected the witness closely, as though contemplating this man's future. Pierce did not envy Lucky Joba.

The same worry seemed to follow Moses Tulu to the witness stand: he sat with folded hands and hunched shoulders, as though wishing to become smaller. His voice was thin as he echoed Joba's story: yes, he had been with Joba outside Bobby's home; yes, he had heard Bobby's directive; yes, the white man, whose name he did not know, had offered only to pay "expenses." The last was said with so little conviction that Ngara looked as uncomfortable as his witness. When Pierce rose to cross-examine, the prosecutor eyed him with visible wariness.

Strolling toward the witness, Pierce asked, "After your first meeting with Okimbo and the white man, did you meet with them again?"

Out of the corner of Pierce's vision, Ngara's

pencil froze. Shrinking back slightly, the witness asked, "What do you mean?"

"What do you *think* I mean? Let's try this: did you and Joba later meet with Okimbo, this *oyibo,* and an Asari named Sunday Opuba?"

Tulu stared past Pierce. "Yes," he finally acknowledged.

"Explain to us how Sunday got involved."

The witness shook his head. "I don't remember."

"Then let me help you: in a bar in Elu, Joba told Sunday Opuba that he could profit from Bobby Okari's downfall and should come with you to meet Okimbo."

Tulu looked around himself, as though awaiting rescue. His brow furrowed in a pantomime of concentration. "Thing is, I was drinking too much gin. I don't bring back our words."

"Were you drunk when the three of you went to see Okimbo and the white man?"

The witness spread his hands in entreaty; surely Pierce must understand, the gesture said, that to answer could be fatal. "No, sir."

"That's a relief. At this same meeting, Joba repeated to Sunday Opuba your story about overhearing Bobby, correct?"

"This was mentioned, yes."

"It surely was. And then Colonel Okimbo suggested to Sunday that he, too, should tell this story in court."

Tulu looked away. "I forget things," he said hollowly. "I was scared."

"I'll bet. But just to be clear, you don't claim that Sunday Opuba was present when you and Tulu supposedly heard Bobby Okari solicit murder?"

"No, sir."

"Then let me suggest that you haven't 'forgotten' hearing Colonel Okimbo tell Sunday to lie. You heard him do that, didn't you?"

The witness seemed to hunch, as if to ward off blows. Turning, Pierce said to Orta, "Please direct the witness to answer, Your Honor."

Orta looked toward Colonel Nubola, who glared at him with obvious dissatisfaction. Then he glanced at Uza, who, after an instant, nodded. Softly, Orta told the witness, "The tribunal wishes to hear your answer."

Tulu stared at his lap, caught between maintaining an obvious fiction and acknowledging the truth in Okimbo's presence. At length, he mumbled, "I remember nothing of what the colonel said."

"Then let's try the *oyibo*. Didn't he offer Sunday fifteen thousand dollars to lie about Bobby Okari?"

Pierce sensed a stirring in the gallery. "I don't remember this," the witness insisted.

"Do you deny it happened?"

Ngara stood. "Asked and answered. Counsel is harassing the witness."

Orta pursed his lips. "Yes," he said to Pierce. "It is clear the witness has no memory of this meeting."

Pierce stared at the presiding judge. "With respect, Your Honor, it is clear that this witness is lying."

Orta looked cornered. "That is argument, Mr. Pierce. Make it at the end of trial, with less insolence. For now, move on or sit."

Pierce tried to conceal his anger and disgust. To the witness, he said, "Let's move to this so-called directive from Mr. Okari. Do you know who was on the other end of the call?"

Tulu shook his head. "No."

"Do you know who lynched those oil workers?"

"How could I know that, sir?"

"You could always make it up, I suppose. But, in truth, you don't know whether those murders are connected to Bobby Okari. *Or* to this supposed call."

Tulu looked down. "All I can know is what we heard him say. Nothing more."

Pierce stepped in front of Moses Tulu. "Be a man," he said softly. "Look me in the face when you tell lies."

"Counsel," Orta interrupted in a tone of judicial outrage. "This is not a question, it is a performance. This tribunal will have none of it."

Pierce ignored him. Eyes fixed on the witness, he said, "Isn't it true, Mr. Tulu, that your accusation against Bobby Okari is a lie?"

The witness still did not look up. "No, sir. I heard this."

"You must have been quite startled, then. Did you tell anyone about Bobby's so-called order except Okimbo, the *oyibo,* and Mr. Ngara?"

"No, sir."

"I thought not. By the way, did you tell Mr. Ngara that the white man was paying you to testify?"

At last Tulu looked up at Pierce. "No, sir," he said hesitantly. "But this was expenses only."

"How much money has the *oyibo* given you so far?"

The witness's eyes moistened. "Please, sir. Like Joba, I did not count."

From the back of the courtroom came a sarcastic bark of laughter. Sharply, Orta cracked his gavel. Turning to the judge, Pierce said, "You can't stop the world from laughing, Your Honor. No further questions."

Pivoting again, he walked back to the defense table, conscious of the silence, Okimbo's stare, Marissa's look of gratitude.

AFTER NGARA'S PERFUNCTORY effort to restore the witness's credibility, Orta adjourned for the day. In the buzz of chatter from the gallery, Bobby said, "You do this well, Damon." Then two soldiers took him away.

Still sitting, Pierce and Bara ran through their

checklist for the night. Pierce would do press interviews; Bara would try to locate Beke Femu. "And I will e-mail Jomo yet again," Bara said. "If Sunday Opuba is brave enough to testify, that would complete your destruction of these liars."

Pierce nodded. But Bara's tone held the faintest trace of doubt; perhaps he still wondered, as Pierce did, whether these witnesses had been paid to tell some version of the truth. The question—the tribunal's pretext for conviction—would linger unless Pierce and Bara could identify a suspect.

Ngara was standing over them. Civilly, he said, "Tomorrow's witness is Eric Aboh. He, too, will corroborate the charges."

He spoke without conviction, like an actor reading lines in a play he did not like. Almost gently, Pierce said, "Do you have any witnesses not on Van Daan's payroll? In the real world, Patric, you'd dismiss this case right now."

Ngara gave him a look of quiet anger. "The case is not over," he said, and walked away.

Pierce got up to seek out Clark Hamilton. Sitting in the gallery, PGL's lawyer slid his notepad into a leather briefcase. Pierce waited until Hamilton looked up. "Your client is paying for this travesty," Pierce said. "Tell Gladstone to fix this before it becomes *his* nightmare."

3

"THE WORSE THE TRIAL LOOKS," PIERCE TOLD ATIKU Bara, "and the deeper PGL's involvement, the better our chances of saving Bobby's life. If I were Michael Gladstone, I'd put the thumbscrews to Van Daan, trying to find out how deeply he's involved."

They were sitting on the Okaris' patio after dinner, reviewing their strategy in light of the day's testimony. "True," Bara answered. "But how bad it looks for PGL depends on whether we can tie its people to the massacre. We may never get the chance—it's easy to imagine Orta ruling that Goro isn't relevant to lynchings that happened a week before. Why would this judge put his own neck on the chopping block?"

The depressing truth of this silenced Pierce: the reasoned strategy of an American lawyer was confounded by Karama's tribunal, a distortion of the law so complete yet so unpredictable that Pierce felt as if he had stepped through the looking glass. The only jury Bobby had—PGL, Western governments, and a scattering of world media—did not have the power to override a dictator.

Marissa appeared on the patio. "There's someone downstairs to see you," she told Pierce. "She would not risk coming here unless it were important."

• • •

THE WOMAN AT the kitchen table, a plump Luandian in her thirties, wore a bright print dress, a head scarf, and thick glasses that accentuated a look of assertive intelligence. As Pierce entered with Marissa, she stood, shaking his hand briskly. "I'm Dora Adako," she said. "Has Marissa explained my work?"

"No. But perhaps you can."

Adako gave what seemed to Pierce a bitter smile. "Not so easy in these terrible days. I'm with an NGO called Progress Through Peace, founded to promote nonviolent solutions to the problems of the delta. Among my missions is trying to persuade young men that joining these militia groups leads to nowhere but death." She began speaking hurriedly, as though anxious to leave. "In Luandia, violence has many patrons. But even the guys who join militias sometimes remain my friends. One of them wants to see you."

Pierce glanced at Marissa. "Concerning what?" he asked.

"That I don't know—he contacted me only because I'm a friend of the Okaris'. But I believe this boy is serious, and that his request is urgent."

Pierce felt caught between interest and mistrust. "Who is he?"

"A member of a militia group that has broken away from FREE." Adako's eyes locked onto

Pierce's. "I know what you're thinking: trust no one."

Pierce hesitated. Softly, Marissa told him, "Dora is our friend."

Pierce nodded. "When does he want to meet?"

"Tonight. You are to walk with Marissa on the beach—away from the flaring, where it's dark. He'll find you." Adako took Pierce's hand in both of hers. "You're defending a great man. Without him, the delta has no hope."

PIERCE AND MARISSA took the wooden stairs down to the beach, then turned away from the flaring. As they walked, the night grew darker. The only lights they saw came from Petrol Island and oil tankers moored miles out to sea; the only sound was the lapping of waves dying on the sand. It was the first time they been alone since the night they had made love.

"How are you?" Marissa asked.

He looked at her. "I don't have time to think about that. When you're in trial, self-reflection is a luxury."

She took his hand. They walked like that for minutes—together, yet alone with their own thoughts. Marissa was the first to stop, as though listening for a sound.

A moment later, Pierce heard the faint idling of an outboard motor. Turning with Marissa, he saw the outline of an open boat as it glided toward them, then the form of a man, one hand on the throttle. He shut it off, propping up the motor. "Get in," he called in a low voice.

Pierce hesitated: whoever this was could murder them both and throw their bodies overboard. But Marissa released his hand and walked swiftly to the boat, her feet splashing the water before the man helped her inside. Pierce had no choice but to follow.

They sat in front, their pilot in back, the motor puttering quietly as he took them out to sea. "Who *are* you?" Pierce demanded.

The man leaned forward, his features becoming visible in the light of a quarter moon. His handsome young face was lineless, his eyes sensitive but watchful. For an instant Pierce thought of a bright graduate student; then he reminded himself that this man had no doubt killed other men, and would survive by killing more. "Jonathan Adopu," he answered, "leader of the People's Front."

The boat kept moving out to sea. Adopu turned, steering toward where the ocean seemed the darkest. "Why did you want to see us?" Marissa asked.

Adopu cut the motor again; suddenly the boat was quiet, drifting with the tide. He seemed to answer for Pierce's benefit. "What they say about the militias isn't true. Some are only criminals, some not. It isn't fair to tar us all." He turned to Marissa. "I believe in your husband's words. But he has no voice without a gun; that's the way in Luandia. Now Karama means to kill him. That is why I did not follow him to the slaughter."

His tone commingled apology and defiance. Evenly, Marissa said, "To what end? Look at the life you've chosen. All of you will kill one another; the boys who replace you will do the same; Karama or someone like him will kill the last man standing. The cycle of violence will consume everyone and everything, until there's no one left who remembers that once there was the hope of something better." Her bluntness, though etched with strain and exhaustion, struck Pierce for its passion. "None of you will bring us peace; the oil you steal makes your crooked patrons rich. You'll die without ever knowing whose interests you serve."

Another thought hit Pierce: she was, indeed, Bobby Okari's wife. "Your husband is an educated man," Adopu answered quietly, "a public man. I'm a militiaman, not a Mandela.

"I joined FREE after Karama's soldiers raped and murdered my sister. By now there are too many dead sisters to count. What are we doing? I ask myself. How did men who joined the militias to keep other men from stealing their shoes become hostage takers? I don't want to live this life. Bobby Okari did not wish me to live it. But what choices does this brute Karama leave me? Who cares for us—the U.S., or PGL, or the white and yellow men filling their tanks with Luandian oil? All your husband's words won't save himself or any of us." His voice grew softer yet. "But if he dies, something fine will die with him. That's why I wanted this meeting."

With its touch of eloquence, Adopu's words left Pierce with a sense of waste, a deeper grasp of why Bobby and Marissa fought for something better. Leaning forward, Marissa asked, "What did you come to tell us?"

Adopu gazed at her. "I have friends within FREE," he answered. "I believe that General Freedom may have deceived you."

"Why?"

"Freedom and Okimbo are friends of convenience—for what reason, and to what degree, I do not know. But others claim to have seen them together. Some whisper that they are allies, and that both work for someone else. Perhaps Jomo, whoever *he* is."

Pierce struggled to make sense of this. General Freedom's intervention, leading Pierce to Sunday Opuba, had been no favor to Okimbo. "What do *you* think?" he asked.

Adopu faced him. "That General Freedom seems to operate with impunity, while Okimbo kills his rivals. How could he prosper without Okimbo's tolerance? How did he escape from prison? How was FREE able to raid Petrol Island or seize the government's radio station long enough to broadcast threats against PGL? Who besides Karama gains if Okimbo slaughters the Asari and executes Bobby Okari? Obviously FREE—as long as they're not blamed for it. Think how good it will be for them to invoke a martyr's name to justify their actions."

"If Okimbo and General Freedom are allied," Pierce rejoined, "Okimbo is betraying Karama."

"Maybe so, maybe not. FREE can't exist without collusion in high places, criminals in office who take their cut. Why not Karama himself?"

Pierce bent forward, elbows on his knees, thinking as he absorbed the rocking of the boat. From the tangle of his thoughts he retrieved the name of Karama's national security adviser, Ugwo Ajukwa—Roos Van Daan's patron, a man with ties to Okimbo and, perhaps, to a speculator in oil futures with influence at the White House. "Does General Freedom also work with Roos Van Daan?" Pierce asked.

"PGL's security man? That I don't know."

"Do you know a man named Sunday Opuba?"

Adopu looked from Marissa to Pierce. "He's dead," he answered quietly. "Buried in quicksand on the orders of General Freedom."

"That can't be," Pierce blurted reflexively, then realized how foolish this sounded. In the moonlight, Marissa looked pale.

"How do you know this?" Pierce asked Adopu.

"A friend told me, the man who led you to Sunday. He's angry about Opuba's murder."

The man from the Rhino Bar, Pierce thought. "Why was he killed?"

Adopu shrugged. "My friend doesn't know. Maybe Opuba didn't realize that Okimbo is the general's friend. Maybe General Freedom used Opuba to mislead you, sabotaging your defense while the general poses as *your* friend. If I hadn't told you this, you might still believe that the leader of FREE wishes Bobby well."

Pierce glanced at Marissa. He sensed her thinking with him: without Sunday Opuba to discredit Lucky Joba and Moses Tulu, their story, however tarnished, would be accepted by a tribunal frightened of Savior Karama. Adopu watched his face. "You want to save Okari," he said. "Perhaps there's another way."

"What's that?"

Adopu turned to Marissa. "There are many of us, madam, better armed than Okimbo's soldiers. When they escort Bobby from the courthouse to the prison, we can kill his guards and take him to the creeklands. Tell him this. If he wants us to act, pass the word to me through Dora."

Pierce was buffeted by the gravest doubts: that this could be a trap; that Adopu might be an agent of Okimbo or Karama; that he could have killed Opuba himself; that his entire story could be a lie, precipitated by the revelations of Bobby's trial; that Bobby's death in a violent escape attempt would tarnish his image and spare Karama international revulsion. But Marissa seemed to trust him. "You could die," she said.

Adopu shrugged. "Your husband *will* die. As for me, my life may not be long. At least this way I'd die for a man I once believed could save us."

Marissa touched his arm. "We'll tell him."

For a moment they continued drifting in the darkness, water lapping at the boat. Then Adopu started the motor and, its snarl low, guided them to the beach.

Pierce got out first, reaching back to help Marissa. Taking his hand, she turned to Adopu. "Be safe."

Adopu laughed softly. "A pretty thought," he answered.

4

AN HOUR BEFORE THE TRIAL RECOMMENCED, PIERCE arranged to visit Bobby Okari. This time, there was no interference; civilly, Major Bangida escorted Pierce to Bobby's cell. There was light now, and a cot for Bobby to sleep on; though it still smelled of feces and urine, Pierce saw that the cell now had a portable toilet. Grasping the bars, Bobby said, "It's become a virtual hotel. Having me collapse at trial would make a bad impression."

Nor could Karama execute a corpse, Pierce thought grimly. "I have some news."

Quietly, he told Bobby about Jonathan Adopu.

"If Sunday's dead," Pierce concluded in a low voice, "we've got no witness to discredit Joba and Tulu. That leaves Adopu's offer to break you out." Pierce's tone became softer yet. "That's nothing I'd be part of in America. But once this trial is over, any chance of an escape is gone."

Bobby gazed at his feet, an absent smile playing on his mouth. "'Shot trying to escape,'" he murmured. "That would make a bad impression." He slowly shook his head. "Perhaps I'd live; perhaps not. But either fate would finish me as a leader for the Asari. Not so an execution."

Pierce felt a sense of dread. "That's a very fine distinction."

"Not to me." He looked into Pierce's face, a plea for understanding. "The manner of a man's death should be consistent with his life. Tell our new friend no."

There was nothing more for Pierce to say.

WHEN COURT RESUMED, all was as before: the armed soldiers, the puppet tribunal, the grim sense of premonition. Watching from the jury box, Okimbo appraised Marissa with a proprietary smile, as though she were a prize to be awarded at the trial's end. Perhaps it was this that made Pierce feel queasy even before he saw Eric Aboh.

A doctor by education, Aboh was a slender man in his forties with a high forehead, a scholar's demeanor, and a certain elegant precision in his movements and speech. But something about him seemed insubstantial, and he did not look at Bobby. Perhaps fear and shame, Pierce reflected, had hollowed him out.

In cautious tones, he traced his background for Ngara: a physician who ministered to the Asari, he had become Bobby Okari's lieutenant—a principal adviser in all strategic decisions; a participant, though with increasing doubts, in the planning for Asari Day. Next to Pierce, Bara listened with veiled eyes. Pierce recalled that, like Aboh, Bara had feared where Asari Day might lead.

"Over the time you knew Okari," Ngara asked, "did his character change?"

"Slowly, yes." Aboh steepled his fingers. "He became more enamored with his international reputation, and listened to us less. The world was watching, he would say, as if he were playing to a gallery."

Judges Orta and Uza, Pierce noted, were unusually attentive—perhaps hoping that the witness could cloak the trial in a certain dignity. "How did these changes affect Okari's leadership?" Ngara asked.

Aboh compressed his lips. "The idealistic leader I once knew came to see himself as infallible, a virtual saint. Saints, I learned to my sorrow, are incapable of compromise. By the end, he was prepared to do anything to maintain control over the movement. To Bobby, *he* was the Asari, prepared to drag us to the precipice."

Noting Bara's guarded look, Pierce felt his cocounsel's disquiet: stripped of pejoratives, the core of Aboh's answer reflected Bara's assessment of Bobby. But Bobby's expression was one of contempt, as though this were the kind of cowardice a strong leader must expect. "Did *you* seek compromise?" Ngara asked Aboh.

"After the lynchings, yes." Pausing, Aboh glanced at Okimbo, who watched him closely. "I met with Colonel Okimbo and Roos Van Daan, PGL's chief of security in the delta. I also spoke by telephone to PGL's managing director, Michael Gladstone. The essence of our discussions was that only a cessation of militant activity among the Asari would prevent some further tragedy."

"Did you try to get Okari to concur?"

Aboh hesitated. "Only after we signed the agreement. I did not wish him to abort our negotiations with PGL, or do anything extreme and unexpected. In this I was right. When he saw the agreement, he labeled me a traitor."

Ngara put his hands on hips. "Do *you* consider yourself a traitor?"

"No," Aboh answered firmly. "I acted because I knew what had happened on Asari Day, and why those oil workers had been lynched."

At once Pierce felt on edge. "Will you explain?" Ngara asked.

In the stillness of the courtroom, Aboh's expression was grave. "A week before Asari Day, Bobby called me, very agitated. Our youth had become impatient, he said. It was time for us to turn PGL's employees into an example.

" 'Isn't FREE already doing that?' I asked.

" 'Kidnapping for money is rational,' Bobby answered. Then he said it was time for us to make PGL fear the irrational, and he knew the young men who could act without hesitance." Aboh's voice slowed, as though he were reluctant to finish. "I asked him what he meant. He simply laughed, and said, 'It will be the climax of Asari Day.' Only when the lynchings occurred did I understand his meaning."

Pierce considered moving for the answer to be stricken, then decided to make his point on cross-examination. "No further questions," Ngara said. Murmurs of disquiet issued from the gallery; as though to underscore them, Orta declared a recess.

Turning, Pierce saw a burning anger in Bobby's eyes. "He's lying," Bobby spat.

Pierce touched his wrist. "Did anything like this conversation happen?"

"*Something* like," Bobby answered. "But I meant seizing the platform and pump stations and any PGL employees who were there. To PGL, *that* kind of action is irrational." His voice hardened. "I was not suggesting murder. If Eric is desperate enough to think otherwise, it is only to save his worthless skin."

WHEN THE PROCEEDINGS resumed, Pierce rose to cross-examine. "Before the lynchings, did you tell anyone about this conversation with Bobby?"

Aboh's eyes narrowed, as though he were plumbing his memory. "I can't recall. So perhaps not."

"So you didn't take Bobby's comments to mean that he was planning murder."

Aboh spread his hands. "I couldn't be sure what he intended."

"During your 'peace negotiations' with Okimbo, Van Daan, and Gladstone, did you warn PGL that Bobby might be proposing acts of violence?"

Aboh hesitated. "No."

"Did you warn any other Asari?"

"No."

Pierce moved closer. "In short, the first time you specifically thought Bobby might have intended murders was *after* the lynchings occurred?"

Aboh considered this. "What I would say," he temporized, "is that the lynchings made my fears concrete."

"But you don't know *who* killed those workers, do you?"

"Not by name, no."

"Or," Pierce said with open scorn, "by age, gender, ethnicity, or description."

Aboh blinked. "No."

"In fact, you have no clue whatsoever as to the persons who hung those men."

"I do not."

"Nor do you—or can you—know their motivation."

"With absolute moral certainty? I can only know what I know."

"Which is precious little. Doesn't it bother you, Dr. Aboh, to come before this tribunal with speculation that you *do* know—to an 'absolute moral certainty'—may lead to Bobby Okari's conviction and, quite possibly, his death?"

Aboh drew a breath. "Do me a favor," Pierce snapped. "Look at Mr. Okari for once."

Ngara stood, preparing to intervene. But Aboh, as though hypnotized, turned his gaze to Bobby Okari. In a dry voice, he answered, "It is my duty as a citizen to say what I know. I have not come here with any joy."

"At least you get to leave," Pierce said. "So let's return to your efforts to spread 'peace' throughout Asariland. In your discussions with Okimbo and Van Daan, did you also discuss whether PGL would give you money?"

Aboh sat straighter, a portrait of offended dignity. "This was not a bribe, if that's what you're implying, but compensation for advice on maintaining social stability."

"You also paid some money to Lucky Joba, right?"

"Yes. And other youths."

"Did they help you 'maintain social stability'?"

Aboh bristled visibly. "In a real sense, yes. Our youth are unemployed; many are restless. If paying money will help curb them, it is preferable to violence."

Pierce smiled a little. "How much did *you* get before signing this 'peace agreement'?"

Aboh met his eyes. "Fifty thousand dollars U.S."

"That'll buy a little peace. Did that payment help influence your decision?"

"Mr. Pierce," Aboh said in an aggrieved tone, "sanity was needed. I'd have signed the agreement without receiving a dime. The money was for my further assistance or for, as you say, 'buying a little peace.' I apologize for neither."

Pierce stared at him. "Who exactly did you need to pacify?"

"I don't understand your question."

"Then let me ask another. When was the last time you went to Goro?"

For a moment Aboh looked away. "A week before Asari Day."

"Were the villagers armed?"

At once Judge Orta glanced toward Okimbo. "Objection," Ngara called out. "The question is irrelevant to the charges against Mr. Okari."

Orta turned to Pierce. "Not so," Pierce answered smoothly. "The witness has testified that he feared Mr. Okari's propensity for violence; implied that the defendant knew unnamed people who could carry out violent acts; and said that he, Eric Aboh, took money from PGL to curb the threat of violence among the Asari. It is fair to ask him whether he saw armaments in Okari's home village."

Orta's features slackened; though he understood the implications of the question, Pierce's rationale for asking it was unimpeachable, thus challenging Orta's pose of impartial jurist. Turning, he conferred with Uza, then spoke to Nubola, whose eyes became hard. Facing Ngara, Orta said, "Objection overruled."

Aboh slowly shook his head. "I saw no arms in Goro."

"To your knowledge, were the activists who seized the platform and pumping station on Asari Day armed?"

"No."

"By the way, is it possible that those acts of resistance were the so-called 'irrational' actions Mr. Okari referenced in his conversation?"

Aboh's mouth tightened. "His words implied actions more extreme."

"But you agree that nothing he said specified a particular act."

"Not in plain language, no."

"But certain *nonviolent* actions followed."

"Yes."

"So why are you so certain that the murders that followed this conversation were what Mr. Okari meant?"

Aboh looked disoriented. "Because that was the tenor of his statement."

"To whom did you first offer this interpretation?"

"Colonel Okimbo and Mr. Van Daan."

"But not during your peace negotiations, correct? In fact, you never suggested that Okari was complicit in these murders until after Okimbo 'arrested' him."

Aboh hesitated. "Yes."

Pierce adopted a tone of mild curiosity. "What did you hear about the events surrounding that arrest?"

"Objection," Ngara called out sharply. "Again, this is irrelevant to the events that *caused* the arrest."

With an air of bewilderment, Pierce faced Orta. "I don't understand Mr. Ngara's objection. Clearly, any question that relates to Dr. Aboh's state of mind prior to his accusation of Mr. Okari is highly relevant. It relates directly to what he believed and what he said to Colonel Okimbo."

Orta glanced toward Colonel Nubola. "I fail to see relevance," Nubola told Pierce sharply.

It was the first time Nubola had spoken since the trial began. Pierce steeled himself. "With respect, Colonel, Judges Orta and Uza have the advantage of a legal education. I suppose that's why they're here. Perhaps you should defer to them."

Though mild in tone, the remark was by its

nature so insulting that Nubola glared at him. "You are here at our sufferance, Mr. Pierce."

Pierce stifled his own fears. "True. But not yours. I've merely asked your fellow judges for a ruling, which they're more than capable of making without military intervention. In other jurisdictions, this is a matter of law."

Someone in the gallery coughed nervously. Nubola's glare intensified. With obvious difficulty, he struggled to maintain the fiction that Orta commanded the courtroom; Orta hesitated, as though contemplating the cost of this pretense. Then he placed his hand on Nubola's arm, saying to Pierce, "Your remarks were out of order. You will apologize to Colonel Nubola or find yourself in jail."

Pierce faced Nubola. "Forgive me, Colonel, if my certainty that this question is relevant caused me to forget myself."

Nubola nodded curtly. Turning to the witness, Orta paused for a final moment. "Please answer, Dr. Aboh."

Aboh's eyes darted from Okimbo to Pierce. In a muffled tone, he answered, "I heard only rumors."

With equal quiet, Pierce asked, "That the villagers had been massacred?"

"Objection." Ngara quickly approached the bench. "This tribunal has been most lenient in giving counsel leeway. But counsel's accusation is intended only to discredit this proceeding and

slander the government of Luandia. I ask that this be stopped."

Pierce forced himself not to glance at Okimbo. Stepping forward, he stood beside Ngara. "The witness first made his accusation to Colonel Okimbo. It is relevant to ask whether he was *frightened* of Okimbo. If he heard that the colonel had ordered his soldiers to kill hundreds of Asari, the truth or falsity of such a report does not matter. But whether this witness *feared* that it was true matters a great deal."

As a matter of law, Pierce knew, this rationale was flawless. From the sheer misery of his expression, Orta knew it, too. Were he to rule correctly, the shadow of Goro would enter the courtroom for good. In the silence, Orta sat back, eyes half shut, slowly rocking in his leather chair. Softly, he said, "Objection overruled."

Pierce fought to conceal his astonishment. Facing the witness, he said, "Please answer, Dr. Aboh."

Once again, Aboh glanced at Okimbo. In a barely audible voice, he responded, "I heard rumors of violence."

"What kind of violence?"

Now Aboh could look at no one. "The murder of villagers. Also rape."

"Did you ask Colonel Okimbo about this rumor?"

"No."

Pierce cocked his head. "Were you at least a little curious?"

Briefly, Aboh closed his eyes. "I didn't think such questions productive."

Pierce shook his head in wonder. "Tell me, Dr. Aboh, how did the subject of your conversation with Bobby Okari arise between you, Okimbo, and Van Daan?"

The witness reached for a glass of water. He took a sip, licking his lips. "They asked if I knew anything about Bobby's involvement in the lynchings. It was clear that they already believed that he had done this. So I told them what I knew."

"I see. Since Van Daan gave you fifty thousand dollars in connection with the peace negotiation, has he paid you anything more?"

Once again, Aboh hesitated. "Yes."

"How much?"

"Twenty thousand U.S. For further services on behalf of peace."

Pierce moved closer to the witness. "Of what nature?"

"I haven't performed them yet. I'm waiting for emotions to die down."

"Or just for Bobby to die?" Before Ngara could object, Pierce asked, "Did Van Daan pay this money after you reported your conversation with Mr. Okari?"

For an instant, Aboh's lips moved but made no sound. In a near whisper, he answered, "Yes."

Pierce considered his position. He had seldom discredited a witness so completely; the real question was whether it mattered. Turning to Orta, he said, "Thank you, Your Honor. That's all I have for Dr. Aboh."

At once, Ngara was on his feet. "Do you believe, Dr. Aboh, that the 'irrational' actions urged by Mr. Okari meant an act of violence?"

"Yes." Aboh paused to compose himself, looking at no one. "The conversation happened as I said it did, with far more menace in Bobby's voice than I'm able to convey. Three deaths swiftly followed."

Ngara nodded, a pantomime of satisfaction. "No further questions."

Aboh left the courtroom, passing Bobby with downcast eyes. Bobby's gaze was more sorrowful than angry. "A pity," he said. "Eric's already dead. It's just that he's still breathing."

"Your Honor," Ngara announced, "that concludes the case for the prosecution."

Pierce was both amazed and unprepared: as thin as Ngara's case was, Pierce still had no defense witnesses other than the Okaris. Thinking swiftly, he told Judge Orta, "In that case, I ask the tribunal to dismiss this case at once."

Orta's eyes opened slightly. "On what grounds?"

"The obvious one, Your Honor. The prosecution's evidence, taken alone, does not establish a prima facie case—let alone establish my client's guilt beyond a reasonable doubt. We've heard only three witnesses, all recruited by Colonel Okimbo, all paid for by PGL. Their credibility is nil." Pierce's voice grew more impassioned. "But even if you credit every word they said, all the tribunal knows is that the lynchings occurred. No one heard Bobby Okari order them. No one knows who carried them out. No one can connect them to Mr. Okari's supposed words."

Orta's eyes dulled, the look of someone who wished to be anywhere but in this courtroom. "How can I defend a case," Pierce asked, "where there is no case to defend? The world is watching, Your Honor. The only matter for this tribunal to decide is whether it's a court of law or an instrument whose sole function is to eliminate Bobby Okari by imprisonment or death. If this is a court of law, it will set him free."

Abruptly, Pierce turned and walked back to his client. But instead of Bobby, he looked at Marissa. Her eyes said all that he could wish for.

When Ngara stood, Pierce could feel his ambivalence; no decent man enters the law for this. "We believe our case sufficient," he said. "If the defense can offer an alibi or explanation, they should. If all they have is silence, that is Okari's confession."

This brief rejoinder, stunning in its sophistry, drew Pierce to his feet. But for the moment Orta had used up his last reserve of courage. Holding up his hand for silence, he told Pierce, "The prosecutor has offered evidence that, if unopposed, is sufficient to warrant conviction. Will you offer a defense?"

Pierce felt near panic overtake him, commingled with a sense of the surreal. "Yes, Your Honor. I ask the court to give us until tomorrow morning to begin."

"Very well," Orta responded with courtesy. "You may start at nine A.M."

Abruptly, he banged the gavel. Quietly, Pierce told Bara, "I don't care how you find Beke Femu. Do it."

Pierce clasped Bobby's shoulder, then went to find Clark Hamilton. A young white man stopped him, extending a hand. "I'm Bob McGill," he said, "political officer at the U.S. embassy. Ambassador Caraway wants to buy you dinner."

5

SORRY FOR THE LACK OF AMBIENCE," GRAYSON Caraway told Pierce. "But the State Department is warning Americans not to travel to the delta and ordering diplomatic personnel to stay away from public places. They're afraid I'll be kidnapped, or just shot."

They sat at a conference table in a sterile corner of the American consulate in Port George, sampling the Luandian version of takeout. "It's better this way," Pierce answered. "When I left the court-room today the look Okimbo gave me was all the warning I'll ever need. If I die in some sort of 'accident,' you'll know why."

Caraway nodded, a grim acknowledgment of the truth. "Stay alive," he said. "Bob McGill says you're doing well in court. If you can keep it up, you'll stoke the Western media and provide those of us who give a damn further basis for questioning this proceeding."

"This isn't a 'proceeding,'" Pierce replied. "It's a lynching. Okari should have walked out of there today a free man. The fact that he didn't should tell the State Department all it needs to know. If anyone there is still awake, tell them I've got no witnesses, let alone a way of proving Bobby's innocence."

Caraway scooped some rice onto his plate, carefully adding a dash of hot sauce. "I should be straight with you," he said. "State's under a great deal of pressure. Luandia's foreign minister has filed a protest, calling your lawsuit a 'gross interference' in the country's internal affairs. His message to me—clearly dictated by Karama—was 'America is not our colonial master.' They're particularly unhappy with you."

"What the hell am I supposed to do?"

"Exactly what you're doing—if you weren't throwing sand in the gears of Luandian 'justice,' Okari might be dead by now. But Karama has begun to make not-so-subtle threats about preferring the Chinese oil cartel to PGL. Hence the Defense Department and the oil strategists don't like you either. They've reduced the complexities surrounding Okari to a very simple test: they'll support whatever helps ensure that America gets the lion's share of oil. You flunk."

Worry and fatigue, Pierce discovered, had frayed his temper. "What about our vaunted devotion to human rights? Or is that just bullshit we peddle to idealists like Bobby before we throw them to the wolves?"

Caraway's reaction was not defensiveness but silence. "The problem's not just us," he said at length. "The Brits won't support anything that might really help Okari. Neither will the French or Germans. As for the Chinese, they're thrilled: supporting murderers like Karama *is* their human rights agenda. We've already discussed Darfur—the Chinese take the Sudanese government's oil, then use their power at the U.N. to help the Sudanese slaughter their own people. There's no chance that oil-consuming nations will agree to sanctions against Karama." His tone became more clipped. "Then there are the Africans. Even statesmen like Mandela, Okari's hero, won't say a word on his behalf. It's 'political correctness' at its most perverse: they'd rather let an autocrat like Mugabe destroy Zimbabwe than join the West in criticizing an African regime. Karama is the latest beneficiary."

Pierce had stopped eating. "I guess the Okaris made a mistake," he said bitterly.

Caraway considered him. "Okari miscalculated," he amended. "He's far from naive. But I sometimes believe he came to see the world's admiration as literal life insurance. It's not.

"As for the United States, he overrates our leverage. There's too much we need from Savior Karama. We need Luandian soldiers, believe it or not, as peacekeepers in African countries torn by conflict. We need Karama's cooperation in fighting the spread of AIDS. The Pentagon, ironically enough, wants his support in keeping American soldiers accused of crimes in places like Iraq from being tried in foreign courts—"

"But this kangaroo court is okay for Bobby Okari?"

"He's not an American soldier," Caraway said evenly. "At the risk of making you angrier still, we also want Karama to crack down on oil bunkering—"

"Angry? It's a joke. His own officials, people like Ugwo Ajukwa, are waist-deep in bunkered oil. Don't our people *know* that? PGL surely must."

"We all do," Caraway answered tiredly. "Which brings us to PGL. So far, you're making its people look complicit—Gladstone's painfully aware of that, believe me. The longer this trial and Okari's lawsuit go on, the worse it gets for them. That's your hole card. But it's also become a problem."

"How so?"

"Because no American company wants public scrutiny of how they're forced to operate in a place like this. They certainly don't want to be sued for human rights abuses by business partners like Karama, or punished by foreign governments embarrassed in U.S. courts. Nor do they like having their employees hung from trees. So they absolutely hate Okari's lawsuit." Caraway put down his fork. "I'll give you one example. Last week I flew to Washington, hoping to persuade the West African desk to support some meaningful measures to help extricate Okari, at least if he doesn't wind up looking guilty—"

"Which he won't."

"The current evidence is pretty feeble," Caraway responded, "though I can't cross him off my list of suspects. Anyhow, I also used the trip to attend a luncheon meeting of an influential group called the Corporate Council for Africa—American companies who do business over here. Within the limits of my position, I tried to interest them in using their collective influence to promote lenience for Okari.

"I got back the usual boilerplate about not interfering with the judicial process of a foreign country." Caraway smiled without humor. "One pompous fellow, some sort of financier, pronounced himself a great authority: I didn't understand Luandia, he told me—he had a personal relationship with Karama and other highly placed officials, and intervening on Okari's behalf would be an enormous mistake. He proceeded to recite Karama's party line on the Asari movement—the secessionist threat, the likelihood of Okari's guilt, et cetera, et cetera—so faithfully I could have been listening to Karama or Ajukwa themselves. It's better in the original. Unfortunately, I also learned that this self-anointed expert has the ear of the White House."

Pierce looked at him curiously. "A commodities trader named Henry Karlin?"

Caraway seemed to search his memory. "I'm not sure about his business," he said at length. "But, yes, I believe that was his name."

Despite Caraway's studied vagueness, he seemed unsurprised by the question. At once Pierce grasped that the ambassador's anecdote was not casual and that, perhaps in league with Dave Rubin, he was conveying information that might somehow be important. "Does Karlin have a relationship with Ajukwa?" Pierce asked.

"I don't know for sure. But it's fair to assume that." Caraway gave him a significant look. "You should also assume that Karlin is actively working against Okari, using whatever political influence he possesses with our current administration. That could be a problem. Another problem is time—you're running out." Caraway paused for emphasis. "The wheels of diplomacy grind with painful slowness; too often our favorite policy is waiting on events. Some people at the State Department resort to hoping that once Karama steals enough, he'll give us that 'free and fair election' he keeps dangling, then trot off to Monte Carlo with his stolen billions."

"Do *you* believe that?"

Caraway laughed briefly. "No. Karama *likes* having the community of nations kiss his feet. In a far less healthy, far more authoritarian way, he's as addicted to the world spotlight as Okari. The effect on both men is malign. Your client doesn't think he'll die; Karama wants to kill him. What better way to show the world who's boss?"

This assessment depressed Pierce still further. "You've made me realize something," he told Caraway. "Luandia is so lethal, and this trial so rigged, that I find myself indulging in magical thinking: that the beneficent United States of America—that beacon of freedom that embraced my immigrant father and sent his youngest child to Harvard—will somehow save a black man who's risked his life for the ideals we claim to live by. Pathetic, really. I'm too old for fairy tales."

For a time they simply sat there in the bleak fluorescent light. "Neither of us," Caraway said at last, "is too old for hope. We need a way to keep Okari alive, even if he's in a Luandian prison. If we can do that, the next step will be persuading Savior Karama to send the Okaris into exile, positioning Bobby as a force for good in the post-Karama Luandia that America's hoping for without doing very much."

"I'd be thrilled with that," Pierce answered. "But whatever happens to Bobby, I'm worried about Marissa. I want her out of here."

"You *should* want that." Caraway paused. "At least she's an American citizen. If the time comes, I'll do whatever I can."

Another silence ensued. "You know what the problem is?" Caraway said at length. "Not only with us, but our allies. It's not just grubby pragmatism. We're also anti-historical: for all we should have learned, too many Western leaders imagine that the Hitlers, Stalins, and Pol Pots were mutants—that the mass murderers of history are somehow different than standard-issue tyrants like Savior Karama. Very few appreciate that—however insane these monsters were—like Karama they made very sophisticated calculations of the forces against them and concluded that they could advance their aims through murder.

"The only difference is a matter of scale. Hitler and Pol Pot were millions of bodies into it before they went too far; Stalin and Mao killed millions more and still died of old age. Karama understands this. In his peculiar calculus, killing Bobby Okari is a pittance." Caraway's tone became weary. "The West's ultimate delusion is that Karama *won't* kill him—that it would simply be too blatant. By the time we face reality, Karama may be watching his home video of Okari's execution.

"I'll help whenever I can, Damon. But your best hope is PGL. With the proper motivation, and Okari's acquiescence, PGL might yet induce Karama to kick him out."

CONCERNED FOR PIERCE'S safety, Bob McGill offered to drive him to the Okaris' compound. "If they kill you," he said blithely, "they'll have to get me, too. Even in Luandia, murdering diplomats is awkward."

The young, Pierce reflected, believe that they're immortal. When McGill pulled up to the compound, Pierce thanked him. "No problem," McGill responded with a grin. "I like watching you in court. Kind of makes me wish I'd gone to law school."

Opening the car door, Pierce mustered a smile. "Keep watching," he advised. "You'll get over it."

Edo, the houseboy, let him in. Pierce did not ask for Marissa; he did not yet have the heart to describe his meeting with Caraway. Instead, he went to the patio, gazing out at the lights of Petrol Island as he sorted through his options.

The ringing of his cell phone broke his concentration. "Yes?" he answered.

There was silence on the other end, then the brief crackle of static. "Is this Damon Pierce?" a man's voice said.

"Yes."

"This is Trevor Hill. I assume you know who I am."

Pierce was startled. "You're in charge of PGL's operations in the delta."

Another pause. "I'd like to see you. Tonight."

Swiftly, Pierce considered the ethics of meeting a key PGL executive—a witness in Bobby's lawsuit—outside the presence of Clark Hamilton. That this could lead to Pierce's punishment by the California Bar was not, after the day's events, nearly enough to stop him.

"Tell me where," he answered.

6

HILL SENT TWO YOUNG LUANDIAN SOLDIERS TO drive Pierce from the compound.

Sitting in the rear of the jeep, Pierce considered the entwinement between PGL, who no doubt paid these men, and the Luandian military. But they served a purpose besides providing transportation: the state security men outside the Okaris' gate did not follow. The soldier stationed at the entrance to PGL's walled compound waved them through without question.

Inside the walls, Pierce felt as if he had entered a world utterly foreign to the menacing squalor of Port George. It was past eleven; the well-lit streets, manicured gardens, and uniform ranch houses reminded Pierce of a middle-class American suburb whose residents, all respectably employed, had retired to bed. He wondered at the schizoid life of a white petroleum engineer who, leaving his family in this ersatz version of home, risked kidnapping or worse outside these walls.

The jeep entered a tree-lined cul-de-sac that ended at a sprawling villa, shadowed by palms, whose windows showed the faint glow of light from the inside. One of the soldiers pointed toward a pathway to a carved wooden door. "It's unlocked," he said. "You can enter."

Pierce followed the path in a darkness so quiet that it sharpened his sense of a surreptitious meeting. Reaching the door, he hesitated. Then he turned the iron knob and stepped inside.

He stood in a tiled alcove. To the right, illuminated by a single lamp, was a spacious living room. Even in the shadows, the decor bespoke a love of Africa: wooden masks; statuary carved from mahogany; wall hangings of patterned mudcloth or woven mats; a framed map of colonial Luandia, faded to sepia by time. To Pierce the surroundings reflected a man who had embraced Luandia as his home. Then Pierce saw Hill, sitting in a high-backed African chair with a tumbler of amber liquid in his hand. "Evening, Mr. Pierce," he said in a grainy British accent.

Hill stood, putting down his drink with exaggerated care. When he crossed the living room to shake Pierce's hand, Pierce caught the scent of whiskey. Pierce's first impression was of ruddy, weathered skin, reddish hair, sky-blue eyes, and the frank expression of someone schooled in practicality rather than politesse. Hill's calloused grip was firm. "Care for a drink?" he said. "I've been at it since sundown."

His enunciation was clear enough, though its deliberation, perhaps a compensation for drink, also conveyed a sense of quiet despair. "Whatever you're having," Pierce said.

Hill walked to a thatched bar tucked into a corner of the room, producing a heavy crystal glass and a bottle of Bushmills. "Good choice. Do you drink whiskey like a Brit or an American?"

"Neat is fine," Pierce said. "Ice melts."

Briefly, Hill laughed, then handed Pierce the tumbler with an air of decorous courtesy. He waved Pierce to a chair near his own, its twin. "I suppose you're wondering what this is about."

Though Hill seemed steady enough, Pierce sensed a man on the edge of a psychic implosion, drinking either to dull his apprehension or to liberate his conscience. "A little."

Hill looked at him sharply. "You missed my deposition. A deposition, I discovered, is no place for subtle truths. All it does is deepen one's disquiet."

Pierce smiled a little. "How many times, I wonder, have I told my clients things like 'Only answer the question asked' or 'Never volunteer information' or 'There are many ways to tell the truth.' You probably heard all three. The effect is often to leave the witness with his job intact and a guilty conscience. Assuming he has one."

Hill's expression turned inward. "Ever read *Heart of Darkness*?"

"In high school, yes."

"Then I assume you remember Mr. Kurtz, who immersed himself in Africa only to experience man's descent into the barbarism that lies waiting in our souls. By the end, all Kurtz could do was mumble, 'The horror, the horror.'"

Pierce tried to ascertain the rules for this surreal but oddly civilized conversation. "Is that your experience of Luandia?"

"Not until now." Though suffused with melancholy, Hill's tone was calm and lucid. "I was born here, when Luandia was still a British colony. My parents were missionaries in Port George before anyone struck oil; to me, this was home. I loved the outdoors, the creeklands, the fishing. Most of all I loved the people, fractious though they were, the traditions through which they found harmony with the earth. Compared to now, living outside modernity was not so mean a fate. And then came oil, the serpent in what—if not the Garden of Eden—was a place that did not destroy its peoples' souls.

"I was near college age. I thought, as did my father, that this elixir would provide roads and health care and education." His tone filled with rueful memory. "So I went off to become an oil geologist, planning to return here. By the time I did, after years in the Middle East, the delta was in the last throes of a wasting disease that had devoured nature and man himself."

This explanation as expiation, Pierce intuited, was a precursor to discussing Bobby Okari. Standing abruptly, Hill returned to the bar, his careful movements seeming to derive from muscle memory. He poured himself a full tumbler of whiskey and brought the bottle back with him, placing it on the table between his chair and Pierce's. Then he sat back a moment, gazing about, as though he perceived something in the light and shadows that no one else could see. "Still," he said in a tone of weary rumination, "I felt the bad old days of oil extraction were slowly coming to an end. What I didn't fully appreciate was that PGL had become inextricably entangled in a nightmare of our creation that we lacked the power to end. Before anything else, my charge was securing the safe operations of PGL in a moral twilight—not just our equipment but the lives and safety of our people. And so I, too, became complicit in the horror."

Pierce took a swallow of whiskey, feeling once more the shadow of Goro. "Gladstone might say you had no choice."

Hill's bark of laughter was surprisingly harsh. "I

could have resigned—or been fired. But I told myself that *that* would be like deserting my troops in a foxhole, surrounded by enemies and enemies posing as friends: thieves, kidnappers, a government contemptuous of its people, 'protectors' who oscillate between being predators and murderers and whose secret alliances may change from day to day." His voice softened. "Survival is a dirty business, Mr. Pierce. No one in my job stays clean."

Pierce poured himself another inch of Bushmills. "I think I understand."

Hill shook his head, a gesture of reproof. "I sat in that deposition the other day, answering questions from your smart young partner, Ms. Rahv. And every answer, however true in itself, falsified an environment she'll never understand. She can't—you can't—imagine what it is to live without law." Suddenly, his voice quickened with anger and remorse. "You arm men who should have no arms. When you call on them to protect your people, as we did after Asari Day, you're nauseous with fear about what they'll do. And no one else wants you to get out. Not the government; not the West; not FREE; not the other crooks and kidnappers; not our management or shareholders getting rich at a safe distance; not the avatars of American oil strategy who imagine us the Praetorian Guard of national security. Who would you have in your place, they ask, the Chinese? They'd destroy what's left of the environment and empower Karama to do whatever he wants.

"So PGL and the government have become like a couple trapped in an abusive marriage. The partners despise each other yet wallow in their dysfunction, afraid of what will happen if they divorce. For Karama, we're reliable and technologically superior—quite reasonably, he doubts whether the Chinese could generate as much for him to steal. For PetroGlobal, the longer it stays, the more it makes: if the world price of oil spikes because of some fresh tragedy in Luandia, it profits; if operations are more stable, production rises and it profits. At whatever cost, a corrupt regime with a brutal military delivers a certain predictability—God only knows what might follow Karama. So, like any toxic relationship, it ends up changing who you are."

"And you?" Pierce asked.

After taking another sip, Hill spoke more quietly: "I've become a man in a catatonic trance, perfectly aware of the evil all around me but unable to speak or move. I still know what the delta needs: leaders who care, revenue sharing, and a sense of community. But that's like dreaming of Utopia in a Hobbesian state of nature. In the end, only Okari claimed to still believe in Utopia."

They were approaching the heart of Hill's malaise, Pierce sensed. " 'Claimed'?" he repeated.

Hill poured himself a more cautious share of

whiskey. Pierce took stock of the toll liquor was adding to his own fatigue; his tongue and brain felt a few clicks slower. "Perhaps he's innocent," Hill responded. "Perhaps not. Perhaps he caused the deaths without wishing to know that. Violent death happens here almost at random, as though you're stepping off a sidewalk when a careless driver careens around a corner. Karama and Okimbo don't have a monopoly on killing."

"But what do *you* think?"

Hill cradled the tumbler in his lap. "That Okari is the only person who proposed, by his actions, to transcend the savagery of the delta. Personally, I thought him gifted with intelligence, charisma, and a *very* considerable ego." Hill gave a rueful smile. "Only a man with an elevated self-concept could truly imagine healing this place. So I took him for a more or less honorable man.

"Of course, who knows about anyone, really? There's only one thing I'm sure of: that Okari, like Gladstone, is caught up in forces beyond his control."

Warmed by whiskey, Pierce chose to reveal some of his own uncertainty. "Gladstone puzzles me," he conceded. "I can't figure out whether he's a decent man or merely a polished businessman."

"You look for polarities," Hill said in mild rebuke. "As though he were a character from a book for boys. By now not even Michael knows what he is for sure.

"I'm sure you plan to question his American superior, John Colson, the chairman of PetroGlobal. I assure you that Colson would much prefer to make money in Luandia by doing the right things. The man beneath Gladstone—me—is too mired in the swamp to believe that possible. So Michael passes on our chairman's well-intended policies, fearful that they may become a 'Chinese whisper': when you tell Karama or Okimbo that your people 'need protection,' it's like Henry the Second in *Becket* asking, 'Will no one rid me of this meddlesome priest?'"

"Henry knew," Pierce retorted. "So does Gladstone. As for the chairman of PetroGlobal, I've represented far too many executives to think he's so naive."

Hill pondered his tumbler of whiskey. "To PetroGlobal," he said at length, "PGL's become a mutation that frightens its parent. PetroGlobal can't control it, can't fix it, and can't get rid of it. So its executives don't want to know the truth—that part of PGL's genetic makeup comes from men like Okimbo and Van Daan. It seems you mean to show them."

"I mean to save Bobby Okari," Pierce answered. "How did Van Daan come to work for you?"

Hill paused, as though facing a decision. "It's as I told Ms. Rahv," he answered. "Okimbo said he wanted to work with him—as though I'd consider a reference from someone I sensed might be a mur-

435

derous psychopath. When I told Gladstone not to hire Van Daan, Michael replied that Ugwo Ajukwa was pressing him to do so."

"What was *your* problem with Van Daan?"

"Other than that Okimbo knew him? Most Afrikaners I know are good people; they've accepted that apartheid had to go. But Van Daan's among the worst, involved in half the dirty wars in Africa—as if there's any other kind. A whiff of racism and brutality follows him into the room."

"Did you say that to Gladstone?"

Hill gazed pensively at nothing. Pierce sensed his divided loyalties: on one side was his loathing for what had happened; on the other, a life of loyalty to PGL. "What I told Michael," he said at length, "was that I didn't think we could control him. It wasn't only that Van Daan was Ajukwa and Okimbo's man, and therefore that I questioned his allegiance. I didn't believe we could predict his methods—by temperament and background, he wasn't likely to internalize corporate memos on 'human rights and community relations.' But Ajukwa insisted, and Gladstone acquiesced."

This last was said in a tone of fatalism, as though it were a turning point. After a moment, Pierce asked, "When did you come to believe that Okimbo had carried out a massacre at Lana?"

Hill no longer looked at him. "There was an oil spill in Lana. Most likely the villagers had sabotaged a pipeline, hoping to get a 'cleanup contract' from PGL. I told Okimbo I didn't want to pay them, that extortion was part of the sickness—impoverished villagers destroying their own environment for money. His response was that I should pay *him* and he would make these saboteurs see reason.

"I refused. Though I doubted it, the leak might have been an accident; too many of our pipes are old. So I decided to visit Lana and see for myself." Hill turned to Pierce, regret etched in his weathered face. "Before I could travel there, reports came back that the village had been destroyed, with many dead. Okimbo told me that another ethnic group, the Ondani, had attacked Lana in a squabble over the proceeds of the anticipated 'cleanup contract.' Just as well, he said; Lana would be no more trouble."

"Did you accept that?"

"No. I thought it was a transparent cover story, not meant to be believed. But I had no way to disprove it. Weeks later, rumors filtered back to me through Okari's people that the attackers had been dressed as civilians but acted like soldiers. In this account, a survivor claimed to have seen a big man with an eye patch directing the attack." Hill's tone was weary. "If so, my complaint to Okimbo had become my own Chinese whisper; when I failed to give Okimbo carte blanche, he used Lana to demonstrate how effective his methods could be. The next time, his tacit message went, PGL should pay him to make our problems disappear. It was my failure to pay for Lana, I believe, that led to Van Daan's ascent."

"But when you told Gladstone about these rumors, he assigned Van Daan to investigate."

"Yes. You know the result: Van Daan reported that it was Asari propaganda." Hill's voice mingled despair and disgust. "'Those people kill each other,' Van Daan told me, 'whenever they get bored.' In Van Daan's account, Okari was exploiting ethnic violence to advance his cause through lies."

Hill poured himself another measure of Irish whiskey and, without asking, one for Pierce. Pierce sipped his for a time, then broke the silence by asking softly, "When those workers were hung, who did you think did it?"

"Possibly the Asari. Possibly not." Hill sat back, his lids heavy. He started to bring the tumbler to his mouth, then stopped. "It occurred to me," he said baldly, "that anyone who could decimate Lana, then blame it on someone else, could do the same thing by killing three of our workers. To pin their deaths on Okari would give Okimbo the equivalent of a hunting license."

Pierce leaned forward. "Did you say that to Gladstone?"

Hill slowly shook his head. "Not in those words. By then my position was tenuous. Ajukwa was agitating to have me fired—inspired by Van Daan, I think. But Gladstone wanted to save my job. His compromise was to give Van Daan his own budget, cutting me out of the loop on 'security matters' relating to the Asari. Making such an accusation would be fatal, I told myself—I could do no good as an ex-employee." He paused, still staring straight ahead. "So I made my own compromise and wrote the now famous 'rubber bullet' memo. My reward for this act of courage was to be confined to quarters with the other employees—for my own protection, Van Daan insisted. My castration was complete."

Though stated without self-pity, the quiet words exposed Hill's internal wreckage more nakedly than a show of feeling. "And Goro followed," Pierce said.

In profile, Hill nodded. "In the literal sense, I still don't know what happened. But essentially, I do. Okimbo and Van Daan planned the massacre your clients saw."

"And Gladstone?"

"Didn't know. Now, like me, he grasps too late the price of his Faustian bargain. Like mine, his job was to protect PGL for the benefit of all those who want us in Luandia. So he turned to the men others had forced on him." Hill faced Pierce at last. "If there was a conspiracy against Okari, Gladstone wasn't part of it. The conspiracy is between Okimbo, Van Daan, and whoever else they work for—or with. Take your pick."

Pierce leaned forward. "What do you know about the trial?"

"That you're making it appear that Van Daan is helping pay for evidence. It seems Michael's quite upset." His gaze broke. "I'm on the sidelines now. As you see, I've turned to drink—Michael thinks I've lost my grip, like a soldier in Iraq suffering from combat fatigue. Soon PetroGlobal will rotate me out of Luandia. If they knew you were here, they'd wish Michael had acted sooner."

"Is *that* all they'd wish for?" Pierce said with real anger. "What about PGL's obligation to stop this legal charade it's part of?"

Hill gave him a mirthless smile. "Because they think it *is* a charade. If PGL sits tight, Karama has intimated to Gladstone, Okari will be convicted and expelled. A tidy solution for all."

"What do *you* believe?"

Hill seemed to reach within himself. "That this is Karama's heartless joke. He means to execute Okari and then, if required, blackmail PGL with Van Daan's complicity. That perhaps you can spoil that last touch a bit."

In this statement, Pierce heard a latent meaning. "Beyond what I've already done?"

Hill sat back with his whiskey. Though Pierce sensed his tremor of doubt, the severing of a last tie, Hill spoke in a discursive manner. "I'm sure you're familiar with the Foreign Corrupt Practices Act—America's effort to keep its corporate citizens from bribing the officials of host countries. In the life of PetroGlobal Luandia, that requires me to keep scrupulous records of payments to people like Okimbo, as well as the purchase of AK-47s, bullets, grenades, and tear gas. All the weapons used to subdue the fearsome villagers of Goro."

"Yes. We've seen the records."

"All of them?" Hill inquired mildly. "Even those maintained by Van Daan after he got his own budget?"

Pierce felt the dullness of the whiskey evaporate. "That's what we were told."

"So were PGL's lawyers. What's eluded them, I find, is that Van Daan kept his own private files." Hill waited for Pierce to absorb this. "After those men were hung and I was confined here for my own protection, I resolved to satisfy my increasingly intense curiosity. So I visited Van Daan's office in his absence. It was there I made my first discovery."

"Which was?"

"That Van Daan keeps his own set of books and records—double bookkeeping, you might say, separate from PGL's." Rising slowly, Hill walked to the other side of the bar, reaching down as though for a fresh bottle of whiskey. What he held up instead was a manila folder. "I want you to forget where these came from, at least for a time. PGL needs to be freed from Okimbo and Van Daan. But not everyone will share my definition of loyalty, especially given what I found on my last nocturnal visit to Van Daan's office. After I heard about Goro."

Every fiber of Pierce's being was now alert. "What, precisely?"

Walking to Pierce, less steadily now, Hill handed him the folder. "I don't think I need explain. Once you've returned to the Okaris', read what's inside. From what I hear about the trial, you'll know what to do."

7

RECOMMENCING THE TRIAL, JUDGE ORTA FIXED Pierce with a gelid stare. "Does the defense have any witnesses?"

His tone was as uninviting as his expression. Standing, Pierce gathered himself, fighting back fear and the dull ache of a hangover, the residue of his evening with Trevor Hill. "I call Colonel Paul Okimbo."

Orta blinked. "For what reason?"

Pierce placed his palms on the defense table. "Colonel Okimbo found the victims, 'arrested' the defendant, and investigated the crime at issue. Without him, there would be no prosecution."

This terse summation caused Orta to glance at Okimbo, as though for cues. But Okimbo's eye was fixed on Pierce; sadists, Pierce thought, fear what they cannot dominate. "If the colonel declines to testify," he told the judge, "then I renew our motion to dismiss all charges."

In answer, Okimbo stood, walking to the witness stand with the catlike movements of a predator. In a hollow show of dignity, Orta said, "Colonel Okimbo may testify."

Pierce approached the stand with his gaze trained on Okimbo. Images flashed through his head: Okimbo raping Omo, torturing Bobby, degrading Marissa. Pierce had never hated another man this much. Quietly, he asked, "How did you first meet Roos Van Daan?"

Okimbo looked contemptuous, like someone forced to swat a fly. "I don't remember."

"Did you meet him through Ugwo Ajukwa, national security adviser to General Karama?"

For an instant, Okimbo hesitated. His voice became indifferent. "Perhaps."

"Did Ajukwa tell you he was recommending Van Daan to be PGL's chief of security in the delta?"

"He may have."

" 'May have'? Didn't you recommend Van Daan to Trevor Hill?"

Pierce caught the first glint of uncertainty. "I may have."

"On what basis? Did you know Van Daan before Ajukwa mentioned him?"

Hemmed in, Okimbo answered dismissively, "It must have been Ajukwa."

"Prior to Asari Day, did you discuss with Mr. Ajukwa whether PGL should fire Mr. Hill?"

Free of any need to impress the tribunal with his candor, Okimbo weighed his answer. "I might have."

" 'Might have'?" Pierce repeated. " 'May have'? 'Must have'? I'm not asking about someone else; I'm asking about you. Did you discuss with Ajukwa asking PGL to fire Hill?"

Sudden fury surfaced in Okimbo's eye. "Yes."

Pierce had found his opening; Okimbo could not stand derision. "In short, you and Ajukwa installed Van Daan at PGL, then moved to sideline Mr. Hill."

"Yes, and good riddance. Hill was weak."

Pierce paused, as though struck by a new thought. "Do you know a militia leader who calls himself General Freedom?"

Okimbo looked wary. "Yes. He was a prisoner in the barracks at Port George."

"Why isn't he still there?"

"He escaped."

"The barracks seem impregnable. Did FREE liberate him?"

"No."

Pierce cocked his head. "Then how did he get out?"

"I don't know."

"Really?" Pierce asked incredulously. "And Karama didn't fire you for that?"

Okimbo watched him. "No."

Pierce saw that Orta looked disturbed, as though entrapped in a dynamic that, from Okimbo's manner, might have grave consequences for each member of the tribunal. "Tell me," Pierce inquired, "did General Freedom escape before or after Karama made Ajukwa his security adviser?"

"This is irrelevant," Ngara called out, "and intrudes on matters of state security."

Turning to Ngara, Pierce intuited that he, like Orta, sensed danger. "What matters of state security? I'm merely placing this escape in time."

Orta fidgeted with the rim of his bowler. "The witness may answer."

As Okimbo knew, this was a matter of public record. "After."

"And did you discuss General Freedom's escape with Mr. Ajukwa?"

"Yes, of course."

Pierce smiled again. "Before or after its occurrence?"

Someone in the gallery emitted a nervous laugh. But it took Okimbo a moment to grasp the implications of the question. With barely disguised anger, he said, "Your question is a stupid one."

"That depends on the answer, Colonel."

Swiftly, Ngara stepped forward. "I ask the court to intervene. Mr. Pierce insults the dignity of the state."

"Not so," Pierce responded softly. "As a representative of the state, I hoped you might be curious as to whether the colonel and Ajukwa allowed General Freedom to escape."

Glancing from Pierce to Ngara, Orta told Pierce firmly, "This accusation—reprehensible in itself—has no relationship to your defense of Mr. Okari."

Perhaps the media felt otherwise, Pierce thought. Turning on Okimbo, he asked abruptly, "Who hung those oil workers?"

"You heard the witnesses," Okimbo snapped. "Don't play the fool."

For an instant, Pierce remembered Okimbo locking him in Bobby's cell. "Perhaps I lack your powers of perception. Didn't Moses Tulu and Lucky Joba first approach you *after* you arrested Bobby Okari?"

"Yes."

"Then on what basis did you arrest him?"

Okimbo frowned. "Because of his violent and seditious statements."

"In other words," Pierce said, "when you 'arrested' Bobby Okari, you had no witnesses against him."

Okimbo leaned forward in a posture of aggression. "They would come, I knew."

"And so they did. According to Joba and Tulu, you first met them in your office with a white man. Was that Roos Van Daan?"

"Yes."

"Why was he there?"

446

Okimbo scowled. "The victims were PGL employees. This was his concern."

"Did he offer to pay the witnesses money?"

"Expenses," Okimbo corrected. "I don't recall the details."

Pierce gave him a curious look. "Did Joba and Tulu simply materialize in your office, or had you spoken to them before?"

Okimbo's gaze narrowed. "Joba called me before. To say he had information."

"During that conversation, did Joba ask whether PGL would pay for his testimony?"

"I don't remember."

Pierce stared at him in mock amazement. "You don't recall if a man who offered to accuse Okari of murder wanted to be paid for doing that?"

"No."

"But when you met them in your office, Van Daan gave both men cash?"

"Expenses."

Pierce raised his eyebrows. "Did Van Daan just happen to have money in his wallet? Or had you suggested that he bring some?"

Stymied, Okimbo glared at Orta. Though he glanced at Colonel Nubola, Orta did not intervene. "I do not remember," Okimbo replied. "You can ask these questions until your tongue falls out."

"Without your assistance, I hope. How much money did Van Daan give them?"

"I don't know."

"Weren't you concerned that the amount might give them an incentive to lie?"

"I already knew the truth. Okari was a perpetrator of violence and sedition. That was why I arrested him at Goro."

The deliberate mention of Goro, Pierce sensed, was intended to remind Pierce to be frightened. It was also a mistake. In a puzzled tone, Pierce asked, "But didn't you arrest Mr. Okari in response to the lynchings?"

"Of course."

"Then why did you plan a military operation in Goro before the murders?"

Ngara stood at once. "The arrest happened *after* the murders for which the defendant stands accused, and therefore is irrelevant to the charges."

Pierce approached the bench, looking from the presiding judge, Orta, to Judge Uza. Stifling his apprehension, he said, "Not if this arrest was planned *before* the lynchings happened. I hardly need spell out the implications."

As Orta turned to Uza, irresolute, Nubola put a hand on his arm. Still facing Uza, Orta flinched. When Uza slowly nodded, Orta turned to Okimbo, briefly glancing at Nubola's hand before he said, "You may answer."

This act of defiance caused Okimbo to fix Orta with an expression of silent warning. Facing Pierce, he insisted, "Okari was arrested for the murders."

Pierce walked back to the defense table. As Bara and Bobby watched, he drew a one-page memo from a plain manila folder. "One month before the lynchings, did you propose to Roos Van Daan that you 'carry out a wasting operation against the village of Goro'?"

Okimbo seemed transfixed by the paper in Pierce's hand. "Tell me from what you are reading."

"Answer the question," Pierce snapped.

Orta held up his hand for silence. Turning to Okimbo, he said softly, "The court desires your answer."

Okimbo glanced at Nubola, as though marking his silence. "No," he told Pierce flatly.

" 'No'?" Pierce repeated. "Didn't you demand that Van Daan give you 'prompt inputs of cash' before *and* after this 'wasting operation' at Goro?"

"No," Okimbo's voice was rough with anger. "I was paid only for protection."

Once more, Pierce read from the piece of paper. "Did that protection include 'ruthless military actions' to 'cause terror among the Asari' and 'alienate Okari from his people'?"

"No."

"No again?" Pierce said with open contempt. "Did you not, in fact, demand that Van Daan pay you twenty-five thousand American dollars for—quote—'setting up the proposed attack on Goro'?"

Okimbo looked at each judge in turn, the movements of his head as jerky as those of a mechanized toy. "I asked for no such payment."

"Enough cat and mouse," Ngara interjected. "I demand to see this document."

Pierce approached the bench and gave the original to Orta. Scanning the document, Orta seemed to blanch. Nubola read over his shoulder, then said derisively, "Who knows where this came from."

"Your Honor," a deep voice interrupted. "May I approach the bench?"

Orta looked up. "Who are you?"

"Clark Hamilton, outside counsel to PGL." Moving beside Pierce, Hamilton added, "I may be able to shed light on this."

Orta handed down the document. As he read, Hamilton drained his face of all expression. "I'm certain I haven't seen it," he told Pierce. "This document can't be from our files—it doesn't have PGL's production stamp."

Pierce shrugged. "Maybe one of your associates slipped up. Anyhow, it's the colonel's memo. Why don't we ask him?"

Pierce looked up at the tribunal. Though clearly enraged, Nubola was out of his depth; the two judges, Orta and Uza, held a whispered conference. Then Orta instructed Pierce, "Show this to Colonel Okimbo."

Taking the memo, Pierce gave it to the witness. "I show you this memo, dated February 7, addressed by you to Roos Van Daan. Can you identify it for the court?"

Staring at the memo, Okimbo gripped it in both hands. "It's a forgery."

"Including the signature 'Paul Okimbo' at the bottom?"

"Yes."

Pierce turned to Orta. "I request that the court order Colonel Okimbo to submit writing samples, and allow us to retain a handwriting expert."

"We strongly object," Ngara interposed at once. "We shouldn't bog this tribunal down with ancillary witnesses. This purported memo—whatever its provenance—is irrelevant to the charge against Mr. Okari."

"Not if the charges were a pretext for Goro," Pierce shot back. "In case it has eluded Mr. Ngara, we're suggesting that this witness conspired to frame Bobby Okari."

Deflated, Orta clasped his hands. "Pending further proof, the court will take this matter under submission. Proceed, Mr. Pierce."

Aware that his time was running out, Pierce turned back to Okimbo. "Let's focus on the day of the operation in Goro. How did you arrive at the staging area?"

"By helicopter."

Relying on the information provided by Beke Femu, Pierce inquired, "Was the helicopter flown by Roos Van Daan?"

Okimbo looked startled, then settled back. "I don't recall."

"Didn't you and Van Daan jointly plan this operation?"

"No," Okimbo insisted. "The plan was mine—to make a lawful arrest."

"With PGL's helicopters and sea trucks? How did you get ahold of them?"

"Mr. Van Daan authorized their use."

Pierce stepped forward. "Did he ask why you needed this equipment to enter an Asari village populated by civilians?"

Okimbo crossed his arms. "We meant to counter any resistance with force."

"There was no resistance," Pierce said evenly. "So you ordered your soldiers to massacre the residents, behead Okari's father, hang Okari from a ceiling fan, and burn Goro to the ground, while you amused yourself by raping a fifteen-year-old named Omo before you slit her throat. Does that about sum it up?"

The courtroom was still. Okimbo leaned forward in the witness box, his stare more lethal than words. "No," he said softly. "It does not."

As Okimbo had intended, the ambiguous answer made Pierce's skin crawl. Ngara jackknifed from his seat as though propelled by tension, addressing Orta in a strained voice: "This slander is too much, Your Honor. I implore you to rule such questions out of order. They have no relationship to the murders at issue."

"Then I'll return to the lynchings." Facing Okimbo, Pierce asked mildly, "Was stringing up those workers your idea, or did someone else suggest it?"

"Enough," Orta directed. "You've established no foundation for such questions."

Pierce faced the judge. "In that case, I request that the court excuse this witness pending the testimony of Roos Van Daan. Given Mr. Hamilton's interest in this matter, I'm sure he can produce him quickly. If not, I'll renew our motion to dismiss the charges."

Seemingly agitated, Orta searched out Hamilton in the gallery. "Have you any objection to counsel's request?"

Hamilton placed his hands on the railing. "Naturally, Your Honor, I must consult with PGL and Mr. Van Daan. I ask that you give us until the morning."

Orta slowly nodded. "The tribunal will adjourn until nine A.M."

Orta brought down the gavel. Abruptly, Pierce was aware of everything around him: Okimbo's silent rage; Bara's fear; Bobby's ironic smile; Marissa's look of gratitude and worry. Approaching Hamilton, Pierce put a hand on his shoulder. "Get me Van Daan, and then a meeting with Gladstone. Or this gets worse for everyone."

8

PIERCE SPENT THE NEXT HOUR WITH REPORTERS from CNN, the Associated Press, and Reuters, after that giving phone interviews to media outlets in England and America. When he returned to the Okari compound with Bara and Marissa, a columnist for the London *Times* drove them, combining the opportunity for access with the man's obligation, as he put it, to "dissuade Karama's minions from hanging you for traffic offenses." With a smile unreflective of his mood, Pierce proposed a daily car pool.

Arriving, the two lawyers and Marissa went to the patio. "Any word from Beke Femu?" Pierce asked Bara in an urgent tone. "We need him to place Van Daan at Goro."

"Nothing," Bara answered. "I'll keep e-mailing his contact. Perhaps when he hears about our defense . . ."

His voice trailed off. No one at the table held out much hope that the soldier would publicly accuse Okimbo and Van Daan of perpetrating a massacre. It was astonishing enough that, with obvious trepidation, Orta had let them come this far. At length, Bara inquired, "Where did you get that document?"

Pierce had told Bara and Marissa nothing. "I have someone to protect," he answered. "I'm also protecting you. For Bobby's sake, I've faxed a copy to my assistant in San Francisco, with instructions to distribute it if anything happens to me."

Marissa stared at the table. Softly, Bara said, "If you've sensed in me a lack of trust, I regret that. But now I see you understand. This is how we live."

Pierce nodded. He still did not know whether to trust Bara.

THAT NIGHT MARISSA came to him. Sitting on the edge of the bed, she murmured, "Are you awake?"

"Uh-huh. I'll sleep once I'm in America."

He waited for her to speak again. "I was thinking about you," she said.

"About what, exactly?"

"Among other things, all the stupid things I said to you at Berkeley about your haut bourgeois aspirations. What an angry, self-important bitch I was."

Pierce laughed softly. "Sometimes. But you were right about me. I was naive."

"But never shallow or unkind." Marissa paused. "What I want to say, I guess, is that I was drawn to you without knowing all the reasons why. I understood that Bobby was remarkable; now it's good for me to know how right that was. But you should know, whatever happens, that what I feel about you is something all its own."

The depth of Pierce's need to hear this revealed to him how much he had repressed. Quietly, he asked, "Will we ever talk about what happened?"

Marissa was silent for a moment. "Perhaps when we get some distance from all of this. I can't make sense of anything now, and it would be wrong to try."

Pierce squeezed her hand. "I know that," he said. "I'd just like to be at peace with you, in time."

He felt her bend to him, soft hair meeting his forehead. Gently, she kissed him, then left the room.

THE NEXT MORNING, when court opened, Roos Van Daan sat next to Hamilton in the gallery, each leaning away from the other in silent dissociation. "I'll bet *that* was a cheery conversation," Pierce murmured to Bobby Okari.

Bobby scrutinized Van Daan. "Why is this criminal here, I wonder."

"Because PGL gave him no choice. They might feel otherwise if they knew what else I'm sitting on."

Bobby gave him a quizzical look that conveyed a glimmer of hope. "Tell me."

"Best to wait. A lot depends on how well Orta slept last night." Pierce looked into his client's weary face. "How well did *you* sleep?"

Returning Pierce's gaze, Bobby smiled a little. "About as well as you did, I imagine. But I envy you Marissa's company. Will I ever see her again, I wonder, outside a prison or a courtroom?"

Pierce touched his shoulder. "That's what we're both working toward."

TAKING THE WITNESS stand, Van Daan looked sullen and dyspeptic; he had not expected to be facing Pierce in such uncertainty. For the first hour, Pierce toyed with him, reading questions and answers from Van Daan's deposition aloud, then asking if each passage was his testimony. By the end of this deceptively understated process, the stillness with which Van Daan studied his interrogator suggested a quarry assessing his escape routes. Sitting in the jury box, Okimbo watched them both closely.

Placing Van Daan's deposition on the defense table, Pierce approached the witness. Quietly, he said, "You know that Bobby Okari is innocent of these murders, don't you."

The startling statement seemed to deepen Van Daan's uncertainty. Tonelessly, he said, "Not according to the witnesses."

"Which you paid for. We already know how much you gave Aboh. How about Joba and Tulu?"

Van Daan remained still. "I paid expenses."

"How much?"

Van Daan hesitated. "Fifteen thousand dollars."

Pierce smiled at this. "In expenses? If I told you that the annual income of the average Luandian male is less than one-tenth of that amount, would you disagree?"

"I couldn't say."

Pierce glanced at Orta. "Never mind—the court can take judicial notice of that fact. Let's try this: what was the annual salary of the three workers who were lynched?"

Van Daan pursed his fleshy lips. "About twenty-five hundred U.S."

"And the money you gave the widows for funeral expenses?"

Van Daan paused again. "Five hundred."

"Too bad for the living," Pierce remarked. "By your reckoning, bus fare to Port George costs thirty times more than burial. How long will it take before you admit to paying those men to lie?"

Van Daan's jaw tightened. "I don't consider them liars."

"Then truth comes at a premium." Pierce moved closer. "On the day of the lynchings, you were in Goro, correct?"

"Over it," Van Daan amended. "In a helicopter."

"And you were also near Goro on the day of Okari's 'arrest.' "

"Yes," Van Daan answered impatiently. "I told you that before."

"Trouble seems to follow you, doesn't it. You also flew Okimbo to the staging area for the operation in Goro. Which you'd already approved."

Van Daan gripped the arms of the witness chair. "No. And I approved nothing."

"Let's not mince words. You paid for that operation, didn't you."

Van Daan shook his head. "No."

Pierce gave him a look of weary patience, then walked back to the defense table, removing Okimbo's memo from the folder. When he turned, Van Daan spoke again, his voice rising: "I know there's this memo Okimbo says is forged. I know nothing about it."

"Humor me." Stepping forward, Pierce handed Van Daan the memo. "According to this, one month before the lynchings Colonel Okimbo asked you to pay him for conducting a 'wasting operation' against Goro. I'd think such a colorful request would stick in your memory."

"It doesn't," Van Daan insisted. "I've never seen this piece of paper."

Pierce skipped a beat. "Then why was it in your files?"

As Orta peered at the witness, a red stain colored Van Daan's cheeks. "If it was, someone put it there to frame me."

Pierce resisted the temptation presented by the word 'frame'; for now it was sufficient to learn, as he just had, that Van Daan had also lied to Hamilton. "Between the date of this memo and Asari Day," he asked, "did you pay money to Colonel Okimbo?"

"If I did, it was merely for protection."

"And you maintain records of all such payments, true?"

Van Daan looked wary. "Most."

Once again, Pierce returned to the defense table. Opening the manila file, he produced another memo. He scanned it, attenuating the witness's tension, then asked, "Did these records reflect a payment to Okimbo for—quote—'miscellaneous services, including planning for an operation in Goro'?"

Okimbo leaned forward; Pierce was immediately certain that he recalled this record well. Perceptibly sagging, Van Daan answered, "I recall nothing like that."

Walking forward, Pierce described the memo for the record before giving it to Van Daan. "Then tell me what this is."

Briefly, Van Daan glanced at it. "I can't."

"Aren't the words I quoted in your hand-writing?"

Van Daan would not look at the document. "Someone else must have written them."

"Then why was this receipt also in your files?"

"I don't know."

"Look again at the document, above the line 'received by.' Didn't you ask Okimbo to sign this to verify that you gave him ten thousand dollars in advance of the operation in Goro?"

Van Daan thrust the document at Pierce. "Take

this," he said in a voice that shook with anger. "It's your forgery."

Someone in the gallery emitted a bark of contempt. To punctuate the moment, Pierce gazed at the tribunal: Orta was frowning, Uza staring at the bench, Nubola looking impatiently toward Ngara. Pierce handed Orta the document. "Please read this, Your Honor. Two witnesses have now claimed that their handwriting is forged on two documents that are damning on their face. I renew my request for an expert to verify the handwriting of Okimbo and Van Daan."

With palpable unhappiness, Orta read the memo. Then he huddled with Uza and Nubola, who seemed to speak with vehemence. When the judge faced Pierce, he appeared shaken. "As before, we will take your request under submission, in light of Mr. Ngara's assertion that the facts surrounding Mr. Okari's arrest are irrelevant to three murders that happened a week before."

Pierce knew this to be a veiled signal to Ngara. In measured tones, Pierce asked Van Daan, "Did the 'miscellaneous services' performed by Colonel Okimbo include lynching those oil workers?"

Ngara leapt up. "*Objection.* The witness can't identify this document. There is no foundation for such an inflammatory question."

"Sustained," Orta said with vehemence. "Enough, Mr. Pierce."

Pierce took the document, returning to the witness table to replace it in his folder. Turning to Van Daan, he asked, "Did you pay Okimbo for the operation in Goro *after* he conducted it?"

"Objection," Ngara said heatedly. "Again, Goro is irrelevant."

Pierce faced Orta again. "A man's life is in your hands. If you'll allow me to proceed, I believe we can show that the events at Goro are inseparable from the murders with which Bobby Okari is charged."

The judge paused, seeming to weigh the risks of appearing to do justice. "With the understanding that his response may later be struck from the record, the witness may answer."

"The answer is no," Van Daan snapped.

Pierce flipped open the folder, still watching Van Daan. "Let me refresh your recollection. One week after the operation in Goro, did you pay Colonel Okimbo fifteen thousand dollars for—quote— 'military operations in Goro carried out by Okimbo and sixty-three soldiers'?"

Reflexively, Van Daan shot a look at Okimbo. "I may have paid him for protection. That is all."

Pierce approached the bench, handing the document to Orta. "As with the two preceding documents, I ask you to note this for the record."

Orta read the memo with narrow eyes and handed it back. Then Pierce gave it to Van Daan. "This is also from your files, Mr. Van Daan. On its face, it's a handwritten receipt for the payment to

Colonel Okimbo of fifteen thousand dollars, with a line above which appears the signature 'Paul Okimbo.' Please explain to the court what *this* is."

With an air of distaste, Van Daan let the document flutter to the floor. "Another forgery."

Nubola glared at Ngara. "We object to *all* these documents," the prosecutor said tautly.

Pierce paused a moment, inhaling to ease his tension. "Then I should be clear," he told Orta. "Our defense is this: that Okimbo and Van Daan conspired with others to lynch the workers, use their murders as a pretext for Okari's 'arrest,' and use the arrest as cover for a massacre intended to crush the Asari movement at Goro. If these documents are authentic—and I am convinced they are—then Okimbo and Van Daan planned the massacre one month *before* the lynchings. All that's needed is a handwriting expert to confirm their authenticity." Pierce trained his eyes on Orta. "Mr. Ngara's objection is the predicate for executing an innocent man. He knows it; the court knows it; everyone here knows it. Just as all of us know that Okimbo and Van Daan are lying. The only question is whether this tribunal will let them."

For an instant, Orta looked stricken. Then he said sternly, "Do not lecture us, Mr. Pierce. Or we will remand you to the custody of a man you slander so freely. As for your defense, you have yet to prove that this 'massacre' occurred. Where are your witnesses to *that*?"

This retort, a cover for Orta's embarrassment, put Pierce on the defensive. "I have two—"

"We know," Orta interrupted with a dismissive wave. "The defendant and his wife. But who else?"

The soldier Beke Femu, Pierce thought. "At the outset of the trial," he answered, "we moved for a delay so that we could locate other witnesses. I renew that motion now."

"And I deny it now," Orta said in a chilly tone. "You will have until tomorrow to persuade us with credible evidence. Until then, the tribunal will hold the matter of Goro in abeyance. Be glad of our forbearance, counsel."

"Thank you," Pierce said, the hollow courtesy of the courtroom. He had sixteen hours to persuade a guilt-stricken soldier to risk his life for Bobby Okari.

9

AFTER DINNER, PIERCE SAT WITH MARISSA ON THE patio, preparing her to testify should Beke Femu not appear. Atiku Bara had vanished; no one knew where. Their only comfort was an article on the Internet edition of the *New York Times.* Beneath the heading "Luandian Dissident's Lawyer Challenges Regime," the article noted the flimsiness of the evidence, the weakness of the witnesses, the dubious nature of the proceedings, and questions about the military's conduct in Goro.

The most pointed sentence was a quote from Pierce: "A striking aspect of this sham prosecution is PGL's apparent involvement in concocting it." But this would only increase the pressures on Orta. Pierce had heard nothing from Gladstone.

"Will they let me testify?" Marissa asked him.

Pierce put down his coffee. "They would in any normal court. But Orta is walking a tightrope, hoping for a veneer of credibility without ending up dead or in prison. At some point he'll fall off."

Footsteps sounded on the patio. Turning, Pierce saw Bara.

"What is it?" Marissa asked him.

"The soldier. Beke Femu." Bara looked from Marissa to Pierce. "In the morning, I'll bring him to court."

Pierce felt relief mingling with a sense of dread. "Why is he willing?"

"Because he has no family."

Silence followed. Bara sat beside Pierce. "I know you've never trusted me. After tonight, you'll have more reason. I'm sending my wife and children to England."

Marissa touched his arm. "Why now, Atiku?"

"Because of Femu," Bara said simply. "I'm afraid of what will happen next."

As Marissa nodded, Pierce felt both her compassion and her solitude. "So here we are," he said. "The few but the proud."

No one answered.

• • •

WHEN PIERCE AND Marissa entered the courtroom, Bara was nowhere in sight. When two soldiers brought in Bobby Okari, Pierce took his place beside him. Inclining his head to Bobby's, Pierce murmured, "We have a witness to the massacre. Now we'll see if he shows up."

Bobby absorbed this, the gratitude in his eyes replaced by sadness. "For the sake of my people, I hope he does. But not for his."

The tribunal took the bench, Orta between a sickly-looking Uza and the stern Nubola. "Well, Mr. Pierce, what do you have for us?"

Pierce stood. "A witness to Goro, I believe. We're awaiting his arrival."

"You may be. This court is not. Continue your defense, or we'll invite the prosecutor's closing argument."

Glancing at Marissa, Pierce saw her face set in resignation and resolve. "Then we call Marissa Okari."

Distracted, Orta was looking beyond him. Pierce heard a stirring in the gallery, then saw Atiku Bara enter with a slender Luandian soldier.

Unsettled, Pierce had his first clear look at Beke Femu, now central to Bobby's defense. He was an unprepossessing figure: almost comically thin, with big ears, limpid brown eyes, and awkward movements. As he looked about his new environment, his entire being radiated fear and confusion;

despite his lawyer's carapace, Pierce felt a stab of remorse. "This is our witness," Pierce told Orta. "I ask the tribunal to hear him now."

Displeasure and uncertainty distorted Orta's features. "Put him on, if you wish," he said in a tone of warning. "But we'll see how far this goes."

Somber, Bara brought the witness forward, pointing him to the chair. As though in a trance, Femu sat. "As part of the witness's testimony," Pierce said, "we ask that the outside counsel for PGL bring Roos Van Daan before the court."

Orta scowled. "For what purpose?"

"Identification by the witness. By the end of Mr. Femu's testimony, there will be no doubt of its relevance."

Once more, Orta looked trapped; there was no plausible reason to refuse. Addressing Clark Hamilton, he said, "You will bring Mr. Van Daan back here. What use we'll make of him is yet to be decided."

Mystified, Femu looked from Orta to Pierce. With daunting coldness, Orta told Femu, "You will tell the truth, and only that. You will not guess; you will not disrespect the court by lying. Prison is the punishment for perjury. Do you understand this?"

Mute, Femu nodded.

"Do you have the power of speech?" Orta inquired cuttingly. "The court reporter does not decipher movements of the head."

The knob in Femu's throat worked. "Yes, sir."

"Good." To Pierce, Orta said, "Begin, counsel. And have a care with how you ask your questions."

Facing Femu, Pierce asked, "Can you tell us your name and occupation?"

"Beke Femu." His voice was close to inaudible. "I am a private in the army."

"In what battalion?"

Femu gave a meaningless nod, as though prompting himself to speak. "The Ninth Ondani, sir. Under the command of Captain Igina."

"Was the Ninth Ondani sent to Goro to effect the arrest of Bobby Okari?"

"Objection." Quickly, Ngara was up, approaching the bench. "These questions are inimical to state security and, we reiterate, irrelevant to the heinous murders of which the defendant stands accused. Mr. Pierce's sole and insidious purpose is to distract from Okari's guilt by demeaning Luandia in the eyes of the world. By now you've seen the press reports treating these lies as truth. Put this slander to an end."

To Pierce, the prosecutor's peremptory tone betrayed his own anxiety, or the knowledge that Orta had been warned. "Is Mr. Ngara now the judge?" Pierce inquired. "Yesterday, this court challenged us to offer a witness to the events at Goro. Now we have. The court should hear his testimony—"

"The court," Orta interjected, "will hear only as

much as it requires." He stopped abruptly, as though realizing that he could not reverse himself at once without appearing craven. "You will proceed, one question at a time."

Mentally, Pierce edited his cross-examination, aiming for its heart. Turning to Femu, he asked, "Before entering Goro, did you assemble in a staging area?"

"Yes."

"What were your orders?"

The witness fidgeted with a cuff. "We were to enter Goro, Captain Igina said. Then we were to arrest Okari. That was all."

Watching, Orta nodded his satisfaction. Stepping between them, Pierce asked, "Did someone change Igina's orders?"

Femu's eyes shut. "Yes."

Orta stiffened, newly apprehensive. Searching for a question not objectionable on its face, Pierce hoped that Femu would have the courage to answer. Softly, he asked, "What were your new orders?"

Femu's eyes snapped open, as though he'd just woken from a nightmare. He looked at everyone and no one. "Did you hear the question?" Pierce asked.

"Yes," Femu answered tonelessly. "We were to kill the people of Goro and burn their village to the ground."

"Jesus," a British voice murmured.

"Who gave those orders?" Pierce asked at once.

Femu swallowed. "The one-eyed colonel."

Pierce felt a constriction in his own throat. Orta seemed too mesmerized to extricate himself; though Nubola leaned forward, signaling the judge to intercede, Orta did not see him. Pierce crossed the courtroom to the jury box, from which Okimbo stared at the witness with a fury beyond reason. Pointing to Okimbo, Pierce asked, "Is this the one-eyed colonel?"

Someone coughed. Miserably, Femu croaked, "Yes."

Ngara half-stood, as though preparing to object, then seemed to choose another course. With as much calm as he could muster, Pierce asked Femu, "Did the Ninth Ondani follow the colonel's orders?"

Femu licked his lips. "Yes. After the sun went dark."

Pierce came forward again, standing near the witness. "Please tell the court what your unit did in Goro."

Were this another country, Pierce knew, he'd be asking Femu to confess to murder; in Luandia, the consequences of answering were much worse. But now Femu seemed ensnared by the memory of his guilt. "We murdered. Some also raped—girls and old women, it did not matter. I saw my friends chop arms off the living. People ran from burning houses and were shot." His voice trembled. "I tried to shoot past them. The colonel saw this—"

He stopped abruptly. Gently, Pierce asked, "What happened then?"

Sweat shone on Femu's forehead. " 'Bring Okari's father,' the colonel tells me. We find the village chief, wearing robe and headdress. He's too afraid to walk. So the colonel says to sacrifice him at the altar of the church."

The courtroom was still. Pierce felt startled—he had not expected this testimony. "Did you do that?"

Femu stared past him. "We make him kneel there. Oda takes out his machete. The chief starts to crawl away, and his headdress falls off. Ado sees a hammer and nails. 'Hold him,' he tells me. So I do, though the chief struggles. Then Oda puts the headdress back on and drives a nail through it.

"The chief screams in pain. Oda drives more nails; the old man crawls like a chicken with no head. Oda gives me the machete to end his screaming."

"What happened then?"

"After this I puke." Femu looked down. "Sergeant Doyah says Okimbo wants the head. Doyah puts it under this arm, like a soccer ball. I think about being in church when I was a boy, how I can never go inside a church now . . ."

Pierce glanced at Bobby. His eyes were moist; whether this was for his father or Femu, Pierce could not know. Quietly, he asked, "What happened then?"

"The village is only ashes and the dead. I follow Sergeant Doyah. He goes inside another house. Through the door I see Bobby Okari. He is tied by his wrists to a ceiling fan. The one-eyed colonel watches him turn."

This was enough, Pierce decided. Scanning the gallery, he saw that Hamilton had returned with Roos Van Daan. "I want you to think back," he told the witness. "When did you first see Colonel Okimbo?"

Femu clasped his hands. "He came by helicopter. An *oyibo* flew him."

Pierce walked to the rail separating the courtroom from the gallery, noting the bleak expressions of those around Van Daan. Pointing to the Afrikaner, Pierce asked, "Is this man the *oyibo*?"

Femu stared, as if at a ghost. "Yes."

Pierce let the silence build, forcing Orta to meet his eyes. "No further questions," he told the judge.

Orta called a recess.

AT ONCE PIERCE felt reality changing.

In the jury box, Okimbo beckoned to Ngara. The tribunal disappeared through the door to the judges' chambers; Okimbo and Ngara followed. They were gone for over an hour. The courtroom remained eerily silent, the gallery filled with the sickened and subdued; for Pierce the scene evoked the memory of watching his forensics team unearth bodies in the Balkans. There were no words.

Femu remained in the witness chair, guarded by two soldiers. Watching him, Bobby said softly, "This is torment." Fingers steepled to his lips, Bara bent his head in the attitude of prayer.

Okimbo emerged first, then Ngara. Moments later the tribunal returned. Uza looked dissociated; Nubola, expectant; Orta, collected but subdued. Orta told the prosecutor, "You may cross-examine, Mr. Ngara."

Ngara rose, expressionless. Without moving from the prosecution table, he asked Femu, "While you were in the staging area, did you have anything to smoke or drink?"

The witness blinked. Pierce watched comprehension creep into his eyes; the question had come from Okimbo. His "Yes" was a near whisper.

"What precisely?"

"Weed. Also gin." Femu looked about. "The colonel—"

"Just answer the question, Private Femu." Ngara's demeaning tone stressed Femu's rank. "How much 'weed' and gin?"

Helplessly, Femu shook his head. "I don't remember."

"And yet you remember these supposed horrors so perfectly." Ngara moved toward him. "Had you ever used alcohol and marijuana together?"

"I don't think so."

"How did you get to Goro?"

The witness hesitated. "I flew."

Ngara smiled grimly. "By flapping your arms? Or did you require assistance?"

Pierce stood. "Objection. The prosecution may find demeaning this witness amusing. After this morning, the tribunal should not."

Orta turned to Femu. Coldly, he asked, "How did you get to the village?"

The witness paused again, as though each question was a trap. "Helicopter."

Ngara moved closer to Femu. "How did you know the man you claim to have beheaded was Okari's father?"

The witness stared at him, frightened and bewildered. "Now I'm not remembering."

"You're not remembering anything, are you?" Now Ngara hovered over the witness. "How much did Okari's lawyers promise you for this fabrication?"

"Objection," Pierce called out.

Orta held up his hand for silence, staring at the witness. "Only expenses," Femu said.

"'Expenses,'" Ngara repeated derisively. "According to counsel, an invitation to perjury. But this time genuine. When did Mr. Pierce coach you in these lies?"

The witness spread his hands. "We met at a garbage dump."

Ngara looked genuinely astounded. "At a garbage dump," he repeated softly. "How much weed had you smoked *then*?"

Anxious, Pierce stood. "I was there, Your Honor."

Ngara fixed him with a scornful look, then turned to Orta. "When counsel first proffered this tale, I warned where it would lead. Now the farce has ripened. I ask the court to remand the witness to Colonel Okimbo for investigation of perjury."

Gripped by anger, Pierce stepped forward. "This is criminal," he protested. "The prosecution asks you to dismiss this witness before he's done, turning him over to the man he's just accused of mass murder—whose own testimony is so packed with lies that *he* should be in jail."

"Enough," Orta snapped.

"Not enough." Heedless, Pierce went on. "The potential for coercion is obvious—that's Mr. Ngara's purpose. To abet him truly would be a 'farce' unworthy of any court."

Orta stared at Pierce, then addressed Ngara. "Beyond what we have witnessed, do you have grounds for alleging perjury?"

"We do," Ngara said firmly. "But we don't wish to compromise our inquiry by declaring them now."

"Very well," Orta said. "The witness will go with Colonel Okimbo."

Pierce heard scattered murmurs of disbelief. "I ask to be heard—"

"We can hear you," Orta cut in. "But when you are finished, we will revoke your privilege to appear before us. Do you value our attention that much? Or will you remain as Okari's counsel?"

Pierce gazed at the witness, feeling the weight of his own culpability. Quietly, he said, "I'll remain."

"Fine. But the witness will not."

Two soldiers took Femu away. In the jury box, Okimbo moved his lips to smile at Pierce.

Turning from him, Pierce sat with Bobby. Pained, Bobby watched the witness. "Now it begins. I pity him."

10

AFTER A SOMBER PARTING WITH MARISSA, PIERCE flew to Waro for the weekend.

The trial had shaken him badly. He spent much of the flight fearful that Bobby, or perhaps Beke Femu, would die in prison. Finally, he returned to the task before him. On Sunday night, he would participate by videoconference in the hearing before Judge Taylor to argue for an injunction against PGL. But his broader purpose was to pull together the threads of what he had learned, searching for new pressure points that might cause PGL and the American government to use all the influence they possessed. The last day had made Karama's intentions clear—however shameful the proceedings, the tribunal seemed compelled by fear to push them to their preordained conclusion. The handful of reporters present, concerned for Pierce, had abandoned their posture of neutrality long enough to shepherd Pierce to the airport; when Vorster and Clellan greeted Pierce in Waro, Vorster offered to return with him for the duration of the trial. "I might improve the odds a little," Vorster put it tersely. "No point throwing your life after Okari's."

Pierce promised to hold the thought.

When he arrived at the hotel in Waro it was close to midnight. His team from Kenyon & Walker was pulling together a filing for the court; Rachel Rahv briefed him at the hotel bar. "We've served a subpoena on Henry Karlin," she reported, "asking for every piece of paper related to his trades in oil futures and communications with Luandian officials—including Ajukwa. We also sent your letter to the Commodities Futures Trading Commission, formally requesting that they investigate Karlin."

Pierce nodded. "Now Karlin will use his influence at the White House—either on Bobby's behalf or to shut down the inquiry into his trades. I have no idea which."

"And we still don't know if Karlin's trades relate to Bobby," Rachel answered. "Stay here long enough, and you begin perceiving patterns where none exist. Have you made any sense of the missing witness from FREE?"

"Missing," Pierce amended grimly, "and presumed dead. That seems the likely fate of witnesses for Bobby. For me, the only question is who killed this one. If it was General Freedom, that suggests he's involved with Okimbo and Ajukwa in a web of corruption that includes God knows *who* else." He gave her a tired smile. "I know, Rache—conspiracy theories are the first sign of dementia. But this conspiracy theory explains General Freedom's escape from Okimbo's custody, the ease with which FREE blew up that facility on Petrol Island, Karlin's uncanny prescience, Van Daan's shadowy relationship to both Ajukwa and Okimbo—"

"There's one glaring problem," Rachel interrupted. "If we follow your theory to its logical conclusion, it also explains what's happened to Okari—the lynchings, the massacre, the tribunal. But *that* doesn't account for Karama. *He* pushed Okimbo as PGL's protector. *He* came up with this tribunal, appointed those chickenshit judges, and controls Okari's fate. Either he's the leader of your conspiracy or it's happening all around him. If the latter, maybe it's not happening at all.

"Remember Occam's razor: often the true explanation is the simplest. The simplest explanation is that, whether Bobby's innocent or guilty, Karama set out to kill him. Everything else is imaginary or irrelevant."

The depressing accuracy of this hit Pierce hard. "You're saying I'm trapped in my own theories."

Rachel touched his hand with sympathy. "Or maybe you're getting closer to the truth. The hell of this place is that it's so hard to know."

Pierce thought of Trevor Hill. "After this, you think we'll ever be the same?"

Rachel gave him a shrewd look. "I will, more or less. But not you. You've seen too much."

Silently he remembered being locked with Bobby in his cell, then the warmth of Marissa's body against his. Pierce imagined them now—Bobby in prison, Marissa desperate and alone—waiting for events only Pierce could influence.

"Let's talk about the hearing," he told Rachel.

ON SUNDAY NIGHT, the lawyers clustered around a conference table at PGL's headquarters, Pierce and Rachel Rahv facing Hamilton and Vasquez. At the appointed time, Judge Taylor materialized on the screen like the Wizard of Oz.

Her manner brisk, she sat in her chambers with a stenographic reporter. "This hearing," she said without preface, "is to rule on plaintiff Bobby Okari's request to enjoin PetroGlobal from participating in acts of murder, such as those that allegedly occurred at Goro, or in violations of due process in connection with Mr. Okari's trial. We'll begin with argument relating to Goro. You first, Mr. Pierce."

Pierce looked into the video camera. "Taken in sequence, Your Honor, the facts show that PGL was deeply involved in an atrocity ordered by Colonel Okimbo—"

"PGL," Taylor interjected sharply, "or Van Daan? PGL claims that whatever he may have done was unknown to anyone above him."

Across from Pierce, Clark Hamilton smiled faintly. "With respect to Bobby Okari," Pierce responded, "Van Daan *was* PGL. Gladstone hired him at the suggestion of Ugwo Ajukwa, Karama's adviser, to supervise security in the delta. In London, when PGL asked for protection, Karama put Okimbo in charge, and Okimbo asked that PGL assign Van Daan to work with him directly. Not only did Gladstone comply, but he gave Van Daan authority to pay Okimbo and arm his soldiers—"

"PGL," Taylor interrupted, "contends it had no other means of protection."

"That's no excuse for abdicating its responsibilities as completely as Gladstone did. At Okimbo's urging, Gladstone removed Trevor Hill from involvement in security matters. Before the operation in Goro, Hill reiterated to Gladstone his belief that Okimbo had ordered a massacre at Lana, and suggested that PGL encourage Okimbo to use tear gas and rubber bullets in any actions against the Asari. Once again, Gladstone sided with Van Daan. So Van Daan authorized Okimbo to use PGL's boats and helicopters in a slaughter carried out with weaponry paid for by PGL."

"That doesn't make PGL cognizant of how they might be used."

"The reports about Lana should have. Instead, Gladstone put a man in charge who wanted more civilians slaughtered. Memoranda from Van Daan's files show that Okimbo proposed a 'wasting operation' against Goro in return for twenty-five thousand dollars, and that Van Daan paid Okimbo ten thousand of that *before* the attack." Pierce slowed his speech for emphasis. "On Friday, at the risk of his life, a soldier described that 'wasting operation' to Karama's handpicked tribunal: the slaughter of civilians, the beheading of Okimbo's father, the torture of Okari himself. According to this witness, Van Daan flew Okimbo to Goro. A massacre ensued. Shortly thereafter, Van Daan paid Okimbo the balance of his fees."

The screen magnified Judge Taylor's look of gravity. "Mr. Hamilton?"

His voice sober, Hamilton said, "The essence of Mr. Pierce's argument is that the lynchings were the pretext for a massacre. If you accept that thesis, you must accept the existence of a conspiracy against Okari *and* PGL.

"After the lynchings, as before, Mr. Gladstone had no choice but to rely on the Luandian military. At every point he emphasized PGL's commitment to human rights; at no point did he authorize the slaughter of civilians. Whatever happened at

Goro—and we have only the word of a soldier addled by alcohol and marijuana—there is *no* evidence whatsoever that *any* responsible person from PGL was in any way involved.

"As to Mr. Van Daan, Mr. Gladstone has suspended him pending an internal investigation. Whatever his role at Goro, he will not be involved in further military operations." Hamilton's voice became firm. "The purpose of an injunction is *not* to compensate for harm that has already occurred but to prevent harm in the future. There's no longer any basis for enjoining PGL."

This last was a key argument; Pierce found Taylor's ensuing silence troubling. "Let's move to Okari's trial," she said finally. "The question is what role, if any, PGL played in the prosecution of Mr. Okari. Mr. Pierce?"

"The answer is simple, Your Honor. Okimbo suborned perjury from these witnesses; Van Daan paid them for it. The result was testimony so preposterous that the gallery laughed. The only moment more ludicrous was Van Daan's assertion that the fifteen-thousand-dollar bribes were actually for 'expenses.'"

"Never mind the defects of the evidence," Taylor cut in. "What's your proof that anyone but Van Daan was involved?"

Pierce felt another stab of dismay. "We don't need any, Your Honor. Van Daan acted on authority granted by Mr. Gladstone. PGL can't disown him now."

Taylor raised her eyebrows. "Mr. Hamilton."

"Our *response* is simple: Mr. Gladstone is not involved, and he's suspended Van Daan. This court's only power is to enjoin PGL if—and only if—there's a risk that it will act improperly in the future. There's no such risk."

"Your Honor," Pierce began, "on the question of risk—"

"I've heard enough," Taylor interrupted. "So I'll address myself to you, Mr. Hamilton.

"The essence of your argument is PGL's obliviousness. I hope that doesn't include you. It's clear that the only reason Mr. Pierce knows so much is that someone slipped him documents PGL never produced. I accept your word that you've never seen them. But I don't believe, and you don't seriously argue, that they're forgeries. So I've begun to worry that neither your client nor you have a clue about what's being done in PGL's name, and with its money."

Astonished, Pierce watched the apprehension appear in Hamilton's eyes. "Your ostrich defense won't fly," Taylor went on. "Gladstone made Van Daan the company's agent. Far from being an excuse, conditions in Luandia—including the murder of its workers—magnified Gladstone's responsibility to be a hands-on crisis manager. The alleged massacre at Goro and this disgrace of a tribunal appear to be part of a scheme designed to eliminate Okari in which Van Daan plays a pivotal role.

"I don't know that Okari's innocent—at this juncture, I don't much care. Injunctive relief includes the power not only to enjoin PGL from further wrongful actions but to undo the wrongs already committed by Van Daan." Pausing, Taylor sat straighter. "Accordingly, the court enjoins PGL from any collaboration in Mr. Okari's prosecution that violates Mr. Okari's rights under international law.

"But that's not all," the judge continued in a chilly voice. "I direct PGL to use its good offices with the Luandian government to seek a recess in the trial in order to investigate whether it has access to further evidence helpful to Okari's defense, and to make that evidence available to Mr. Pierce. If PGL does not comply, the court will consider initiating criminal contempt proceedings against PetroGlobal *and* its officers."

Across the table, Hamilton took notes, his only defense against humiliation. "Your client should also know," Taylor told him, "that we will do everything in our power to limit the consequences of its actions to Bobby Okari. By letter and by telephone, this court will ask the secretary of state to formally request the Luandian government to suspend the tribunal until PGL has complied with its order, and to urge that any future proceedings accord Mr. Okari due process of law. Among *your* responsibilities is to limit the harm to date by working with Mr. Pierce. Is that clear?"

In another context, Pierce might have felt sympathy for Hamilton: not only was Taylor's ruling worse than he could have imagined, but its impact would be disastrous for PGL's reputation and the value of its stock. In yet another context, Pierce might have been elated. All he could feel now was hope.

When Taylor vanished from the screen, Hamilton faced Pierce. "We'll cooperate, of course."

"Of course."

From his expression, Hamilton heard the acid in Pierce's voice. Pierce did not care; this case had stripped him of false politesse. At length, Hamilton said, "Michael wants to see you. Give me a half hour to explain to him what's happened."

GLADSTONE HAD A spacious corner office. When Gladstone's assistant closed the door behind him, Pierce found him gazing at the half-lit skyline of Waro. Without turning, Gladstone said, "It's always better in the dark."

"Much like your business, I suppose."

Gladstone turned, his face expressionless. "You must be quite pleased."

Pierce could imagine his thoughts; whether or not Bobby survived, Gladstone's overlords at

485

PetroGlobal might throw him to the wolves. "I'll be 'pleased,'" Pierce answered, "when Bobby's life is spared."

"I'll do what I can." A sliver of anger entered Gladstone's voice. "As I would have before this judge fueled the media campaign you're no doubt about to launch."

"No doubt. Your choice now is to make it better or worse."

Gladstone was silent. At length he said, "It was Trevor Hill, wasn't it?"

He did not seem to expect an answer. "You got here on your own," Pierce responded. "All you could ever control was PGL. Through a series of miscalculations, you lost that. If you believe that Karama is using this trial merely to kick Okari out of Luandia, that's the worst miscalculation of all."

Gladstone shoved his hands into the pockets of his linen sport coat. "I've arranged to see Karama. If we can help get Okari out of here, will he dismiss his lawsuit?"

"All I can do is ask Okari and wish you good luck with Karama."

Gladstone's smile was bleak. "Okari once told me that we were Siamese twins, our fates inextricably bound. I suppose I should have listened."

11

A T TEN O'CLOCK MONDAY MORNING, PIERCE AND Hamilton stood before the tribunal. "With the support of counsel for PGL," Pierce said, "defendant renews his request for a recess. I ask the court to hear Mr. Hamilton."

Orta fixed Hamilton with a disparaging gaze. "PGL is not a party here."

"True," Hamilton responded. "But Mr. Van Daan is a principal witness, and his role raises important questions about the case against Okari. PGL requests a recess to investigate Mr. Van Daan's activities, and to inform the court and Mr. Pierce of our findings in four crucial areas: the murder of our employees; the events in Goro; the testimony of Lucky Joba, Moses Tulu, and Eric Aboh; and Van Daan's own credibility."

"For our part," Pierce added, "we believe that PGL's investigation will confirm the lack of credible evidence against Mr. Okari. A man's life is at stake, and the truth may be at hand. Justice requires a recess."

As Nubola shook his head, Orta said impassively, "Let us hear from Mr. Ngara."

Ngara stood. "I respectfully request the tribunal to hold this matter in abeyance pending the further testimony of Beke Femu."

Pierce felt numb: that Orta looked unsurprised

confirmed his worst suspicions. "Very well," Orta said, "You may recommence your cross-examination."

Hamilton glanced at Pierce, then shrugged in resignation. Pierce took his place between Bara and Bobby, noting Marissa's stricken face. In this courtroom, Pierce thought, hope vanished quickly. Bara's expression was blank; Bobby's, contemptuous at first, changed when he saw Beke Femu.

Watching Femu take the stand, Pierce thought of a college friend who had suffered a nervous collapse; afterward an affectless stranger had occupied the man's body until, like his former self, this shell vanished from the campus altogether. So it seemed with Femu. He gazed at the courtroom with spectral eyes, as though he remembered nothing from before; only his naked fear when he saw Okimbo betrayed that he did.

"Tell the tribunal," Ngara directed, "if you have anything to add."

"Yes." Femu's voice was almost inaudible. "I lied."

A smile of satisfaction stole across Ngara's face. "And your reason?"

"Personal gain." Femu looked down. "A man gave me money. He said he was working for Mr. Pierce."

This fabrication, Pierce thought, showed a lawyer's touch; he could not disprove the supposed act of someone else. "How much money?" Ngara demanded.

"Ten thousand dollars U.S."

Taking a document from the table, Ngara handed copies to the court, then to Pierce. On its face, it was a record from the Bank of Luandia, dated one week before, showing the deposit of ten thousand dollars by Beke Femu. "A forged document," Bobby murmured. "One can never say they lack a sense of humor."

Ngara gave it to the witness. "Did you deposit that money in your account?"

"Yes," Femu responded mechanically. "This is the record."

"Very well. Tell us what happened at Goro."

The witness swallowed. "There was resistance. We did only what was necessary to subdue the village."

Femu's script lacked the texture and detail of truth. But Colonel Nubola nodded his encouragement; from the jury box, Okimbo watched Bobby Okari with obvious enjoyment. "So," Ngara prodded, "there was no massacre."

The witness still looked down. "No, sir."

"Then where did you get this terrible story?"

"From the man who gave me money," Femu mumbled. "He showed me a legal document signed by Mr. Pierce. He told me to memorize the underlined parts. Then I could add whatever details I liked."

Ngara handed Pierce a copy of the civil complaint in *Okari v. PetroGlobal Oil*. Scanning its pages, Pierce saw that the factual allegations were denoted by highlighter. After handing copies to the tribunal, Ngara asked, "Is this the document?"

"Yes, sir."

"In short," Ngara said harshly, "your testimony was based on a complaint prepared by Okari's lawyer."

Femu nodded. "Yes, sir. I am very sorry."

Turning his back to Femu, Ngara said dismissively, "No further questions."

Standing, Pierce remained by the table. "What did they do to you in prison?"

The witness blanched. "Nothing."

Femu watched Pierce as though expecting him to challenge this. Instead, Pierce asked, "When did you open the bank account mentioned a minute ago?"

Though the witness's mouth opened, he was momentarily silent. "I can't remember."

"This year? Or before that?"

The witness shook his head. "I don't know."

"Do you remember *where* you opened it?"

"No."

Pierce nodded. Softly, he asked, "Because you never opened an account?"

The witness hugged himself, as though the courtroom had turned cold. "I did."

"How much money was in it?"

"I can't remember."

Pausing, Pierce let the gallery absorb this. "The man you say supplied this money, what was his name?"

"He didn't say."

"What did he look like?"

"I don't know." Femu gazed at the ceiling. "Tall, with short hair. Thin."

"How old did he appear to be?"

"I don't know." Femu paused. "Maybe in his thirties?"

Pierce smiled faintly. "Sounds a lot like Mr. Ngara. Would you say they resembled each other?"

From the gallery came a cynical laugh. Briefly, the witness stole a glance at Ngara. "I can't say," he mumbled.

"Then let's go back to your prior testimony. Among other things, you said that a white man flew Colonel Okimbo to the staging area outside Goro. Did you get that from the document you just identified?"

Femu hesitated. "Yes."

Pierce stepped forward, holding out the complaint. When Femu took it from him, his hand trembled. Calmly, Pierce said, "Show me where."

Femu fumbled with the pages. In suffocating silence Pierce returned to the defense table, studying Ngara while awaiting Femu's inevitable answer. In a muffled voice, Femu said, "I can't find this."

"That's because it isn't there. So how did you

know to say a white man came with Okimbo?"

Femu shrugged helplessly. "I guess the stranger told me to say a white man."

"Did he show you a picture?"

Femu's face was a portrait of confusion. "I don't remember."

"Then how did you know what he looked like?"

For a long moment, Femu simply shook his head, confused. "Objection," Ngara said. "The witness now says no such man exists."

Pierce kept staring at Femu. "And yet he identified Van Daan in court. Out of all the *oyibos* in the courtroom, Mr. Femu, how did you pick out the man you said was with Okimbo?"

Femu gave Pierce a pleading look. "You pointed to him."

"And you recognized him," Pierce said softly. "How else could you have known Van Daan wasn't in his office, surrounded by coworkers, when you were in Goro?"

"Is that a question?" Ngara asked sharply.

"Yes." Pierce turned to him with open disdain. "As you know, it's also the truth."

"You will not disparage counsel," Orta snapped. "Objection sustained."

Pierce ignored this. "If you falsely identified Van Daan," he asked Femu, "how could you know he wouldn't have an airtight alibi?"

The witness held out his hands in entreaty. "I'm confused now."

"You're not confused, Mr. Femu. You're afraid."

Femu glanced at Okimbo. "No, sir."

"Yes," Pierce responded quietly. "You and I can go over your testimony, bit by bit, until you're forced to admit that your story today is a lie. So why don't you tell me what Okimbo did to you in prison?"

The witness gaped at him. Pierce felt Bobby grasp his arm. *"Enough."*

Pierce turned, inclining his head to whisper. Bobby's eyes were suffused with pain. "I know too well what Femu can expect," Bobby murmured, "You're signing his death warrant."

"He's signing yours," Pierce snapped. "Femu is dead already."

"Not by my hands. This man did his best." Bobby's voice was low and intense. "Karama has decided my fate. Ngara knows it; so does Orta. Let their victim go."

Slowly, Pierce exhaled. After a moment, he turned to Orta, "No further questions."

With a satisfied expression, Orta folded his hands on his stomach. "You may step down, Private Femu."

Unsteadily, the witness stood. Two Luandian soldiers removed him from the court. Bobby watched him vanish with a look of sympathy and dread. "Your Honor," Ngara said, "I now wish to oppose Mr. Pierce's latest motion for recess. It's clear that the defense, not the prosecution, has offered perjured testimony. The sole witness to this so-called massacre has now refuted his slander; therefore, the events at Goro should have no place in this proceeding." Ngara's tone became imperative. "As a predicate to ruling on this recess, the tribunal should strike from the record all testimony regarding Okari's arrest and bar any further evidence on that subject."

Helpless, Pierce knew that he was witnessing a legal choreography synchronized before the hearing. "Now for Mr. Pierce's request," Ngara continued. "PGL claims to be concerned about the conduct of an employee. But Colonel Okimbo has affirmed that no impropriety occurred. So why does PGL seek delay?" The prosecutor's voice throbbed with theatrical outrage. "Because PGL has been threatened by a judge in the United States who is pushing the rogue lawsuit used as a template for Private Femu's perjury. If counsel has anything truthful to offer us, he should do so now."

Orta nodded his approval. "Have you any response, Mr. Pierce?"

Pierce fought to rein in his anger. "Yes. First, Femu was plainly lying today. Second, Van Daan paid all three witnesses to Mr. Okari's supposed guilt. Third, the memoranda from Okimbo to Van Daan show that both men were involved in an operation against Goro planned prior to the lynchings." Pierce paused, his stare challenging the tribunal. "Unless these are forgeries, the truth is clear. Our request for a handwriting expert is still before the court. How does this tribunal rule?"

Orta looked dyspeptic. "The tribunal will confer in chambers," he said at length. "After that, we will announce our ruling."

He banged the gavel. In the tumult that followed, Pierce turned to Marissa. The fear in her eyes was terrible to see.

WITHIN TEN MINUTES, the judges returned.

Nubola looked commanding, Uza sickly; it occurred to Pierce that he had not spoken aloud in court. Sitting between them, Orta read in a monotone from a document that, Pierce felt certain, had been prepared by Ngara before this morning's session: "Based on Private Femu's recantation, the tribunal will strike from the record any references to the events relating to the defendant's arrest, and will entertain no further testimony on that subject. For this reason, we deny Mr. Pierce's request for a handwriting specialist.

"This leaves the defendant's request for a recess pending an investigation by PGL. In principal part, that request relies on the assertions regarding Goro we now have ruled irrelevant. Moreover, the credibility of Mr. Van Daan does not relate to that of Colonel Okimbo or Messrs. Joba, Tulu, and Aboh." After a pause, Orta tried to infuse the written words with indignation. "As for PGL's intervention, we do not exist to rescue it from the unjust acts of an American court. Nor is this tribunal within the jurisdiction of the United States judicial system. We will tolerate no foreign meddling in these proceedings—especially where, as that judicial system itself recognizes, terrorist threats to national security require special processes. Motion denied." Looking up, Orta stared at Pierce. "You will confine yourself to refuting the evidence that Mr. Okari ordered the murder of three fellow Luandians."

Pierce stood. "What evidence? There is none. I have no witness to refute what the prosecution never tried to show: who murdered these oil workers, and that those unknown persons acted on Mr. Okari's orders—"

"Not so," Orta interjected. "The testimony of three Asari men establishes a prima facie case that Mr. Okari issued such orders."

"To *whom,* Your Honor?"

"Perhaps Okari can tell us," Ngara interjected. "If the defendant wishes to refute this testimony, he can speak for himself."

"I will." Turning, Pierce saw Bobby push himself up. Though the effort seemed to exhaust him, he spoke with passion. "I will not demean myself by answering these charges unless I am free to describe the massacre of my people. If this tribunal does not allow me to do so, it is because your purpose is to bury me along with the truth. I will not join you as a bit player in Karama's charade—"

Orta banged his gavel. "Sit, or I will find you in contempt of this tribunal."

"I will gladly sit," Bobby responded. "But contempt of *this* tribunal is impossible."

A gasp issued from the gallery. Glowering, Orta told Pierce, "You will control your client or go to jail with him. Okari declines to refute the charges against him. Produce another witness, or be done."

Glancing at Marissa, Pierce saw Bobby shake his head. Pierce walked over to him. "I won't allow this," Bobby said, "and you shouldn't want it. To call Marissa would jeopardize her further. Whatever becomes of me, I want her to survive."

There was nothing for Pierce to say. Facing Orta, he said quietly, "We have no other witnesses. Do what you will."

Raising his head, Orta tried to gather the remnants of his dignity. "We will entertain closing arguments at nine A.M. tomorrow," he intoned. "Then we will render our verdict."

12

IT WAS PAST MIDNIGHT, BUT NO ONE AT THE OKARIS' compound slept.

In her bedroom, Marissa called and e-mailed media contacts and supporters in America, alerting them to the fateful pronouncement awaiting Bobby in the morning. Working beside Pierce in Bobby's study, Atiku Bara alerted diplomatic contacts in

Europe and among the nations of the British Commonwealth, seeking more visible support for Bobby in the rush of events. Shutting his mind to its hopelessness, Pierce prepared the final argument, logical but impassioned, that he would have given in an American court. Turning off his cell phone, Bara asked Pierce, "What will you say?"

"That he's innocent. What else is there to say?"

Bara cast a troubled gaze at the carpet. "He should have said so himself."

"To what end?"

"For the world to hear." Bara's eyes met Pierce's. "For me to hear."

The tenor of his voice filled Pierce with unease. "What are you saying, Atiku?"

Bara drew a breath. "Lucky Joba wasn't lying. The phone call he heard Bobby making was to me."

Pierce sat back, stunned. All he could do was stare at Bara, trying to reintegrate his sense of this man in light of the secret he had carried. "He was just so tired," Bara murmured. "Worried the youth were slipping away—"

"According to Joba," Pierce cut in, "Bobby said there must be deaths."

"To me, he was speaking out of anguish, less for himself than imagining the mind of an Asari youth." Bara's tone was soft. "Obviously, I issued no orders. Almost as soon as Bobby said this I could feel his regret. We never spoke of it again."

"Not even after the lynchings?"

"There was too much for us to talk about. Perhaps he didn't remember; perhaps he did not wish to."

Pierce rubbed his eyes. The truth behind his sense that Bara concealed secrets now seemed clear. The burden Bara carried was his fierce loyalty to Bobby; the information he had withheld from Pierce concerned his own doubts. "According to Eric Aboh," Pierce said, "Bobby told him something similar—if more ambiguous."

"True. But Eric is jealous and a coward. All it would take is a healthy fear of Okimbo to cause him to enrich his testimony."

For a moment Pierce was quiet, torn between dread of his question and the need to hear the answer. "Do you think Bobby ordered the killings? Or said anything that might have encouraged them?"

Bara considered his answer. "For all the time I've known him, Bobby's commitment to nonviolence has seemed absolute. In my heart, I still believe this. We've proven that the trial is a farce, and that someone else may well have ordered those men hung. Perhaps that is all we could do. But the barest possibility lingers that Karama and his underlings may have framed a guilty man. For Bobby's sake, and mine, I wish this were not so."

For me now, as well, Pierce thought. But all he said was "You've been a loyal friend, Atiku. You have nothing to regret."

• • •

THE NEXT MORNING, Pierce felt an oppressive fear permeate the courtroom. Soldiers ringed the building; inside, the number of guards had doubled. As if on alert, Okimbo stood instead of sitting, positioned so that the tribunal could not help but see him. The gallery was quiet. Even the judges appeared lifeless: when Orta spoke, inviting closing arguments, his voice was barely audible. Watching, Marissa was so rigidly composed that the effort this must surely require touched Pierce more than tears.

In his closing argument, Ngara was perfunctory, as though he had lost any relish for a drama whose fraudulence was so transparent. After reviewing the testimony against Bobby, he said, "These murders were the inevitable culmination of seditious rhetoric, secessionist ambition, and civil disobedience against the security and economic interests of the state—crimes in themselves punishable by death." He pointed to Bobby Okari. "Now this man, so voluble in his insolence, has refused to speak to the evidence. This court has no choice but to find Bobby Okari guilty and sentence him to death."

Sitting beside Pierce, Bara stared at the table. As Pierce gathered his notes, Bobby touched his arm, his eyes filled with intensity and purpose. "Our final words should come from me."

There was no reason, Pierce realized, to refuse.

Nodding, he stood. "As is his right, Mr. Okari wishes to speak on his own behalf."

Orta's features rearranged themselves: his lips pressed, his eyes narrowed, and the furrow in his forehead deepened. Then he mustered a curt nod.

Bobby stood with difficulty, resting his palms on the table for support. His gaze swept the tribunal, first resting on Nubola, then Uza, and finally Orta. Softly, he told them, "I knew that someday we would meet before they ever brought me to this place.

"Long ago, by speaking for my people, I signed a pact with death. I knew full well the fate of those who protest in Luandia. You are merely Karama's pawns, interchangeable cogs in the machinery of death."

The courtroom was hushed. Watching Okimbo, Pierce waited for him to halt the proceedings, or for Orta to do so out of fear. Bobby's speech gathered a relentless force. "I've committed no crime but to rally the oppressed to seek an end to misery. The punishment was the slaughter of my people." His voice filled with searing anger. "The men who are your overlords have fouled our land; poisoned our water; ravaged our daughters; killed our men, women, and children and driven their survivors into hiding. And now the 'judicial system' for which you are the front men has beaten, starved, and tortured me; stripped my wife naked for trying to see me; intimidated and bribed fearful men to

501

bear false witness against me; and trampled every right due any man in its indecent haste to kill me."

On the bench, Orta reached for his gavel, staring at Bobby. "Even now," Bobby asked him, "are you still afraid of truth? If you find me guilty, as Karama has ordered you to, the world will see your cravenness and shame. And if you sentence me to death, you are as guilty of murder as whoever hung those men."

Okimbo stepped into the well of the courtroom, nodding peremptorily to Orta. But the judge still held the gavel. "I stand before you," Bobby continued, "appalled by our poverty; distressed by our political subjugation; angered by the devastation of our land; sorrowing for the loss of our heritage; compelled to uphold our right to a decent way of life; and determined to help give our country a government that protects us all. So I am not the only man on trial."

When Pierce glanced at Marissa, her eyes were shining with pride and anguish. "All of us," Bobby said firmly, "stand trial before history. The government and PGL are on trial. So are the politicians, soldiers, businessmen, lawyers, and judges—too greedy to act, too afraid to speak the truth—who abet the cruelty and corruption of the state. And so are all the nations of the world who take our oil to fuel their cars and factories and arms and lust for power, leaving us with nothing but men like you."

Angrily, Orta cracked his gavel, *"Silence."*

Bobby shook his head. "We are almost done here, you and I. For you and for your colleagues, this is the last chance to expunge your own guilt. For your sake, and that of our people, I ask that you take it."

Wearily, Bobby sat down. Breaking the silence, someone applauded. Furious, Orta banged his gavel.

This time the silence was complete. Filled with dread, Pierce watched the judges talk among themselves. When Orta faced the courtroom, he did not look toward Bobby, and his voice was devoid of feeling. "We find the defendant Robert Okari guilty of murder and sedition. The sentence for these crimes is death by hanging."

Pierce heard a gasp. Glancing up, he saw Okimbo smile; his foot tapped, as though keeping time to music only he could hear. Fighting his outrage, Pierce stood. "We ask for time to petition the government. What is the scheduled date of execution?"

Humiliation passed through Orta's eyes. "By decree of the executive, the court has no discretion in this matter. We await instructions from President Karama."

Orta banged the gavel. The tribunal stood at once and retreated from the courtroom.

On Okimbo's order, four soldiers came for Bobby. Stoically, he quickly embraced Bara, then Pierce. As the soldiers encircled Bobby, he turned to see Marissa.

She stood there, motionless, until Bobby disappeared. Pierce knew he would always remember the desperation in her eyes, the look of a wife who might never again see her husband.

13

IN TAUT SILENCE, VORSTER AND CLELLAN DROVE Pierce, Atiku Bara, and Marissa away from the courthouse. Marissa stared ahead, ignoring the barricades and soldiers. But when they reached the compound, armed soldiers under Okimbo's command were stationed at the iron gate.

Lowering the window, Clellan waited. A lieutenant in combat fatigues approached. Peering in at Marissa, he said, "Mrs. Okari is under house arrest. Once inside, she stays there."

Pierce got out, facing the lieutenant. "On whose orders?"

The man shook his head. "Don't question us," he said curtly. "Unless you want to join her."

He barked a command to a soldier inside the gate, and the iron bars slowly parted. As Bara and Marissa got out, Pierce leaned inside the van. "Wait here," he told Vorster. "I'll call you."

Vorster nodded; there was nothing else to do. "Let's go inside," Pierce told Marissa.

Her look was both fearful and questioning. "You're sure?"

"Yes."

Together, Marissa and the two lawyers walked through the gate, and then it closed behind them.

ONCE INSIDE, PIERCE asked Marissa for a moment with Bara. The two men went to the patio. The noontime heat was sweltering; beads of sweat appeared on Bara's forehead. "You could be next," Pierce told him.

"And you?"

"I'm an American. My chances are better than yours. God knows what will happen in the delta now."

Bara put his hands in his pockets. "The only alternative to Karama will be FREE. Perhaps that's why those murders happened." His gaze met Pierce's. "It took such courage for Bobby to speak today. Once he said such things because he believed that, in the end, words of hope would triumph over weapons. Now hope will die with him." Tears surfaced in Bara's eyes. "I must try to remember Asari Day—men and women, young and old, all demanding justice. Then others may remember, too."

His tone was valedictory, as though Bobby were already a memory. "He's not dead yet," Pierce said. "There's a meeting of the Commonwealth nations, in Australia. If you can leave, go there, and talk to any leader you can find about speaking out on Bobby's behalf. If enough of them do, maybe we can save him."

Bara looked down. Neither man said what both believed: that the purpose of this mission would be to save not Bobby Okari but Atiku Bara. "And Marissa?" Bara asked.

"I'll take care of her."

Slowly, Bara nodded. "There's something else you can do," he told Pierce. "Among the Asari, it is tradition that we are buried in our home village. Otherwise the dead man's soul can never sleep. If they murder Bobby, try to see that he's laid to rest in Goro." His voice softened. "This should have been my duty, Damon."

"You have a family in London." Facing Bara, Pierce felt a renewed fear for him. "Vorster's waiting outside. Say good-bye to Marissa and go."

Awkwardly, the two men embraced. "Do me a favor in return," Pierce told Bara. "If they murder Bobby, don't come back. Leave this last to me."

WHEN BARA HAD gone, Pierce went to Marissa's bedroom.

She sat in the window, gazing out at the Atlantic. "How are you?" he asked.

After a moment, she turned to him. "I was thinking about the three of us, back in Berkeley."

"What, exactly?"

"A thousand things." She hesitated. "I found myself imagining that I'd chosen not to come here. Then I felt ashamed."

"Human, you mean?"

506

"I guess. In my more selfless moments, I imagine you'd never met me. Or maybe that's just self-pity."

Pierce waited a moment. "I have to leave, Marissa."

Her eyes glistened. "I know."

Watching her face, Pierce realized that, dislocated by all that had happened, she thought he was returning to America. "Not home," he said. "I'm flying to Savior City before those soldiers shut me in here."

"For what?"

"To see Caraway, and maybe Gladstone—he's got a meeting with Karama." Pausing, he searched for words of hope. "That today was so awful helps us in the eyes of the world, I think. Whatever else, it should be the end of delusions."

"The end of mine." Marissa bowed her head. "I find myself waiting for the telephone to ring, Okimbo inviting me to collect my husband's body from him. I can't stop seeing Bobby hanging from those gallows. I wonder if it's better knowing the hour that he's scheduled to die, or to die with him hour by hour."

Pierce did not know what to say. By leaving, he could lose himself in action; Marissa was forced to wait alone, dreading what would happen to Bobby, and herself. At length, Pierce said, "I'll do whatever I can for him. Then I'm coming back for you."

"Only if it's safe." Looking up at him, she tried to smile. "Don't become a burden to me. It's enough to worry about the other man I love."

Looking into her face, Pierce understood, as much as he could, how she must have felt watching her husband taken from the courtroom. "When I said I was coming back," he told her, "I was promising myself."

"Then I won't say good-bye," she answered softly. "We've done that too often already."

THAT EVENING PIERCE boarded a plane for Savior City.

The soldiers had let him leave without incident; the question was whether he could return. Flying with Vorster, he found his thoughts oscillating between Bobby and Marissa—fearing that Bobby might be dead by the time he arrived; imagining what might happen to Marissa. To leave her effectively in Okimbo's custody filled him with foreboding. As the plane taxied to the gate, he found a message on his cell phone and was certain it meant the worst for both Okaris.

But the message was from Gladstone. "I saw Karama," he said simply.

THEY MET IN the dimly lit restaurant of a luxury hotel. Though his attire remained elegant, Gladstone looked as though he had not slept, and his voice and manner were subdued. "It was after midnight," he said, "in Karama's backyard zoo. As we spoke, he threw scraps of meat to a pair of tigers. Karama called Okari a secessionist. His fate was not a question of commerce, Karama said, nor could he take into account our fears of an American court.

"It was like talking to a monomaniac—no give at all. I tried to resurrect his previous hint that, were we quiescent, he might content himself with exiling Okari. He answered that this was before you and this American she-judge conspired to embarrass him." Gladstone sipped his mineral water. "I took that as a suggestion for us to be silent. So do my superiors."

"Then it seems they've got a choice," Pierce answered. "Please Karama and fuel my lawsuit, or do the morally decent thing."

"Which is?"

"Speak out against Bobby's execution, here and in America. Not just for show—PetroGlobal has friends at the White House and in Congress." Pierce's voice hardened. "By tomorrow Okari may be dead. All I can do then is amend my lawsuit to include his execution, with the widow Okari as plaintiff. The result for PetroGlobal will be worse than you imagine. I don't think its officers will enjoy answering for Okari's murder."

Gladstone shot him a resentful look. "*I* don't enjoy answering for Roos Van Daan. You can be sure that our chairman and our board are acutely aware of the problem you've created. They're less persuaded of Okari's innocence; oddly enough, the hanging of our employees troubles them as much as the prospect of Okari's." Gladstone's tone became sardonic. "Sentiment aside, our board isn't interested in trying to save Bobby if all they get is more of you. They want this lawsuit gone."

"And I want both Okaris alive. Did Karama say anything about *her*?"

"No. Not even to suggest that she's the bone he'll throw us in return for silence."

Pierce absorbed this. "I'm not the client. But tell your people this: *if* they help both Okaris get out alive, I'll find some way to end this lawsuit."

Gladstone stared at him. "That's all?" he inquired tartly.

"Not quite. I want a meeting with Karama. I know you can accomplish *that* much, Michael. So please don't tell me no."

Gladstone's expression filled with misgiving. "The man's a psychopath," he said flatly. "If I succeed, bring something to feed the tigers besides yourself."

His cell phone rang. Taking it from his suit coat, Gladstone glanced at the number, then pushed the talk button. "What is it?" he asked brusquely.

Gladstone listened. After a moment, his eyes froze. Before hanging up, he said softly, "Thank you."

"Is Okari dead?" Pierce asked at once.

"No. But you'd better get to Caraway as quickly as you can."

"What is it?"

"Six American military advisers have been kidnapped in the north, allegedly by Islamic terrorists." Gladstone shook his head in dismay. "I'm no geopolitical strategist, but I'd say this changes everything."

14

IT WAS NINE P.M. BEFORE PIERCE REACHED CARAWAY, nine-thirty when Pierce and Vorster headed for the embassy. Vorster had again concealed a gun beneath the seat of his SUV. But the broad streets of Savior City were light in traffic and largely free of crime; unlike Waro, this artificial city existed to glorify Karama, and the dictator's presence fed an oppressive fear of displeasing him. As they neared the embassy, the distant lights of Karama's redoubt glowed against the dark shadow of Savior Rock. "He'll be up all night," Vorster said. "Even without a crisis, Karama's like Dracula."

Pierce's cell phone rang. When he hit the talk button, he recognized Jeff Schlosser's voice, its rhythm more rapid than normal. "What the hell's happening over there? Those soldiers are all over the news."

"I just heard," Pierce said. "All I know is this can't be good for Bobby."

"That was my reaction," Schlosser said. "Actually, I need to know what you did to stir up Henry Karlin."

"Nothing that points to you," Pierce assured him. "We sent Karlin a subpoena, then wrote to the chairman of your agency asking that it investigate Karlin's trades. So what's he done?"

"Gone ballistic. The chairman came to my office personally, wanting to know what we had on Karlin. When I reviewed the trades with him, he said it was a bullshit case. Then he told me to shut this down before we damage Karlin's reputation based on unprovable speculation from Luandia." Schlosser's voice was etched with cynicism. "I'm sure it had nothing to do with the fact that our chairman was the finance director for the president's last campaign, and that Karlin was a major fund-raiser. Money's only supposed to buy access, not an entire federal agency. You'd think this was Luandia."

Pierce felt his own anger merge with a growing sense of helplessness. "So what do you think?"

"We hit a nerve." Schlosser paused briefly. "Might as well give you the rest. The day before your letter arrived, Karlin made another futures bet—the option to buy six million barrels at four bucks higher than the current market price."

As Pierce digested this, the SUV glided to a stop in front of the American embassy. "When does the option come due?"

"Three days from now. Just like before, when Karlin bought the options, there's no apparent reason why the price of oil would spike above four bucks in so short a time. Which strongly suggests that he knows something the average speculator doesn't. What's your guess?"

Pierce felt sick. "That in three days Bobby Okari will be dead."

Pierce felt Vorster staring at him. Speaking more slowly, Schlosser said, "You really think that."

"I wish I didn't. But if Bobby's executed, the price of oil will go way up. Karlin is tied to Ajukwa, who's tied to Van Daan, who's tied to Okimbo, who may have ties to General Freedom. One story has it that General Freedom slips bunkered oil out in barges and tankers owned by Ajukwa; another that Ajukwa is the mysterious Jomo." Pierce paused briefly. "Put all that together, and it helps make sense of Karlin's trades. Look at the events that happened between the time Karlin bought the first three options and when he cashed them in at a profit: FREE sabotaged PGL facilities; someone lynched three oil workers; and FREE raided Petrol Island. If Ajukwa knew in advance that all this would happen, he could have tipped Karlin off that the world price of oil was likely to go up. Karlin wouldn't even have to know why."

"What would be in it for Ajukwa?"

"Kickbacks. Karlin's connections in Washington. Bigger profits on the oil he ships after

513

FREE has stolen it." Pierce paused. "Perhaps more power. Suppose being Karama's key adviser isn't quite enough for him?"

Pierce heard the silence of thought. "A lot of guesswork," Schlosser observed, "to account for an execution."

Turning, Pierce gazed through the rear window at the lights of Karama's redoubt. "This is the place for it," he answered.

PIERCE WAITED IN Caraway's office for over an hour before the ambassador rushed through the door. "Meetings," he said hurriedly. "I apologize."

"What's happening with our hostages?"

Caraway perched on the edge of his couch as though ready to depart at a moment's notice. His face was tired, his speech uncharacteristically clipped. "We're still sorting through the scraps of intelligence. The short of it is that Americans are training Luandian soldiers in the Muslim north. Six were snatched from their vehicle near a town named Rakaad. A group calling itself Al Qaeda in Luandia is taking the credit. Our intelligence people have never heard of them."

"Meaning they don't exist?"

"No one knows for sure. But the name Al Qaeda gives Karama more leverage in America. When Bhutto was assassinated and the Pakistanis blamed Al Qaeda, plenty of Americans were conditioned to believe it—it's like ringing the dinner bell for

Pavlov's dogs. Same here." Steepling his fingers, Caraway ventured musingly, "The pity is that we were making progress on Okari. That trial—especially the verdict—raised the chances that the U.S. would speak out much more strongly. I even hoped we might induce the president to call Karama himself."

The regret in Caraway's tone deepened Pierce's despair. "But not now," Pierce said.

"Not likely. The kidnapping of American soldiers trumps Okari's plight, and empowers the DOD as their protector. We need Karama's cooperation to get our soldiers back alive. The president is not in a great position to pressure Karama about Okari: if he loses these men, his advisers worry, he'll be crucified by his critics in Congress and the media." Caraway stopped himself. "That's telling you perhaps more than I should. But that 9/11 has changed the nature of our government is no surprise to you."

"None," Pierce said. "But the timing of these kidnappings makes me wonder."

Caraway gave him a quizzical smile. "Everything in Luandia doesn't happen because of Bobby Okari. Most likely this is a tragic coincidence."

"And if it isn't?"

Though Caraway seemed to ponder this, Pierce sensed that he already had. "The 'terrorist' kidnappings of American soldiers diverts us from trying to save Okari. *If* you're determined to take that road, one can posit that our enemies want to destabilize Luandia, and that Okari's death will help perpetuate lawlessness in the delta, perhaps driving out companies like PetroGlobal." Caraway's tone became dismissive. "Should you want to get even more conspiratorial, you could argue that Islamic terrorists—or whoever the kidnappers are—are doing this to help empower FREE. And if your goal is achieving paranoia, you could choose to believe that Islamic terrorists and FREE have some alliance regarding the use of bunkered oil.

"But that's the difficulty. Some of our most highly placed strategists tend to see Al Qaeda where it isn't. So we invade Iraq and, by doing that, create more soldiers for Al Qaeda and open the country to terrorists who weren't there before. Which brings us back to where we started—who are 'Al Qaeda in Luandia,' and are they Al Qaeda at all?"

"And if they're not?"

Caution showed in Caraway's eyes. "That's for our intelligence people."

Pierce gazed out the window; even here, he could see the lights of Karama's fortified palace. "Suppose they're working for Karama," Pierce said. "Or someone close to him."

Caraway looked at him hard. "Why would you say that?"

516

"Your Pakistani example. Whether it's real or not, Al Qaeda in Luandia empowers Karama more than it embarrasses him. Like Musharraf, Karama becomes an indispensable ally in the war on terror, empowering him to dispose of Bobby as he likes. That's true even if Karama himself doesn't know who these kidnappers are." Pierce leaned forward. "What's Ugwo Ajukwa's role in the hostage crisis?"

Caraway appraised him closely. "Ajukwa is pivotal," he answered. "He's Karama's national security adviser. He's also a Muslim from the north, with deep connections there."

"And what's his involvement with respect to Bobby?"

Caraway paused. "According to the foreign minister, Ajukwa is urging Karama to execute him. Not that Karama needs encouragement." He glanced at his watch. "I'm due to see Karama about the hostage situation in less than an hour—maybe I'll learn more then. But no matter who these kidnappers are, Karama knows that whatever he does with Okari, many of our oil strategists see him as our best hope of stability."

Pierce felt his time running out. "What will you say about Bobby?"

Caraway gave a brief shake of his head. "I've been given a laundry list of requests. Full protection of other Americans in Luandia, including military personnel. Permission to bring in our top

517

military intelligence people. A commitment that Karama will use all his resources to find out where our people are. And, if we need it, Karama's authorization to bring in the special forces for a rescue operation." Despite the flatness of Caraway's tone, Pierce heard a note of apology. "American lives are at stake. In diplomatic parlance, I'm not authorized to make Okari a formal subject of this meeting."

"There's another American life at stake," Pierce said sharply. "Marissa Okari's."

"I'm well aware of that," Caraway answered. "After they put her under house arrest, I called the foreign minister. Adu tells me that Ms. Okari is also in Karama's hands. You already know that Luandians don't recognize dual citizenship. To their mind and, I'm afraid, to ours, she's different from these soldiers."

"But not to me."

Caraway nodded. "If there's a way to slip in a word about the Okaris, I will. After I see Karama, I'll feel out the foreign minister again. I'll tell you whatever I learn, good or bad." He stood abruptly, extending his hand. "I'm very sorry this has happened, Mr. Pierce. It's far from what I hoped for. Please stay in touch."

CHECKING INTO THE hotel, Pierce turned on CNN.

The international broadcast carried six photos of the kidnapped soldiers: two African-Americans, three Hispanics, and a blond corporal with a crew cut who, despite his expression of martial resolve, looked as innocent as a farm boy. For a moment, Pierce imagined millions of Americans filled with empathy for the soldiers' families and anger at their abductors. Then he pulled out his cell phone to call Dave Rubin. "Who's 'Al Qaeda in Luandia'?" Pierce asked.

"Damned if I know," Rubin answered. "As I told you before, there's evidence of a jihadist presence in the north. But I'm wondering if someone made these guys up."

Pierce heard the beep of an incoming call. "Hang on, Dave." Pushing the flash button, he answered.

His caller's voice was resonant. "Is this Damon Pierce?"

"Yes."

"I am Ugwo Ajukwa, national security adviser to President Karama. Come to Savior Rock at half past midnight and General Karama will grant you fifteen minutes."

Without awaiting an answer, Ajukwa hung up.

15

J UST BEFORE MIDNIGHT, PIERCE AND VORSTER reached the high metal gate that protected the entrance to Savior Rock.

The barrier was guarded by soldiers in combat fatigues. After an officer checked by telephone with someone inside, the electronic fence opened, and Vorster and Pierce drove into four square miles surrounded by a twenty-foot concrete wall and shrouded in darkness. A winding road flanked by palms led to the distant palace, brightly lit against the looming outline of Savior Rock, fifteen hundred feet of black stone. Three times Pierce and Vorster stopped at gated checkpoints manned by sentries. Three times they passed large buildings: the compound of the state security services, bristling with satellite equipment intended to alert Karama to a coup; the home of the vice president, built inside Karama's compound to make its resident his virtual prisoner; the Congress building, where "elected" members could not come or go unless the president permitted it. To Pierce, the compound was the physical expression of Karama's need to maintain power through fear. Pierce felt that fear himself; catching his mood, Vorster murmured, "Into the belly of the beast."

After another half mile of darkness, they passed through the final gate, entering a driveway to Karama's sprawling palace. Set against the black mass of Savior Rock, it was bathed in spotlights that illuminated the lushly landscaped grounds as brightly as a football stadium at night. Reaching this fortress, Vorster let Pierce out.

Pierce stopped at the foot of the marble steps. Stationed amid the plants and trees, video cameras captured every stride he took. The palace itself, grand in the manner of nineteenth-century France, displayed what appeared to be a system of alarms and sensors. Pierce slowly climbed the steps to a twenty-foot-high metal door, in front of which stood three uniformed Asians with automatic weapons, Karama's North Korean bodyguards, their faces as blank as their eyes were hard. Passing between the guards, Pierce saw the metal doors parting without the apparent involvement of a human being.

Inside was a white marble entryway the size of a basketball court, with forty-foot ceilings and a marble stairway, covered in deep red carpet, that rose to the president's quarters. A watchful man in impeccable dress materialized from a side entrance and led Pierce up the stairs. At their head were more Koreans. Without acknowledging their presence, the man led Pierce into Savior Karama's waiting room.

It was, as Caraway had described it, as gaudy as the court of Louis XIV. But tonight it was not filled with sycophants or favor seekers. When the assistant led Pierce to a thickly upholstered armchair and left him there, Pierce was alone.

He was at Karama's mercy. Repressing his apprehension, Pierce focused on what he must try to accomplish, uncertain of what effect his words would have on a person so brutal and unpredictable. Then, Pierce saw, rather than heard, a tall man enter the room. Wearing long white robes and an African cap, he seemed less to walk than to glide, his appearance of ease contradicted by a look of enmity directed at Pierce. Even before he spoke, in a deep American-accented voice, Pierce recognized him as Ugwo Ajukwa. "You are Mr. Pierce," Ajukwa said in a cool tone. "You know, I think, who I am."

He did not extend his hand. Nodding, Pierce said simply, "I do."

As he followed Ajukwa, Pierce recalled Bobby's account of being summoned by Karama: they walked through a sumptuous sitting room and into an illuminated garden that ended at the iron bars of Karama's zoo. With his back to Pierce and Ajukwa, a uniformed man gazed into its darkness, motionless, as though listening for the sounds of animals at night. As Ajukwa approached him, Pierce stopped amid the garden. "Mr. President?" Ajukwa said.

Karama did not turn; at first, Pierce thought he had not heard. Then Karama ordered, "Bring him."

Ajukwa beckoned to Pierce. Pierce walked forward, stopping a few feet from Karama. "This is Okari's lawyer," Ajukwa said.

At last Karama turned. Though Pierce had seen him on a giant screen, he was not prepared for the impact of looking Savior Karama in the face. Even without knowing of Karama's cruelty, Pierce would have felt it. The aviator sunglasses, concealing his eyes, deepened the impassivity of someone utterly indifferent to human contact; the tribal scars on the man's face underscored the gulf between him and Pierce. Ajukwa stood behind Karama, even taller and much lighter of skin—a dagger to Karama's bludgeon, so different in appearance, and so intently watchful, that Pierce intuited a distrust grounded in ethnicity and ambition. His voice etched with disdain, Karama said, "You came to plead for Okari's life. So plead."

Fighting a sudden queasiness, Pierce glanced at Ajukwa. "I came to speak with you alone."

Ajukwa's eyes narrowed. "Speak," he interjected, "and be done with it—"

Still watching Pierce, Karama raised his hand for silence. "First you spew insults," he said to Pierce. "Now you set conditions. Soon you will shit from fear."

To show fear, Pierce sensed, would mean failure and perhaps increase the danger to Bobby and himself. "What I have to say is between you and Bobby Okari. No one else is meant to hear it."

Karama showed no flicker of expression. Then he held up his hand again, snapping his fingers. "Go," he said.

At first Pierce did not know for whom these words were intended. Then Ajukwa spoke sharply: "This is a trick."

Still Karama stared at Pierce. With deadly softness, he said, "So I am not equipped to deal with tricks? Then perhaps you think I should not be president."

Ajukwa's expression became veiled; over Karama's shoulder, he gave Pierce a measured nod, as though he had marked him well. Ajukwa's footsteps as he left made no sound.

"Speak," Karama said.

Pierce felt his time trickling away. "All Bobby wants," Pierce said, "is hope for the delta. To kill him would be like executing Mandela. You'll unleash hell."

"Nelson Mandela?" Karama repeated with contempt. "I have yet to hear from him. So perhaps Okari is not as important as he imagines himself. Only *I* can make him so by keeping him alive; the world will think him too sacred for me to hang. Okari is only useful to me dead."

Karama's implacable reasoning gave Pierce pause. "You can make him useful alive," Pierce answered. "Spare him, and the world will see you differently."

"You babble Okari's pieties," Karama snapped, "mistaking poetry for power. He believes himself to be the world's darling, too rare a soul to be executed by a simple military man. But who is to stop me? PetroGlobal? They owe their stockholders the profits I can give them. The Chinese? They kill their own Okaris by the thousands, including in Tibet. The Africans? South Africa helped keep Mugabe in business, and Mugabe has no oil.

America? As long as they get their oil and save their precious soldiers, the day after I hang Okari he'll be just another black corpse.

"True, there will be noble speeches about his sacrifice, the indomitability of his spirit, the obligation of those who survive never to forget. But the world is a forgetful place. Your cars will run; your youth will go to the movies; your president will thank me for my friendship. Soon Okari's people will remember him, if at all, as the murderer of three Asari oil workers. If this pathetic plea is all you came for, you've wasted my time."

Pierce had no time for hesitation: Karama's last phrase, seemingly a throwaway, might be an invitation. "There's something more," Pierce told him.

From the darkness of the zoo came the bestial growl of a lion. "There is only one thing of interest to me," Karama said in a low voice. "What you implied at the trial."

Pierce reached for his last reserves of determination. "Some of this I know," he said. "Some I believe. What I know for certain is that you're surrounded by a web of deceit. Ajukwa urged you to trust Okimbo. Ajukwa forced PGL to hire Van Daan. Ajukwa ships oil stolen by General Freedom. Okimbo let General Freedom escape from prison. General Freedom hit PGL's facilities and raided Petrol Island. Every step empowered Ajukwa and FREE. And every military action by

FREE enabled Henry Karlin—Ajukwa's American partner—to make a killing in oil futures."

Karama's face showed nothing. "There's one more thing," Pierce continued. "Okimbo and Van Daan planned to wipe out Goro a month *before* the lynchings, knowing this would decimate the Asari movement and empower FREE." Pierce slowed his speech, speaking each word emphatically. "Ajukwa knows you well. He knew you wanted to be rid of Bobby; he knew that you believed Bobby wanted the delta to secede. So he ordered Okimbo to lynch those men on Asari Day, certain that you'd blame Okari and give Okimbo a free hand. Then he counseled you to execute Okari. With Okari dead, General Freedom has more power. So does Ajukwa, his ally—"

"Give me evidence, *oyibo*."

"Before the lynchings, Karlin placed another bet on oil futures. He *knew* the price of oil was going up, because Ajukwa knew about the lynchings before they happened. If you get records of Ajukwa's bank account, I'm confident you'll find millions in kickbacks in the last three months—"

"Ajukwa's rich already," Karama interrupted. "I have made him so."

"Not as rich as you are. There's only one way to become that." Pierce softened his voice. "In Luandia, money is power—you know that better than anyone. So are friends in the military, like Okimbo; and a well-armed militia leader, like

General Freedom. Ajukwa wants to be president.

"You know how to make your enemies speak the truth. I suggest you ask Ajukwa if he's Jomo."

Karama stared at him. Pierce had the eerie sense that Karama could read his thoughts—could tell that, despite his weaving of facts and guesswork, Pierce had no idea if his surmise about Ajukwa was true, any more than he could predict what this accusation, reverberating in Karama's brain, might cause this man to do. Then there was the most dangerous imponderable of all: if Karama himself had ordered the lynchings, the whole of Pierce's argument turned to vapor. In a tone of molten anger, Karama said, "You forget Okari's history. Long before these men died, he spat in my face. He refused a position in my government. He used his gifts to hold me up to ridicule." A corrosive envy filled the words. "No matter who carried out the lynchings, Okari disdained me as a man. There is no balm in my soul for that."

Pierce stared into the pieces of black glass. "Nor is it a cure," he answered, "to kill Okari for Ajukwa's reasons."

Impassive, Karama folded his arms. "Do you wish Okari to live?" he said at last. "Then tell him he must start his life all over again, like a baby crawling on his knees. Only now he will crawl to me." His voice became commanding. "It is not enough for him to disown your lawsuit. He must go on television to denounce his movement; ask

527

his followers to abandon their secession; apologize to me for his disrespect; and beg my forgiveness in memory of our former friendship. Oh, yes, and confess to murder." Karama's smile, a gelid movement of his lips, raised the flesh on Pierce's neck. "If his speech is truly pleasing, I will let him rot in jail until the last ember of his movement has died. Then I will set him free to roam the world, yesterday's man, trying to resurrect his tattered reputation until his testicles turn to raisins.

"Tell him that. And if he finds death more attractive, tell him that his wife and I will watch his final spasms on film, in the moments before I enjoy her for myself." Karama's voice became as intimate as a whisper. "Did he tell you we once shared a woman? When he is dead and you are back in America, I will not have to share Marissa Okari. I will leave the rest to your imagination, Mr. Pierce. She will not be able to tell you about it."

Pierce felt the awesome power of this man to inspire fear and hatred overcoming his self-control. *"You cannot do that."*

"Because she's American? Perhaps the people of your country will rise up as one, demanding her salvation, and this single half-black woman will replace the ravaged women and starving children of Darfur." Karama gave a terrible laugh. "I haven't checked today. Has your president sent troops on their behalf?"

Pierce could not respond. Karama watched his

face, and then the trace of a smile played on his mouth. "You are heartsick, I see—no doubt for your friend Okari. But I am not without mercy. If Okari crawls to me, I will forswear his wife and let her return to the country she abandoned. Then, perhaps, you can have her.

"I trust you to persuade Okari on her behalf, and yours. Then you won't have to wish in secret for a client's death." Pointing to the door, Karama said softly, "Go to him while he's still alive. Neither Okari has much time."

Karama turned his back and walked to the edge of his zoo. "Sleep, my darlings," he said into the darkness. "There's much for us to do."

Pierce walked in the other direction, scarcely conscious of his surroundings. From the tangle of emotions one thought surfaced: Karama had not refuted his accusation of Ajukwa.

16

WHEN PIERCE CLIMBED INTO THE SUV, VORSTER looked at him keenly. After that, he asked no questions. Neither spoke. Only after they passed through the entrance to Savior Rock, headed for the hotel, did Pierce take out his cell phone.

Though it was past two A.M., Caraway answered. "This is Damon," Pierce said. "I just saw Karama."

"After I did? What's your impression?"

"He'll kill Okari if it suits him. Karama thinks

we and the rest of the world will do nothing. To him, Bobby's a secessionist, a test of his power. But his feelings are far more personal than that and include Marissa." Pierce struggled to capture his feelings. "It was worse than I'd imagined. He's completely rational, and utterly insane."

"Yes," Caraway responded in a tone of weary recognition. "Tonight he spared me the overt psychosis. But he brought up Okari on his own: he says he needs a free hand to 'stabilize' Luandia, and wants us to back off. It's clear that this is his condition for giving us what we need to rescue our soldiers."

Staring at the empty streets of Savior City, Pierce felt despair seeping into his soul. "We have human rights groups appealing to the presidents of the U.S., South Africa, and France, and the prime ministers of England and Australia. But Karama thinks it's all a joke."

"Karama," Caraway answered, "understands geopolitics. In my latest conversations with the Europeans, they seemed most concerned about being *seen* as caring. We'll get public statements asking for clemency, and nothing with any bite." Caraway's tone betrayed frustration. "As for us, events are moving too quickly. In the best of times, it's hard to focus the full attention of the government on anything less than a Cuban missile crisis. Now our crisis is these soldiers. By the time that's resolved . . ."

His voice trailed off. After a moment, Pierce asked, "Have you figured out who Al Qaeda in Luandia is?"

"No. Karama claims not to know. Perhaps that's even true. But some of our intelligence people wonder if they exist. That leaves some pretty novel theories."

"Including that they belong to Karama," Pierce said. "Or maybe Ajukwa."

Caraway did not answer directly. "If so, we'll get our men back—just as soon as they've served their purpose." His tone grew pointed. "Whatever the case, the kidnappings drove up the price of oil by four dollars a barrel. Okari's death would spike it more."

Pierce hesitated. "When I met with Karama," he said, "I floated a theory about Ajukwa. The short of it is that Ajukwa's involved with Okimbo, Van Daan, and General Freedom in a scheme to acquire more money and more power. One aspect of which is lynching these workers and blaming Okari."

There was a long silence. Softly, Caraway inquired, "How did Karama react?"

"I'm not sure. But I sensed him taking it in."

"God knows what he'll do with that," Caraway answered. "You're toying with the psyche of a murderer."

"No doubt. But Karama offered to spare Okari's life. The offer is so bad it's almost credible: in return for mercy, Bobby has to apologize to

Karama, repudiate his movement, confess to murder, and spend an indefinite time in jail—from which he may never emerge." Pierce paused. "He finished with threats about Marissa. I believe in those."

There was more silence. "If you're asking about Ms. Okari," Caraway said, "there's nothing new. It would be better for all of us if she weren't here."

"Well, she is," Pierce snapped.

Caraway's voice was level. "What I'm saying is that you know people. I'm aware that she's watched by soldiers. But if there's some unofficial way to get her out, we have an embassy in Accra. Ghana's fairly close."

"And if I can't manage that?"

"Then Okari should consider Karama's offer, no matter how humiliating. As my grandmother used to say, you're a long time dead." Caraway paused. "There's a story about Karama. During one of his entertainments—the videotape of a particularly gruesome execution—a colonel fainted. Standing over him, Karama said, 'And he calls himself a soldier.' I don't want the Okaris to become another grisly test." The ambassador's voice flattened. "I've said enough. If I hear something you should know, I'll call."

Hanging up, Pierce sat back, silent. As they neared the hotel, Vorster said, "This doesn't sound good."

"No. But I've got a question for you."

"What is it?"

Pierce turned to him. "If I could get Marissa clear of the compound, is there a way to take her to Accra?"

Vorster puffed his cheeks. "I do business here. So does Dave Rubin. Something as volatile as this can't have our fingerprints on it."

Pierce felt disheartened. "And so?"

Vorster hesitated. "I know someone—a Frenchman with a plane who's crazy and likes money. Maybe . . ." He shrugged. "I don't know that he's still around. If he is, and wants to do it, then he'd have to get himself to Port George. It could take time." He studied Pierce. "How would you slip her past those soldiers? I don't think there's enough money in Luandia for that."

"That's my problem. Can you work on this?"

Vorster frowned. "I'll do what I can."

"Then just drop me at the airport. I've got to see Okari while I can."

IT TOOK SEVEN wasted hours for Pierce to book a flight; another six to reach Port George. Clellan flew with him. By the time they reached the barracks, dusk had fallen.

"I'll wait," Clellan said. "Good luck."

When Pierce presented himself to the sentries, Major Bangida appeared. "Okimbo wants to see you," he said.

This is what Pierce had anticipated, and dreaded. He followed Bangida inside.

Okimbo looked up at Pierce with his hands flat on the desk, as though preparing to rise. His eye did not blink. With silken quiet, he said, "You are here by the grace of President Karama. You'll be allowed to leave only for that reason. But should you break any of our laws, from now until you leave our country, you will belong to me."

That Okimbo expressed this as a simple statement of fact made his words more chilling. "Go see your friend," Okimbo told Pierce. "This is his last chance to save all three of you."

BOBBY SAT IN a corner, his profile illuminated by a single bulb. The stink of his waste was worse; gripping the bars, Pierce felt a wave of nausea. "Forgive me," Bobby said in a wan voice. "But it's hard to stand. It seems I'm not being fattened for the slaughter."

Pierce felt too edgy to respond. "Karama's made an offer, Bobby."

"Which is?"

As Pierce told him, Bobby listened stoically. "If you can believe Karama," Pierce concluded, "at least you'd live."

Pierce followed Bobby's gaze to a dead rat in the corner. "Is this a life?" Bobby asked.

Quietly, Pierce said, "There's also Marissa. Karama reminded me that you and he once shared a woman."

Bobby's eyes closed. "What about diplomacy?"

Pausing, Pierce felt his sense of urgency overwhelm pity. "There is none. The Americans are obsessed with these hostages, and the Europeans are vamping. The calculus is brutally simple: it's Karama, not you, who controls the flow of oil."

Bobby slumped. "Karama asks too much of me. I'm afraid only for Marissa."

"What do you gain by dying?" Pierce demanded. "In some inner-city neighborhood in America, they'll name a charter school the Okari Academy. Maybe your friends will start a scholarship fund for exiles. And in time you'll be forgotten. In far less time than that, your people will lose all hope, and FREE will use your death to justify more violence. Your legacy will be a slaughterhouse."

Bobby seemed to shudder. "And if I renounce my cause by crawling to Karama? What then? Only the hope of living until I'm exiled, the pitiful human remnant of public cowardice. Compared to that, hanging is a mercy." As Bobby gazed at Pierce, a plea surfaced in his eyes. "No, I must believe that each mistake Karama makes will advance our cause. If that requires my death, better than a life of cravenness." He paused, then finished softly: "Before he left, Bara came to see me. If I die, he believes, I may be mentioned for the Nobel Peace Prize."

Somehow this last hope touched Pierce more than what had come before. "There's no peace prize for a pointless death," he forced himself to say. "Or for sacrificing the living."

Bobby watched his face. "Were it not for Marissa, would you say this?"

Pierce weighed his answer. "If it weren't for Marissa, I'd have no right to say it."

"Then you must get her out of the country, any way you can."

"Even if she's a widow?"

"She's sacrificed too much already." Bobby inhaled. "You know of the escape tunnel. Take her, and go."

"And if she refuses?"

"She can't," Bobby insisted. "She must carry on the work. A widow can be a powerful force, and Marissa has the gifts for it."

Even now, Pierce thought, there were more sacrifices for Marissa to make. "Even if I could get her out," he said, "I don't know that she can leave you."

"Then lie to her," Bobby demanded. "Tell her that you've arranged all this with Gladstone, and that I'll be joining her soon."

"I can't do that."

"You *will* do that." With terrible effort, Bobby stood, taking two steps forward before gripping the bars. "For your sake, and mine. If afterward she feels you've betrayed her, at least she'll be alive." Reaching through the bars, Bobby rested his hand on Pierce's shoulder. "Please comfort her for me.

Tell her that I died consoled that she will live, not only for our cause but for herself."

Pierce had no words. Perhaps, despite Atiku Bara's beliefs, Bobby had always known that he would die. Now he was asking Pierce to help him die alone.

Tears came to Bobby's eyes. "So many years, Damon, since we met in Berkeley. So many complications, so much sadness. Perhaps some good will come of it."

Pierce felt his throat constrict. "What should I tell Karama?"

"That I'm reflecting. I'll refuse him once she's safe."

Silently, the two men embraced through the bars, foreheads touching. For a last moment, Pierce looked into Bobby's worn face. Then he turned and walked away, hoping that, by not looking back, he would convey to Bobby Okari a sense of purpose.

CLELLAN DROPPED PIERCE at the Okaris' compound. Under the watchful eyes of the soldiers, Pierce told Clellan quietly, "Go back to the hotel. If I need you, I'll call." Then he walked through the iron gate, perhaps to be imprisoned with Marissa.

He had no time to think of this. When Edo answered the door, Pierce asked, "Where's Madam?"

"Sleeping," the houseboy said gravely. "She took some pills, to rest. I'm to waken her in an hour."

Thanking him, Pierce went to her bedroom.

Marissa lay on top of the covers, stirring slightly. Though she was asleep, Pierce saw the circles of weariness beneath her eyes. He had no heart to wake her. For a quiet moment, he watched her face, peaceful in repose. Then he hurried to Bobby's den.

Glancing around him, he called Vorster. "Time's running out," he said. "Any luck?"

"No." Vorster's voice was flat. "I can't find this Frenchman."

"Keep trying, for God's sake." Pierce stopped himself. "Do whatever you can. I don't want to lose her, too."

Vorster promised and got off.

Sitting at Bobby's desk, Pierce rubbed his temples. Then he placed another call.

17

POCKETING HIS CELL PHONE, PIERCE SWIFTLY climbed the stairs to the patio.

In the distance, the scattered lights of Petrol Island blinked against the vast blackness of the Atlantic. He gazed down at the beach, studying it closely until the orange glow of the oil flares revealed two armed soldiers. Then he hurried to Marissa's bedroom.

Bending, he touched her shoulder. She stirred, still drowsy, then abruptly started, eyes wide with fright until she recognized his face. Pierce spoke under his breath. "You have to dress, Marissa. We're leaving."

She stared at him in incomprehension; then her thoughts cleared. "What about Bobby?"

"He's part of this." Urgency sharpened his voice. "Better that you not know the details. When we get closer, I'll explain."

She got out of bed. Slipping off her nightgown, she turned to him. "What can I take?"

"Only what you're wearing."

She hesitated, as though absorbing what might lie ahead. Then she hurriedly opened a drawer and threw on a blouse and blue jeans. "Let's go," Pierce said. "We're taking the tunnel."

She gave him a questioning look. "What about Edo?"

"He can't know, for his sake. Let's hope he doesn't hear us leave."

Quickly but quietly, they descended the main staircase, briefly looking about the darkened house before going to the kitchen. Marissa snatched two flashlights from a drawer, giving one to Pierce, before they took the back stairs to the cellar.

Kneeling, Pierce pushed aside the barrel lid and removed the stone that hid the darkened shaft. "You first."

Marissa began climbing down the ladder.

Glancing up, she said, "There's no one to cover the tunnel. If they come inside, they'll see it."

Pierce wrestled the lid to a position where it partially obscured the opening. "All we need's an hour," he said. Then he climbed into the hole as Marissa, standing at the bottom, held her flashlight so that he could see. Pausing, he pulled the loose stone into place, covering the opening, then descended until he stood beside Marissa.

The dank smell of moist earth filled Pierce's nostrils, intensifying his claustrophobia. "Have you ever done this before?" he asked.

"No."

"Then follow me."

Holding out his own flashlight, Pierce led her into the darkened maw. His feet splashed into a puddle of water. "We're below sea level," Marissa said.

She did not need to explain; at any time the tunnel could collapse and fill with water. Pierce accelerated his pace, pushing ahead the few feet of yellow light and shadow provided by his flashlight. The tunnel narrowed. His elbow banged into a timber, causing dirt to crumble at his feet. Pierce started; behind him, he heard Marissa gasp.

The wall held. More cautiously, Pierce began moving again. "How long will it take?" she asked.

"Twenty minutes or so."

As he spoke, the musty, suffocating air caught in his throat. How much oxygen was there? he wondered. His steps quickened slightly, splashing water again.

"Deeper," Marissa said tightly.

"If it was flooded," Pierce assured her, "we'd know by now."

He was not certain of this. Silently, they kept moving.

Minutes passed. Their path became mud; the pools of water deepened. Pierce imagined the walls collapsing, sealing them beneath the earth. He had a brief but intense memory of his parents' home, then his apartment in San Francisco. Perhaps this was how insanity felt—glimmers of lucidity in a darkened world. Then Pierce heard the sound of falling earth.

Slowly but completely, the walls behind Marissa began to crumble. Wrenching her forward, Pierce ran headlong, and then his flashlight found the ladder.

Behind them, he saw that the last few feet of tunnel had held. Water began to seep around his feet. Pointing at the ladder he urged, "Take it."

She edged past him, grasped the ladder, and climbed with the swift agility of fright. Pierce aimed the flashlight to help her see. When she reached the top, he said, "Push."

As she did, the floor of the shack opened. Pierce waited until she disappeared. Then he climbed the ladder. At the top, he saw Marissa peering at the lunar landscape of the garbage dump. Closing the cover to the tunnel, Pierce stood beside her, searching the ruins for the forms of human beings.

There was no one. Perhaps two hundred yards away, the spire of the flare pipe rose from the beach, its giant orange flame brilliant against the night sky. Pierce doused his flashlight, then hers. "Follow me," he said.

Together they began to clamber across the field of metal and garbage, nerves jangling at the crunch of their steps on rusted metal. Pierce thought of meeting the soldier Femu in this place; by now he might be dead, or wishing for death. He focused his attention on the flare. As the distance closed, they could hear its roar, feel its heat. Sweat glistened on Marissa's forehead.

Changing course, Pierce began to circle the flare, keeping the same distance. Suddenly he could see the beach. Hurrying, he led Marissa toward the edge of the flare's light, where the beach became shadowy again. As the darkness concealed them, he slowed, breathing hard, then looked back toward the Okari compound. On the far side of the oil flare, it sat on the hill above the beach, a half mile distant. He saw no sign of soldiers.

Pierce faced the ocean and turned on his flashlight. He kept the light on as he counted to ten. When he turned it off, a light appeared above the darkness of the water.

He took Marissa's hand, leading her to the water's edge. The light on the water vanished. As they waded into the surf, Pierce heard the outboard motor, then saw the outline of a boat. It glided toward them, its motor idling. "Get in," a man's voice ordered.

Touching the small of Marissa's back, Pierce urged her forward. A hand reached out from the darkness of the boat, pulling her inside. Pierce climbed in after her. As the man pushed the throttle, his ruddy, weathered face came into the half-light. Turning to Marissa, Pierce nodded toward their pilot. "This is Trevor Hill. He's taking us to Petrol Island." Facing Hill, Pierce asked, "Are you set?"

"As much as I can be," Hill responded. "Needless to say, I didn't file a flight plan. Too much to explain."

Marissa looked bewildered. "Where are we going?"

"To an airstrip on Petrol Island," Pierce responded. He did not wish to tell her that the flight was unauthorized; that Hill was leaving PGL and stealing one of its planes; that this man was risking his life, and theirs. Leaning forward, Pierce murmured, "What about Van Daan?"

"Sleeping, I hope—since we suspended him, he's been confined to Petrol Island under watch. But God knows who he works for, or how they might react." Hill glanced over his shoulder. "Enough talk for now."

Without lights, they navigated the choppy waters

toward Petrol Island, perhaps a mile distant. They moved slowly but steadily; if Hill had been drinking before Pierce called, he showed no sign of it now. Pierce prayed that this was true. If all went well, Hill had a plane to fly, and thick banks of what looked like rain clouds had begun to obscure the moon. Marissa shivered. Though it was not cold, Pierce put his arm around her.

For half an hour, they moved across the water toward Petrol Island, Hill searching for patrol boats. If their escape had been discovered, their pursuers would consider water their most likely course—and since FREE's raid, Hill had told Pierce, at the request of PGL Okimbo had increased the patrols cruising the waters between the island and Port George. "There," Hill said softly.

Some distance away, but close enough to provoke fear, a patrol boat cut the darkness with a beam of light. Hill shut off the motor. Helpless, they drifted, watching the light of the patrol boat scan the water. Marissa grasped Pierce's hand. The patrol boat kept coming closer. The low growl of its motor grew more ominous.

Marissa's grip tightened. The beam of light swept within twenty yards of Hill's boat, then back again. Pierce could see the outlines of the soldiers looking to each side. Then the boat moved on as they continued to float silently, unseen.

Pierce felt Marissa exhale. Hill kept watching

until the boat had nearly vanished. Then he restarted his motor, glancing at the darkened sky.

They forged across the water. A half hour crept by. As Petrol Island grew closer, Pierce spotted the lights of a boatyard.

Cutting back on the throttle, Hill steered the boat toward the side of the dock. When they reached it, Hill inclined his head toward a wooden ladder and threw Pierce a rope line. Climbing onto the dock, Pierce lashed the rope to a post. Marissa followed him up the ladder, then Hill.

At the end of the catwalk was an open jeep. Hill got in the driver's seat, Pierce beside him, as Marissa slipped into the back. Sounding relieved, Hill said, "Just a couple of miles to the airstrip."

Hill navigated the jeep along a narrow road. As they turned onto the main thoroughfare, a four-lane highway, the world of Petrol Island material-ized around them—the refinery to one side, the compound to the other. They headed toward the compound, passing a white man with a woman passenger, likely a prostitute from Hooker Village. Their headlights caught a jeep filled with soldiers coming toward them in the opposite lane. Over his shoulder, Hill snapped at Marissa, "Duck."

She curled sideways, head pressed to the seat. As the jeep came closer, Hill gave the driver a careless wave. When the man waved back, Pierce felt his eyes close.

"Nearly there," Hill murmured.

No one spoke. There was no more traffic on the road. Moments later, Hill turned down a side road. Beyond a field of grass, Pierce saw four small planes sitting on the tarmac. The airstrip was dark. "I closed it down," Hill said. "Bad weather coming. There shouldn't be anyone here."

The road ended at the tarmac. Hill got out, then Pierce and Marissa. They followed him toward a propeller plane at the far end, shrouded in darkness by the lowering clouds. "It's small but stable," Hill observed. "I've flown these all over Africa."

He stopped abruptly. A split second after Hill, Pierce saw the jeep parked beside a wing of the plane. "Going for a spin?" a thick voice asked.

Pierce froze; he knew the voice at once. From the shadow of the plane stepped Roos Van Daan, two young Luandian soldiers at his side. As they approached, the soldiers aimed their handguns at Trevor Hill. "You shouldn't have checked on available planes," Van Daan told Hill. "Why ask when you've closed the airstrip?"

"Who's paying you?" Pierce demanded.

Van Daan's teeth flashed. "That, Counselor, is your last question. And I object." Glancing at the soldiers, he said, "They were trying to escape. Shoot them all."

Pierce reached for Marissa's hand. One of the soldiers looked from Van Daan to Hill. Calmly,

Hill spoke to him in a native dialect. As Van Daan turned to the soldier, puzzled, the man put his gun to Van Daan's temple and fired.

Eyes wide with shock, Van Daan sagged to the ground, blood spurting from his shattered skull. Gazing down at him, Hill said laconically, "I paid them."

Fighting shock, Pierce turned to Marissa. She began to tremble. He gripped her shoulders. "Listen," he said. "Trevor's flying you to Accra. You're to go to the American embassy. They'll get you home from there."

"Home?" She stared at him in confusion. "What about Bobby?"

Pierce felt the first heavy drop of rain on his face. "PetroGlobal's brokering a plan. But Bobby won't go along until you're safe."

Her eyes filled with doubt and worry. Pierce could read her thoughts: she was trying to imagine a bargain that her husband would agree to. "You've trusted me this far," Pierce said. "It's way too late to stop. Now go."

Marissa blinked at the rain spattering her face. "You're not coming with me?"

"I'm staying here." He tried to sound reassuring. "I need to make sure this goes the way it should. I'll see you on the other side."

He glanced at Hill. A look of empathy passed through Hill's eyes: he had just heard Pierce lie about her husband and himself, knowing they both might die. But then so might Hill and Marissa, shot down by Luandian pilots.

Hill spoke to the soldiers in dialect. Each taking a leg, they dragged Van Daan's body toward the grass. "They worked for Van Daan," Hill told Pierce, "providing security for Petrol Island—it seems they learned to hate him. They have no idea what's happening. But they'll get you back to Port George."

The first flash of lightning split the night sky. Thunder followed, then sheets of rain. "We've got to get up," Hill shouted.

Pierce turned to Marissa. "Call me from the embassy," he said quickly. "Please, hurry."

Swiftly, she kissed him, then ran after Hill with her head down against the rain. Pierce watched until she vanished inside the plane.

18

PIERCE'S RETURN TO PORT GEORGE WAS FILLED with foreboding and regret, a deep sadness for that already lost, and that which would be lost. For nearly two hours, he and the soldiers retraced Hill's route in the open boat, soaked by a driving rain that obscured the lights of Port George. Flashes of lightning struck the water, one frighteningly close, followed by thunder so awesome and enveloping that it evoked God's judgment. Constantly Pierce thought of Marissa, buffeted by these brutal skies above the trackless reaches of the delta. Now and then they saw the streaks of beam lights from a patrol boat; once they hid among the floating mass of oil tankers moored offshore. By the time they reached the harbor at Port George, clothes clinging to their bodies, Pierce felt spent. With a residue of good manners, he shook the two men's hands and gave them money from his wallet. Then he climbed a ladder and stood on the dock, alone. It was just past two A.M.

Rain pelted him like bullets. He could not return to the Okaris' compound; but he felt a primal need for shelter, a place to rest and to think. Above the waterfront, the red neon words HOTEL PRESIDENT blinked like a mirage through the sheets of water. Passing between two looming cranes, Pierce headed for the sign.

The hotel was four stories, sterile in its modernity. Pierce paused at its glass entrance. He had nowhere else to go, yet was safe from detection only in the rain. But he could do no good unless he acted—with whatever misgivings—as he would have before Marissa's escape. He walked into the lobby, drawing the silent stare of a security guard, then went to the front desk and hit a bell for service.

A frail old man appeared; after a flicker of astonishment he pretended there was nothing remarkable about a rain-soaked *oyibo*, without luggage, appearing like a fugitive to request a room. Eyes downcast, he asked to see Pierce's passport and a credit card. Pierce had no choice but to comply, knowing that one phone call might bring soldiers to arrest him. Taking a room key, he slipped the old man some cash.

The third-floor room was small and shabby. With the drapes closed, Pierce stripped off his shirt and removed his cell phone from the pocket of his jeans. When he pressed the power button, the phone came on.

He lay back on the bed. His first call was to Rachel Rahv. Hearing her voice mail, he left a terse message: Leave Luandia at once, and take the others with you. Then he called Grayson Caraway.

For a second night, despite the hour, the ambassador was awake. "It's Damon," Pierce began. "Tell your friend in Accra to expect a visitor."

Caraway sounded mildly astounded. "You managed it?"

"So far. It may not work out quite so well for me . . ."

"Where are you?"

"Still in Port George. What do you hear about Okari?"

"Rumors. Two hours ago I called the foreign minister at home. Adu had clearly been drinking, I think out of dread. Ajukwa's been arrested, he said."

Pierce sat up. "What does that mean?"

"That something you said stuck with Karama. Though who knows what or why, or how it relates to Okari. But Ajukwa may already be dead: aides who vanish in the middle of the night tend not to reappear."

For an instant, Pierce absorbed that he might have caused a death without fully comprehending the reason. He pushed the thought aside. "I told Okimbo that Bobby was considering Karama's offer. Once they learn she's gone, that's done. If there's anything else you can do to save him, now's the time."

"I've been trying to reach the president. But he's still focused on the troops." Pausing, Caraway spoke more softly: "It's a strange night. There's more than Ajukwa, I'm afraid. Adu heard that a hangman has been called to Port George. I'm not sure there's anything else I can do."

Pierce felt anxiety overcome him. "What can I do, dammit? I've got no way of reaching anyone except by a cell phone that needs recharging."

The ambassador spoke softly. "Assuming the worst, what does a lawyer usually do in these circumstances? Provide hope, I suppose. Or at least what comfort you can—"

"I'm not a priest," Pierce snapped.

"Surely not. But you knew what Okari's prospects were, and stayed." The ambassador's tone mixed apology and compassion. "I'll pass along any messages you need me to. But I may be of more use if you're arrested. After all, you're an American."

This touch of weary irony left Pierce with nothing to say. "Good luck," the ambassador said. "If I hear anything more, I'll call. Please know, Damon, that I'm sorrier than I can say."

Pierce thanked him, and got off.

Lying back on the bed, he considered his situation. He had no e-mail, no way of reaching out, nothing but a cell phone and this room. It made him think of Bobby Okari—facing so much worse, alone.

He lay there, envisioning Bobby's cell. For a time he debated whether to turn off his phone, preserving power, or keep it on for Caraway and Marissa. It was just past four o'clock. The battery had perhaps five hours to go; by then, all of this might be done. He kept the phone on.

No one called. No one came for him.

A little before five, Pierce forced himself to get up, shower, and put on his damp clothes. Then he went to the lobby and out into the street.

The rain had stopped. A young cabbie waited outside, no doubt hoping for an early fare to the airport. Getting in, Pierce said tersely, "Take me to the barracks."

HE ARRIVED THERE in the first thin light of morning, before the pollution that fouled the air had tinged the dawn with orange. Pierce presented himself to the sentries and asked for Major Bangida.

In moments Bangida appeared, crisply dressed and fully awake. In a sardonic tone, he said, "We've been looking for you. Okimbo wasn't expecting a visit."

Pierce felt his last hope die; from Bangida's manner, they knew about Marissa. Fighting back his fear, he followed the major into the courtyard.

Involuntarily, Pierce stopped at what he saw there. A thick rope dangled from the gallows; a man in a red silk gown, no doubt the hangman, was stationed on the platform. The Black Maria that had taken Bobby to and from the trial was parked with its rear door open, revealing a steel coffin.

Stunned, Pierce turned to Bangida. Nodding, the major said, "This is the day." There was no pleasure in his voice, no emotion at all. "Come— Okimbo is waiting for you."

Pierce made his mind go blank. Mechanically, he followed Bangida inside the prison.

Okimbo was leaning against the stone wall, arms folded. "The houseboy Edo told us," he said in a conversational tone. "Did you think us too foolish to have spies?"

Pierce said nothing. Okimbo nodded curtly to Bangida, dismissing him. "Enabling a treasonous Luandian citizen to escape," he told Pierce, "is punishable by death. It's no help now that you're American, or a lawyer. Though I suppose you can represent yourself to the same effect as you did Okari. Consider this morning a preview."

Pierce felt loathing overtake his fear. "I came to see Okari. You can amuse yourself later."

Okimbo seemed to weigh his choices. Then Bangida returned. Solemnly, he said, "President Karama is calling."

Okimbo's eye widened in surprise. Squaring his shoulders, he headed to his office. Quietly, Bangida told Pierce, "Go to Okari."

Gathering himself, Pierce climbed the steps to Bobby's cell.

Bobby sat on a stool, his hands manacled behind his back. With an air of resignation, Bobby turned at the sound of Pierce's footsteps. Seeing Pierce, he seemed to relax. "Damon," he said softly. "You never fail to surprise."

Pierce gazed at him through the bars. "I wanted you to know about Marissa. She's out."

"Out?"

"Gone." Pierce repressed his own worry. "Soon she'll be at our embassy in Accra. Once she's there, she'll call me."

"And yet you're here."

Though Bobby's voice was filled with wonder, Pierce was not sure what lay behind this comment; nor did he wish Bobby to die with Pierce's fate on his conscience. At length he said, "I'm your lawyer, Bobby. I wanted to be with you."

For a long while, Bobby studied him. Gently, he asked, "Aren't you still in love with her?"

Surprised, Pierce weighed his answer. "There's

been no time to think of that. It hardly matters now."

It was a kindness, Pierce thought, that Bobby did not know the literal truth of his last statement. Bobby shook his head. "I think it will, in time. Marissa's sacrificed far too much, in some ways more than I. I'd like the comfort of knowing that you care for her, as I think she does for you."

Pierce absorbed Bobby Okari's grace, his desire to die in peace. "Yes," he said at last, "I'm in love with her."

Perhaps it was true; at that moment, gripped by a sense of loss Bobby could not perceive, Pierce felt that it was. But he might never know.

Bobby watched his face. "I can see how sad you are, Damon. But you've lightened my conscience, and allowed me to die with dignity. What more could one man do for another?"

Pierce heard footsteps on the stone. Turning, he saw Bangida. "It's time," the major said. "Do you want to be there with him?"

"Yes."

"Then go to the courtyard and wait."

Pierce faced Bobby again. Eyes moist, Bobby tried to smile; for a moment, Pierce smiled in return. Then he followed Bangida outside.

In the morning light, Pierce saw a soldier with a video camera, aimed at the gallows. Only when Pierce heard it whirring did he see what the man was filming.

Okimbo hung from the gallows, his face suffused with agony. Someone had removed his eye patch; the stray eye, exposed, stared crookedly at nothing. His left foot gave a final twitch, then was still.

"It seems I'm now a colonel," Bangida said.

His flesh crawling, Pierce watched the hangman give the rope a tug, confirming that Okimbo had become dead weight. "I have a message from President Karama," Bangida went on. "When we're done here, you must leave Luandia at once—if you want to live. A man of honor, he said to tell you, repays his friends."

Pierce struggled to absorb what had happened. But there was no time. Flanked by two soldiers, Bobby Okari emerged from the prison. As they led him to the steps of the gallows, Bobby gazed up at Okimbo, less with surprise than what seemed a weary recognition of their common fate. Karama, and Luandia, would consume them both.

The hangman lowered Okimbo's corpse. Two soldiers came forward, laying the body on the platform as though it were a sacrifice to Bobby. The video camera kept whirring.

The soldiers pushed Bobby up the stairs. Briefly, he stumbled—whether from fright or exhaustion, Pierce could not tell. Then he straightened, walking the last few steps by himself.

The hangman stepped forward, holding a black hood. "Will you wear this?"

Bobby gazed at the soldier with the video camera, then met the hangman's eyes. "No."

Pierce swallowed. "Tell Karama," he said to Bangida, "that his friend asks one last favor. Bury Okari in Goro, with the others."

Bangida did not answer. As the hangman placed the noose around Bobby's neck, Bangida stepped forward, standing at the foot of the gallows.

Pierce's cell phone rang, shrill in the silence of the courtyard. As Bangida turned to Pierce, so did Bobby. Hastily, Pierce answered.

"I'm here," Marissa told him. "In Accra. Tell me how Bobby is."

Pierce saw Bangida move toward him. "I can't talk now. But it's going as he and I expected. He'll be glad you're safe." Hastily, he switched off the phone.

Bangida turned away. Noose around his neck, Bobby looked toward Pierce. Silent, Pierce nodded.

As if in prayer, Bobby's eyes shut briefly. As the hangman tightened the noose, Bobby gazed at the sky, taking in this last orange dawn. From the foot of the gallows, Bangida asked, "Do you have anything to say?"

Bobby gazed down at him. His face was weary, as though he were ready to die. "Yes," he answered. "I recant nothing."

A fragment of prayer, the legacy of his parents, surfaced from Pierce's subconscious: *Hail Mary,*

Mother of God, pray for us sinners, now and at the hour of our death.

Bangida gave an order. Bobby Okari's last expression in life, perhaps intended as a mercy to Pierce, was the faintest of smiles.

Afterword and Acknowledgments

THE GENESIS OF THIS NOVEL LIES IN TRAGIC EVENTS that occurred in Nigeria almost fifteen years ago, when a courageous environmental and human rights activist, Ken Saro-Wiwa, was hanged by General Sani Abacha, the country's brutal and corrupt dictator. The crime of which Saro-Wiwa stood accused, on flimsy evidence, was ordering the murder of four local chiefs who were members of the Ogoni, Saro-Wiwa's ethnic group. The tribunal that tried him was summoned into existence by Abacha and answerable to him alone; its arbitrary proceedings had little in common with courts as we know them, or with other courts in Nigeria. In the minds of most observers, Saro-Wiwa's true crime was to protest the excesses of the government and petroleum companies in the Niger Delta, and to seek for the Ogoni and others at least some of the benefits from revenues accruing to the petroleum companies and the kleptocratic regime of General Abacha. To this day, the facts surrounding the deaths of the Ogoni chiefs remain obscure.

There remains, as well, some debate about the complex character of Saro-Wiwa. But important things are clear: he was extraordinarily courageous; exceptional in building a mass movement in a country where no such tradition existed; an eloquent advocate for nonviolence; and a uniquely hopeful figure whose execution was devastating to the people of his impoverished region. Sadly, his legacy has been claimed by armed militia groups who have helped plunge the Niger Delta into violence, sustaining themselves by such enterprises as kidnapping and oil theft. Again, there is some debate about the character and intentions of these groups—particularly the Movement for the Emancipation of the Niger Delta (MEND). But there is no doubt that conditions in the delta are bad and getting worse.

I was involved with PEN, in a modest and ancillary way, in protesting Saro-Wiwa's prosecution. But when I decided to use Saro-Wiwa's story as a departure point for *Eclipse,* I confronted the staggering variety of a country with two hundred and fifty ethnic groups and an extremely complex society. Even Americans who know a lot about Nigeria do not pretend to fully understand it. As someone who can make neither claim, I worried about doing a serious injustice to Nigeria and its people. Hence Luandia, a fictional country that serves the purpose of my novel without being a fully realized depiction of an actual place.

Since Ken Saro-Wiwa's death, much has happened. Nonetheless, events in Nigeria continued to inform this novel. The environmental despoliation of the Niger Delta is more widely known, as are the persistent problems of poverty and corruption.

Though Nigeria has returned to civilian control, experienced observers label the 2007 presidential election a particularly blatant example of election rigging. The industrial world's need for oil has combined with post–9/11 concerns to make Nigeria a focal point in the search for "energy security." The pervasive corruption surrounding oil revenues persists unabated.

Indeed, since I completed the novel in January 2008, the conditions it portrays have metastasized. The price of oil has skyrocketed. America's dependence on oil has begun crippling its economy, even as China's needs grow exponentially. The militia, including MEND, have stepped up the ambition and sophistication of their military operations, cutting Nigeria's oil production and influencing the world price of oil. And the pervasive misery and violence of the Niger Delta, by all accounts, deepens.

It was with respect to the delta that I encountered another barrier to portraying Nigeria itself. As part of my research I traveled to that country, visiting Lagos and Abuja, and interviewed as many Nigerians and Americans familiar with the delta as I could find. The focal point of this trip was to be a visit to the delta itself. But two weeks before my trip, armed conflict between and among military and militia groups broke out in Port Harcourt, the delta's principal city. In a separate incident, one of my contacts was shot. Thereafter, the State

Department warned Americans not to travel there. When I persisted in my plans, the security firm I'd engaged to help me insisted I not go—arguing that I could become a target for kidnapping, among other things, and that the state security services might see my interest in militia groups as encouraging seditious elements.

With great ambivalence, I heeded this advice. I became less ambivalent two weeks later when one of my principal contacts was jailed with two German filmmakers, on charges of sedition, for taking them on much the same itinerary she and I had discussed. Nevertheless, the trip to Nigeria was extremely informative, and, through extensive research and interviewing, I did everything possible to compensate for what I missed.

A final word about what separates fact and fiction. Again, Luandia is not Nigeria; I do not pretend to portray the energy and diversity of Nigeria's people. Though I borrowed Ken Saro-Wiwa's eloquence and bravery, Bobby Okari's character and actions are my own invention. Nor was I able to do credit to Nigeria's vibrant and courageous human rights community. Similarly, while I tried to dramatize the diplomatic complexities of a case like Bobby Okari's, it was impossible to convey all the considerations pertaining to Nigeria, one of the most strategically important countries in Africa. But the corruption I depict—including oil bunkering—pervades the Niger

Delta. So does the environmental despoliation. The lawsuit I portray finds its parallel in lawsuits brought by human rights groups on behalf of civilians slaughtered by Nigerian soldiers; while I have simplified the law for the lay audience, the central premise of these suits is that oil companies can be held legally responsible for the excesses of their protectors. Nonetheless, it would be wrong to reflexively villainize the oil companies, some of which have done much to improve their operations and all of which are handicapped by the absence of government bodies dedicated to the betterment of the people. As for the characters other than Bobby Okari, I researched the challenges they would face, then proceeded to invent these people from scratch. I hope that the result, while fiction, contributes to most readers' understanding of the conflict between human rights and the geopolitics of oil in an important area of the developing world.

I COULD NOT have written *Eclipse* without the help of numerous people in Nigeria, America, and England who generously shared their knowledge. Their help greatly enriches the novel; any oversimplifications or errors of fact or interpretation are mine alone.

I begin by thanking many Nigerians who helped me: Omo Agaga, Congressman Ajuji Ahmed, Tem-Tem Amacree, Usman Bugaje, Sunday Dare, Sunny Ofili, former minister of finance Ngozi

Okonjo-Iweala, and Patrick Ukata gave me valuable insights into Nigeria as a whole. And my comprehension of the Niger Delta was deepened by its residents, most of whom are members of its human rights community and several of whom knew Ken Saro-Wiwa well: Dr. Judith Burdin Asuni, Father Matthew Kukah, Patrick Naagbanton, Ben Naanen, Chris Newsom, Damka Pueba, and, especially, Ken Saro-Wiwa's brother Owens Wiwa.

In dealing with the diplomatic aspects of the novel, I was lucky to have the advice of four former American ambassadors to Nigeria: Robert Gribbin, Howard Jeter, Princeton Lyman, and Thomas Pickering. I also profited from the advice of other current national security officers, State Department officials, or members of our foreign service: Sandy Berger, Carolyn Gay, Marc Grossman, Anthony Lake, Donald McHenry, Vic Nelson, Susan Rice, John Shattuck, Andrew Silski, Gayle Smith, and Rudolph Stewart. And three military experts helped fill in the military and strategic considerations inherent in my story: Lieutenant Colonel Mark Ellington, retired Colonel Bill Godbout, and retired General James Jones.

A number of American and English experts helped as well, including academic writers, strategists, and members of the human rights community: Chris Albin-Lackey, Melissa Crow, Dr. Stephen Davis, David Goldwyn, Jean Herskovits, Dan Hoyle, Peter Lewis, Bronwen Manby, Bear

McConnell, Stephen Morrison, Tom O'Neill, Dr. Robert Pastor, Susan Reider, Ken Roth, John Schidlovsky, Jill Shankleman, Robert Tyrer, and Michael Watts. Several judges and lawyers enabled me to better grasp the law: Martha Boersch, Judith Chomsky, Cindy Cohn, Judge Thelton Henderson, Rick Herz, Paul Hoffman, Judge Susan Illston, Dick Martin, and Dan Nardello. Three experts in the oil business were generous in describing the difficulties that business faces in Nigeria: Lew Watts, Nick Welsh, and Robin West. Retired British general Peter Williams was very patient and helpful in describing the daunting security problems plaguing oil companies.

I owe a great debt for the advice, knowledge, good company, and, not least, protection provided by Anthony Boyson, Cobus Claassens, Joe Jobert, and Daniel Revmatas of the Pilgrims Group. Finally, others enabled me to fill in some important gaps: Professor Bob Harmon explained the phenomenon of a solar eclipse, and my friend Alex MacDonald gave Damon Pierce a past, including an eyewitness account of the appearance of Robert Kennedy at the St. Patrick's Day parade attended on March 17, 1968, the date of Damon's birth.

I also benefited from reading fiction and nonfiction books about Africa, Nigeria, Saro-Wiwa, the Ogoni movement, and the geopolitics of oil: *The Politics of Bones,* by J. Timothy Hunt; *Untapped,* by John Ghazvinian; *Violence in Nigeria,* by Toyin Falola; *Ogoni's Agonies,* edited by Abdul Rasheed Na'Allah; *Yellow-Yellow,* by Kaine Agary; *Half of a Yellow Sun,* by Chimamanda Ngozi Adichie; *The Fate of Africa,* by Martin Meredith; *Imperial Reckoning,* by Caroline Elkins; *Nigeria and Oil,* by Anup Shah; *The Next Glut,* by Andy Rowell, James Marriott, and Lorne Stockman; *You Must Set Forth at Dawn,* by Wole Soyinka; *Where Vultures Feast,* by Ike Okonta and Oronto Douglas; and *In the Shadow of a Saint,* Ken Wiwa's honest and affecting portrait of his father. *Black, White, and Jewish,* by Rebecca Walker, and *Dreams from My Father,* by Barack Obama, helped me with Marissa Okari's inner landscape. In this connection, I also borrowed from Ken Saro-Wiwa's speeches to give Bobby Okari his voice.

I also read several important articles: "Curse of the Black Gold: Hope and Betrayal in the Niger Delta," by Tom O'Neill; "Blood Oil," by Sebastian Junger; and "The Megacity," by George Packer. Tom O'Neill was also kind enough to give me the first draft of his article, an immensely helpful and evocative source. The reports I read included "Convergent Interests: U.S. Energy Security and the 'Security' of Nigerian Democracy," by Paul M. Lubeck, Michael J. Watts, and Ronnie Lipschutz, as well as several comprehensive reports by Human Rights Watch and a number of articles in the *New York Times.* Finally, I owe a great debt to

Glenn Ellis for his penetrating and sometimes harrowing documentaries about Ken Saro-Wiwa, the Ogoni movement, and the tragedy of the Niger Delta.

Finally, I wish to thank the core of people with whom I share the madness: my agent, Fred Hill, a mainstay of my career; my terrific editor, John Sterling; and my ever-patient and always discerning assistant, Alison Porter Thomas, whose daily comments help keep me on track. Then there is my wife, Dr. Nancy Clair. As an educational consultant, Nancy has worked in every part of the world; a lover of Africa and its people, Nancy helped encourage me to write *Eclipse.* Once I began, she went with me to Nigeria, a trip vastly improved by her energy, insight, and support. As if that were not enough, she read each chapter as I wrote it. For all of that, and all she has brought to me and to the kids, this book is for her.

Center Point Publishing
600 Brooks Road ● PO Box 1
Thorndike ME 04986-0001 USA

(207) 568-3717

US & Canada:
1 800 929-9108
www.centerpointlargeprint.com